THE SUNDAY HEROES

NOEL B. GERSON

The Sunday Heroes

WILLIAM MORROW & COMPANY, INC.

NEW YORK 1972

For Marilyn
and All of America's Other Sunday Widows

Professional football is no more a sport than is the manufacture of the computers or television sets that make it possible. At worst it is big business, at best a highly specialized industry.

—Robin A. Stephens

1

A sustained roar filled Yankee Stadium as the Giants, with less than three minutes still to play, began another touchdown drive, and although they were beating their AFC rivals, the Chicago Cougars, by a score of 33–6 in the interconference game, none of the paying customers left their seats. The victory would assure the Giants of their NFC divisional championship and a spot in the play-offs, and Super Bowl fever hung in the air.

Robin Stephens stretched, stood and started out of the press-box cubicle reserved for Giant executives. He hurried to the locker room before thousands of fans spilled onto the field and blocked his progress. The public-relations boys were competent, but Robin didn't believe in taking details for granted, and intended to assure himself that the television hookups had been made and that the bourbon and Scotch had been laid out in advance for the working newsmen.

Someone in the adjoining cubicle waved, so Robin took a few extra seconds and opened the door. It simply wouldn't be politic to give a fast brush-off to Daniel Grannett, the Cougars' general manager and former coach, himself enshrined in the Pro Hall of Fame, and according to the old-timers, the best offensive tackle in the history of the game. He was such a fixture, in fact, that he almost lived up to the title, "Mr. Football," that the sports-writers had draped around him.

The grizzled, overweight man extended a huge hand. "Congratulations, Rob, and the same to the Maras. The Giants will go all the way this time around."

"Thanks, Danny. We hope you—and Mr. Klein—will join us for a drink and a snack. Mrs. Grannett and Mrs. Klein, too, naturally. I'm sure the Maras will be expecting you." Robin was paid to think of every angle.

"I'll try to drop in, Rob." A pained expression fleetingly crossed the lined face. "Our boys have taken another bad shellacking today, and this is our last game of the season, so I've got to say a few words to them about next year."

"Sure, Danny." Robin waved, then called, "We'll be looking for you."

If he knew the old man, Danny would be too busy rebuilding the bruised egos of his own charges to make an appearance in the Giant dressing rooms. You couldn't expect anything else from a member of the Old Guard, who had been weaned on the need for "team spirit" from his own high-school and college playing days.

Making his way down to the offices and players' quarters, Robin was relieved he had taken the precaution to wear one of his oldest suits. A general front-office assistant—there were no formal titles in the Giants' organization—couldn't afford to run the risk of ruining one of his several tailor-made English suits. The gooks—the players—would be so exuberant they would pour entire bottles of champagne over everyone who came within reach. At least Robin had taken the additional precaution of buying an inexpensive domestic champagne by the case. There wasn't a single player on the squad who would recognize the taste of a first-rate champagne. Assuming that any of the stuff would be consumed internally.

For the next few minutes, after he reached the office and locker room complex, Robin was so busy he was only vaguely aware of hearing the end of the game on one of the radios that was blaring in the suite. A few moments later the howling players began to troop in, so he tactfully retreated to the farthest reaches before the heavy drinking began, and reminded the players they had to win yet another game before they reached the Super Bowl.

After a very short hiatus the inevitable bedlam broke loose, and Robin wandered into the television room to watch the quarterback, his tight end, and the linebacker who was the team's defensive captain being put through their interview paces. Any gook who played long enough in New York was conscious of the publicity nuances expected of him, and the players handled themselves with aplomb, making the appropriate, respectful remarks about their opponents for the upcoming National Conference championship, the Vikings.

A substitute guard who played on the special teams and who hadn't been able to wangle a pay increase from Robin this past season obtained his own brand of vengeance by squirting a stream of champagne into the face of the man he held responsible. But Robin escaped additional insult, perhaps because he had the ability to make himself virtually invisible when he wished, at least in football circles. By ordinary standards he was reasonably tall, standing at six feet, and at thirty-five he was no older than the team's senior players, but there the resemblance ended. He weighed only one hundred sixty-three, which meant that no one would mistake him for even a defensive back or a runback specialist, and he avoided the mustaches, bushy sideburns, and long hair that had become standard in football players' circles. He looked, in fact, like what he was, an alert, clean-cut business executive; and his appearance was no accident, as he believed it important to cultivate his future.

He conducted the owners of several visiting teams through the madhouse, depositing them with his own employers, the Maras. He avoided saying anything quotable to members of the working press who questioned him, as he believed in the principle that front-office help should remain anonymous, and that the public really didn't care what he thought of the Giants' chances of going all the way this year. Then some of the reporters who traveled with the Cougars joined the party, so he greeted them cordially before turning them over to the public-relations contingent.

In the crush he missed the man who was as tall as the biggest football player on the squad, actually taller in the high-crowned Stetson he always wore. Then the booming laugh that was another of Marcus Aurelius Klein's trademarks cut through the racket, and Robin immediately started toward him, taking a circuitous route that would not be too obvious. It wasn't that there was anything in particular he wanted to sell to Klein, but he made it a policy to call himself to the attention of all the team owners in the league. Unobtrusively, to be sure, and for the simple reason it could do him no long-range harm.

Maybe it was true, as some of Klein's former employees claimed, that the man was a bastard when you worked for him, but as an outsider Robin was fascinated by him. Marcus Aurelius Klein was a genuine powerhouse, a one-man conglomerate whose known interests included an aerospace company, a major meat-packing plant, soap and soup and hardware manufacturers, as well as vast real estate holdings. His football team was one of his hobbies, and unquestionably had changed him from an ogre to a sportsman in the public eye, but it was just as well, if the press could be believed, that he wasn't particularly interested in making a mint with the Cougars. Oh, they were in the black every year, it being impossible for any major-league football team to lose money, but the Cougars were a sorry aggregation, and their profits were minimal.

Precisely as Robin had hoped, Klein saw him from a distance and hailed him, so he made his way to the industrialist's side.

Years of living in Chicago and New York, London and Palm Beach, had not robbed Marcus Aurelius Klein of his rural Texas twang, and his eyes were still a cold, clear blue, in spite of the liquor he had consumed this afternoon. "Boy," he said, "you deserve a share of the credit for this jamboree."

"Thanks, Mr. Klein," Robin said, "but anything we've achieved has been a team effort."

[14]

Klein's eyes bored into him. "Bullshit," he said. "I know who engineered those trades with the Rams and the Oilers. And a little birdie told me who had a hand—at just the right time—in the TV contract negotiations that have meant a bigger bundle for all of this season."

It would be harmful to pretend false modesty, and Robin could not resist the temptation to make it plain that he knew Klein's sources of information. "That little birdie," he said, "must hide away in an aviary known as the Commissioner's office."

Klein grinned, but his eyes remained unchanged. "You've got so many friends in the Commissioner's office that I'm going to rely on you instead of my own people to get me an extra box for twelve for the Super Bowl game, Stephens."

Robin murmured that he'd be delighted to oblige.

"And after the game, boy, look me up. I'd like to buy you that drink you deserve."

Kate Stephens wandered restlessly through the cramped living room of her tiny Manhattan apartment, and when she spoke there was a note of resignation in her voice. "I'm not being bitter, Rob. I'm not vindictive. And God knows I'm not mercenary, so you can't claim I'm trying to gouge more money out of you."

Robin stubbed out his cigarette and lighted another. "Good. Because I haven't got it. If we win the Super Bowl I'm reasonably sure I'll get a bonus, but I don't know how much it'll be. And anyway, I can't count on it right now."

"All I want," Kate said, running a hand through her dark hair, "is this one extra chunk of money beyond what you gave me after the divorce. I have no intention of trying to stick you for alimony, Rob, and you damn well know it. You also know I can't set myself up overnight again as a free-lance commercial artist, and I need five thousand."

"Just like that. All of a sudden you need more for your living expenses, or whatever, so you come to your ex-husband, that perennial soft touch and philanthropist, and you expect him to find you five G's, which he'll not only pick out of nowhere like a cornerback intercepting a pass on a crossover, but he'll hand to you as a present because he's known for his generosity."

Kate's smile was that of a patient wife dealing with a husband who was still a small boy in his relations with others. "I've been wanting this chat with you for a long time, you may remember. In fact, I've been trying to get together for six months, but you've been too busy. First you had player contracts to negotiate. Then you had the TV deals that were life or death. Then you had to run training camp. Just you, apparently, out of that whole, big staff. Every time I tried to reach you during the exhibition season you were out of town, and once the regular season began, it was even worse. You might instruct your secretary to say, 'This is the football season, and Mr. Stephens has taken the veil.'"

"Very funny," Robin said, "but a professional football team doesn't run itself."

"I know," Kate said. "I spent eight years finding out, the hard way, and if I'm not a good girl you'll punish me by forcing me to memorize the figures on how much the concessions for hot dogs and beer—or the men's rooms—are worth every year."

Robin had promised himself he would not allow her to needle him into blowing his cool and making a scene. "Look. If there's such a thing as an amicable divorce, it's what we had. No hard feelings, no grudges. Friends. I made you a decent settlement, and I could call it quits right there—"

"You promised you'd help me out if I ever got into financial trouble."

"That's why I'm here, Kate. I've learned a few things myself. I can't turn off my loyalties after eight years of living with a woman, and I'll gladly help you out to the best of my ability. But I can't dig up five thousand on short notice."

"Unless you've changed your style of living, you've always salted away part of your salary," she persisted.

A flush of annoyance rose to his face, and he struggled harder for self-control. What he did with his income was none of her damned business, and he was sorry he had allowed sentiment to bring him to her apartment. On the other hand, it was true he had promised her, at the time of their divorce, that he wouldn't let her starve. Not that anyone ever went hungry any more, but it would be far easier to live with himself if he helped her in her time of need. "I may have a personal deal cooking on the back burner," he said, "so I may be able to come to the rescue if you'll be patient."

"I've been just that for a long time, and my bills keep multiplying. Which fish are you landing—Detroit, St. Louis or the Chicago Cougars?"

She knew far more about football than her disclaimers would lead anyone to suspect. But Robin had no intention of discussing a deal that was still in the formative stage of development. "As a matter of fact," he said, "the whole thing is on the complicated side. A shift in front-office personnel isn't the same as a player trade, and management always walks on eggs to make sure there are no hard feelings."

"Spare me the details. Not only do I care nothing whatever about the gyrations of sports tycoons, but I'm not especially interested in your own plans. Oh, I wish you well, naturally, but you and I are moving in separate directions. I wouldn't have come to you at all if there had been anyone else, but I had no choice." Her shrug may have been a calculated gesture of helplessness, but she managed it prettily.

Robin admired her artistry, even though he took a dim view of her motives. She knew he was no longer in love with her, of course, but she was banking on the probability that he still found her appealing, so she was turning on the charm. It wasn't the first time and presumably wouldn't be the last, either, but he had been prepared for just such a stunt, and it left him cold. "I'll be in a better position to talk after the Super Bowl game," he said.

Her smile faded, and her dark eyes became bright. "I'm not a natural-born bitch. My bitchiness is an acquired characteristic. So is my knowledge of football. You taught me that the newspapers will print anything about a team that's headed for a championship, so this is my finest hour. You'll have to come through for me now. Even a man who works in the front office is news, and a juicy item about him is worth a column or better in every newspaper in the United States."

She seemed to be threatening him, but he had no idea what might be in her mind, so he braced himself and waited.

The sheen in Kate's eyes hardened, and a brittle quality crept into her voice. "How is Min?" she asked.

She had found a vulnerable area, and he knew it would do no good to pretend innocence. But his training as a negotiator came to his assistance, and he forced her to spell out her thinking. "I may know a lot of people who have that name."

"Maybe, but I doubt it. I'm referring to Minerva Helmsley, the first blonde in your brunette-conscious life. Also the wife of one Hal Helmsley, the Chicago Cougars' star fullback."

Robin raised his invisible guard still higher. "I haven't seen her in some time."

Kate arched an eyebrow. "I assumed she was here for the Giant-Cougar game."

"Hal Helmsley is a player," he said, "so when the Cougars go out of town he travels with the team. And lives with the team. His wife wouldn't have been allowed to get together with him before the game."

"Oh, a girl like Min would be the very last to want him to break training, I'm sure. But she might have a friend who'd show her around town—and prevent her from doing something desperate. Like going out with her husband after the game and maybe even shacking up with him for the night."

The charade had been played long enough. "If you have a point to make, I'm waiting to hear it."

"All right. On the line, then. You've been playing around with Min behind her husband's back. All hell will break if Helmsley finds out. Push that kind of man into the open, and he's got to take action to protect his own public image. That means a divorce suit—naming you as corespondent. Men who work in the front office are supposed to keep their mitts off players' wives, so you'd be penalized for being out of bounds. The publicity would ruin your chances of getting a new job—and you might even get yourself fired."

"Okay, Kate, you make yourself clear." Robin wanted a drink, but refused to help himself to her liquor. "This is plain, old-fashioned blackmail."

Again she shrugged, but this time the gesture was cold. "I'm not interested in pinning on labels. Or in name-calling. All I know is that I need five thousand dollars in cash."

She had him spread-eagled over a fat barrel, but he could not surrender without putting up a fight. "You sound very sure of your facts."

"I am," Kate said, lighting a cigarette and blowing a thin cloud of smoke at the ceiling. "I still have some friends in football, and you and Min haven't been quite as invisible to the naked eye as you seem to think."

He tried to make his nod look casual.

"If you were planning to marry her, Rob, it would be a whole new ball game. But she doesn't have enough class for you, just as I didn't. You still have your sights set on becoming a general manager, and you won't remarry until you find someone who lives up to your concept of a wife who will be an asset to you."

He refused to admit the accuracy of her observation, but damned her for knowing him so well.

"The world is filled with chicks like Min. Or me. You ought to be more careful in your associations."

"So I'm beginning to learn." Robin became crisp. "What would stop you from coming back to me in another six months, and putting the heat on me for still more money?"

"I find this distasteful, that's why." Kate tried to recover her dignity. "I don't enjoy threatening you, and I'm doing it only because I can't go any deeper into debt. You'll have to take my word that I won't bother you again. In fact, under these unpleasant circumstances, neither of us will want to get together again. So let me have the five thousand, and we'll call it quits."

"I'll do what I can," Robin said, hating himself for having been stupid enough to be maneuvered into an untenable position. Picking up his hat, he walked to the door.

Kate could well afford her victory smile. "Before the Super Bowl game," she called.

He walked several blocks before he began to recover his equilibrium. It would be necessary to send her a thousand or two at once to keep her quiet, but perhaps he could stall for a time before paying her the rest. The worst of his situation was his realization that his taste in women was abominable; apparently he lacked the ability to distinguish someone with character from a tramp. He was as lacking in judgment as the players, who always went for the girls with pretty faces, tricky figures and obvious sex appeal.

As Robin's anger cooled he realized he was heading back to his own bachelor apartment. It was the last place on earth he wanted to be, but he couldn't think of anywhere else to go, and it was too late to rustle up a date for the evening who could take his mind off his idiocy. Most of the chicks whose phone numbers were scribbled in his address book were versions of Kate—or Minerva Helmsley, and he was fed up with the type. For the moment, anyway.

Yet he knew himself well enough to realize he would weaken again when the familiar desire for a woman began to take possession of him. His worst mistake had been marrying Kate, and he didn't intend to fall into that pattern; she had been absolutely right when she had said he wouldn't remarry until he found a woman who would offer him more than sex. Come to think of it, however, he didn't know anyone who would even qualify for a life as the mate of a highly paid, universally respected general manager of a major-league football team.

Somewhat to his own surprise, it occurred to Robin that he was leading a lonely existence.

Marcus Aurelius Klein's guests were crammed into the main living room and two auxiliary parlors of the Miami Beach hotel suite, making it almost impossible for the waiters carrying trays of canapés to circulate. But the throngs were even more dense in the vicinity of the bars set up in each of the rooms, where men were lined up four-and-five deep seeking refills.

The male guests fell into three categories, each easily identifiable. Executives of various Klein industries and their associates from other corporations were middle-aged, and wore either conservative business suits or overly loud lightweight jackets. The sporting crowd was impeccably, expensively tailored, drank more rapidly and used broader gestures when speaking. The athletes, taller and stronger than the rest, either emulated the most conservative of the businessmen or did not bother to wear jackets and showed up in sports shirts and bell-bottomed slacks.

The women, regardless of age or station, seemed cut from the same bolt of cloth. All wore heavy, carefully applied makeup, were dressed in the very latest styles and were groomed within the proverbial inch of their lives. They owed their trim figures, which they exhibited in a minimum of attire, to nature in a few cases, and to diet, massage parlors and sauna baths in most instances. Indifferent to sports but supremely conscious of the roles they themselves were playing, they were an attraction at every major spectacle, from Super Bowl game to World Series to heavyweight championship prizefight.

The disparities in vocation, personal background and age were meaningless. Sports was the great common denominator, and everyone was called by his first name. Few bothered to rehash the details of that afternoon's Super Bowl game, but betting odds and the amounts won and lost were the principal topics of earnest conversation, and only the athletes were bored by the talk.

The hotel's newest air-conditioning units tried in vain to cope with the crowd, and Robin Stephens sweltered in a corner of the main living room. He sipped a mild bourbon and water, decided it wasn't worth the bother to fight his way to the bar for more ice, and consequently made no attempt to move. His hand had been shaken by thirty or forty of the men, the women had favored him with their most brilliant, artificial smiles, and his presence thereafter having been forgotten by most of those present, he was content to relax in the company of Mal Ferguson, the Cougar head coach.

There were those who called Ferguson, a one-time player for Danny Grannett, a pale carbon copy of his superior, whose instructions he supposedly followed to the letter. Everyone in the business knew better, however, and believed he deserved his nickname, Mal the Iceberg. He was never discouraged in defeat, never had been known to lose his temper on the field or in the dressing room, and even the veterans who had played on his teams for many years swore they had never heard him raise his voice.

Ferguson had to lean in Robin's direction in order to make himself heard. "With the money this party cost," he said, "they could have bought me a new offensive tackle."

"We'll make you a special bargain price for some gook from our squad." Robin made no attempt to hide his boredom. Mal was one of those good citizens known to sportswriters as "a credit to professional football," but in Robin's very private opinion he was directly responsible for at least one-third of the Cougars' woes. Coaches, who received even more publicity than their biggest star players, were the real field leaders in the game, and it was axiomatic that a coach with charisma sold tickets. Conversely, a colorless head coach, no matter how technically proficient he might be, invariably produced a drab team that failed to earn as much money as it might. And Mal, who might be a regular churchgoer, perfect husband and model father, was supposedly lacking in the personality that inspired a team and produced results at the box office.

"We'll take Schwartzie off your hands any day, Rob," he said.

Robin grinned without humor; only a moron would have taken his remark seriously. "Schwartzie," he said, "won't be sold or traded. He's untouchable."

"That's what I thought." Mal lapsed into glum silence.

Two players chatting on the far side of the room caught

Robin's notice. Hal Helmsley had stopped in for a quick drink, and was the center of an admiring throng. A bandage that concealed a deep cut on his forehead, just below his curly, blond hair, made his face less blank than usual, but nothing could disguise the breadth of his shoulders, which were almost as wide as the door frame behind him. Robin had to hand it to him: the slob had a magnificent build, and for a man of his size was incredibly agile and fast on his feet, doing the one-hundred-yard dash in ten seconds when dressed in full uniform. He deserved his All-Pro rating and his standing as the Cougars' only offensive star of note.

A quick study of the crowd indicated that Minerva had not come with him, even though it was mandatory that the wives of those on Marcus Aurelius Klein's payroll accompany their husbands to a Klein command performance party. It was typical of Min not to bother, but Robin had no complaints. Klein had asked him to stop in for a drink and a private talk, and he didn't want to be distracted by a blonde who was capable of making him forget everything but her own appeal.

A single glance at the man talking to Helmsley caused him to brighten. Fred Finch, known to the press as "Fearless Freddie," had been hailed as the quarterback replacement for the irreplaceable Johnny Unitas when he had been picked up by the Baltimore Colts, but he had sorely disappointed the team, its fans and the Baltimore press. Fearless Freddie, it was charged, had only two worthwhile traits: he could throw a football like a bullet being discharged from a high-powered rifle, and he was the most courageous player on any active major-league roster. But he was also charged with supreme recklessness, an impulsiveness that interfered with his field generalship and a desire to show himself off to good advantage, regardless of what happened to his team in a game.

In Robin's opinion those who made the claims, and they were legion, failed to understand Finch's character. Neither Baltimore nor Boston, which had employed him for several years, had known how to handle him. He was mercurial, to be sure, but

[23]

Robin was convinced, after watching him under fire, that he always kept his head and knew precisely what needed to be done in any given situation. Finch was one of those oddball nonconformists who appeared in pro football from time to time, and what he needed was a head coach who had complete confidence in him, supported by a front office that would grant him the right to run a team on the field as he saw fit, without interference from anyone. Turn him loose in his own way, Robin believed, and he would become another Unitas, Y. A. Tittle or Bart Starr.

Accompanying Finch and clinging to his arm was a flamboyant little redhead in a skin-tight dress, and Robin, who privately admired his taste, knew that the many women in his life hurt his image, as did his unabashed drinking. Coaches and fans had grown tired of playboy quarterbacks, and failed to realize that Finch was serious when he worked. His unfortunate image was his own fault, to be sure; he was rebelling like an adolescent, even though in his mid-twenties, because no one had ever told him it would be in his own best interests to behave with greater discretion off the playing field.

Finch happened to catch Robin's eye and immediately started across the room toward him, the redhead trying to keep pace with him as he threaded through the crowd with the instincts of a broken field runner avoiding a blitzing defensive line. There weren't many front-office people who let it be known they liked Finch.

"Hello, champ. What are you going to do with all your Super Bowl money?" The tall, lean quarterback had an abnormally large hand, and his grip was like that of a vise.

"I think," Robin told him, "I'll spend it on riotous living."

"You hear that, Martie?" Finch turned to the redhead. "We're being invited to an orgy. This is Robin Stephens of the new champs, Martie. And this is Coach Ferguson of the Cougars," he added as an afterthought. "How's everything, Coach?"

Mal Ferguson's stiff nod and almost military bearing indicated his opinion of the quarterback.

But Finch was unabashed. "What do you say?" he demanded, slipping an arm around the girl. "Do we accept the invite?"

"Right on," Martie said, and giggled.

Mal Ferguson's face seemed to freeze. "If you'll forgive me," he muttered, edging away, "I'm being paged in the next room."

"What a dried up old woman," Finch said. "Thank God I don't have to play for him."

What he said or did was none of Robin's concern, but the kid needed a strong shove in the right direction. "Freddie," he said, lowering his voice, "you know you shouldn't talk like that in public about any head coach. The word gets around. Besides, you never know when you might end up on the same team."

"Not me," Finch said. "I'm this year's leper boy, and nobody will take me in a trade. Which is why I'll have to pass for a half-dozen touchdowns per game next year—and break some total yardage figures." Suddenly he became belligerent. "You think I can't do it? Make me an off-the-record bet, and I'll take all your Super Bowl money!"

"If the Commissioner's office ever catches you betting," Robin said calmly, "you'll be placed on permanent suspension. But a bet with me isn't necessary, because I happen to believe you can come up with the best statistics in the game."

"You hear that, chick?"

Robin gave the girl no chance to reply. "Martie," he said, "I wonder if he turns you on just as much when he isn't thumping his chest."

She stared at him, her green eyes enormous. "Sure," she said. "How did you know?"

"Tell him," Robin said.

"Freddie, you turn me on—"

"I get the message, chick." Finch drained his strong Scotch and stared down at the shorter man. "You're all right, Stephens."

"The same to you," Robin said.

"We ought to form our own team, and then we'd show those dehydrated bastards like Ferguson some real football."

Robin was certain several people had overheard the remark,

and winced. By the time it was repeated by a half-dozen guests it would be distorted into even more spectacular shape. "Martie," he said, "if you want to become very, very rich, find some way to shut this cretin's mouth and keep it shut. His bosses will pay you a fortune."

A door opened a few feet to Robin's left, and Marcus Aurelius Klein beckoned.

"Excuse me," Robin said, but before he turned away he saw a quick gleam of comprehension in the quarterback's eyes.

Finch grinned broadly. "There are times when I can really keep my mouth shut," he said.

Robin made no reply as he went into the sitting room, and his host closed the door behind them.

"I hope I haven't kept you waiting too long, but I've been tied up on the transatlantic phone," Klein said. "Most days I wish that damn instrument had never been invented, but if it hadn't, I'd be running a two-bit family business down in Texas. Help yourself." He gestured toward a bar.

It was very quiet in the room as Robin mixed himself a weak bourbon and water, and for some moments there was no sound but the crashing of waves on the sands of Miami Beach, the roar muffled by the closed windows and the hum of the room air conditioner.

Klein regarded his guest over the rim of his highball glass, then raised it in a token toast. "Here's to your Giants, boy. I made a bundle on them today, and I hope you cleaned up, too."

Robin shook his head. "I never bet on a game, Mr. Klein, not even on my own team. It's one of my Ten Commandments for keeping out of trouble with the Commissioner's office."

Klein was pleased, and waved him to a chair. "You're smart, Stephens, so smart that you've probably guessed that my invitation to you for this evening wasn't purely social."

"Hold on, Mr. Klein." Robin remained standing. "Please don't be offended, but I'm on the Giants' payroll, so I'm in no position to have even exploratory talks with anybody else."

Marcus Aurelius Klein chuckled. "By God, boy, what they

say about you is true! But you can relax. I've already had a word with the Maras, since I'm not the kind who'll play secret footsie with friends' hired help. I've told them what I have in mind, and they've given me the green light to have a little chat with you. They won't stand in the way of your advancement."

Robin tried to maintain a poker face. "That's different," he said, and sat down in a chair with a view of the breakers by moonlight.

"How'd you like to join the Cougars?" the industrialist asked abruptly.

Robin worded his reply carefully. "That depends on a great many factors. I have a lot of respect for you, Mr. Klein, and I'd welcome the chance to join an organization where—assuming I proved myself—I might be able to move on from football to even bigger things. Some day."

Klein's laugh was dry. "You know my system."

The younger man saw no need to reply to the obvious. "There are all kinds of angles. The Cougars are in trouble."

"If they had won the Super Bowl today instead of the Giants, I wouldn't be talking to you. What are the problems—as you see them?"

Robin hesitated.

"Level with me, Stephens! Anything we say is between you and me."

"Okay." Robin took a deep breath. "You have the nucleus of a first-rate team, but no more than that, and you can't sell season tickets when a team loses more games than it wins. Season after season. Only your share of the league's television income keeps you profitable—"

"You're telling me," Klein muttered.

"—but that quarter of a million per minute for Super Bowl game sport announcements isn't enough. Your ball-park concessions suffer, your color souvenir programs don't sell, everything slumps. You have only two players with the charisma to draw crowds. Helmsley, your fullback, and the kid linebacker Ted Marcus, who is being called another Sam Huff or Dick Butkus.

Everybody else ought to be traded." He thought he might be moving onto treacherous ground, and halted.

"I'm listening," Klein said.

Robin tried another approach. "One of your basic faults is your old-fashioned scouting system. About one thousand gooks who come out of the colleges every year are pro prospects, and only a computer can evaluate that number. But the Cougars still depend completely on the personal reports of a handful of scouts—who can't possibly cover the field. Now, I'll admit that computer programming doesn't pay off overnight, and is expensive—"

"I've never been known for my refusal to spend money when necessary," Klein interrupted savagely.

Robin was not cowed. "So the grapevine says."

"They also say I don't care if I make money on the Cougars, and that's damned nonsense. Every subsidiary of Klein Enterprises carries its own weight! Or else! I realize football is different from most other businesses, so I'm willing to be patient, but my patience has limits. How much do you suppose I made on the team this year?"

"Net?"

"Net."

"Somewhere in the neighborhood of a couple of hundred thousand," Robin said.

"You're mighty close. How much should we make?"

"Well, Mr. Klein, the teams that hit the Super Bowl pack away profits of a couple of million each, but they aren't the criteria. Any team that gives the fans entertainment values for their money should earn a net of somewhere between seven hundred and fifty thousand to a million every year."

"Hmm. You and my cost analysis boys talk the same language." Klein walked to a bar in the corner of the room, splashed more bourbon into his glass and extended the bottle to his guest.

Robin wanted another drink, but shook his head.

"How long would it take to put the Cougars on that basis?"

"It might be done in two years, but that would be pushing

hard. Ordinarily I'd say three." Again Robin hesitated. "Of course, it could take longer."

Klein stood with his feet wide apart, and hooked his thumb into his belt. "You aren't coming clean with me, Stephens!"

"Well, sir, you're putting me in one hell of a tough spot. I'm a businessman, not a fortune teller." Robin was firm. "You understand that the figures I've cited are predicated on the assumption that TV interest will be maintained at the present peak, or near it. If and when it drops off badly, football will go the way of baseball, where most teams are either losing money or just scraping through."

"Is that going to happen, Stephens?"

"It needn't. Aggressive, tough teams loaded with colorful personalities and led by coaches who can capture the public imagination will keep the pot boiling."

Klein lowered his bulk into a chair too small for him. "What do you think of Danny Grannett?" he asked suddenly.

Robin preferred to avoid embarrassment. "He's probably the grandest of the grand old men since Amos Alonzo Stagg. He—"

"I told you to level with me!"

"Okay. A quarter of a century ago, the difference between the pros and the college game was less pronounced. Maybe the lines Danny built as a coach were the walls of granite they were called by the newspapers. I don't know. I was too young to understand much about the game. But the Cougars have no walls of granite these days, and not much of anything else, either. Danny is a wonderful guy. The newspaper and TV and radio people love him, the public worships him and everybody in the business is very fond of him. But he won't build you a team that'll earn you the money you want the Cougars to make." Robin deliberately rose, crossed the room and poured himself another drink of bourbon. "Is that what you wanted to hear, Mr. Klein?"

"Now we're putting our cards on the table. You're earning twenty thousand in New York. Will you come with the Cougars as assistant general manager at forty thousand?"

"I'm grateful to you, and I could use the money," Robin said.

"But I see no point in robbing you, Mr. Klein. I wouldn't be worth it to you."

"Suppose I think otherwise." Marcus Aurelius Klein became ugly when he was crossed.

"Then you'd be wrong. An assistant advises, but mostly he carries out the general manager's orders. It's the G.M. who makes the trades, makes the deals, supervises public relations, hires the head coach—and all the rest. I'm sure you follow me."

Klein laughed without humor. "In some of my other companies, I've seen what bright young men who have guts and cleverness and foresight can do. They're the boys who are on the way up. All the way to the top."

Robin discovered that his temples were pounding. "What interests me about the Cougars is the long-range potential," he said cautiously.

"Yeah, they have no place to go but up." Klein took two cigars from the flap pocket of his jacket.

"I never use them, thanks."

Klein took his time lighting a cigar, then stared up at the ceiling. "I've been promising myself that—one of these years—I've got to move Danny Grannett up in the hierarchy. He'll be worth his weight—present, not his old playing weight—in solid gold to the Enterprises as a public relations V.P. who visits Congressmen and speaks at banquets. But I can't promote him until I find the right person to take his place with the Cougars."

"Mr. Klein," Robin said, "you've just hired yourself a new assistant general manager."

"My legal department will send you a contract within a week." Suddenly the older man's manner changed, and he became perceptibly harder. "You mentioned Hal Helmsley as one of two Cougars worth keeping."

"Very definitely. He's a cross between Jim Brown and Jimmy Taylor, and there isn't an active fullback in the game today who has his running and blocking ability. Or his verve and color. A whole new team can be built around a player like that!"

Klein stood and jerked a thumb in the direction of the rooms in which the party was in progress. "In there," he said, "I imagine there must be a half-dozen women who could be persuaded to hit the hay with you. The world is full of willing dames. So—if Helmsley is as valuable as you seem to think he is —you'd better kiss her off in a hurry. The assistant general manager of the Cougars can't keep laying Helmsley's wife."

Robin ate dinner with some of the Giants' public relations people and a couple of newspapermen, then returned to his own hotel room overlooking the beach. It was only 11:00 P.M., so the night was still young, but the half-hour he had spent with Marcus Aurelius Klein had already changed his life, and he no longer quite felt like a member of the Giants' organization. Besides, everyone would get stoned tonight to celebrate the winning of the world championship, and he had always been a moderate drinker.

A sense of caution was at least partly responsible for his return to his room, of course. He felt far more elated about his new position with the Cougars than he did about the Giants' victory, and he was afraid he might let something slip to a friend. Sportswriters by the hundreds were on the prowl in Miami Beach tonight, and under no circumstances could he allow one of them to learn prematurely of his move. From what Klein had indicated, it might be a few days before Danny Grannett was told he had a new assistant, and if he read the story in the newspapers before he received official notification, Robin would walk into the Cougar office under a cloud that might make it difficult for him to function efficiently.

He poured himself another drink, then walked to the window and stared out at the gentle, foaming waves that broke, ran out into deeper water and reformed to break again. Maybe he'd go down to the bar for a nightcap before he turned in, but right now he wanted to savor his personal triumph. And he couldn't help making a few plans. He knew the Giants wanted a new cornerback, and would be willing to trade a couple of good players for that speed merchant in the Cougar's secondary who, in spite of his talents, left the fans cold. Other AFC teams would be chary of trading, but maybe he could find some receptive ears in the ranks of the National Conference. With little to lose and a great deal to gain, he'd try the Vikings first.

An insistent tap at the door interrupted his reverie, and Robin felt a strong twinge of annoyance as he answered the summons.

Minerva Helmsley slipped quickly into the room, her short, blond hair tousled and heavy make-up emphasizing her eyes. She was tiny but voluptuous, and a single glance indicated she was leaving little to one's imagination tonight; in fact, she was wearing no more than Miami Beach's very liberal laws prescribed.

"Are you ever hard to find!" she said, flouncing into the room and immediately helping herself to a cigarette. "Like you're invisible or something."

Robin hated being placed on the defensive. "A man in my line of work is a little on the busy side after his team has just won the Super Bowl."

Minerva's blue eyes were scornful as they swept the room. "I can see," she said, "that you're just rushed to death. You promised you'd call me at my hotel. But," she added with ill-concealed resentment, "you forgot."

"Never. But I didn't want to be forced to hang up in a hurry if that two hundred and sixty pounds of fullback answered."

"I'm the one who always answers the phone. You know that by now." She was still aggrieved, but his excuse was legitimate, and had a mollifying effect. "Aren't you even going to offer me a drink?"

In the wake of Marcus Aurelius Klein's warning he didn't want her to become drunk and unmanageable, so he carefully measured bourbon into a glass.

"You could use an eyedropper," Minerva said, watching him.

Robin added a generous splash, but filled the glass with more water than she usually liked.

She took the drink, dropped into a chair, and crossing her legs, let her skirt ride high on her firm, shapely thighs.

"Where's the muscle man tonight?" he asked.

"Out with the boys, naturally, doing a pub crawl. A couple of fellows from the Cougars, and one or two others who are on the Pro Bowl squad with him. They started out from our room, but I paid no attention to the names of the ones I hadn't met. Like they're all sides of beef hanging in a butcher's freezer."

Contempt for the players on whom the professional football industry depended was an attitude they shared, and Robin couldn't help grinning. But he quickly sobered again. "I assumed," he said, "that the gooks would take their wives out for a night on the town tonight."

"Not my gook and his pals. Girls would get in the way, and wives, especially, might inhibit them from doing what they really like when they cut loose."

Hal Helmsley would be important to Robin's future, and his eyes narrowed as he looked at Minerva. On many teams, as he well knew, there was a small group that engaged in homosexual practices, which wasn't surprising. Ever since the times of the ancient Greek runners and the Roman gladiators, men whose bodies earned their livelihood sometimes displayed exceptional interest in the bodies of their colleagues. He had heard no rumors about Helmsley, however, and now was the opportune moment to nail down information that would prove valuable when he moved into his new job.

"Are you saying what I think, Min?"

She shrugged, allowing a thin shoulder-strap to slide down over her upper arm, and handed him her glass for a refill. "I suppose some people might call him acey-deucey, but me, I just say he isn't particular. As long as he has a partner who's alive and human, he doesn't complain. But who cares? I don't interfere with him, and he leaves me alone." She made it plain that any discussion of her husband bored her.

Robin saw she was drinking too fast, and experience had taught him there might be trouble.

He didn't have long to wait. "I feel like kicking up a storm tonight, honey," she said. "Where are you taking me?"

He braced himself. "No place."

[33]

Minerva was incredulous. "You've got to be kidding. There are more night spots per square foot in this town than anywhere else in the whole world."

"And you seem to forget that Hal is out there in the wild blue velvet night, visiting most of them."

"He and the boys are dive-hopping over in Miami," Minerva said scornfully. "They wouldn't pay the three to four dollars a drink that bars on the Beach charge."

"Maybe so." He clung to his new-found resolution. "All the same, there are plenty of owners, front-office people, coaches and players from every team in the business who are on the town tonight. Not to mention enough sportswriters, radio and TV commentators and publicity people to populate a medium-sized city. I know every last one of them, and they all know me."

"But not me. Except for some of the Cougars, I don't know hardly anybody in football."

"You've never faded into the woodwork, Min. And tonight you're as inconspicuous as goal posts being floodlighted for color cameras on a field goal attempt during a night game." He chuckled at the image.

She accepted the description as a compliment, and laughed.

"I mean it. Anyone who doesn't know you would damn well make it his business to find out, and there's bound to be somebody from the Cougar organization around to tell him. You happen to be married, remember, so there could be all kinds of complications, no matter what private arrangements you and Hal have worked out."

A high-heeled slipper tapped on the floor. "Like what kind of complications?"

"I'll just name one. Martin J. Morton. Commissioner of Professional Football. A man who personally and officially is allergic to even the faintest whiff of scandal that might reflect on the purity of the game as the most wholesome of all American institutions!"

[34]

"Some day," the girl said with concentrated venom, "I'm going to blow my mind if I even hear the Commissioner's office being mentioned in polite conversation. Is he some kind of dictator, or something, that he can tell people who they can go out with and where they can go?"

"Correct," Robin said calmly. "He's an absolute dictator with unlimited powers over everyone in the business. If you and I were seen together doing the town, he might investigate us—"

"Well, there's plenty to investigate, that's for sure." She found the notion amusing.

"Exactly. And after digging around, he might suspend Hal and pass the word to the owners that I'm not the kind of fellow they want on their payrolls. Why do you suppose we've always gotten together in towns that don't have major pro teams?"

The smile faded from Minerva's sensual lips. "It wouldn't surprise me if you've got another girl waiting for you to hit the bright spots with her," she said.

"Well, you're wrong. I haven't even had a lunch or dinner date with anyone other than you in months." And that, he thought, was the literal truth.

The revelation pleased her. "How come?"

"Because you're more than enough for any man who keeps regular working hours." How honest could he be?

Her vanity satisfied, Minerva nodded, then jumped to her feet and snapped on a wall radio. "This room really has all the gadgets. Look at all those buttons and switches."

"My company pays for the room," he said.

"Before the night is over we'll try all of them. You'd better order up more ice, honey."

Robin was afraid there might be an explosion if he indicated that she would leave as soon as he could get rid of her. Anyone who failed to take a Marcus Aurelius Klein threat seriously was a complete idiot. "There's plenty of ice."

"We'll melt it." In a sudden gesture of impatience she began snapping switches and twisting knobs. "Why do we need air

[35]

conditioning on a gorgeous night like this? It was snowing when I left O'Hare, and I want to enjoy the trade winds, or whatever it is they've got down here!" She turned, went to a window overlooking the sand and surf, and opened it.

Watching her, he tried to think of a logical excuse that would persuade her to leave, but was afraid he'd be wasting his breath. He could blame no one but himself for her proprietary attitude toward him, and suspected that marriage was lurking somewhere in the back of her mind. Unfortunately, they had become so intimate over a period of so many months and had proved so sexually compatible that it would be difficult to persuade her he had no intention of making her the next Mrs. Robin A. Stephens.

"This breeze," Minerva said, "is positively luscious."

The wind was pressing the thin fabric of her dress against her breasts, so that, for all practical purposes, she might already be undressed, and Robin averted his gaze.

"You want to know something?" Suddenly she turned toward him again.

"Why not?" He tried to keep his voice light.

"I haven't played around either. You've been the only one." Minerva looked at him when he failed to reply, and impatiently ran a hand through her short hair. "Now you're supposed to be dying of curiosity, and ask me how come you've won the jackpot—which is me."

"Okay. How come?"

"Because I haven't wanted anybody else. You sound as stupid as a football player! You've never handed me a phony line, and you've always treated me decently. Ever since the day I made the mistake of marrying Hal, I've felt like another of a star fullback's accessories. You know, like his vicuna coat and his imported turtleneck sweaters. A man in his position is supposed to be married to a blonde who comes on strong with the sex bit when the newspaper photographers snap their pictures together. I'm first-rate scenery, but that's the end of it. I'm useless to Hal as a human being."

[36]

It occurred to Robin, for the first time, that Minerva, in spite of her seeming self-assurance, was as lonely and frustrated in her way as he was in his. Perhaps her situation was even worse, since he had an active career that kept him busy.

"Don't look at me like that!" she commanded, her voice suddenly sharp.

"What am I doing?"

"The last thing I want is sympathy—from you or anybody else. I can get along just fine."

It would be cruel to destroy her illusion, he thought, even though he suspected she herself realized it was false. "I've never known anyone more self-sufficient than you, Min," he said, trying to prevent a note of kindness from creeping into his voice.

"You can say that again. Loud and clear." She heard the shrillness in her own voice, and smiled ruefully. "I'll tell you something, baby. Maybe I act whorish sometimes when you and I get together—because I know it turns both of us on when I do. But I'm not a whore."

"I never thought you were," Robin lied.

"I don't like these sneaky dates any more than you do."

When a woman became soft, she had the ability to confuse him. "That's one reason we can't keep meeting the way we've been doing. There's no long-range percentage in it."

Minerva leaned against the window ledge, half-sitting, half propping herself. "One of these days I'm going to make a clean break with Hal, and then you and I can be seen together anywhere. How does that sound?"

"Well, we'd be saved a lot of complications, but don't put me on a spot, Min. I don't want to be tagged as the cause of a marriage breaking up."

"Hal and I are finished, no matter what. My leaving him has nothing to do with you, not directly. I can get a job as a model, or something like that, but I'm not looking forward to it. So it will be a matter of timing. Hal is due for a big raise when he hassles for his new contract, and I think he'll be glad to give me a good chunk of money to be rid of me. My God, that makes me sound mercenary." She rubbed her bare arms, her expression unexpectedly wistful as she stared past him.

Robin was reminded of Kate, and some of his new-found sympathy for Minerva vanished.

"I don't want you to get the wrong idea, either," she said. "I'm not asking whether you'll marry me after I'm free. For right now, I'll take the fun, and let the future work itself out."

Nothing was further from his mind than marriage to her, and her sensible attitude relieved him. All the same, he thought it wise to take additional precautions. "When someone has been burned in marriage, as I have," he said carefully, "you don't want to rush into another mistake."

"You aren't the only one," she said. "Just because you and I hit it off in the hay doesn't mean we'd make out in other ways."

"Precisely."

"Even though I think we'd get along just great." There was a trace of smugness in her smile.

Robin couldn't imagine her as the wife of an assistant general manager, participating in the social events that were an integral part of the conference get-togethers of team owners and their principal business administrators. The ladies at these gatherings were atypical of the sporting scene, and were inclined to be conservative in appearance, dress and manner, so Minerva would stand out—in all the wrong ways. Therefore she would be more of a hindrance than a help to a husband who was moving up the ladder. But there was no present need to tell her his thoughts. It was a lucky break that she wasn't looking ahead in long-range terms, and he could concentrate on extricating himself from his present situation. Klein's warning had been emphatic, and he had no desire to let Kate retain possession of the club she was brandishing over his head.

He yawned, hoping she might take the hint. "This has been one mighty rough day," he said. "I'm dead beat."

"If you were a football player, you could take some pep pills.

But you won't need them." Her mood changing, Minerva twisted around and looked out at the beach again.

Robin felt a twinge of uneasiness; apparently she had some firm ideas of her own.

"Just look at that beach. And the water." Minerva paused, and a seductive note crept into her voice. "Guess what, honey."

He braced himself. "If you tell me, I won't have to guess."

"First we're going skinny-dipping. And then we're going to screw on those nice, warm sands."

"Like hell we're going to do either!" Robin said. "Not only could everybody in the hotel look out of the windows at us, but this town has some laws that are strictly enforced. The beaches are closed after dark, and they mean it. The police send patrols up and down all night."

"Oh, well." Not bothering to ask for another refill, she prepared herself a third drink, then returned to the window and her contemplation of the surf.

Still on his guard, he sank into a chair as he watched her. That tricky figure inevitably gave him ideas, but he never knew what stunt she might pull next, so it was best to be prepared.

"If the beach is out, we'll do it the next best way," she said. "On the floor in front of the open window. Now that I think of it, we've never tried it that way, have we?"

Robin found himself trapped, but continued to put up inner resistance as he shook his head.

Minerva moved toward him, deliberately tantalizing. "You know what I like, honey. Warm me up. We're going to make this one of our star-spangled jamborees."

"Look here, Min," Robin protested, his defenses rapidly crumbling. "I've got a million things to do tomorrow."

"If I hear any more excuses," she said, "I'll make you pay through the nose—and some other places. I'll get you so worked up that you'll do whatever I want. I'll make you get down on all fours, and you'll chase me around the room for an hour before I'll give it to you. Remember?"

At that moment he hated her, but he despised himself even more because he had granted her the power to gain a sexual domination over him that was beyond reason. He was cautious in his dealings, always self-controlled, but he had allowed her to possess him erotically, and knew he lacked the will to reject her demands.

His expression told her she had won, and she savored her triumph. She approached still closer, until her body was only inches from his face, and her hips began to undulate slowly. "Turn me on, honey," she murmured.

Robin knew what was expected of him, but made a last attempt to hold back. Veins bulged at his temples, his forehead was bathed in sweat and he clenched his fists, his nails biting into his palms.

"I have a little surprise for you," Minerva said.

He capitulated, knowing what the "surprise" would be, and when he ran his hands up the sides of her legs and thighs he found, as he had anticipated, that she was wearing no underwear. His fingers extended, he grasped her bare buttocks and pulled her closer.

She strained toward him. "You like this." It was a flat statement.

"Mmm," Robin said, and buried his face between her thighs.

Soon Minerva felt the flicking of his tongue, and a shudder shook her entire body. "Honey," she whispered, her hands pressing his head still closer, "together we're the greatest. I'm never going to let you go."

Danny Grannett had never cured himself of the professional football player's habit of eating a mammoth breakfast, but a great many years had passed since he had observed training table rules, and steaks and eggs were no longer enough to satisfy him. Frequently he ate hot cereal, too, and he liked to joke that the honey he poured on his waffles gave him quick energy.

Muriel Grannett listened to her husband place the order with room service, and when the meal came she fled as soon as she had gulped down a small tomato juice and a cup of coffee. After thirty-five years of marriage, she told him, there was no law that forced her to watch him make a pig of himself, and she could maintain a figure that belied the existence of four grandchildren only if she absented herself. Most of the shops on Collins Avenue wouldn't open for another hour, but that didn't matter, Muriel said, and went down to the outdoor pool to enjoy the early morning sun.

So Danny took his time, savoring every bite as he read the newspaper accounts of the previous day's Super Bowl game, and was still engrossed in his meal and the sports pages when Ellen Hibbs arrived. Chic in a green linen pantsuit, with a matching ribbon holding her long, reddish-blond hair in place, she looked far younger than her twenty-eight years, and a stranger seeing her in the hotel elevator could not have guessed that she had forgotten more about professional football than most men knew. At first glance she resembled an actress or ballet dancer, and occasionally she was mistaken for a model, but she had no interest in the stage.

The daughter of a Big Ten coach who had died of a heart attack shortly before he was scheduled to succeed Danny Grannett on the Cougars' bench, she had made football her entire life. Danny had been accused of rank sentimentalism when he had hired her, but seven years had passed since that time, and Ellen had won such universal acceptance that even the other members of the staff forgot whether she was called Danny's personal assistant or his executive secretary. Even the players thought of her as part of the scenery, and the rookies soon learned that anyone who made persistent passes at her was in peril of being dropped from the roster, regardless of his talents. A man's character, Danny often said, was more important than anything he did either on or off the field.

Ellen let herself into the suite, joined her boss at his breakfast table, and after pouring herself a cup of coffee, waited for him to recognize her presence.

Still studying the accounts of the game, he raised a hand in casual greeting. "Best waffles I've eaten in years," he said. "Have some."

She knew, as did his wife, that it was useless to protest she would lose her figure if she ate as he did. "I saw Muriel on her way to the pool just now, and she said to tell you she had to buy a new bathing cap."

The subject was of no interest to him, and he merely grunted.

"Because she forgot to bring one with her, of course." Ellen sipped her coffee. "Most of the columnists were terribly unfair to the Cincinnati defensive line this morning. They were as good as they've been all season; they played a cohesive game, but they were no match for that Giant offensive line."

Danny did not look up from his newspapers. "You're dead wrong," he said.

Few people anywhere would have argued football with a man who was known as a living legend, but Ellen Hibbs was the exception. "The front four diagnosed practically every play, but they were buried!"

"Cincinnati," Danny said patiently, "made the mistake of playing New York's game. They tried to contain the Giants on the ground, when they should have blitzed, red-dogged, stunted —anything to get the ball."

Ellen wished that, just once, she might be endowed with football knowledge equal to his.

While she sought an adequate reply, the door buzzer sounded.

"I asked Chuck Blanchard to join us," Danny said. "Mal Ferguson, too, but he flew home last night."

The girl went to the door and admitted the Cougar's director of public relations. There were hollows beneath Blanchard's puffy eyes, his skin was pale and it was evident that, like many of his colleagues, he had consumed more than his fair share of grain and grape the previous night.

But he was alert enough to ask Ellen a silent question: "Are we announcing a new trade already—or what?"

Her almost imperceptible shrug indicated that she was also in the dark. Being a realist, however, she was content to wait, and poured Blanchard a cup of black coffee while the men exchanged desultory greetings.

The public relations director gratefully sipped his scalding coffee. "I haven't seen the A.M.'s, but I suppose the New York papers are hailing the Giants as the wonder team of the decade."

"They just might be, at that," Danny said. "They've suffered no serious injuries, their team is so young that not one man is retiring, and they've got a couple of players tucked away on their taxi squad who would be stars anywhere else. They can afford to stand pat, and it doesn't much matter who they net in this winter's draft."

Ellen gazed wistfully out of the window, her expression like that of a woman who wants to buy a dress she can't afford. "How I wish we could wangle that Black defensive end, Jeffers, from them. He's mammoth, but he has all the instincts of a lightweight defensive back, and when he tackles you'd think he wrote the textbook."

"We couldn't get Byron Jeffers," Blanchard said, "if we offered Marcus Aurelius Klein's soup company in a trade for him."

"Don't be too sure of that," Danny said, and although he realized both of the others were staring at him, he took his time wiping his mouth and hands before settling back in his chair and smiling at them.

Ellen was careful, as a rule, not to smoke in his presence, but his provocative statement excited her, and she reached into her shoulder bag for a cigarette.

Blanchard needed no encouragement to light it for her, then light one of his own.

Reproving them in silence, Danny snapped off the air conditioning and opened a window before resuming his seat. "Last night," he said, "Muriel and I paid a courtesy call on Marc Klein during that fandango he was throwing. We hate big brawls like that, so we just stopped in for a few minutes. And Marc surprised me by hauling me off for a private conference."

Again Ellen and Blanchard exchanged glances.

"You can guess all day without coming close," Danny said. "We're going to be beefing up the front office, and we're getting a man who might be just the one to tell us how we could land Byron Jeffers."

Ellen snapped her long fingers. "I spent a few minutes at the Klein party, too, and as I was arriving, early in the evening, I saw Robin Stephens of the Giants ducking out."

"He's our new boy," Danny said, his eyes showing no emotion.

Ellen's loyalty to Danny Grannett was always her first consideration. "In what capacity, may I ask?" she demanded, her voice rising from alto to soprano.

"Marc has decided to give him the title of assistant general manager."

"I don't like this one bit," she said.

"Now, Ellen," Danny said, and shook his head. "He's been examined under the Klein corporate microscope, so you can bet he's an efficient, alert fellow."

"Football," she said, "isn't a sport that needs executives who have been reared and nurtured under microscopes."

"That may have been true once upon a time. As recently as the days when Otto Graham and Bob Waterfield were playing, football was primarily a game. But now it's become far more." Danny paused and made a valiant attempt to grin. "I'm told on all sides there's a need for the executives who can read corporate charts and work out profit and loss statements faster than the computers."

Ellen made no attempt to hide her irritation. "You didn't build your walls of granite with computers!"

"Simmer down," Danny said, and patted her hand.

Blanchard's hangover was forgotten, and he watched them, taking no active part in the conversation himself, but missing no nuance. The hiring of a new assistant G.M. might be interpreted in many ways, but Ellen's upset state pointed in just one direction. The Cougars had been floundering in a sea of mediocrity for a long time, and although nothing injurious to Danny had

[44]

appeared in print, he knew that any number of the Chicago sportswriters and their colleagues in other cities privately believed the landmark should be labeled as historic and set aside.

Suddenly Ellen turned to the public relations director. "What do you know about Stephens?"

Blanchard didn't intend to say anything that might be misquoted to Marc Klein's new boy. "I've never worked with him myself, but the Giants' P.R. people seem to like him very much."

"That's been my own impression," Danny said, still soothing the girl, "and I have every expectation that he'll fit into our own organization smoothly."

Ellen's loud sniff said far more than words could have expressed.

Danny pretended to ignore her. "We expect him to show up in a couple of weeks. The corporation brass will notify me of the exact date, and then I'll let you know."

"Shall I see him in advance, Danny, so we can get a news release ready? And maybe set up a tentative press-conference schedule?" the public-relations director asked.

Danny Grannett shook his head. "Under no circumstances, Chuck. Stephens belongs to the Giants until he submits his resignation and the Maras accept it. He doesn't become one of us until he signs the contract the legal department is preparing. *Then* he'll be a Cougar, and it will be okay to talk to him. Commissioner Morton has set up strict regulations in matters of front-office personnel transferring from one club to another, and I insist that my staff obey those rules to the letter!"

"Sure, boss." The old man's Boy Scout approach could be tiresome, Blanchard thought.

"For the present," Danny continued, "keep this information strictly to yourselves. If any rumors leak out and the press comes to you, Chuck, don't lie outright, but side-step."

"Okay, but may I ask why?"

"Marc Klein's orders," Danny said, indicating that their employer's command needed no amplification.

"Fair enough." Blanchard's head reminded him he needed a stiff Bloody Mary at the lobby bar, the only place in the hotel that served drinks this early in the day. "If you need me, I'll be around all day. I'm not flying back to Chicago until late tonight." He made a groggy but dignified departure.

Ellen could scarcely wait until the door of the sitting room closed behind him. "Now, Uncle Danny," she said, "what's the real story?"

"No more and no less than I've told you. And I hope you know all those cigarettes are as bad for your blood pressure as they are for your lungs."

"My blood pressure couldn't rise much higher than it is right now," Ellen said. "Why do we need a new assistant general manager?"

"I can think of many reasons. The farm teams need coordinated supervision—"

"You've already promoted Billy Leeds to the new job of farm-team supervisor!"

"Somebody has got to work out the details of building the new stadium with the city. And the banks. And the architects. And the ecologists who claim we'll be putting up a new eyesore on the Chicago lakefront. And the Congressmen who want their share of the credit. And all the others, so many that I can't keep them straight in my own mind. To be truthful with you, Ellen, I don't have the time or the talent for that kind of work. Or the interest. I prefer to work with the coaching staff on next month's draft."

"Stephens—or someone like him—could have been hired to handle the new stadium without making him assistant general manager!"

"I'm the one who'll be giving him this assignment," Danny said, absently tugging at the open collar of his sport shirt. "Nobody except you even knows that'll be one of his jobs. And squabbling with the concessionaires over their new contracts will be another. That's been one of the nightmares of my job."

Ellen moved to a place directly opposite him and stared at

[46]

him until he returned her gaze. "My nightmare," she said, "is that one of the hot-shot characters who carries an attaché case and wears English-tailored suits is going to bump you onto the shelf, Uncle Danny."

There was a hint of self-consciousness in his deprecating laugh. "Well, Muriel has been after me to retire, all right, but I wouldn't know what to do with myself after spending my whole life in football. Anyway, Marc didn't mention anything about my retirement last night, or even grooming young Stephens to succeed me. I expect to be around long enough to produce one championship Cougar team, and then I'll be ready to step down." He rubbed his massive, bare forearms. "Looking at our prospects realistically, that means I'll be in harness for a long, long time to come."

"I hope so, Uncle Danny! You get more fan mail—to this day —than almost any of the coaches or players, and the Commissioner's office should subsidize you as an inspiration to all the youngsters who want to play football."

Danny Grannett chuckled. "I ought to hire you as a personal press agent." Slowly his smile faded, and his eyes seemed to sink deeper into his grizzled face. "Do you know something I don't, Ellen?"

She pushed back a long strand of her reddish-blond hair. "Not really. I guess it was listening to some of those wise punks last night, the bright boys of the Klein conglomerate who weren't even born when you were making football history. They thought I was just another of the dozens of girls who had been imported for the party, so they didn't much care what they said in front of me. But I just burned when they said how old-fashioned you are, and how you can't handle a general manager's job any more, and how you ought to be turned out to pasture. On and on, Uncle Danny. All kinds of nasty remarks like that, and I see no reason to get you all whooped up, too, by repeating them to you."

The old man stood, drawing his massive frame to its full height. "I can't blame those young fellows," he said. "The old

Chicago Cardinals had a following before the team changed leagues and went to St. Louis, and there was no American Conference franchise in Chicago until Marc started the Cougars. People who don't like the Bears—or want two first-rate teams in town, or just naturally love football—are anxious to root for us. But winning is the name of this game, as it is in any competitive game, and it isn't easy to cheer for a collection of sad sacks who have never won more games than they've lost in a single season."

"You've developed some wonderful players, Uncle Danny. Like Hal Helmsley, for instance. And if the fans will just be patient—"

"Ah, that's a big if, Ellen. I hope they'll bear with me, because it takes time to build a solid, championship team, and I've got to do my job in my own way."

"Of course you do!" Ellen said, and dropping the subject, unwilling to tell him that her feminine intuition, which had no place in football, was screaming that Robin Stephens represented a grave threat to his future.

Chuck Blanchard stirred his second Bloody Mary with the muddler, and his head began to clear enough for him to think coherently. A one-time sportswriter who had worked for the Klein conglomerate as a publicist for the soap company and a lobbyist for the aerospace manufacturing subsidiary, he had been plucked out of his anonymous Washington job and had become the Cougars' director of public relations. He loved his present post as much as he despised Marcus Aurelius Klein, and long had nurtured the dream of moving higher in the football team's front office, where the rewards were greater and the work less demanding than any he had known.

The day would come, he had promised himself, when he would add ticket sales to his present responsibilities, and when seats became hard to obtain, he could make a real killing. There were ticket sales managers and even box-office treasurers who had retired after a few championship seasons, and Blanchard had seen himself moving in that happy direction. Danny Grannett had confidence in him, and even though the Cougars weren't yet a promising team, you never knew what would happen in football. In any event, they would play two games with Cincinnati, the AFC champions, this coming year, and both the Giants and Vikings were scheduled for interconference games in Chicago. The demand to see the front-running teams would be heavy, and if he could gain command of seating between now and early summer, he'd be in a position to turn big blocs over to the ticket brokers, and could insist on an even split in under-the-table earnings. It would be no trick at all by a year from now, no matter how the Cougars fared, to acquire enough for a new house and that sports convertible he coveted.

But the unexpected appearance of Robin Stephens on the Cougar scene might change everything, and Blanchard found himself unable to evaluate the man. He could sound out the Giants' publicity staff, of course, but they would give him no more than a surface portrait. Would he ride with Danny's decisions or try to buck them? Would he be content to work with the present Cougar front-office staff, or would he try to inject his own people into the organization? It was likely that no one, with the possible exception of Marc Klein, knew the answers.

The air conditioning in the lobby had not yet been turned up all the way, and Blanchard mopped his bald head with a handkerchief. Then, as he raised his glass to his lips again, a couple who emerged from an elevator caught his eye, and he watched them as they crossed the lobby to the broad, half-spiral staircase that led to the front entrance. Both were wearing dark sunglasses, but were vaguely familiar, and the girl, clad in the flimsiest of short dresses, had a spectacular figure; Blanchard had never been drawn to the short, Dresden-doll type, but told himself this one was something else.

Suddenly he recognized her, and hitched forward on his bar stool, holding his glass in front of his face. Unless he was very much mistaken, and he had seen her on many occasions over the past two or three years, she was Hal Helmsley's wife. Her companion was more difficult to identify, but he perspired even more profusely when, with a sudden sense of shock, he recognized Robin Stephens.

He continued to watch as Stephens put the blonde into a taxi that pulled up in front of the entrance, and he smiled sourly to himself when he noted that the couple took care to avoid any physical contact. He'd been through the same sort of thing himself, and could understand their precautions, even though it had to be obvious to anyone who noticed them that the girl had spent the night in the man's room. This was not an hour of morning when anyone escorted a casual visitor or even a breakfast date to a taxi, not when she was a blonde like Helmsley's wife who oozed sex from every pore.

By the time Robin slowly made his way to the bar, Blanchard had turned in the opposite direction and was innocently studying an abstract mural done in mosaics on the far lobby wall. The publicity man paid strict attention to his drink, and carefully allowed Robin to discover his presence. Then, very casually, he asked, "May I join you?"

"Sure." Robin was in no mood for a chat, and concentrated on his own Bloody Mary.

For a time Blanchard was silent, too. "Congratulations," he said at last.

"Thanks." Robin's reply was mechanical. "The team had it coming, and everybody played a great game out there yesterday."

Even the bartender had moved out of earshot, but Blanchard took no chances and lowered his voice. "That isn't what I meant," he said.

Robin peered at him through the dark glasses.

"I just heard from Danny about some interesting developments. I realize they're still confidential, but I'm delighted."

Robin was surprised that Grannett had already been told of his move, and the knowledge dictated a slight change in plans. When he returned to his own room he'd make a token call to Grannett to express his own pleasure; then his new general manager would have the ball, and would decide whether he wanted to get together now or preferred to wait until the move became official.

"I'll sit tight," Blanchard said, "until I'm given the green light. Then we'll work up the press conference and all the rest. We'll suit your convenience, naturally."

Robin had almost forgotten the public relations man's presence. "That's very nice of you," he said, and removing his glasses, passed a weary hand across his face. Min Helmsley was the only member of the human race who had ever discovered the secret of perpetual motion and put it into practice, he thought, and he was beat. Not even a professional athlete endowed with Hal Helmsley's stamina, he told himself, could keep up with Min when she went on one of her rampages.

Blanchard saw the deep shadows beneath the bloodshot eyes of his outfit's new assistant general manager, and his own apprehension subsided somewhat. It was comforting to realize that Stephens was very human, and convenient to have learned some fascinating facts about his private life. It always helped to know someone's weaknesses.

"I'm afraid you'll have to forgive me if I'm only half-here this morning." Robin wanted another drink to overcome the effects of all the bourbon he had consumed, but was afraid it might knock him out. On the other hand, there was no reason he couldn't drop off for a few hours beside the pool, and in any event, he had no one but himself to blame for trying to match Min drink for drink. He had long known that her shapely legs were hollow, and he grimaced as he signaled to the bartender. "Hit me again, and another for my friend."

"Thanks," Blanchard said, and pretended to look away as he asked, "Tough night?"

"There are many ways to celebrate the winning of the Super Bowl," Robin replied, his voice heavy with irony, "all of them active."

Blanchard's myopic eyes narrowed. "I can imagine," he said.

2

They held two press conferences to announce the appointment, the first in New York. The second, in Chicago, took place in a lounge at O'Hare Airport on Robin's arrival, and was delayed twenty-four hours because of a snag that upset his plans just prior to his departure. Kate Stephens learned of his new job by reading the newspapers, and threatened him again, forcing him to pay her the last of the five thousand dollars she had demanded.

The Chicago press conference was a model of brevity in which he called all the right plays. "I'm here," he said, "because I believe the Cougars have a potential that will be realized before most people expect us to start winning championships. I'm here because I've always liked Chicago, and because I'm looking forward, as you are, to the building of our new stadium. But I'd like to emphasize that I have no plans of my own. I'm also here to take orders and learn from the wisest and finest man in football, Danny Grannett."

He fielded questions with aplomb, and only Phil Donegan, "the dean of Chicago sportscasters," proved troublesome. As Donegan's followers had known for many years, his ruddy, smiling face and genial manner concealed a sharp tongue and equally acute news sense. He held the title of sports director for WWW, one of Chicago's leading combination television and radio broad-casting companies, and keeping his hand in, he served as the anchorman and commentator for all televised Cougar games.

"What have you heard, Mr. Stephens, about Danny Grannett's retirement?" he asked.

"No one has mentioned it to me," Robin replied. "If there's any validity to the story, which I very much doubt, I suggest you ask Danny about it."

Donegan shifted his attack to the opposite side of the field. "How do you think you'll get along with him?"

"I always make it my business to get along with my boss!" Robin retorted. "And in this case it will be a great experience. Name somebody in this business who wouldn't want Dan Grannett as his teacher!"

"Then you don't expect to replace him?" The sportscaster had been stopped on the ground, and tried an aerial attack.

"Hardly. Let me remind you that I've been hired as *assistant* general manager."

Donegan appeared to accept the loss of the ball, then unleashed his bomb. "Do you have any major trades up your sleeve?"

Robin held his temper in check, having been warned by Chuck Blanchard that he would be subjected to a grilling. Donegan, who liked to call himself "the sports voice of Triple-W" not only worked the Cougar games on television but had the biggest radio audience in the greater Chicago area for his nightly radio program, which had attained its popularity because of his can-dor. Until his claws could be clipped, a task that Robin promised himself he would enjoy, he was obliged to treat the assassin with care.

To the delight of the three TV news cameramen who were taping the session, he slowly removed his jacket, unfastened his cuff links and pulled his sleeves above his elbows. "I just wanted to prove that I have nothing up my sleeves," he said.

Donegan joined in the general laughter, but he was persistent, and started to ask still another question.

"I'm not finished," Robin said, cutting him off. "I want to

make something clear for the permanent record. I've seen the Cougars in action just twice in the past two years, so I'm not yet really familiar with the team's personnel. I haven't yet had a meeting with Dan Grannett, so I don't know what my duties will be. Therefore I can't tell you whether I'll have a voice in trades. I don't know myself. If I have any ideas on the subject they're strictly my own business as of now, and if I'm asked to express them, they'll be passed along to just one person—the general manager of the Cougars." The time had come to end the session. "Now, gentlemen, thank you for your courtesy, and drop in to see me any time you come up to the Cougar offices."

He escaped without further interrogation. Blanchard's assistant was waiting with a car, and he was driven to the Ambassador East, where he found a note from one of the executives at Klein headquarters urging him to stay there as long as he wished at company expense before searching for a permanent place to live. Apparently it was true that the conglomerate spared no expense in its dealings with those whom it employed in the upper echelons, but Robin preferred not to avail himself of the corporation's generosity. It was unsound business procedure to fall into anyone's debt, and, in any event, he spent so much of his time traveling that even the best hotels did not appeal to him, so he intended to find an apartment as quickly as possible.

Blanchard suggested lunch at the Pump Room, but Robin wanted to keep a measurable distance between himself and subordinate members of the Cougar staff until he became familiar with the organization. It was difficult to cool a business intimacy that developed too quickly. So he had a sandwich sent up to his room, and spent an hour leafing through the mounds of congratulatory letters and telegrams the hotel had been holding for him. A few had been sent by friends and acquaintances, others had been sent by companies that did business with the Cougars and the rest had been sent by total strangers, people who belonged to that blurred mass, the general public, and were responsible for the continuing existence of professional football.

Robin felt a need for exercise, but the January wind that blew in from Lake Michigan was numbing, so he took a taxi to Klein Tower, a new skyscraper on Wacker Drive. An express elevator lifted him to the Cougar headquarters on the forty-third floor, where it became obvious that the staff had been alerted. The exotic redhead who presided over the reception desk greeted him by name and, for good measure, gave him an expert eye, which he pretended not to notice. Every executive who wanted to climb higher in the company's hierarchy was familiar with the Commandment, Thou Shalt Not Play Around With the Hired Help.

An attractive Black secretary appeared to escort him, and he was relieved to discover that the color barrier had been broken here. Approximately half of the players on the rosters of the National Football League teams were Black, and the eradication of prejudice in the front offices made life easier for those who spent several months each year negotiating contracts with men of all hues.

"I'm Patricia Thompson, Mr. Stephens," she said, "and I've been assigned to you until you bring in a permanent secretary."

He made a point of shaking hands with her before she conducted him past the endless rows of file cabinets, interspersed with the desks of clerks and stenographers and statisticians.

"You may not have heard that Mr. Grannett is on vacation," she told him. "He left rather suddenly just day before yesterday for Hawaii."

"No, I hadn't heard. Thanks." He felt vaguely resentful because no one had told him.

The girl seemed to read his mind. "Miss Hibbs passed the word to keep it quiet. I'm guessing now, but I suspect he wasn't feeling too well."

Robin looked at her with a feeling of growing respect. She was pretty and trimly dressed, and obviously she used her brains. He might do worse than make her the permanent cornerstone of his permanent personal staff.

"Miss Hibbs asked me to bring you straight to her office," the the girl said. "So maybe you'd be more comfortable if you let me relieve you of your things."

Robin handed her his hat, coat and attaché case, then deliberately tested her. "Give me a rundown on her."

Patricia Thompson met the challenge without hesitation. "Miss Hibbs? Mr. Grannett couldn't get along without her, and neither could the Cougars. If you don't believe me, she'll tell you herself."

He nodded and grinned.

She returned his smile demurely, but said nothing more as she led him past a long row of private offices, halting at the entrance to one near the far end. "Mr. Stephens is here, Miss Hibbs," she said, and departed without waiting for a reply.

Robin thought the girl fluttered an eyelid before she took off, but put her out of his mind for the present. His first impression of the office he entered was its masculine atmosphere. Action photographs of the Cougars filled the walls, and the furniture consisted of overstuffed leather chairs and dark woods. But a single rose stood in a pale vase at the far end of the room, and the young woman who stood and extended a hand to him seemed very feminine. She was wearing a dress of a soft material that made it plain she had no reason to be ashamed of her figure, charm bracelets jangled on her wrist and her reddish-blond hair fell in waves below her shoulders.

"Welcome to Cougar country, Mr. Stephens," she said, and waved him to a visitor's chair.

Her voice was so impersonal that Robin felt as though she had slapped him across the face, a reaction he recognized as absurd. So he compensated for it with his most charming smile.

Ellen Hibbs was impervious to it. "Dan is sorry he isn't here to pipe you aboard in person, but he and Muriel had a chance to fly to Hawaii day before yesterday with a party Mr. Klein was taking on one of the company jets, so they grabbed the opportunity."

"I don't blame them. I'd have done the same." It appeared that Grannett still enjoyed the confidence of Marcus Aurelius, which was a trifle surprising.

She took a cigarette from a bone china box on her desk, but did not offer him one, and her manner remained courteous, yet remote. "Dan has left you enough to get your feet wet," she said.

Robin deliberately stood and lighted her cigarette, then took one for himself from the pack in his pocket. "I'm ready to start swimming."

"Your biggest, immediate job is going to be the negotiations for the new stadium," Ellen said crisply. "I've left all the file folders in your office, and as I know a little something about the talks so far, I'll be glad to discuss the problems with you after you've done your homework."

"That'll be a help." Studying her covertly, he wondered why she behaved as though ice water ran in her veins. She didn't look all that cold, so perhaps it was the defense mechanism of a woman who held a highly responsible post in professional football, which was unusual.

"In a separate folder," she said, "are last year's contracts with the concessionaires. They'll be anxious to start hammering out this year's deals whenever you're ready to see them. Danny is turning all that over to you, too."

"Good." A shrewd negotiator could increase a team's profits by six figures if he wangled the right contracts with concessionaires. "Maybe you can give me a few pointers there, too."

"Certainly, Mr. Stephens, if you wish."

"The name is Robin," he said.

Ellen nodded, but her expression remained unchanged.

Again he felt rebuffed. "Anything else on my agenda?"

"I'm sure," she said severely, "there will be more than enough to occupy you until Danny returns." She handed him a small sheaf of cards. "Fill these out for personnel and payroll, please. We've assigned you a temporary secretary, but feel free to get someone else, if you prefer, although it's a Klein practice to promote from within the organization."

"Then that's what I'll do."

"You may feel you'll want an assistant for work on the new stadium, and if so, I'll send you a list of candidates we've prepared."

"Send it along," Robin said. "As I understand it, I'll have to contend with three banks, the city administration and the park board, not to mention two opposing factions of conglomerate brass. Both of which presumably have their offices somewhere on the floors above us."

"You catch on quickly." She paid him the compliment grudgingly.

He shrugged, refusing to let her open hostility irritate him. "I assume that's why they hired me. And speaking of lists, I'd very much like to see the coaching staff's draft choices."

"Danny reserves the supervision of that area of operations for himself!" The green in her eyes deepened when she became upset.

Robin began to understand her defensive attitude. "I wouldn't interfere," he said, "even if I could. But I happen to know a little something about this year's crop of college seniors myself."

She made no reply.

"So," he continued, determined to force a showdown that would establish his authority, "I might have something to contribute to the Cougar cause."

Ellen realized that, pending Danny Grannett's return, she could not prevent the newcomer from meddling. "I'll bring those lists to you myself. I'm sure you realize they're confidential."

Robin stood and looked down his nose at her. "My dear young woman," he said, "I've earned my living in this business for the past twelve years!"

The dignity of his rapid exit was somewhat marred by his ignorance of the Cougar office geography, and he didn't know where to go when he reached the corridor. But Patricia Thompson materialized out of nowhere, and silently led him to a handsome corner suite.

"This is yours, Mr. Stephens," she said.

He closed the door behind them. "How did you know I was going to need you?"

The girl flashed a broad smile. "It figured," she said cryptically.

There was no need to question her prematurely, he decided; everything would fall into place. Meanwhile he could enjoy the inspection of an overwhelmingly impressive office. The outer room was an unoccupied secretary's office, with a couch for waiting visitors, and the large inner chamber had cross-ventilation, always a sign of an executive's stature, and also boasted a private bathroom. In due time, he thought, it would be perfect for cowing players and others who came here to negotiate contracts.

"This won't be half-bad," he said, "after I move in a few personal belongings and put up some pictures. Where do you hang out, Patricia?"

"In the bullpen."

"Move your stuff in here," he said.

The girl's eyes widened. "We assumed, all of us, that you'd bring somebody in from New York with you."

"I prefer a secretary who knows the local scene. You're a Chicagoan?"

She nodded.

"How long have you worked here?"

"Three years." She straightened. "I'm Frank Thompson's widow."

Everybody in football remembered Franklin D. Thompson, the promising Cougar halfback who had been called to active Army duty as a lieutenant and had been killed in Vietnam. What was astonishing was that no one in the front office had the basic public relations sense to have rescued his widow from the anonymity of the secretarial bullpen.

"You're elected," he said, "and I hope you're free to have dinner with me tonight."

She was delighted to have been awarded the job, but the invitation confused her. "I couldn't go anywhere in what I'm wearing."

Robin wanted to put her on the right track immediately. "You look fine," he said. "And let's get this straight—I don't make passes at secretaries, including my own. But we're going to be working together, so we ought to get acquainted. And I'll want you to fill me in on everything you think I ought to know about this place."

The question was settled, and he spent the afternoon looking through the stacks of documents already piled high on his new desk. A number of key papers needed more thorough study, so he threw them into his attaché case to take back to the hotel with him, and time passed so quickly that he was surprised when he glanced at his watch and saw it was six o'clock.

Few members of the sports fraternity frequented the Pump Room, so he decided to take Patricia there for dinner, and they chatted easily in the elegantly furnished eighteenth-century room. Over cocktails and dinner she answered his questions about various staff members, but he waited patiently to bring up several topics he considered important. Finally, over brandy, he opened an invisible door.

"Tomorrow," he said, "I wonder if you'd do me a favor. Get hold of some real estate agents, and go apartment hunting for me. All I'll need is a place with a bedroom, a kitchen and a living room big enough for throwing an occasional business party. This is the part of Chicago I know best, so I'd like to live somewhere on the near North Side."

"I'll be glad to do it for you," Patricia said, "but maybe you've picked the wrong secretary, Mr. Stephens. If the real estate people think the apartment is for me—or for a boyfriend—all of a sudden it may be rented out from under us. A lot of buildings on the Gold Coast are still allergic to Blacks."

This was precisely the opening Robin wanted. "To hell with them," he said. "I wouldn't want to live in one of those buildings."

She peered at him, and saw he was sincere. "Well," she said. "I think I've got me a boss I'm going to like."

"You can bet on it. And since we're being frank about color, that brings up something else. I've heard rumors there have been factions on the Cougars. How about it?"

Her hesitation was itself an answer. Finally she said, "It was worse a few years ago."

"But it still isn't good?"

"Things could be better."

Robin knew of one team, potential champions, that had been

ruined by the feuding of whites and blacks. "What are the coaches doing about it?"

"Oh, they try, and they're pretty fair. A couple of the assistant coaches are Black themselves, and that helps." Patricia sipped her brandy. "What trouble there is these days is caused by some of the veterans—both Blacks and whites—who've been around for quite a time. Fellows who were there when Frank was still alive."

"Can they be hauled into line and made to cooperate?"

"I've never known anyone who could be forced into losing his prejudices," Patricia said, "but some of them can be silenced because they'd be afraid to say too much if they knew their jobs depended on their good behavior."

"You're really okay." A secretary with the ability to think independently and reach sound conclusions was priceless. "Let's get down to basics and name names."

The girl averted her face.

"An infectious disease can't be stamped out unless the carriers are identified," Robin said firmly. "Until I know who is responsible for the racial feelings on both sides, my hands are tied."

Patricia raised her head and studied him for a moment. "I suspect you can be ruthless."

"I'm not paid my salary to be charming and friendly." Perhaps he was overstepping the bounds of his authority by demanding the identities of the racial troublemakers; disciplining them was Mal Ferguson's job, and Dan Grannett was ultimately responsible. Nevertheless, he'd be better able to judge his own competence in the situation when he was armed with the facts.

She sighed and slowly twirled her glass.

"Name some names, please. And don't get the feeling that you're ratting on anybody. Your loyalty is to me, and through me to the Cougars."

Patricia took a deep breath. "Well, the head of the white faction is Tony Zimmerman."

The team's number two quarterback, the durable Zimmerman was one of the oldest veteran players still active in professional football. "I'm not too surprised," Robin said. "He went to one of those little redneck colleges in Mississippi or thereabouts, and back in his day it was automatic that every athlete on campus joined the Klan."

She was surprised that he knew so much about Zimmerman's background. "Have you been doing research on Tony?"

"No more than on anyone else." He saw no reason to mention that he was familiar with the records of virtually every player in major-league professional football. "Keep talking."

Patricia sucked in her breath. "The worst of the Blacks isn't one of the old-timers, although they rally to him. It's Ted Marcus."

Robin felt as though he had been dealt a physical blow. In his first season as a pro, Marcus had already established himself as a star, and was sure to develop into one of the top linebackers in the game. "Are you quite sure?"

"Positive!" she declared. "Tony and his friends on the other side of the fence were tamped down before Ted Marcus joined the Cougars. In fact, Tony was actually kind of friendly with my Frank. They kidded each other about color—you know, half-joking. Then Ted showed up—they say he was a member of the militant wing of a Black Nationalist organization for several years, although I can't swear to that—and all the old hatred on both sides flared up again."

He was silent for a moment. "Couldn't the coaches and the front office stop the feuding?"

"That isn't Mr. Grannett's way. He has no prejudices himself, so he refuses to take anybody else's seriously. And Mr. Ferguson just concentrates on football. He has a one-track mind, and doesn't think of anything else."

Robin did not want to be too open in his criticism of new colleagues before giving his secretary time to develop ironclad loyalties to him, so he shifted into another gear. "The front office must be aware of the situation."

"Oh, I'm sure of it."

"Well, then." He spread his hands.

She slid the metal chain of her shoulder bag between her

fingers. "I guess," she said, "you don't know Mr. Grannett very well."

"I've met him any number of times, at league meetings and the like. But aside from that, I only know what I've read. Which is what everybody else knows."

"And that's misleading. I—I don't want to talk out of turn, Mr. Stephens—"

"You aren't, I assure you."

"Well, Mr. Grannett is so old-fashioned in some ways you wouldn't believe it. He doesn't think in terms of race problems, so in his mind there aren't any. Football is more than a game to him. Frank used to say that it was Mr. Grannett's religion. And anybody who wears his uniform is a football player, no more and no less. He isn't a Black man and he isn't a white man."

"Ultimately," Robin said, "that's the only possible attitude an intelligent person can take. Race doesn't matter in football."

The girl shook her head. "There's a difference between what you're saying and what I'm saying. *You* say race shouldn't mean anything—and you're right. But Mr. Grannett can't even see it exists. So the sore continues to fester."

Robin offered her a cigarette, which she refused, then dropped the pack into his pocket. "Can't the very efficient Miss Hibbs open his eyes?"

Patricia surprised him by laughing. "I just knew this would happen!" She saw he was confused, and became apologetic. "I'm sorry, but if you'd been around the office the past few weeks, you'd understand. Ellen becomes a little paranoid when she thinks anyone is threatening Mr. Grannett. For a whole year she wanted to ban our leading sportscaster from Cougar games because he was needling Mr. Grannett—"

"Having met Phil Donegan today, I know how she felt."

"Anyway," Patricia said, "she'll relax with you and get along just fine once she realizes you aren't trying to grab the top job for yourself."

"Her presence in the business may be a triumph for Women's Lib, but it doesn't prove anything else."

"I felt sure she'd annoy you, Mr. Stephens. But Ellen is okay, and you'll discover she's far more competent than you imagine."

"I'm willing to be convinced," he said, and dropped the subject. At no time would he reveal his long-range goals to his new secretary, no matter how much loyalty and trust he inspired in her. But he had already made up his mind to keep a close watch on Ellen Hibbs, and if she really stood in his way he would deal ruthlessly with her when the situation demanded it.

After they finished their coffee and brandy Robin sent Patricia home in a taxi, paying the driver in advance. He stopped at the hotel desk for telephone messages, and leafed through them on his way up to his room. One in particular caught his eye: *Welcome from a golfing grass widow.*

No name was signed, but the number looked familiar, and when he checked it in his memo book he found, as he had expected, that it was the unlisted Helmsley number. Minerva was making it plain to him that her husband had gone away on a trip and that she was at home alone.

Dropping the message into a pile with all the rest, Robin read the accounts of his arrival in the Chicago newspapers, and then looked at his watch. It was only eleven o'clock, so the evening was still fairly young, and the Helmsleys lived in the same near North Side neighborhood, no more than a ten minute walk or two-minute taxi ride from the hotel.

He pushed the thought out of his mind, but it crept back into his consciousness. It was unlikely that he was under surveillance, but Marc Klein was unpredictable, and having issued a warning, might want to make certain it was being heeded. So that would make it difficult for Minerva to come to the hotel. But if it was true she was alone at her apartment, he'd be safe enough paying her a visit there.

Damning himself for his own weakness, he cursed Minerva, too, for tempting him. He had told her nothing about Klein's stern injunction, so it was high time she learned there would be serious trouble ahead if they continued to see each other. In any event, that was the excuse he offered himself as he walked to the telephone and dialed her number.

*　*　*

The news broke first through the press, and Chuck Blanchard, after a moment's hesitation to determine the priority, made calls in quick succession to Robin, Ellen Hibbs, the public-information vice-president of the Klein conglomerate and the Blanchards' daughter, who was married to a local sporting goods manufacturer. All of his own telephones were already ringing, but he told his harassed secretary to hold the calls while he passed along the urgent message. "The AP has just notified me that a bulletin from Honolulu says Dan Grannett has suffered a heart attack there. That's all I know for now."

Robin immediately switched off his own telephones, sat quietly behind his desk while he smoked a cigarette, and then waited a few moments longer to calm himself. His mind was seething, but he needed more precise information before he could look ahead, so he went down the corridor to the office of Ellen Hibbs.

He found her already on the phone, placing a call to Muriel Grannett in Honolulu, and although it was obvious she would have preferred privacy, it would have been too much to ask him to leave.

The Cougar switchboard operator performed a minor miracle, and the call went through so quickly that Robin barely had time to light another cigarette before Ellen was on the line with "Aunt Muriel."

It was difficult to follow the fragmented, sometimes emotional conversation, so Robin exercised supreme self-control as he stared out of the window at the Michigan Avenue skyline. The Chicago wind was blowing vigorously, as usual, and a few snowflakes were swirling in the air, but he did not see them. Perhaps his great chance had come too soon, before he could prove himself, and in that event someone else might be brought in over his head. But speculation was useless, and under no circumstances could he allow himself to become panicky.

At last Ellen wearily replaced the telephone in its cradle and sank back in her chair. "Two heart specialists agree that Uncle Danny suffered what they called a minor coronary attack," she

[65]

said. "With proper rest and treatment he'll recover. Thank God."

"Thank God." Questions crowded Robin's mind, but he asked none of them.

"He'll have to spend six-to-eight weeks in the hospital, and then he'll have to loaf for another three months. He should be coming back to work while we're in summer training camp."

"The important thing," Robin said, "is that he'll be back. Is there anything that anyone can do for him?"

"No, he's very comfortable, but Aunt Muriel says he's not allowed to take any telephone calls or receive any visitors. And the doctors aren't allowing him to talk business with anyone."

"Of course." For the moment Robin tried to put business considerations into the back of his mind. "If you happen to know his reading tastes, I'll appreciate it if you'll give me some idea, so I can send him a half-dozen books."

Ellen's eyes widened slightly. "That's very thoughtful of you."

"Well, Danny has never struck me as the kind of fellow who has any great love for flowers, and there must be thousands of them around a hospital in Hawaii. So books seem like the best idea."

"I'll give your secretary a list before lunchtime," she said.

"Thanks." He stood and walked to the window. "The press will be clamoring for information. Any suggestions?"

"First," Ellen said without hesitation, "I believe we should refer all medical questions to the specialists in Honolulu. I have their names." She tore a slip of paper from her memo pad and handed it to him.

"Fair enough. But I believe we ought to pass along the word, informally, that he'll be okay."

"I'm not sure that's ethical," Ellen said.

He turned and faced her. "If we don't, there will be screaming headlines—before we can stop them—saying Dan Grannett is dying."

She was reluctant to agree, but he made sense. "I suppose you're right." For a moment she, too, was lost in thought. "The players and some of the staff, not to mention the people we do business with, may get jittery. So I think we should also issue a statement to the effect that pending Danny's return, the Cougars will follow the guidelines he's already laid down."

"Whatever that means," Robin said.

She stared hard at him.

"If there are any such guidelines, I haven't seen them."

"I meant in general." Ellen looked uneasy.

"Well, the concessionaire contracts won't be terribly different from last year's, of course."

She was willing to pay the new assistant general manager a grudging tribute. "You've driven a harder bargain with all of them."

"That's why I'm paid a salary," Robin said. "As for the new lakefront stadium, the political in-fighting and the financial complications are going to make it impossible for us to be in operation this coming season. We'll be lucky if construction even starts by the time Danny gets back."

Her gesture was an acknowledgment of his exclusive responsibility in that area. "I was thinking more in terms of the team itself," she said. "The draft. Trades. All that kind of thing."

"To the best of my knowledge," Robin replied, realizing a genuine showdown was at hand, "Danny hadn't coordinated his draft list with the coaching staff's list."

Ellen was shocked. "Have you been talking to Mal Ferguson or his assistants?"

Right now was the time to indicate he was not accepting the restrictions she had placed on his areas of command. "Only in overall terms. We haven't dug into specifics. Yet."

"Danny has always insisted on controlling trades and the draft himself," Ellen said, her green eyes stubborn.

"Sure." It was better to sound reasonable than show his frustrated anger. "But—as of the past half-hour—everything is changed. The draft drawings will take place next week, and the trading season is wide open right now. But Danny isn't coming back in time to take charge. Mal Ferguson was expecting to have a long session with him this coming Monday, but Danny won't be here on Monday. And Mal swears he doesn't know what Danny has had in his mind. Incredible though that may be."

His criticism of the Grannett methods caused her to flush. "No two football teams operate in the same way, Robin."

"I could debate that point with you, Ellen. I could point out to you in rather considerable detail that virtually all teams have adopted systematic approaches to the problems of acquiring the players who are necessary to this business. Danny has had his own approach, and if you insist that his reputation warrants any approach he chooses, I'm not going to argue with you. Because all that is irrelevant. Apparently he was carrying a list of potential trades around in his head, but that won't do the rest of us any good."

Ellen continued to stand up to him. "I believe I have a fairly good idea of what he had in mind."

"Then dictate a memo to me right now, telling me everything you know. Or think you know."

"If you insist," she said, and glared at him.

"I do." His smile was tight.

"I hope," Ellen said, "you'll do Dan Grannett the courtesy of allowing me to sit in on any meetings you may have with Mal Ferguson and his coaches."

"I'll keep a complete record of everything that goes on," he said, "so Danny can be brought up to date whenever he's well enough to be informed. In the meantime, however, I want to make it very clear that I didn't take this job of mine so I could have the rather dubious privilege of submitting to the authority of a woman—who may *think* she understands the football business!"

He left before she could reply, and stormed into Patricia's office.

His secretary was fending off someone on the telephone, and handed him a thick sheaf of messages that had accumulated in the short time he had been elsewhere.

He waved aside the slips. "Get Blanchard in here," he said, "so

I can give him a statement for the press. Then find out when Mr. Klein can see me—the sooner the better. And while you're at it, don't let anyone know that *I'm* asking for the meeting with *him*."

A large Picasso painting occupied one wall, and at right angles to it was a medieval tapestry, a juxtaposition that Marcus Aurelius Klein found amusing. One bank of windows gave him an unobstructed view of the Chicago River, its bridges and the buildings that rose high above both sides, while the other looked out on his private helicopter landing pad. The office was enormous, which was expected, and sparsely furnished, which was not. Only the padded leather swivel chair behind the oversized, marble-topped table that served as a desk looked comfortable, while the visitors' chairs and settees, all of blond wood in Scandinavian design, looked positively forbidding. It was rarely necessary for the master of the empire to remind visitors that he conducted his business there, and did not expect them to relax.

The marble-topped table was virtually bare, and Klein, looking up from a paper he was studying, glanced at the onyx clock that stood beside his electronic intercom. "I lost a bet with myself, Stephens," he said. "I was sure you'd call for an appointment ten minutes earlier, or else come straight up without phoning."

Robin walked the length of the office, the thick Oriental rug sinking beneath his weight, and accepted the plain wooden chair at one side of the table that was offered to him. "I wanted to make certain the press was squared away."

"And now that you've satisfied the reporters, you want to know for yourself where things stand." Klein enjoyed being a jump ahead.

"Yes, that's part of it. I also wanted to tell you that Danny's assistant has spoken to Mrs. Grannett in Honolulu, and—"

"I've had a chat with Muriel myself. I've sent a specialist from San Francisco to consult with the doctors who are already working on the case, and I've told Muriel to send all the bills to me. Personally." Klein took a cigar from a lead-lined humidor. "Now, young man, what can I do for *you*?"

Robin had heard that delicacy did not pay off in this office, and tact was not appreciated. "I'd like to know where I stand, Mr. Klein."

"If you're asking whether I intend to replace Danny, I'm not. You're number two, and until number one comes back, you move for the time being into his slot. What else?"

Robin minced no words. "What are the limits of my authority?"

Klein looked at him with an expression that might have indicated approval. "Hell," he said, "you have the responsibility, and anything that goes wrong will come out of your hide."

"I've had the green light from Danny in certain areas from the day I walked in, which was only a week and a half ago. But there are some functions he didn't delegate. Like running the college draft, which comes off next week, and making trades. He was on vacation when this illness struck, so we've had no chance to get together. The only person who knows what was in his mind, or claims she knows—"

"I'm very fond of Ellen Hibbs," Klein said, and chuckled.

Robin made a mental note to the effect that it might be far more difficult to get rid of the girl than he had assumed. "I have no way of knowing where Dan Grannett's views end and her opinions begin." It was best to know at once where he stood, and he would either return to the Giants or find another job before being forced into a spot where he could be blamed for the mistakes made by others.

Klein probably knew what he wanted, but waited for him to clarify his position.

"I can't perform miracles," Robin said. "Even Vince Lombardi needed time for that. I can't even promise you the Cougars will end next season with a better win-and-loss record than they had this past season. But if I handle the personnel situation in my own way, I can make you several flat guarantees. We'll be laying the foundations for a future championship team. And we'll have immediate returns at the box-office."

"I wear several hats." the older man's eyes were opaque. "M. A. Klein, sportsman, wants a winner. Naturally. M. A. Klein, public figure, cringes when his name is associated with a mediocre product." Suddenly he straightened. "And M. A. Klein, businessman, wants every last one of his enterprises to pull as much freight as it can carry!"

For the first time since the start of the crisis, Robin felt a stab of elation. "I won't be bothering you again, Mr. Klein," he said. "I hope you'll pay us a visit at training camp—which I plan to move to a more convenient and less expensive location."

"Oh, drop in any time you have a free minute," Klein said. "I'll be particularly interested to hear how you and Ellen Hibbs are getting along."

Mal Ferguson had been a substitute lineman on Dan Grannett's teams for eight years before being promoted to defensive coach, where his real talents had been revealed, and he had made such steady progress that no one else had been considered for the post of head coach when Danny had decided to confine himself to the Cougar general managership. Ferguson's critics claimed he was a plodder who lacked initiative, and not even his most enthusiastic defenders claimed he was colorful, but within the business he was respected as a man who knew football.

Robin shared that opinion, and felt a trifle sorry for the husky, graying man who sat opposite him behind the closed door of his office. Life could not have been easy for any coach who had been forced to live and work under the ever-present scrutiny of as expert a second-guesser as Dan Grannett. All the same, there was an opportunity to perform major surgery, so personal feelings were unimportant.

"What I can't understand about this draft list," Robin said, tapping several stapled, closely typed sheets of paper, "is why it should be so radically different from all the others in the league."

[71]

Ferguson clamped his teeth on the heavy pipe that protruded from one side of his mouth, and puffed on it for a moment before removing it to facilitate his speech. "I guess our scouts didn't agree with any of the others," he replied.

"That's too simple, Mal, and you know it," Robin said. "All of the others have banded together in groups of threes and fours to form scouting companies that cover every college campus in the country, because no one team can afford to hire that many scouts. And they use the latest, most sophisticated computers to analyze the data they pour into the machines."

Ferguson grinned. "Wait until you hear Danny express his opinion of computerized football. He doesn't often cuss. But man, does he ever let loose!"

"Danny is entitled to think what he pleases. Nobody has a better right. All the same," Robin said, scanning the draft list, "I find Andy Lincoln of Grambling listed as number two-seventy-three. He's second on the Giants' list, but the champions draw last, of course, so they don't stand a chance of getting him. I understand Dallas, Oakland and Buffalo are hot for him, and Baltimore is willing to give up their first and third draft choices for him if somebody else gets him first. That's how highly the computers rate Andy Lincoln!"

"What can I tell you?" Ferguson gestured broadly with a huge hand. "Jeez, I don't have to stand on ceremony with you, Rob. I'm too busy on weekends to watch any of the college teams."

"I'm not for a minute blaming you, Mal. All I'm saying is that the Cougar's draft list is exceptionally weak, and we've got to do something about it. I saw Mr. Klein this morning, after we got word of Danny's illness, and I don't mind telling you he wants a team that's going to start drawing sell-out crowds. This season."

"That's a tall order."

"Sure, but it can be done. I'll grant you there may be a few sleepers on our list, players nobody else knows or wants, and we have nothing to lose by gambling on them. But I propose we build in a hurry by trading."

The coach's square-jawed face was hidden for a moment behind a cloud of smoke. "I've thought about trades, Rob, don't think I haven't! But we don't have that many men who are worth the players we'd want."

"I propose to sweeten the pot by throwing in most of our draft picks," Robin said. "We'll hold out a few for our top selections—and release all the rest."

Ferguson was startled. "That's pretty drastic."

"You've only heard the beginning. Write down the names of all the men on the present roster you want to keep."

The coach agreed to the unusual procedure, and struggled for some minutes with pencil and paper, producing a list of fifteen names.

Robin swiftly crossed off all but three, those of Hal Helmsley and two linemen. "If there are any others you think are potential material for a championship squad, I'm prepared to listen to your arguments," he said.

Ferguson's eyes bulged, and he forgot to draw on his pipe. "You can't break up the team!"

"Just you watch me." Robin softened a trifle and smiled. "Could you use Byron Jeffers?"

"What team couldn't?" Ferguson countered.

"The Giants will give him to us for these two gooks and a top draft choice. I'll offer them the third, and settle for the second. Would that Buffalo punter and place-kicker, Adam Renewzski, be of any use to you?"

"You got to be kidding. He's great!"

"He's ours, in return for our fifth choice and their pick of any two men they want from our defensive backfield. I sounded them out just before you got here this afternoon."

"Excuse me if I feel like I've been kicked in the stomach," Ferguson said.

"Sure, it's a lot to absorb in one sitting." Robin sounded sympathetic.

The coach picked up the sheet of paper on which he had labored. "We can't dump Tony Zimmerman," he said at last.

"Well I wouldn't be surprised if no other team is interested in a back-up quarterback who claims he's thirty-nine and is probably a couple of years older."

"That isn't what I mean," the coach said. "He's been with the Cougars ever since Mr. Klein bought the franchise. He's as much a part of the team as Danny. Or me."

"If you feel sentimental about him, add him to your coaching staff, but deactivate him as a player. I question his worth on the field, and if no other team wants him in a trade, we save a valuable place on the roster."

"The fans will scream if we get rid of Zimmerman, Rob."

Deliberate brutality could have a therapeutic shock value. "Unfortunately, the Cougars don't have enough fans to make their screams heard above the normal sounds of Chicago's winds." Robin paused, then said quietly, "I assume you refer to our white fans."

"There was a lot of talk about Tony a few years ago when there were race feelings on the team," Ferguson said, becoming defensive. "But nobody could ever prove he was mixed up in any of that crap. And ever since then he's kept his nose mighty clean. Just because he's a Southerner, you know, some of the Black ends thought they weren't getting their fair share of passes from him."

"There was more to it than that," Robin said.

The coach was silent for a moment. "On my way in here, I noticed that Thompson's widow is working as your secretary. I guess you wouldn't know that Thompson and Tony Zimmerman had a real feud going. For a long time."

Robin refused to argue a matter that could be neither verified nor disproved. "One quick, sure way to improve the Cougar image," he said, "is to get rid of all the dissidents, white or Black, and make this a team that welcomes any man for his playing ability, regardless of his color."

"Sure, and I'll go most of the way with you," Ferguson said, "but I hate to dump Zimmerman. Suppose that quarterback we're bringing up from the Peoria farm club isn't ready for another season. We'll need Tony to fall back on."

"Zimmerman will not be a member of the Cougars' squad this coming season."

Mal's jawline grew white as he clamped his teeth on the stem of his pipe. "If the kid quarterback doesn't make the grade for us—"

"In my opinion it's the worst of all possible mistakes to depend on a rookie quarterback. Not even one in ten can make the grade in his first year. Look at the statistics."

"You front office guys are great believers in figures, but we deal with people down on the field." Mal stirred as he began to assert himself. "Personally, I have faith in the kid. That's point number one. Point number two is that we'll need Tony Zimmerman to help him."

"My decision on Zimmerman is final." Robin slapped the table for emphasis.

"Then we're up a tree, and we may as well be content to land in the cellar this coming season. Good, experienced quarterbacks don't grow up out of the ground like mushrooms."

"I expect to trade for a quarterback, and I'm going to get one of the very best."

"Using what for trade bait? We'd have to give up Helmsley!"

"No," Robin said, speaking very softly. "Even juicier bait than Helmsley. Ted Marcus."

Mal Ferguson placed his pipe in an ashtray and stared hard at the younger man. "I thought it was an oversight or a fluke of some kind that Marcus wasn't on the approved list. He's the key to our whole defense, and he'll keep improving for years. You can't be serious about trading him, Stephens!"

"He's going," Robin said.

The head coach of the Cougars clenched and opened his fists. "Why?"

"For the same reason we're getting rid of Zimmerman. No team crippled by racial antagonisms has ever made it to the top."

"Maybe you've been listening to some of the newspaper people around town who are inclined to exaggerate this kind of thing—"

"My sources of information are accurate," Robin interrupted.

"What a man wants to believe off the field is his business, not ours," Ferguson said heatedly. "The minute he puts on his uniform, he becomes a football player."

"As you yourself mentioned just a little while ago, you deal with human beings on the field."

"Sure! My yardstick—and Dan Grannett's—is a player's dedication to football. I don't give a damn if he's a Commie or a fascist or one of the Black Power boys—or whatever. How does he tackle? Can he block? Does he give one hundred percent all the time? Those are the things that count!"

"A white offensive lineman who hates Blacks won't go all out when he's blocking for a Black halfback, Mal, and you know it."

"I disagree!" Mal sat back in his chair and glowered.

"I hoped I could persuade you to see this my way. Sorry you can't." Robin's tone was deceptively mild.

There was a long, uncomfortable silence before Mal said, "I suppose you have some mastermind deal all worked out in your head."

"I certainly do. I'm going to approach Baltimore, and ask them for Big Horse Collins."

Mal was shocked. "My God, Stephens! Oh, Collins is good, all right. He's a first-class linebacker, he's smart and he's still young. But he's not in Ted Marcus' class!"

"A basic fact of life that any flesh peddler in the business will gladly confirm. So I won't make a one-for-one trade. If they want Marcus—"

"Everybody wants him. He'd give Baltimore the best defensive line in the American Conference!"

"—they'll have to throw in another player to sweeten the pot."

Mal seemed to sense what was coming, and grew even stiffer. "They have a lot of good players."

"There's only one I want," Robin said. "Fred Finch."

The head coach was speechless.

"Not only do we need a quarterback, but he's ten feet taller than anyone else on the active rosters."

Mal passed a hand over his eyes. "You can't do this," he muttered.

"He has more than a potential. He's arrived, and with the right handling he can hit superstar level with us his first year," Robin said.

"Who'll handle him?" Mal demanded. "I'll tell it to you plain —I can't!"

"If necessary," Robin replied, "I'll do it. I'm convinced he's the hottest property in football today."

The head coach cursed quietly but fluently.

"Bigger than Marcus and Helmsley put together. You may get five thousand fans who'll come to see a linebacker in action. Or ten thousand to watch a fullback grind out the yardage. But you'll fill every stadium in the United States and Canada from your first exhibition game of the season to the Super Bowl if you put the right quarterback on the field. You can even fill the bleachers during summer practice, at a couple of dollars per seat. Fearless Freddie, surrounded by a peerless cast of supporting players, is exactly what we need."

Mal was still dazed. "Fred Finch," he said, "isn't the Cougar type."

Robin's smile was tight. "What type is that?"

"The kind who'd rather play football than eat."

"When you were a boy that may have been true. But there ain't no such animal these days. Football is as much of a business for the gooks as it is for us."

Mal shook his head. "You'll have to speak for yourself. I'm talking about men who believe in Dan Grannett's principles, and follow them."

"Dan is paid to haul in as big a profit as he can for Marcus A. Klein, just as we are. And, if he can bring in a championship team at the same time, so much the better."

"I don't think you understand what this game is all about, Stephens."

"Until somebody can convince me I'm wrong," Robin said, "I'll have to do things my way. Which means I'm going to trade for Fearless Freddie Finch."

"He drinks during the season—"

"So does everybody else."

"Not publicly!" the head coach snapped. "And not to excess. He runs around with flashy girls—"

"Speaking as a bachelor, I admire his taste."

"He's not only a swinger, which gives football a bad image," Mal said, "but he mocks the game and everybody in it at his press conferences. Which is why the Colts had to shut him up. Before they sat him on the bench. No matter how talented he's supposed to be."

"I'm familiar with all the answers," Robin said. "The difference between Finch and Joe Namath is that Namath is a serious, dedicated man the minute he climbs into uniform, while Freddie never stops kidding around. Mal, you've been working with young men all your life, and you surely don't need me to tell you that all Finch needs is to be encouraged into taking the right path—and then given his head."

"Not in my rule book," Mal Ferguson said.

They had reached an impasse, and stared at each other in silence, with Mal's stubborn hostility matched by Robin's seemingly cool indifference to the views of anyone else.

For an afternoon, the better part of the evening and most of the next morning Robin sat behind the closed door of his office, talking on the telephone. He survived on endless cardboard containers of coffee, augmented by the sandwiches Patricia brought him, but he ate almost nothing, and at times he was in danger of losing his voice. But the file of pink memo cards denoting players traded or sold grew, the list of draft choices available to the Cougars shrank, and the yellow cards signifying players acquired expanded equally rapidly.

The press began to pick up rumors which Chuck Blanchard and his staff could neither confirm nor deny, and Phil Donegan twice demanded an immediate interview with Robin, but was told, "Mr. Stephens can't see anyone." What made the rejection particularly galling was the complete lack of any attempt to offer a gracious excuse. Robin might have permitted the veteran sportscaster to save face, and it would have been a simple matter to claim it was necessary to acclimate to new responsibilities in the wake of Dan Grannett's sudden illness. But Robin inaugurated his regime in his own way: he was busy, and even those who were important in the world of communications would have to wait.

At noon Patricia brought her new superior another sandwich, and he decided to wait until she left the office before he threw it into the wastebasket. "By one o'clock, our time," he said, "San Francisco will be in business for the day. Be sure you get them on the line promptly. I'm offering them two of our remaining draft choices for their nifty young tight end."

"You have time to go out for something to eat, you know," the secretary told him.

He shook his head. "I'm not hungry, and I'd fall flat on my face if I went down to the bar for a drink. You've been great, Pat, and once we're through with all these deals and the dust settles, you can take some days off."

"I'm having fun," she said, and grinned. "I haven't seen as much happening around here in all the time I've worked for the Cougars." She placed another container of coffee on the desk. "I suppose you're too busy to see Hal Helmsley."

"When?"

"I tried to set an appointment for next week, but he's out in my office, and he insists on seeing you now."

Robin glanced at the small, chiming clock on the oak table opposite his desk. "Send him in, but you may have to run him out at one, when the San Francisco call comes through."

"Just send for me," she said as she moved to the door, "any time you want a two hundred and twenty pound fullback pushed around."

Hal Helmsley, dapper as well as massive in a suede suit and bulky, cable-stitch sweater, seemed completely at ease as he strolled into the office. "You're harder to see than the Commissioner, Robin."

"My door is aways open to you, Hal," Robin replied, shaking hands and waving his visitor to a chair. "Can I order you some coffee?"

"No, thanks."

"Take this sandwich, then. I won't be eating it."

The fullback was about to refuse, but opened the waxed paper wrapping first. "I have a weakness for turkey on rye bread," he said, and began to consume the sandwich in large bites.

Robin did not act like a man badly pressed for time. "How's your golf game?"

"Not too bad. I shot in the low eighties out in Palm Springs last week." Helmsley glanced across the desk, then spoke again, without discernible malice. "There'd be no point in telling you how my wife is getting along, because you probably know better than I do."

Robin's face became expressionless.

The fullback waved a huge hand. "Don't worry, buddy, I haven't come here to scrap about Minnie. She and I have had it, and we're just waiting for the right time to separate. You're welcome to her—if you want her. And even if you don't, you'll probably have her. Our Min knows what she wants, and these days she wants you. I'm giving you a free tip—because I'm such a good guy."

"Thanks," Robin said, admitting nothing.

"Now you can do me a favor in return. What the hell is popping around here? A few hours after I heard that poor old Danny Grannett was sick, I started getting phone calls from newspaper and TV and radio people all over the country. They tell me Marcus and I have been traded for the whole Patriots team. I'm being sent to San Diego, and Tony Zimmerman is being retired because nobody wants him. And so on."

Robin forced a laugh.

"Football has taught me not to duck issues," Hal said, running a hand through his thick, blond hair. "So I've come straight to the oracle. Are you busting up the team?"

[80]

"That's a loaded question, Hal."

"Sure, buddy. Like my asking if you've stopped beating my wife. You won't tell me who is being traded?"

"It would be unethical and premature. But I'll gladly make one thing very clear. You're staying in a Cougar uniform."

"Good. I'm building a following in this town, and I'm going to capitalize on it. I'm opening a men's store, and I have some other plans. I'm also counting on you to take Minnie off my hands so I won't have to pay her a lot of alimony."

Robin smiled politely, but said nothing that could be either quoted or misquoted.

"If I'm staying, maybe this would be the wrong time to start talking new contract terms."

Robin glanced at the clock. "We have a few minutes. You're getting forty thousand now. How much do you want?"

"What are the Cougars offering?"

"A new three-year contract at fifty thousand a year."

"You have got to have blown your mind. I carried for almost twelve hundred yards this past season—"

"With an average of five point six yards per carry. And a cardboard line in front of you. I know all the statistics."

"Then you ought to know I can't be had cheap." Hal demolished the last of the sandwich and wiped his mouth with the back of his hand.

Robin threw a paper napkin across the desk to him. "What do you think you're worth?"

"Seventy-five G's. For three years."

Robin whistled softly, concealing his elation. It would be easier to come to terms with the star fullback than he had feared.

"Treat me right," Hal continued, "and I'll make a special deal with the acting general manager. I'll try to talk Minnie into getting off your back."

Robin stiffened. "We're discussing a player contract with the Cougars. Nothing concerning your private life or mine is relevant."

"The shade of Danny Grannett is still haunting the place, I can see. The new management believes in the Boy Scout virtues that were sacred to the old!"

"You won't get seventy-five as a straight salary." Robin remained crisp. "I might go to sixty, with a bonus arrangement that can make up the difference, provided we get peak seasonal performances from you."

"Man," Hal said, "I do believe I can be had!"

"We'll work out the details in the next week or two, after a few other matters are settled," Robin said.

Before Hal could reply, the door opened abruptly, and Ellen Hibbs stormed into the office without having bothered to knock. She carried a sheaf of interoffice memoranda in her hand, and barely bothering to nod in Hal's direction, she glared at Robin. "It's urgent," she said, "that I see you immediately!"

Hal laughed as he retrieved the fur-lined coat he had thrown over a chair. "I'll retire, knowing the acting G.M. is in good hands. Robin, why don't you drop around for dinner tomorrow night? I promise I won't be home." He departed, chuckling at his own humor.

Ellen's shocked expression indicated she had heard rumors about Robin and Minerva Helmsley.

Robin was embarrassed, but had more important matters on his mind. "I trust I'll always be courteous enough not to barge into your office when the door is closed."

"You'll have to forgive my manners, but these memos on the trades you've been making since yesterday have driven everything else out of my mind." Ellen waved the sheaf. "Are you trying to destroy the Cougars?"

"To the best of my knowledge and ability," Robin replied, resuming his seat, "I'm building a new team."

"While tearing down everything Danny Grannett has tried for years to accomplish."

"But didn't. He had a mediocre team that did ordinary business at the box office. Chicago is like New York. A city of this size demands a winner." He sipped his coffee, discovered it was cold and put down the container. "Anything else?"

"Danny isn't dead, you know, and he hasn't retired. When he comes back there won't be more than a handful of players he'll recognize."

He studied her for a moment, then commanded, "Sit down!" She made no move.

"You and I are going to reach an understanding right now. First, I told you to sit!"

Rather than make an issue of the matter she perched on the edge of a chair and tugged at her short skirt. "What you're doing to the Cougars is the most outrageous—"

"If I make a mess of the team, it'll be my funeral," Robin declared, his voice icy, "and I have no doubt you'll invite everyone in the business to sit in box seats—as your personal guest. I know the risks I'm taking, and if I fail, I fully expect you to do your damndest to drive me out of the industry. Now, let's talk about you. For the present, I'm quarterbacking this operation, and I expect the members of my team to obey the signals I call. You're efficient, and I can find no fault with your work. But your attitude makes it impossible for me to place any confidence in you. I prefer not to rock any front-office boats, and for Dan's sake I'd like you to be here when he returns next summer—or whenever. But you'll have to start remembering you're working for me, and you aren't here as his personal representative."

"I hope you realize," she said, matching his chill, "that absolutely nobody is going to stand still and accept your ax job."

"That depends on who you mean by nobody."

"The newspapers will have fits, and so will the commentators on the air—"

"They'll change their tune when the team improves."

"And the Cougar fans will be up in arms!"

"That, my dear girl, is where you're wrong, and betray your ignorance of a sports-minded public." Robin stood and pointed out of the nearest window. "People out there," he declared, "will snap up every seat we put on sale if we give them a tough, aggressive, colorful team that will start winning more games than it loses. They may be unhappy for a short while, but those who cry the loudest will be the first to cheer the new Cougars. You can believe me or not, as you wish, because I don't care what you think."

"You'll be hanged in effigy—and maybe in person—for trading away Ted Marcus and Tony Zimmerman."

"With you supplying the rope?"

"Your humor is overwhelming, but this sparring is accomplishing nothing. I've come to you in the hope I can persuade you to reconsider." Her expression made it plain she was swallowing her pride. "I realize you've already made most of your deals, but they aren't final until you confirm them in writing, and—"

"If I were to back out now, I'd be committing suicide in football." He controlled his anger, and propping his elbows on the desk, spoke more gently. "Accept the idea that—for right now, anyway—I'm in charge of the store."

"I've already gone upstairs, and if I hadn't realized your decisions are final, I know it now." Ellen tried a more conciliatory approach. "I can understand you don't have a very high opinion of a woman in football, and I'm not blaming you for it. It's a cross I've had to bear ever since I came to work here. I'm not necessarily questioning your judgments, even though I may think some of your trades are crazy. My one worry is Uncle Danny. I'm afraid he'll literally have another heart attack when he learns what you've done to his team."

"Well," Robin said, "I don't pretend to be an expert on the personality of Dan Grannett. But he's been in this business far longer than both of us put together, so he must know that when a team doesn't produce at the box office, it'll be broken up."

She stood, smoothing her skirt, and shook her head.

It occurred to him that, at this instant, she looked feminine, defenseless and appealing. If she moved into some other line of work she could become an exceptionally attractive girl.

"For a lot of reasons," Ellen said, "some of them connected with Uncle Danny and some of them personal, I'm going to hang around. So I'm afraid you'll be stuck with me. All I can promise you is that I'll try to accept your decisions, even though it won't be easy. What I may think or say isn't important, though." She paused at the door. "Far more serious opposition is forming, and you've got your work cut out for you."

Robin did not complete the last of his trades until nine o'clock that night, and after stopping for a quick dinner, he went straight to his new apartment on Astor Street. There, over a quiet nightcap, he would condense the data preparatory to a meeting in the morning with Chuck Blanchard and his assistants. A press conference had already been called at noon, and at that time he would announce the wholesale shake-up that would put a new Cougar team on the field. He would have preferred to wait until he had held personal talks with some of the key players he had acquired, but the rumors were flying in a half-dozen National Football League cities, so it was essential that the blockbuster announcement be made by the Cougars, rather than leaked to the press by their opponents.

Mixing himself a mild bourbon and water, Robin emptied the contents of his attaché case on a coffee table, and began to compile a list that included the information he wanted to stress on the background and records of each of the new players. Although he was tired he soon became absorbed in the task, and forgot the passage of time until the house telephone at his elbow jangled.

"Mal Ferguson," the metallic voice at the other end of the wire announced. "I'm in the lobby, and I'd like to see you for a couple of minutes."

"Sure, come on up." Robin was not unduly surprised by the unexpected visit, and returned to his work until he heard the elevator door open and close.

The head coach looked wan, and there were deep, dark shadows beneath his eyes. "I won't pretend I just happened to be in the neighborhood," he said with a weary smile. "You had just left the office when I tried to get you there, and I've stopped off downstairs here a couple of times."

"Let me get you a drink," Robin said, taking his hat and coat. "And find yourself a chair. My secretary has been buying furniture for me, but things have been on the hectic side, so there aren't too many places to sit as yet."

Mal lowered himself into the only easy chair in the living room. "This isn't a social call, and I'm not so sure you'll want to offer me a drink when you hear what I'm going to say."

"If I remember rightly, you never take anything stronger than beer." Robin went off to the kitchen, returning with an opened can. "Pardon the informality, but the glasses and dishes Pat ordered from Marshall Field haven't come yet, so I'm still camping out."

Accepting the beer, Mal took his time stuffing and lighting his pipe. "It's this way," he said uncomfortably. "I can't show up at the press conference tomorrow."

Robin said nothing as he waited for the explanation.

"Some of your trades were just tremendous. Getting Byron Jeffers was a stroke of genius, and Adam Renewzski will be worth his weight in gold to the Cougars. But one of your deals sticks in my craw. I just can't buy Finch and Collins for Ted Marcus."

Robin resumed his place on the sofa. "You still don't like the idea of our getting Fred Finch."

"I'm so opposed to it," the coach said, his face solemn, "that I'm submitting my resignation. As of right now."

Robin's expression did not change. "I won't accept it, Mal. You still have two years to go on your present five-year contract."

"When somebody in my position asks to be released, his request is usually honored."

"I'm not going by the unwritten book." Robin's smile was bloodless. "I'm protecting myself in the clinches, Mal. I had an idea you might want to pull something like this, so I've been prepared for it. If you walk out, the stink will get the new Cougars off to a bad start. You're popular with the fans, and no matter how good the new players may be, ticket sales will be hurt for at least a season if you quit."

"I made it plain to you that Finch isn't my idea of a quarterback."

"You've spent a long time on Klein's payroll, and at your age you'd be a nut to jeopardize your pension plan." Robin sipped his drink. "If you insist on stepping down as head coach, I can't stop you. But I'll insist you honor your contract, and you can work it out for the next couple of years as chief scout."

Mal looked at him with reluctant admiration. "I've got to hand it to you," he said. "You can be a ruthless bastard."

"I'm not trying to win any personal popularity contests. Now, drink your beer and listen to me for a minute. Suppose Finch behaves himself off the field, and doesn't pull any of those wild stunts of his to please the crowds—"

"Egomaniac quarterbacks who can't understand there are ten other men on the team are like leopards. They can't change their spots."

"I'm just asking you to suppose. Let's say he does change. Let's also say he operates within the boundaries of your overall offensive operations and sticks to your individual game plans. Would you be willing to give him his head and let him call his own game on the field?"

"Of course." Mal looked haggard. "But you're setting up all kinds of conditions that won't and can't be met!"

Robin's manner changed, and his voice hardened. "If necessary, I'll bring in a head coach who will work with our new players, and you can mark time scouting until your contract expires. But I'd rather you stayed on."

"I can't see why."

"Very simple," Robin said. "The basic public appeal of football is emotional. A great many people support a team because of sentiment, which may or may not be rational. I'd face a lot of grave problems if I completely did away with Cougar tradition, and I see you as the natural bridge between the old and the new."

"You aren't just ruthless. You're clever."

"Also," Robin continued, playing his trump card, "Dan Grannett will be back on the job one day. So it strikes me that somebody who is undeviatingly loyal to him would want to be here when he returns."

"That's the only thing that stopped me from walking out when you told me you wanted Finch. Don't think it's easy for me to—"

"Then don't!" Robin stood so he would gain the advantage of looking down at the other man. "I'm prepared to make you a binding gentleman's agreement. String along with the new team, and I'll accept complete responsibility for Finch's conduct. If he steps out of line at any time, you can quit. Without notice."

Mal chewed on the stem of his pipe. "There has to be a catch in all this."

"I'm leveling with you. Say the word, and I'll pay off your contract in full immediately. All I ask is that you give the new setup a whirl."

"How are you going to put the brakes on Finch?"

Under no circumstances could Robin reveal that he had no specific plan in mind, but was relying exclusively on his confidence in his own ability to deal with people. "Leave Fearless Freddie to me."

"I'm tempted," Mal said. "For one reason. Dan Grannett ought be back in harness before the exhibition season starts, and he'll get rid of Finch overnight if there's any of the crap he's pulled wherever he's played." His face disappeared for a moment behind a cloud of smoke. "What I really don't understand is why you're doing all this, Robin. Dan will be back when the doctors give their okay, so you won't be in the driver's seat long enough to make a name for yourself, either good or bad."

Robin smiled. "Do you accept my terms?"

"Well. I guess so. Hell, I have nothing to lose."

The immediate crisis was ended, and Robin was too tired to look beyond it. "Then I'll see you at the press conference tomorrow. At twelve sharp."

3

Phil Donegan's resonant baritone voice, heard regularly on WWW-TV as well as on the station's radio outlet, led the chorus of opposition to what became known as the "Cougar catastrophe." Other commentators joined in denouncing Robin Stephens for the destruction of the team and the undoing of all that Dan Grannett had tried to accomplish. The loss of Ted Marcus was regarded as criminal negligence, and three radical Black organizations picketed Klein Tower for a week in protest. The acquisition of Byron Jeffers, the Giants' great defensive end, and Gerald "Big Horse" Collins of the Colts were minor compensations, but the fact that place-kicker Adam Renewzski had also become a Cougar was virtually ignored.

The critics aimed their principal fire at the deal which had brought Fred Finch to Chicago, and Fearless Freddie was being damned as a liability who would lead the Cougars straight to the occupation of the American Conference cellar. Even a power-crazed acting general manager suffering from delusions of glory, Donegan said nightly on his popular program, should have known better than to hire an exhibitionist who failed to understand the principles of team play.

The Chicago newspapers were somewhat more conservative

in their approach, but they demonstrated no enthusiasm for the formation of the new team. They refused to launch an assault, but their dispassionate, remote attitude was damaging. Then, by coincidence, the *Tribune* and the *Sun-Times* published editorials on the same day, both suggesting that the team might continue to suffer under an inexperienced general manager, and expressing the wish that Dan Grannett would recover his health in the immediate future.

Robin rode out the storm in silence, rejecting the advice of Chuck Blanchard, who urged him to wage an aggressive campaign in which he would strike back at his critics. The gale would subside far more quickly, he said, if he pretended the winds weren't blowing; in due time the exploits of the new Cougar team would prove he had known his business. One night, in an unguarded moment, he admitted to Minerva Helmsley that he was irritated by the endless versions of a joke making the rounds in Chicago and environs, all of them based on the theme, "What do you suppose will happen to Robin Stephens when Danny Grannett comes back?"

The sale of season tickets for the forthcoming season slowed to a crawl, and the receipts in hand were lower than they had been for any comparable time of year since Marcus Aurelius Klein had established the team. Robin was careful to show no concern at staff meetings, and made no protest when a sales chart appeared on the wall of Ellen Hibbs' office. He could have told her to remove it, but, as he remarked to his secretary, he didn't want to give her the satisfaction.

Early in April, when the N.B.A. basketball play-offs and the opening of the major-league baseball season were diverting the attention of sports fans, Robin arranged for a contract talk with Fred Finch that, he knew, would be of critical importance in determining the fate of the Cougars for the year. Finch was expected to arrive on a Thursday evening, and had been instructed not only to avoid all reporters but to go straight to Robin's apartment from O'Hare Airport.

Late on Wednesday morning, however, Patricia Thompson

walked into her superior's office, trying to appear calm as she said, "Fred Finch is here to see you."

Robin stared at her.

"He also has a girl with him."

He continued to stare. "Who is she?"

Patricia shrugged. "She has very red hair and he calls her Martie."

Robin cursed under his breath, then recovered. "Who knows they're here?"

"Nobody except the receptionist."

"Okay, tell her to keep her mouth shut. Pat, I want you to get out of here for the rest of the day, and take that jazzy broad with you." He reached for his wallet, then handed her a number of bills and two credit cards. "Take her shopping, and buy her enough to keep her interested. Nothing extravagant, but make sure she's occupied. Don't let anyone from the communications media get within ten feet of her, and at the end of the day make sure she goes back to your apartment with you. I don't care if you have to gag her and put handcuffs on her, but keep her isolated. Can you manage?"

The secretary's bright smile was reassuring. "Trust me, boss."

"I do, Pat, but only you. Everybody else in this town is howling for my scalp."

In a sudden gesture of sympathy she reached out and patted his shoulder. "We'll show 'em," she said.

Moments later Robin was slouched in his swivel chair behind his desk, and did not look up as Fred Finch, resplendent in a new, hand-tailored suit, bounded into the office. "Shut the door, you stupid son-of-a-bitch. You have the brains of an offensive tackle and the imagination of an offensive guard."

"What a way to greet the Cougars' wave of the future."

Robin ignored his outstretched hand. "You were told to travel alone, get here Thursday night and come to my apartment, not the office. So you've already disobeyed all three orders."

The quarterback's good humor vanished. "What difference does it make?"

"Obviously," Robin said, glancing at him for the first time, "I didn't give you instructions just for the hell of it. I intend to keep you under security wraps. Now. All through training. All through the exhibition season, too, at the very least. After that, we'll see. There are eight million people in the Chicago area, boy, and you may not realize it, but all eight million of them are gunning for you and me."

"What of it? We'll thumb our noses at them, and anybody who doesn't like us can kiss our asses!"

Robin stood, went to the door and bolted it. "Listen to me carefully, Fearless Freddie, because I don't intend to mince words. Four years ago, when you won your Heisman Trophy, you were the hottest new prospect in pro football. Since that time you've been with three teams, and you've done nothing but acquire a reputation as a vain, reckless hothead, a personal show-off and a slob who can't get along with other players."

"That isn't fair—"

"I'm doing the talking." Robin paced the length of the carpeted office. "It should be plain, even to someone of your limited intelligence, that I have a somewhat higher opinion of you. I'm betting the future of the Cougars on you. And my own future." He halted directly in front of the quarterback and pointed a forefinger at him. "There's no doubt in my mind that you can be the number-one player in the game today, and the biggest box-office draw. A combination of Namath, Tarkenton and Unitas at his peak. Super-passer, super-scrambler, super-field-general, an inspiration to your team and the idol of every football fan on the North American continent!"

"Now you're talking to me," Freddie said, and taking a cigarette from a case, flicked a gold lighter.

"You're off tobacco as long as you're on the Cougar roster, and that's just the beginning," Robin said, his voice rough.

The quarterback looked at him in astonishment. "You can't be serious."

Ignoring the comment, Robin stepped up his attack. "Are you marrying that redhead you brought with you?"

[93]

"Hell no! We've been shacking up since the middle of last season, but—"

"That stops, too. No more traveling with her, and when you take an apartment here—which won't be until just before the season opens—you'll live there alone. I don't care if she has a place in the same building, but you're going to have a new image."

"The Boy Scout image of Dan Grannett. They got to you, Rob."

"The image will apply exclusively to you. You have the opportunity of a lifetime here, provided you don't blow it. You'll do what Mal Ferguson tells you. You'll cooperate with him and with your team, you'll earn the respect and faith of the other thirty-nine men on the squad, and you'll become a leader. And you'll do it fast, or I won't be able to protect your hide. Step out of line just once, and when Dan Grannett comes back, he'll ease you out of pro ball. What's more, you'll stay out."

Freddie stifled a flippant retort, and looked pale beneath his heavy sun tan.

"When the mobs in the Roman circus howled for a gladiator's blood," Robin said, "he couldn't afford to make mistakes, and he had to win their favor in a hurry. Then, after he became a champion, he could get away with anything he wanted. Understand me?"

"I'm beginning to get the drift."

"I'll spell it out. This season—not some future season—you've got to show what you can do. End the year as number one, two or three in passing yardage, pass completions and touchdowns. Show you can direct a ground offense. And, at the very minimum, win at least two more games than you lose. You've got to be better than anybody else in the business because the Cougar fans are down on you, thanks to the Ted Marcus deal that brought you here, and they'll discount fifty percent of what you do."

"Screw 'em."

"No!" Robin slapped the desk. "You'll smile, keep your

mouth shut and run up your scores. You're holding all the cards. Your own passing, Hal Helmsley's running and Adam Renewzski's toe that'll give you a field goal any time you're inside the forty-yard line. Plus a defensive team that will hold down opposition scores."

"I know you're putting together a team that can do big things in a few years—"

"Enough concrete results *this year* to fill the stadium will make you an authentic hero. Then we'll set our sights on a championship in a maximum of two more years."

Freddie took a cigarette from his case again, but thought better of it. "Why the big pep talk?"

"Because I've put my neck on the chopping block, and I insist you justify my faith in you." Robin's manner changed, and for the first time he softened. "What do you want out of football, Freddie?"

The quarterback fingered his watered silk necktie. "A lot of things. Money, Glory. Fun. One of those juicy pensions when I'm older."

"Sure. A big salary. The chicks lined up at your apartment door. Lots of testimonial advertising. And breaking all the records in the books. Would that sum it up?"

"More or less."

"You can have all of it, without waiting, if you'll work for it. I'm demanding results—without excuses—because I know you can give them to me, and I'm willing to prove my faith in you. The Colts paid you twenty-five thousand last year. I'll give you a one-year contract for forty, and if you'll come through with what I demand, I'll add a bonus of ten thousand at the end of the season. Produce for me, and next year you can write your own ticket. How does that strike you?"

Freddie sat upright in his chair. "I was all set to haggle with you when I came in here, but you've just knocked all the air out of the football. Who can object to a raise of one hundred percent?"

"All right, that's settled. Now, you'll be working for Mal

Ferguson, who doesn't appreciate your humor or your way of life. In fact, he's convinced you can't change your personality."

"He's got something there, Robin."

"Mal and a lot of other people think I'm insane to be placing all my bets on a quarterback they consider unstable. It happens that I don't share their opinion of you. It also happens that I think you've been hampered by just one thing, a refusal to curb your natural flamboyance. Well, I'll tell you something I wouldn't say to anyone else. I know damned well you can't change your personality or your temperament. All I require is that you tamp down that exuberance for one season."

Freddie sat back in his chair and grinned. "Now," he said, "you sound like the general manager I thought I was getting when you traded for me."

"Produce on the field, Freddie, and I won't care how you live by this time next year. Fill the stadium for us, infect our fans with championship fever, and I'll back you up if you decide you want to keep a whole harem."

"I'll remember that."

"Just remember you work for Mal. Don't try to pit us against each other, because he'll have my complete support. But if you want advice or help in anything not directly concerned with your playing, my door will always be open to you. Okay?"

Freddie stood and extended his hand. "I'd be a prime gook who deserved demotion to the Atlantic Coast League," he said, "if I didn't follow through your way."

"Your contract will be ready for signature tomorrow. Meanwhile, tonight, you'll have dinner with Mal Ferguson. Just the two of you. And you'll convince him you'll break your tail playing his brand of football."

Freddie struggled for a moment, then capitulated. "You're the boss," he said at last.

It was no hardship to dine with a pretty girl, but Robin couldn't quite overcome the feeling that he was acting as a baby-sitter. Not that the redhead was all that young, but he was standing in as her escort for the evening while Fred Finch, following instructions, tried to achieve some measure of rapport with Mal Ferguson. Martie's appearance was so spectacular that Robin was afraid she might be recognized as Finch's girl if they were seen in any of the places frequented by members of the sports fraternity, so he took her first to a small bar near his apartment and then a quiet, pseudo-French restaurant in the neighborhood.

For a time the girl seemed uneasy in the company of her friend's employer, but several cocktails, a bottle of wine with dinner and the realization that her companion found her attractive helped her to relax, and she began to chat freely about her past. "Would you believe I came from the Middle West?" she asked as they sipped after-dinner brandy. "A little town in Missouri."

"How did you happen to meet Freddie?" Robin glanced at his watch and knew they had at least two to three hours to kill before Fred would join them at his apartment.

"Well, it's kind of crazy. Everybody always told me I ought to be an actress, you see, so I went out to Los Angeles to get into pictures and television." Martie flicked back a thick strand of her copper-colored hair. "One day I got this walk-on part in an hour special, and Bud was doing a part in it, too."

Apparently she thought her explanation was adequate, but Robin had no idea what she meant.

She sensed his confusion. "It was just a week or two after the Rams' season ended, and Bud was never an actor, of course, but he set all kinds of records as a tight end that year, so he was in demand for television shows."

A light dawned: she was talking about Bud Timkin, the All-Pro.

"So we started going together, and I went to San Diego with him when he was traded to the Chargers. Fred was with the Chargers that year, and we got to be friends after Bud and I

[97]

broke up. So then I came East with Fred when Baltimore bought him."

"I see." Robin saw far more than he indicated to her. He had heard that professional football had its own groupies, camp followers who transferred their loyalties from player to player as circumstances dictated, but this was the first time he had actually met a member of the sorority. Curiosity led him to ask, "How do you happen to be interested in football?"

Her dress was so tight-fitting it was difficult for her to shrug, but the redhead executed the move prettily. "Way back in high school I went with the captain of our team, and I got spoiled for other fellows. There's something about a man in football that makes him more special than anybody else."

It was obvious that she was hooked by the glamour of the publicity that surrounded the players.

"What position were you?" she wanted to know.

Robin smiled. "By the time I got to college I realized I wasn't tall enough or heavy enough, so I became the student manager of the team."

Martie looked him up and down, her green eyes taking in every detail. "Maybe you're a little light, and you could stand another inch or two, but you have the build of a split end. Or maybe a safety man."

Her candor amused him. "It's a little late for all that now."

"But you aren't old! I remembered meeting you in Miami Beach, and when you inherited the top job with the Cougars and traded for Fred, I thought it was just great. All the general managers I've ever met before were old."

His colleagues, most of them in their fifties, would not have appreciated the observation. "I'm just an acting G.M.," Robin told her. "I'll get sent back to the bench when Dan Grannett recovers from his heart attack." He signaled to their waiter for two more brandies.

"You'll have your own team. You'll see."

"What makes you think so?"

"I have a feeling about things like that. Just like I told Fred he was going to be traded this winter, and he'd be number one on a different team. You'll be a general manager on your own."

"That would be nice," he said carefully, and wondered whether he should prepare the ground for Fred, who would be forced to tell her they could no longer live together openly.

"Could I tell you something?"

Her grave tone surprised him. "Sure."

"Quarterbacks aren't like other players. They love themselves too much. So I'm not sure I'll still be with Fred by the time this next season ends."

Perhaps it wasn't going to be necessary to say anything to her about her future relationship with the man on whom the Cougars' immediate future depended.

"Anyway, I don't like it much in the East. I think of California as home. The weather there is so much nicer, and I just hate all this cold." Martie went through the motions of shivering before sipping from her refilled brandy snifter. "And," she added as an afterthought, "my career is out there, too."

"Of course." Robin wondered how long she would rely on the illusion that she was an actress.

Suddenly she brightened. "Anyway, I know most of the fellows on the Rams and the Chargers. And about half of the Raiders' team."

She would encounter few problems establishing a new liaison when she and Fred parted, and for a number of years she might continue to drift. Then, when she realized she was growing older and less attractive, she might be able to persuade some player lacking in perspicacity to marry her. She was a victim of the public-relations campaigns that made folk heroes of football stars, but Robin refused to accept any share of responsibility for her plight, even though he was one of those responsible for the public image of the professional gladiator. If football were a low-key sport, girls like Martie would become baseball or basketball groupies. The appeal of one game as opposed to that of another was irrelevant; the attitudes of millions were shaped by the insistence of entrepreneurs that professional sports be regarded as pastimes rather than branches of the mammoth entertainment industry.

"Anyway," Martie said, "I'm glad you and I could get together tonight. You're cute."

"Thanks." He was abrupt, wanting to keep this brief relationship impersonal.

His unresponsiveness surprised the girl, and her green eyes reflected her hurt. "What do you think of me?" she demanded, sliding closer to him on the banquette.

"You don't need me to tell you that you're unusually attractive." Robin tried to ignore her proximity.

"No, but it's always nice to hear." She sighed happily and let a hand rest on his thigh. "I knew you liked me. I can always tell."

He didn't want to become involved with another player's girl, even one who was thinking of terminating her affair. Under the best of circumstances Fred Finch was going to be difficult to handle. But Robin could think of no way to remove her hand without offending her, and he couldn't allow himself to forget that a scorned woman was capable of kicking up a storm.

With her free hand Martie picked up her snifter and sipped. "Your wife must have been crazy to divorce you."

He was surprised. "You know about me?"

"I know everything about everybody in football. And not just from the sports pages and listening to the players. I read about all of you in the columns, too. I'll prove it. I saw a hint about you being interested in somebody—I can't remember offhand where I read it—but it didn't mention her name."

Robin pretended ignorance. He had no intention of indicating to this girl, of all people, that he had been upset by a veiled reference to his own affair with Minerva Helmsley. "The gossip columnists," he said, "make up stories about people when they have no hard news to write. I've been happy to be a bachelor again, and there's nobody in my life these days."

Martie giggled. "But there could be." Moving swiftly, she opened the zipper of his trousers and slid her hand inside.

He was so startled that, after automatically pressing the base of his spine against the back of the banquette in a futile attempt to escape, he remained motionless.

"I knew what you'd like," the redhead said. "I have an instinct for it."

"We'll be thrown out of the restaurant."

"Don't be silly. Your napkin is covering us." Her deft fingers became active, stroking and manipulating with a light touch.

In spite of his distress, Robin felt himself responding to her.

"That's more like it," Martie murmured.

"If you want me to say uncle, I've said it. I wish you'd remember you're Fred Finch's girl—"

Her laugh cut him off. "He cheats on me all the time, so what I do is my own business."

The possible complications continued to alarm him.

But Martie was relentless, and her ministrations became more insistent.

He squirmed on the banquette, unable to free himself. He knew he was hard now, fully extended, and recognized a danger sign: he wanted her to continue, no matter how great his embarrassment and fear of entanglements.

"Fun?"

He nodded, and gulped the rest of his brandy.

"Then say it!"

Robin wondered, fleetingly, why it was his fate to attract sadistic women who tried to dominate him. In every other phase of living he was in command of himself and others, but women like Martie—and Minerva—seemed to sense his one weakness and delighted in taking advantage of it. "Great fun," he said in a strangled voice.

Her half-smile, irregular breathing and the sheen that brightened her eyes were indications of the satisfactions she felt because she was in charge. "You told me we'd go over to your house to wait for Fred. Shouldn't we be leaving?"

His writhing became still more pronounced, but he wanted to avoid an even more compromising situation. "We'd better leave well enough alone." It was becoming difficult to speak.

Martie shook a cigarette out of a pack and applied the flame made by a small, gold lighter to the end. Any of the restaurant's other patrons who happened to glance in her direction at that moment would have called her cool and remote.

Only Robin knew otherwise. Her grip had tightened, she slid her hand back and forth, and he knew he was completely at her mercy. He could not tolerate mortification in a public place, and privacy was preferable, regardless of the consequences. "You win," he said. "We'll leave right now."

She relaxed her hold slightly. "Get the check," she ordered.

He obeyed, signaling the waiter.

Martie did not release him, however, and had one final surprise in store for him. As he paid the bill she began to tease him again, her fingertips caressing him as, with her free hand, she absently applied gloss to her lips.

"If you don't stop," he muttered, "it'll be too late."

She regarded him with a superior smile and squeezed hard.

Robin's gasp was involuntary.

Still smiling, Martie withdrew. "A general manager," she said, "can be even more of a blast than a brute of a player."

Robin discovered he was trembling, and had to wait until the tremors subsided before he closed his zipper. Slumping against the banquette, he closed his eyes for a moment as he tried to regain his self-control.

"That," Martie said, "was just the beginning."

He nodded, unwilling to verbalize his surrender yet knowing that what had happened was only a prelude. He understood the girl better than she knew herself, and realized she had chosen to associate with men in football because she saw them as symbols of virility. "How long were you planning all this?" he asked wearily.

Her giggle sounded ingenuous. "Ever since you and Fred told me he had to go off for a few hours. I told you I have hunches about people, so I knew what it would be like for you and me."

Robin's physical desire began to ebb somewhat, although he continued to throb. "Before we get out of here," he said, "I want to make one thing clear. I've staked my entire future on what Freddie does for us this season, and I can't afford to let you or anyone else come between us. When he shows up tonight to take you East on a late flight, that will be the end of anything between you and me."

"I believe in helping a man's career, not hurting him!" Martie sounded genuinely indignant. "Besides, Fred is buying me a gorgeous gold bracelet I saw in the window of a Baltimore jewelry store."

Their waiter brought the change, and Robin's guilt impelled him to leave an exceptionally generous tip.

"So I can't waste time wondering whether you and I will get together again in three months or six months or whenever," the redhead said. "Right now I've got too many other things on my mind. Like what I'm going to do to you when I get you alone."

Muriel Grannett's telegram arrived a few hours before Ellen Hibbs was scheduled to leave for a late spring vacation, and was addressed to the younger woman:

"DAN HAS SUFFERED RELAPSE STOP HIS CONDITION NOT SERIOUS BUT DOCTORS AGREE HE MUST REMAIN IN HONOLULU FOR ADDITIONAL PERIOD OF THREE TO FOUR MONTHS STOP HE CAN'T RETURN TO WORK BEFORE OCTOBER AT EARLIEST STOP SO I RECOMMEND COUGARS MAKE ALL PLANS FOR COMING SEASON WITHOUT HIM STOP I AM NOTIFYING MARC KLEIN IN SEPARATE WIRE STOP DAN IS RECONCILED TO LONGER CONVALESCENCE AND SENDS LOVE AS DO I."

That night, after dinner, Minerva Helmsley stopped in to see Robin at his apartment, and he told her about the message. "That Hibbs gal is really strange," he said. "And cold-blooded. She sent me a copy of the telegram, but she went off on her vacation without even sticking her head in the door of my office."

"My guess," Minerva told him, "is that she was afraid you'd

gloat. Hal told me after we saw the headlines in tonight's newspapers that it means you'll be in charge for all of this coming season."

"That's exactly what it means, so I'll have the chance to show —all on my own—how much of a profit the team can make this year. It's a great break for me, and I'm grateful for it. But Ellen ought to know I'm not going to leap up and down with glee on Danny Grannett's prostrate body."

"You could be right," Minerva said, "in which case I have no idea why she left without seeing you. I've never been able to dig her type."

"Neither have I, and I don't want to."

"You prefer mine."

Robin glanced at her warily, then crossed his living room and turned on his television set. "Phil Donegan will be on in a couple of minutes. I want to hear what he says about the new development."

"That's why I'm here," Minerva said.

Again he looked at her, then adjusted the dials as the screen came alive.

"Donegan called Hal an hour or so ago and asked him all sorts of questions."

"Like what?" Robin demanded.

"Oh, all kinds of things. His contract, and was it true that we're splitting."

It was difficult not to shout. "What did Hal tell him?"

"Nothing, really. He said his contract was his business. And the Cougars'. He said he agrees with your policy of not releasing salary figures."

Robin was relieved. "I'm glad he knows when to keep his mouth shut."

"He wasn't all that careful, Robbie. And that's why I'm here. Hal let it slip that he won't be coming back to me at the apartment after he goes off to training camp. And Donegan crawled all over him, wanting to know if you had come between us."

He felt as though he had been kicked in the stomach. "Isn't that great."

"Don't worry. Hal assured him that nobody is responsible, and that we're breaking up because our marriage isn't right, not because of any third party."

Before Robin could reply, Phil Donegan appeared on the television screen, seated behind his familiar sportscaster's desk, crowded with miniature figures representing Chicago's baseball, football, basketball and hockey teams. Robin turned up the volume, and they heard Donegan's deep, slightly rasping voice:

"Cougar fans, and I'm one of them, have been counting the weeks until the return of the team's general manager, Dan Grannett, Mr. Football himself. This afternoon all of us suffered a severe blow when we learned that Dan will be confined in a Honolulu hospital longer than expected, and won't return this season.

"We're grateful for his sake and that of his lovely wife, Muriel, that Dan's ultimate recovery seems assured. That's the biggest news of the day, and I know all of you out there will rejoice with me.

"But our happiness is marred by the fact that the Cougars will be sailing into the season's storms without an experienced pilot at the helm. I've been accused of being antagonistic to young Robin Stephens, the acting general manager, and I guess I am, with cause."

"Phony candor," Robin said, not looking at the girl who sat beside him. "Always goes great with the fans."

"I accused Stephens of rank incompetence when he lost Ted Marcus, the Cougars' superstar defensive player, and in return for him got Big Horse Collins, a competent enough linebacker, and the quarterback who would be a liability to any team, Fred Finch. What the Cougars do in the months ahead will prove whether I'm right.

"Now I make an even more serious accusation. I charge Stephens with misuse of his temporary power for his personal sake."

Minerva nervously lighted a cigarette, and Robin leaned forward in his seat, straining so hard toward the television set that the girl placed a restraining hand on his arm.

"Statistics prove that Hal Helmsley is not only the finest full-back in pro football today, but the best player ever to wear a Cougar uniform. I wondered, when Stephens broke up the team that Dan Grannett spent years assembling, why Helmsley had been spared. Not only spared, but given a new contract! And what a contract!"

He proceeded to outline the terms in full detail, and Robin turned in astonishment to Minerva. "Are you sure Hal didn't tell him all this?"

"Positive! I was right there when he talked to Donegan on the phone!"

"Then where in hell could he—" Robin cut himself short as Donegan continued.

"Just this evening I confirmed, on unimpeachable authority, a rumor that has been making the rounds in recent months. Helmsley and his wife are separating. Now, an athlete's private life isn't usually our concern. We're interested only in his performance on the field. But, in this instance, I can't help wondering many things.

"I wonder if still another story is true, that Mrs. Helmsley and Robin Stephens have been seeing each other. If they have, I can't help wondering whether Stephens made a very special deal with Helmsley, signing him to a very juicy new contract so he'd look the other way. I'm not criticizing the right of any man and woman to get together, and that includes Stephens and Mrs. Helmsley. But if Stephens signed his fullback to the most lucrative contract in Cougar history because he had ulterior motives, owner Marcus Aurelius Klein should intervene immediately.

"It's bad enough to see the Cougars being ruined by an acting general manager who should have been restrained long ago. If my present suspicions are correct, Football Commissioner Martin J. Morton should conduct a full-scale investigation . . . I'll be back with today's baseball scores after this message . . ."

Robin leaped to his feet and snapped off the television set. "The son-of-a-bitch," he said.

Minerva, pale beneath her make-up, lighted another cigarette from the butt of the one she was finishing. "This means trouble, doesn't it?"

"For Phil Donegan, in the long run. And for somebody else as fast as I can arrange it!"

"If the Commissioner steps in—"

"I'll be happy to see him. I signed a fair contract with Hal, and I can justify every clause of it. I'd like to see any club sign a thousand-yard fullback for much less!"

The ringing of the telephone startled them.

Robin picked up the instrument. "Yes. Hello, Chuck . . . Yes, I heard the bastard. I'm making no statement, and I want you to get hold of Helmsley. Tell him to keep his mouth shut, too. We're not going to dignify anything Donegan says by replying to him . . . that's right. To hell with him . . . and one thing more. Find out where Mr. Klein is. All I know is that he went out of town today. Wherever he is, I intend to see him—and settle something once and for all." The telephone crashed into its cradle.

"That must have been Chuck Blanchard," Minerva said. "What does he think—"

"He's paid to follow my orders. When I want the benefit of his thinking, I'll ask him. You heard what I told him, Min."

The girl took a deep drag on her cigarette. "I'm scared, Robbie. If the Commissioner makes a fuss there could be a nasty scandal that—"

"I'll see the Commissioner before he sends for me. But there's something else I've got to do first. Don't you realize what's happening?"

She shook her blond head.

"This was a deliberate, vicious attempt to cut my throat, and it was planned with care. By somebody who wants to see me disgraced and fired. If Hal didn't give Donegan those contract figures—"

"I swear he didn't! He may be a gook, but he isn't that stupid."

"Then it had to be an inside job. Someone in the Cougar office who was familiar with the contract terms and passed them along to Phil Donegan." Robin's voice dropped to a near whisper. "The contract is good, but not extraordinary. Hal could have wangled the same terms from any general manager in the league. Bringing you into all this is nothing more or less than an attempt to kill me off."

"Who would want to do that?"

"I can think of just one person in the Cougar organization. Ellen Hibbs. But this is one effort that's going to backfire—because I intend to strike first!"

The house itself was a sprawling, relatively modest structure of pink stucco that resembled a small, immaculately kept hotel. What made the place impressive was that the entire area was a private estate, and only a Marcus Aurelius Klein could own such an island off the coast of southern Georgia. The formal gardens in front of the main structure covered several acres, while off to one side, above the beach, were the two swimming pools, one filled with purified sea water, the other with fresh water. Behind the greenhouse at the rear was the landing field; at the far end stood the hangar, in which an executive jet, a smaller airplane and a helicopter were sitting. And from the broad veranda on the other side of the house, one could catch a glimpse, through a screen of trees, of the eighteenth green. Golf enthusiasts called the course magnificent, Robin knew.

The major-domo had invited him to play a round while he awaited Klein's return from a day's outing on his boat, but Robin wanted to be on hand the moment he disembarked, and refused to leave the immediate vicinity of the house. A swim in the sea water pool gave him a chance to work off some of his frustrations, but he couldn't really enjoy the water, and the idea of stretching out in the sun didn't appeal to him, either.

He preferred to maintain a vigil beside the pool at a vantage point from which he could watch the dock, which was located on the inner shore of a tiny bay formed by a curving spit of land that curled past the beach. Solicitous servants brought him a late lunch, newspapers and magazines, but he had little appetite and could not concentrate on reading matter. In his present perturbed state of mind he could enjoy nothing, even though he was awed by the quiet display of wealth.

At last his wait was rewarded, and late in the afternoon a small, white yacht appeared on the horizon and sailed toward the dock. It seemed to grow as it drew closer, and Robin smiled wryly; he should have known that Marc Klein wouldn't be satisfied with a craft that even a substantial citizen could afford. Two people were standing on the forward deck, a man in shorts and sport shirt, and a woman in a terry-cloth robe with a hood that concealed her face. The man waved, and when Robin recognized Klein he returned the gesture.

The presence of the woman was an unexpected complication, but Robin could not permit her to stand in his way. Klein and his wife were separated, he knew, so the identity of his companion was not important, and all that mattered was the urgent business that had brought him here.

The uniformed officer in the wheelhouse maneuvered the vessel into her berth, a sailor jumped onto the dock to make her fast, and then Klein and the woman came ashore, holding hands. Robin started toward them, warning himself not to rush. They sauntered in his direction, laughing and chatting, and their intimacy made him feel like an interloper, but he could not turn away for fear he would embarrass them.

As they came within earshot the woman glanced at Robin, and then she, too, smiled and waved. He was stunned when he recognized Ellen Hibbs.

"Are they taking good care of you?" Klein called. "I left orders for the staff to look after you when they notified me on the radiophone that you were here."

"I couldn't ask for anything more," Robin replied, but that was not the truth. He wished the ground would open beneath his feet and swallow him.

"It's too bad you didn't get here a little earlier," Ellen said, unabashed at having been discovered spending her vacation with

Klein. "You could have gone out for the day with us. The one thing I've missed is a swim. Anybody want to join me?"

"We'll order a drink for you," Klein said.

She peeled off her robe, sprinted to the sea water pool and jumped in.

Although Robin was still too numb to think clearly, he could not help noting that her figure, revealed in a bikini that left little to the imagination, was superb. Perhaps their mutual antagonisms had blinded him to her charms.

Klein took his arm and guided him to a table at the side of the pool. "You're still drinking bourbon?"

Never had Robin wanted a drink so badly. "Yes, please. And I'm sorry if I've barged in on you at an inconvenient time, Marc."

"Oh, you haven't inconvenienced me in the least." Klein was surprisingly casual. "In fact, Ellen and I have been expecting you. Ever since a videotape of the Donegan telecast was flown down to us." They had reached the pool side, and he picked up a house telephone to give the butler a drink order.

"I'm seeing the Commissioner late tomorrow afternoon." Robin was grim. "I called his office to make the appointment before I left Chicago, and I defy him—or anyone else—to say the Helmsley contract isn't legitimate."

"It certainly seemed reasonable and fair to me, and Ellen agrees. Dan Grannett might have shaved five thousand from the gross, but I have no intention of peering over your shoulder and telling you that Dan would have done this or that differently."

"Thanks." This was the opportune moment, Robin realized, to express himself freely on Ellen, who was the reason for his visit to Klein's island. But the revelation of her intimacy with the Cougar's owner forced him to revise his tactics. He still believed she was responsible for telling Phil Donegan the terms of Helmsley's contract, but he preferred to make no flat accusations while she was swimming. He would wait until she joined them, and if Klein chose to discharge him after he fired his artillery, at least he would have the satisfaction of knowing he had not acted behind her back. His entire future in football was at stake, he knew, but he had to speak his mind bluntly, regardless of the outcome. A man's self-respect was more important than any job.

"There are angles I want to discuss, Marc," he said. "But I'd rather wait until Ellen joins us."

Klein nodded, then brightened when the butler approached with a tray of drinks. He shouted to Ellen, who was displaying a proficient crawl stroke, and she climbed out of the water, drying herself with a towel and retrieving her robe before she came to them and stretched out on a canvas-backed chaise.

"That pool," she said, "is the greatest luxury in the world. You should have come in with me, Robin."

"Maybe you can persuade him to take a dip before breakfast tomorrow," Klein said, and added to Robin, "Personally, I know of nothing less civilized than a swim first thing in the morning."

Robin took a deep breath. "Ellen might not want to swim with me after she hears what's on my mind." Leaving his drink untouched, he looked straight at the girl. "I was shocked when Donegan came on the air with the accurate details of Hal Helmsley's contract. Not more than a half-dozen people know them—"

"And you thought, naturally, that I passed the information along to him," she interrupted.

"I'm afraid that's exactly what I thought. And it's the reason I'm here."

Klein was seemingly unperturbed as he sipped his drink. "What motive might she have?"

"Loyalty to Dan Grannett," Robin replied without flinching. "Combined with complete disapproval of what I've been doing to the Cougars."

"That makes sense." Klein took his time lighting a cigar.

Ellen tasted her drink. "You're right, Robin—except for one factor. You've learned something about me in the past half-hour, and it should be plain to you that I wouldn't have to go to Phil Donegan in order to discredit you where it counts. I have far more effective means at my disposal."

"Provided I'd listen to you. Which I wouldn't," Klein said, and half-turning in his chair, grinned at her. "Did you give Donegan the contract information?"

"No, Marc," she said. "I don't operate that way, and you know it."

"So I do." The owner of the Cougars turned to Robin. "There's your answer."

"Then who did get in touch with him?" Robin demanded, finally relieving the ache in his throat by taking a swallow of his drink.

The girl shrugged. "It could have been any one of a number of people in the office. It shouldn't be news to you that—with the exception of your own secretary—most of the staff resent what you've done to Uncle Danny's team."

Robin had to admit the validity of her argument. "It's a cockeyed way to get even. The Cougars are stuck with my players this year, regardless of whether I'm still around to watch them. And I very much dislike the idea of having a spy for an antagonistic sportscaster running around my office."

"What are you going to do about it?" Klein asked.

Robin knew he was on the spot, and that he had to accept the challenge. He could not demand that the woman who was Klein's mistress be discharged, as that would be asking too much. But one approach was still open. "Whoever has been talking will go to great lengths to keep his or her identity from me," he said. "On the other hand, everybody in the place knows that Ellen and I haven't been hitting it off." It couldn't be helped if his candor caused additional trouble, and he still sounded calm as he turned back to the girl. "When you return from your vacation, I'd like you to find out who did it. Nobody enjoys being an undercover policeman, but you're the obvious choice for this assignment."

She was silent for a moment as she sipped her drink. "I hate the idea," she said, "but I'll do it." She left the self-evident unspoken: by finding the guilty party, she would automatically remove suspicion from herself.

Robin had escaped his employer's censure, apparently, and was able to breathe more easily. His original instinct had been right, and he was glad he had brought his charge against her into the open.

"There's another angle I don't like," Klein said. "God knows I'm no prude, and I refuse to be a hypocrite, either. It shouldn't be very hard for you to figure out what's up between Ellen and me, Robin. All I'll say about that is that we'd be in one hell of a jam if we ever hit the public prints—or Phil Donegan started talking about us on the air. People in professional sports—and this goes for team owners and businessmen as well as the players —must keep their public images clean. Our puritanical tradition demands it. People won't support any team—regardless of whether it's baseball, hockey, basketball, much less football— if they think there's any hanky-panky going on."

It was obvious he had been upset by Donegan's hints about Minerva, and Robin braced himself.

"When you first came to the Cougars," Klein said, "I told you to stop seeing Mrs. Helmsley. Well, you haven't, and I'm not blaming you for it, really. Every man is entitled to associate with anyone he wants to see. But there are rules he's got to be willing to follow."

"Marc is worried about the reaction of the fans," Ellen explained.

"And about the Commissioner," Klein said. "Morton holds his job because he's straight-laced. Not just in his dealings with the individual teams, but in his own personal life. He's a living, walking example of the pure Christian, and he thinks everyone else should behave as he does."

"We talked about all this after we saw the Donegan video-tape," Ellen said, "and my best advice is that we ignore the Donegan innuendo."

"I agree," Robin said. "I've already told the publicity department I refuse to issue a rebuttal, and I'll make no statement on the subject."

"I can't argue with that," Klein said. "It never hurts any man to keep his mouth shut. But that isn't going far enough. When a situation requires action, I expect an executive who works for me to do what's necessary."

Robin took another long swallow of his drink.

"I've never given a long-term contract to anyone who has shirked responsibility or lacked the courage of his convictions." Klein stood, picked up the ice bucket from the tray on the table and began to drop cubes in their glasses as he added, almost casually, "It seems to me the perfect way to recover public good will and make a liar of Donegan would be for you to marry Mrs. Helmsley. Think of the bombshell you'd explode in M. J. Morton's lap when you see him tomorrow!"

Robin's frankness in dealing with Ellen had saved his job, at least for the present, but he resented the pressure being applied to his personal life. He hadn't seriously considered whether he wanted to marry Minerva; maybe he did, and maybe he didn't. But he sure as hell didn't enjoy having his arm twisted. Not that Klein had presented him with an ultimatum. Not exactly. It was still a free country, and a man could marry anybody he pleased—or stay a bachelor for the rest of his life, if that was what he wanted.

Marc Klein had always interfered in the private lives of key employees, however, and obviously had no intention of changing his tactics now. So his message came across loud and clear: if you want to stay with me and my organization, he was saying, you'll be wise to follow my advice.

Robin didn't have to make up his mind instantly, to be sure, but he knew he'd be smart if he settled the question before he returned to Chicago. It was one thing to marry Minerva in order to keep and solidify his job as general manager of the Cougars. But he had to keep in mind the strong possibility that Dan Grannett would return some day, and his temporary replacement might be out in the street that same afternoon. Would he feel he'd been stuck with Min, that he'd been short-changed, or would he be willing and able to accept her as his wife on a long-range basis, even though he'd be forced to look for another job?

The question had to be weighed with care, and it was useless to curse Klein for forcing his hand. He knew he'd have to make up his mind before he saw her again, and he realized that a practical man didn't waste his substance cursing his fate, but faced a crisis realistically.

Adam Renewzski opened his beer can with practiced fingers and glanced appreciatively around the living room of Hal Helmsley's apartment before raising the can to his lips. It didn't matter if the star fullback's former wife had furnished the place. He lived in style, and nobody appreciated comfort more than the place kicker, who had spent the first fifteen of his twenty-six years living in poverty in an industrial suburb of Warsaw.

Gerald "Big Horse" Collins, the Cougars' new middle line-backer, seemed unaware of his surroundings. His two hundred and forty-three pound bulk was sprawled inelegantly in an easy chair, and his belch, after swallowing a quantity of beer, was loud enough to rattle the ornamental cups and saucers that sat on the mantel. "I never knew," he said, "that a city apartment could have a fireplace. I've always wanted one."

"I was lucky," Hal Helmsley said. "I was afraid my wife would want to keep this place after the divorce, but she let me have it without a murmur."

"If I am not rude," Adam Renewzski said in his precise, heavily accented English, "you pay a large price for this apartment?"

"Not too bad," Hal said. "Five hundred a month."

The place-kicker whistled soundlessly.

Hal didn't want his new teammates to think he was putting on airs just because he earned a superstar's salary. "I'll probably ask somebody to move in with me. And share the rent."

"Put me on the list," Collins said.

"Okay, Horse, I will." Hal glanced at his guest.

Collins returned his gaze, and grinned.

Suddenly there were tensions in the air, and Renewzski broke the silence. "The reason we have imposed ourselves on you, Hal, is to learn what you can tell us about management before we negotiate our contracts."

"Sure." Hal sipped his beer. "I don't know what the new system will be. Dan Grannett and Mal Ferguson used to call the guys in for conferences, and both of them would try to overwhelm you. I have a hunch that Stephens will handle contracts alone, and that's okay, too. Mal has never done much except sit there—and stare at you."

"Is that supposed to scare you?" Collins asked.

Hal shrugged.

The linebacker drained his beer and belched again. "I've heard that Ferguson is just a carbon copy of old Dan Grannett."

"Not from anybody who's ever played for him!" Hal leaned forward, and his chair creaked as he shifted his weight. "Don't ever fool yourself about Mal. He's quiet, and he holds the world's lousiest press conferences, but he knows his football. And he'll chew out your ass if he thinks you're giving less than one hundred percent."

"What is his policy on fines?" Renewzski wanted to know.

"He's fair, but he'll fine you in a hurry if he thinks you deserve it. One great thing about him—he never publicizes a fine. It's between him and the individual player."

"A gentleman. I like that." Renewzski ran a hand through his long, black hair.

Collins went to the bar-refrigerator in the far corner of the room and helped himself to another beer. "You won't have any trouble with him, Adam, and neither will I. He needs us this year."

"Only if you work your tail off for him," Hal interjected. "Anybody who doesn't put out with the old gung-ho for him will sit on the bench."

Collins threw his beer can into the air, then caught it with one hand, behind his back. "I haven't seen any of the rah-rah college spirit on a team since I got out of school."

Renewzski frowned. "It may be that Ferguson will be changed this year, with Grannett not here."

Again Hal shrugged.

Collins nodded. "You got something there, Adam. A lot of coaches take their cues from the general manager."

The place kicker's eyes were thoughtful. "This Stephens. What sort is he? My friends on the Giants like him, but a man changes sometimes when he becomes G.M."

"Yeah, a nice fellow turns into a triple-distilled bastard," Collins said. "What's your opinion of him, Hal?"

"Well, my ex-wife seems to be mighty damn fond of him, which isn't news any more." Hal spoke with unabashed candor. "Me, I don't really know him professionally. Yet. He has guts, breaking up a Dan Grannett team in a Dan Grannett town, I'll say that for him."

Collins absently scratched the back of his bull-like neck. "Well, God help him if we don't pay off for him."

"Precisely so." A gleam of shrewd amusement appeared in Renewzski's dark eyes. "It is my analysis that we will get what we wish in salaries and benefits. The Cougars have a greater need for us than we have for them."

Hal was unconvinced. "Maybe, maybe not. A guy who can tear a whole team apart once might do it again. We won't really know until the season gets under way whether Rob Stephens is stupid—or ruthless."

She was standing in the small crowd at the gate as the passengers came into the O'Hare Airport terminal from their plane, and Robin spotted her at once because she was dressed too flashily. She was incapable of making herself inconspicuous, he thought, and felt another wave of the discomfort that had been assailing him for the past twenty-four hours.

But he smiled, and surprised Minerva by kissing her, thereby breaking his own rule that prohibited them from making public gestures of affection.

"Well," Minerva said. "Turn you loose in the sun for a day, and it acts like an aphrodisiac. That's worth remembering."

Carrying his small suitcase in one hand, he took her arm with the other. "We can talk in the taxi," he said.

"I got your telegram telling me to meet you, and I'm dying to know what—"

"Wait," he commanded.

"You got a sun tan. All in one day, too. I've been envying you, Robbie. Last year the whole team, wives and kids and everybody, went there for a party after the season ended, and it was fabulous. Did Mr. Klein have any other guests?"

"If you'll just be patient, I'll tell you everything that happened." It was wrong to take out his frustrations on Minerva, and he tried to curb the anger that had been mounting in him since the previous day. In all fairness, he couldn't blame her for their predicament.

Minerva realized he was out of sorts, and had the sense to remain silent while they made their way through the airport's long corridors to the taxi stand. As soon as they settled into the cab she slid closer to him. "Now, tell Mama."

"Is Hal in town?"

"He was still asleep when I left to come out here for you."

He was relieved to know the issue could be settled without delay. "When can you leave for Nevada?"

Minerva didn't understand the abrupt question. "Why would I go out there?"

"For your divorce."

"Oh, we're still hassling over alimony. Hal swears the most he'll pay me—"

"To hell with alimony," Robin said. "Pack your clothes and any keepsakes you want, and get out today. I want you on a plane to Reno by tonight. My secretary will make a hotel reservation for you, and before you leave I'll have an appointment

[118]

made for you with a lawyer out there. You're filing suit for divorce. At once."

Her confusion became greater. "Hal and I agreed to wait until he left for training camp."

"Your plans have been changed," Robin said.

Sudden anger appeared in her blue eyes. "Thanks for telling me. Maybe you and Mr. Klein have made some decisions, but they have no part of me. A player may be a slave who belongs to his team, but wives are their own bosses. At least this one is!"

"The sooner you get your divorce," he said, curbing his own temper, "the sooner you and I can be married."

For a long time she sat in silence, looking out at the other cars on the busy highway into Chicago. "After you've been married," she observed at last, still staring out of the window, "a bachelor girl's existence has a lot of drawbacks, and I wasn't especially looking forward to that kind of a life again. All the same, it would have been nice if you'd proposed."

Robin realized he could not take her for granted, and placed an arm around her shoulders. "You know I've wanted to marry you, Min—"

"Bull. You've avoided the subject for months, and I've let you get away with it because I haven't been any too certain, either, that I want to end up with you."

He twisted her toward him. "If the Cougars show an improvement at the box office and the league standings this season," he said, "I stand a good chance of being named permanent general manager. Not that Klein said it in so many words, any more than he indicated that Dan will be kicked upstairs, but the message came through to me, loud and clear."

Minerva studied him, making no attempt to free herself. "And I'm part of the deal?"

"I wouldn't put it that way!" He knew he had bungled, and searched his mind for some way to make amends. "What's the advantage of waiting for months when we can kill a lot of vicious gossip by going through with it now?"

"A general manager," Minerva said, "may not earn as much as a star fullback, but he doesn't break bones, and his career isn't limited by the spring in his legs." There was a hint of bitterness in her eyes as well as in her voice as she raised her face for his kiss and murmured, "Here comes the bride."

The ghost of Caesar's wife hovered over the oak-panel offices of the Commissioner of Professional Football, and even the pretty receptionist was a genteel, subdued young lady. A replica of the Super Bowl trophy that stood in a corner cabinet was the only reminder that this was the regulatory headquarters of a major sport. The private offices that lined the main corridor were sound-proofed, and the men who worked in them were sober, conservatively dressed and efficient citizens, in their own persons guaranteeing the world that the interests of the public were being protected by vigilant guardians.

The inner sanctum of the Commissioner might have been the office of a bank president, and Martin J. Morton himself resembled a successful surgeon. Indeed, he had attended medical school for two years before turning instead to the law, where he had earned an international reputation as a mediator in major labor disputes, and his few intimates still knew him as Doc. On formal occasions the players and management called him Commissioner, but of late he had been making a conscious effort to soften his severe image, and in private he encouraged everyone in the industry to address him by his initials.

His informality was strained, however, and his smile was as stiff as the starched collar of his shirt as he extended his hand to Robin.

"Thanks for seeing me on short notice, M. J."

"We're both in luck. I'm flying to Cincinnati later today to speak before a banquet group tonight." The Commissioner led his guest to the highly polished conference table that occupied an entire section of his L-shaped office.

"I just got back from Georgia a couple of hours ago myself," Robin said.

Morton eyed him through steel-rimmed glasses. "You've had a meeting with Marcus Klein?"

"Yes, for obvious reasons. We're very annoyed by the unwarranted attack made by Phil Donegan on the Cougars—and on me."

"I'm always amazed by the size of Donegan's audience," the Commissioner said. "Our switchboard has been jammed by calls ever since his program of the other evening, and sacks of mail are piling up faster than our staff can read the letters."

Robin opened his attaché case and took out a sheaf of papers. "I knew you'd want to see the Helmsley contract."

Morton scanned the document, then laid it aside. "I have no quarrel with your terms, as such," he said, speaking with precision. "There are several players in the league who are earning more than Helmsley, although their records are less impressive than his. I'm upset by the implications that lie behind the drawing of this contract."

"In confidence and not for publication," Robin said, his tone matching the Commissioner's frigidity, "Mrs. Helmsley is leaving tonight for Nevada, and we intend to be married as soon as she gets her divorce."

"That will halt a great deal of the criticism," Morton said, "but many people are going to continue to wonder whether you bought Helmsley's acquiescence."

Robin was irritated. "They'll damned well have to get over wondering," he said. "No one has been dishonest, there have no under-the-table agreements, and the lady is going to become my wife. I don't see what more I can do."

The Commissioner sat back in his chair, pondered briefly and then offered his visitor a cigarette from a silver box.

"I never use them," Robin said.

Morton was pleased. "Neither do I. Stephens, you've come to me voluntarily, which I appreciate, and I can find nothing in your situation that warrants the taking of official action by this office. Since you dealt with us only in minor matters before you moved to the Cougars, I hope you'll forgive me if I point out to you that the primary duties of the Commissioner aren't punitive. Our basic function is the performance of large-scale public relations. We try to create confidence in football as a sport. We want people in general to believe, as we do, that those who are connected with the game are men of integrity who live in accordance with high personal standards. That's our obligation to the thousands who play the game in colleges and high schools, and to the millions of fans who watch those games."

Robin had heard some of his colleagues remark that Morton was incapable of making conversation and always sounded as though he were delivering a speech from a formal podium, and the observation was unfortunately accurate. The man was completely lacking in personal warmth. "I'll gladly listen to any suggestions you care to make, M. J."

"That simplifies my task, Stephens. It would be virtually impossible for me to prove you've done anything illegal, so the hands of this office are tied. But I am in a position to offer you a bit of friendly advice. It never pays to engage in feuds with the press or prominent commentators. They always have the last word. So I urge you to mend your relations with Phil Donegan."

Had the speaker been anyone but the Commissioner, Robin would have stalked out. "I've had no feud with Donegan. He's disliked me since the day I showed up on the Cougars' payroll, and more recently he's made himself my enemy because he doesn't like my trades. I can hardly be blamed for using my own judgment, and it isn't my fault that I wasn't a loyal member of Dan Grannett's staff for years."

"Oh, I know that Donegan has gone beyond the bounds of taste and propriety," Morton said. "Try to remember he's an enthusiastic Cougar supporter who is limited by his own temperament and prejudices."

"Just as I'm limited by mine," Robin said firmly.

A chill seemed to settle on the Commissioner's shoulders. "A general manager can afford neither prejudices nor displays of temperament. He must be prepared to make sacrifices for the good name of football."

"Donegan has been doing a hatchet job on my professional and personal integrity," Robin said, "so I can't hail him as a blood brother. He owes me an apology. I'm happy not to press for a public statement, you understand. I think too much has already been said for general consumption. But Donegan will have to express regrets to me in private, and until he does, M. J., he can fry in hell."

Morton shook his head, his manner doleful. "You're making a grave error to demand an apology, Stephens. When you or the Cougars find you're in real trouble, and it comes eventually to every team, Donegan will skin you alive." His tone indicated that the Commissioner's office also would be reluctant to extend a hand to the team or its general manager.

Robin had already convinced himself he was making enough of a sacrifice by marrying Minerva. "I can't lower my pride to Phil Donegan's level," he said.

The Commissioner became even colder. "I can do no more than warn you, Stephens."

A heavily tanned Ellen Hibbs returned from her vacation without fanfare, and Robin sent Patricia to her office with copies of memos and other documents that might concern her. He had already made up his mind not to change his approach to her, in spite of the fact that he had learned she was Klein's mistress. Actually, now that he knew he would be in charge of the team for the entire season, he wished he could find new duties for her to perform. It would be too difficult to utilize her services as a personal assistant, partly because he wasn't Dan Grannett, and even more important, because he would feel she was looking over his shoulder, waiting to report on everything he said and did to Marc Klein.

So he did not go down the corridor to Ellen's office, and instead waited for her to report to him. Meanwhile there was work to be done, and he sent for Chuck Blanchard. "I have some information for a press release," he told the public relations director. "I've just closed a deal with Central Illinois College for the use of their playing fields and a dormitory. We're moving our training camp there. Patricia can give you the details on the size of the dorm and anything else you may need."

Blanchard was upset. "We aren't going back to the Joliet University campus?"

"Not for publication," Robin said, "we're saving a big chunk of money. I'm getting the facilities at Central for far less than we paid at Joliet."

The publicity man seemed even more disturbed. "I wish you'd told me you were thinking of changing."

The location of the team's training camp was none of his concern, and Robin raised an eyebrow.

"I have some friends at Joliet, and I'm sure they'd have worked out new terms with you."

"Mal Ferguson is satisfied with the facilities at Central, and so am I." Robin's tone indicated the subject was closed. "Let me give you something far more important than a training site to worry about. Season ticket sales are way off the mark, and with Donegan still sniping at us on the air every night, they won't pick up appreciably unless we mount a strong campaign. You might book speeches for some of the players before various men's clubs. That's usually sure-fire."

"Uh-huh. The trouble is that most of our players are new, and haven't yet built a Cougar following." Blanchard recovered from his disappointment over the training camp. "But I'm sure I can move the tickets, and that brings up something I've wanted to discuss with you, Robin. Would you be willing to give me final responsibility for seat sales?"

Robin was surprised by the unusual request. "Let me think about it," he said. "I'll get back to you."

The publicity man apparently wanted to say more, but refrained, and went off to his own office.

Robin looked at the view of Chicago's skyscrapers that had become familiar to him, and suddenly rang for Patricia. She appeared immediately, and he motioned her to a chair. "What's your opinion of Blanchard?" he asked her.

"I'm not competent to judge his work," the secretary said, "but everybody likes him."

"Including you?"

"Yes."

"What do you know about his social life, scale of living and all that?"

"Well," Patricia said, "he spends a lot of time in the newspapermen's bars, of course, but there isn't much else I can tell you. He has an apartment on Lake Shore Drive, but I've never been there. I'm afraid I'm not being very helpful, Mr. Stephens."

"Don't let it disturb you," Robin said.

They were interrupted by a tap at the door, and the secretary opened it on her way out, revealing Ellen in the frame.

"Welcome home and come in," Robin said, hoping he sounded more cordial than he felt.

"I can come back later if you're busy," Ellen said.

He waved her to a chair, deciding on the spur of the moment to make no mention of her vacation. It would be far easier to get along with her on a day-to-day basis if he pretended he hadn't seen her on Marc Klein's island. "You're catching up, I see." He gestured toward the thick sheaf of papers she was carrying.

"I'll have some homework to do, that's certain." She began to look through the papers, which indicated to him that she, too, did not intend to mention Klein. "Congratulations on the training camp you set up at Central. I assume you'll want me to follow through with the school on the hiring of cooks, cleaning help, and so on."

"Yes, please." On sudden impulse he asked, "Did anyone here have any close ties at Joliet University?"

She shook her head. "Not to my knowledge. Why?"

"What would you think if someone here was upset by our move to a new camp?"

"It would depend on how paranoid I was feeling on any given day. Since I'm enjoying a screaming paranoia this morning, I

[125]

jump to the conclusion that he was getting a private rake-off from someone in the athletic department at Joliet."

"That's what occurred to me," Robin said, and abruptly changed the subject. "Obviously you've had no chance to examine the ticket-sale patterns."

"I've seen them," Ellen said, "but it will take me a few hours to analyze them."

"Whenever you get to it."

She looked at a double column of figures. "We're down eleven percent from the same date last year."

"I'd like to boost sales, of course, but I'm not really worried. The demand will go up like a rocket when the new offensive team starts clicking in exhibition games."

Ellen bit her lower lip but made no reply, making it clear she failed to share his optimism.

"Anything else on your mind?" In spite of Robin's determination to remain civil, he could not help speaking curtly.

"Several things. I've already put out several feelers on the special assignment you gave me. I don't mind telling you I had some ideas of my own when I saw the videotape of Donegan's program. Ideas," she added with care, "that I've told no one. I'd rather not start pointing a finger until I'm more sure of my ground. But I can't necessarily produce results overnight. It may take me some time."

"The sooner the better, naturally." It was unnecessary for him to spell out to her that he wouldn't be comfortable until they found the culprit who had passed along confidential information to a sportscaster.

Ellen rose abruptly and walked to the windows, standing with her back to the room, so he could not see her face. "There's something else I've been considering, and please hear me out before you say anything. You may not want me under foot at all. I hadn't expected poor Uncle Danny's recovery to be so slow, and there doesn't seem to be any question that you'll be in charge here for the full season. By now you can't help but know that I look out for his interests and try to protect his image of the Cougars. That's the way I'm made. You're trying to do a job, and I know you're sincere, so I don't doubt your motives. What I don't like is your methods, which is unfortunate. But that's the way things are. If I were you, I wouldn't want me around, needling you and getting in your way. So I'm willing to step aside as long as you're acting general manager. I can take a leave of absence from my job, and I imagine a temporary place could be found for me in the parent organization."

Robin wanted to laugh at her delicacy. He felt certain Marc Klein would transfer her to another of his companies whenever she indicated a desire to move.

Ellen turned to face him, and her simplicity was that of a little girl as she said, "It's up to you."

He tapped on his desk with a letter opener, trying to gauge his response to the unexpected offer. In all probability she had made it because he had become aware of her relationship with Klein and realized he might be inhibited by the presence of his employer's mistress, who would observe and criticize every move he made. In addition, he was far from certain that she was free of guilt in the passing of information to Phil Donegan, so it would be doubly helpful to be rid of her.

On the other hand, his instinct urged him to keep her on the staff. The gesture would indicate to her—and to Klein—that he had the self-confidence to be the master in his own house. She was a competent administrator, and by indicating he trusted her he might win enough of her respect to persuade her to work on his behalf. Certainly he needed all the help he could get.

"If the season had just ended," he said, "I might bring in someone from another team to help me. But we'll be going into training camp in another couple of months—"

"The rookies report seven weeks from today," Ellen interrupted.

"—so it's too late to hire anyone familiar with the Cougar operation. I'd rather have you stay right where you are."

Her astonishment indicated she had assumed he would be delighted by the opportunity to get rid of her. Recovering swiftly, she dropped all pretense. "Marc says that what he admires most about you is your guts, and he's right, as usual. I'll try not to be too much of a gadfly, although I'll have to be honest, and I just hope you won't regret this decision."

"Well," Robin said, matching her candor, "I'm taking so many risks that one more doesn't increase the odds against me by too much."

In the weeks preceding the establishment of training camp Robin mailed contracts to all the veteran players on the Cougars' roster, and more or less as he had anticipated, about half signed without further ado for the new season. Exchanges of correspondence, buttressed by a flurry of long-distance telephone calls, were necessary in other instances, but little headway was made with the key players acquired in the winter trades, and they came to Chicago, one by one, for personal conferences with the acting general manager.

Robin quickly came to terms with Byron Jeffers, the mammoth defense end obtained from the Giants, but Big Horse Collins thought he had been the key figure in the deal that had brought him and Fred Finch to the Cougars in return for Ted Marcus, and demanded an increase of ten thousand dollars. Robin was forced to disillusion the linebacker, but finally agreed to give him a raise of five thousand, bringing his salary to thirty thousand. Place kicker Adam Renewzski, who knew his worth, insisted on a salary of thirty-five thousand, and after consulting with Mal Ferguson, Robin followed the coach's suggestion and gave in, provided Renewzski also agreed to do the punting. Thereafter the other newcomers fell into line, each of them receiving increases of three to five thousand dollars.

Treating the figures as completely confidential, Robin kept them in a locked file drawer to which only Ellen Hibbs and Patricia had access. Nothing specific regarding salaries was leaked to the press or commentators, although Phil Donegan waged a relentless campaign on the air, insisting that Robin was squandering money in order to buy the loyalty of his team. Donegan's inability to obtain accurate financial data was something of a satisfaction, however, and at the least it seemed to indicate that Ellen had not been responsible for the original leak.

But she found it impossible to refrain from expressing her own feelings, and one afternoon, when she learned that two relatively obscure linemen had received substantial raises, she came into Robin's office to protest. "You're going to hate me for saying this," she said, "but I know Uncle Dan would tell you that you're being too soft. Every last one of the players would have capitulated and accepted smaller salaries if you'd held firm."

"There's no doubt of it," Robin told her, and grinned. He was beginning to understand Ellen, and it gave him pleasure to tease her.

"You're admitting there's substance to the nasty charges Donegan is making on the air every night!"

"Not at all." He tried to exercise patience. "Dan Grannett has one concept of football, and believes he can inspire a man to play his best. Maybe so. I won't get into an argument with football's greatest living legend. But I'm just a businessman, and I realize the gooks are playing for more than fun. Most of them have wives and kids to support, and they're in football for the same reason I am. Money. They'll give their all on the field—for me—only if their wallets are full. I'm trying to build a team in a hurry, and I don't know any other way to do it. Whether I'm right or wrong doesn't much matter. It's my system, and I'm stuck with it."

His stand was unassailable, and Ellen was forced to retire, even though she could not accept his thesis.

While the negotiations with the players were still in progress Minerva Helmsley returned from Reno with her divorce, and Robin proceeded with his plans to marry her. It was true that she wasn't what he wanted as a wife, but she was flamboyantly attractive and sexually dominating, qualities he found appealing, so he consoled himself with the thought that he could do worse.

Regardless of how he felt, however, Marc Klein had given him no real choice: if he hoped to prolong his career with the Cougars he was being forced to marry her. So he tried to make the best of the situation.

"My apartment is a little small for two people," he told her, "but I don't want to get tied up on a long-term lease in a bigger place until I see whether I'm offered a new contract at the end of the season. Can you manage in that amount of space?"

"Why not? When I was modeling, I lived with three other girls in a place half that size." Minerva proved surprisingly agreeable.

"If I'm signed up as G.M. on my own," he said, "you can pick our new apartment, and the sky will be the limit."

Robin used his real first name, Bascom, when they applied at City Hall for a marriage license, and the strategem succeeded in fooling the press, so nothing appeared in print. The ceremony was performed by a judge of the Municipal Court, with Patricia Thompson and a reluctant Mal Ferguson acting as witnesses. Still avoiding publicity, the newlyweds retired to their apartment, and the following day Minerva moved in her clothes, which filled every closet and made the purchase of additional wooden wardrobes an immediate necessity.

The continuing contract negotiations made it impossible for Robin to get away for a honeymoon, but he bought his bride a diamond and ruby watch, and she was mollified. After the season ended, he told her, they would make an appropriate trip somewhere.

"I thought the players were the only ones who kept talking about 'after the season,'" Minerva said. "But I guess everyone in football is in the same boat."

Not until four days after the wedding took place did the press belatedly discover that the Cougars' acting general manager and the former wife of star fullback Hal Helmsley had been married. Chuck Blanchard arranged for a session with the photographers, and then everyone retired to a nearby bar for a drink. That night Phil Donegan carried the news on his sportscast, and although his smile was ironic and his tone of voice biting, he gave the facts without adding a comment of his own.

Robin and Minerva watched the program on the portable set in their living room, and both were relieved when Donegan refrained from launching a new attack on them.

"The bastard is clever," Robin said. "He knew he'd make sympathy waves for us if he did his usual knife job."

Telegrams of congratulations began to arrive that same night, and the following day the first gifts appeared. Among them was a silver bowl from Marc Klein, and with it a card that read, "*You're very wise.*" Ellen Hibbs sent a modest cheese board, together with a simple message, "*Best wishes.*" Hal Helmsley proved he was unperturbed by a possible revival of unsavory rumors by sending a telegram that Minerva pinned to the bedroom wall. It read: "MY BLESSINGS ON TWO OF MY FAVORITE PEOPLE."

The changes in Robin's daily routines were few. Minerva arose in time to drink a cup of coffee with him every morning before he went off to the office, and then went back to bed. They dined in restaurants every evening, sometimes going on to a bar for a few rounds of drinks, sometimes going straight home. But, no matter what time they retired, Minerva's sexual appetites were ravenous, and she demanded that Robin make love to her nightly. Now and then he rebelled, saying he was too tired, and on these occasions she became even more aggressive than usual, delighting in arousing him against his will.

There was no other friction, however, so their relationship was tranquil, and their first quarrel did not develop until they had been married for two weeks. They were dining in the neighborhood French restaurant to which Robin had taken Fred Finch's mistress, Martie, and the trouble began when two men seated opposite the couple stared surreptitiously and without interruption at Minerva.

Robin made no comment until the men departed. "I didn't

want to make a scene," he said, "but I wanted to slug those guys."

Minerva laughed happily. "They were harmless, honey. They were just looking."

"I know, but it was the way they were looking that spooked me. Not that I blamed them."

She sensed something critical in his tone. "What does that mean?"

"Any man is going to pop his eyeballs at a girl with your figure—when she wears a dress cut that low."

Minerva bristled. "Don't you like my dress?"

"It would be okay at a jazzy cocktail party or some place like that." Their coffee arrived, and he added saccharin to his cup. "I've been meaning to mention something about your clothes anyway. You've got to be a little more careful. For instance the day the press photographers took our pictures, you were wearing a very short, tight skirt, and it made quite a leg show in print the next day."

"I'm not ashamed of my legs!" The last of Minerva's good humor vanished.

"Neither am I, and there's no reason you should be. But you've got to remember my position demands a certain dignity. I'm not a gook who earns his living smashing through a line of even bigger gooks. For instance, the outfit you wore the other night to the little party the office staff gave for us was too provocative. It didn't fit the occasion."

"Mr. Stephens," Minerva said, "Mrs. Stephens has just blown her cool, and she wants you to listen. Very carefully. I know my assets, and I refuse to hide them. It wasn't so long ago that you flipped because of them. Right?"

"Sure, but—"

"Never mind the excuses! I refuse to pretend I'm something that I'm not! You'll have to take me the way I am, because I have no intention of changing. I like it when I'm the center of attention. I like it when I'm admired. You've known it ever

[132]

since we started seeing each other, so I'm not telling you anything new. So get this through your head—I'm not a corporation
wife, or a businessman's wife, or a general manager's wife. I'm
me. I happen to be married to a man who happens to have a
certain kind of job. That's his business. Exclusively. But how I
look is my business. Exclusively."

Robin had never seen her so overwrought. "Keep your voice
down, Min."

"Why should I? There's no secret about the way I feel. If
you wanted one of those anemic white-gloves-and-Easter-hat
girls, you shouldn't have reached into the grab bag for me. Anybody who wants to think I'm flaky is entitled to his opinion at
no extra charge."

"All I ask is a recognition that there are times when a sedate
appearance and attitude can be helpful."

"Don't you believe it, honey! The chicks look at me and turn
green. The men look at me and drool. That's what helps you
to stand out from the crowd. What do you care if some of
them don't like me? They remember me—and you. As long
as I don't play around, nobody has a right to criticize me. I was
faithful to Hal—until you came along, and I'll do better as your
wife. If you didn't trust me, you shouldn't have married me,
but it's too late for regrets now. We're in this together, so
you'll just have to take me for what I am."

Patricia Thompson could cope with any situation, but she was
thoroughly flustered, one morning a scant ten days before the
opening of training camp, when she burst into Robin's office.
"Dan Grannett is here to see you!" she exclaimed.

For a moment he was too startled to reply, but regained a
surface equilibrium. "We mustn't keep him waiting."

A gaunt Mr. Football limped into the office, leaning heavily
on a stout walking stick. He had lost so much weight that his
shirt collar was several sizes too large for him, and his bones
seemed on the verge of protruding through his loose, wrinkled

skin. "Sorry to break in on you like this, Robin." His voice had lost none of its resonance. "But we're in town for a couple of days, and I didn't want to pass through without seeing you."

Robin shook his hand and guided him to the most comfortable chair in the office.

"Don't make a fuss. I'm not that much of an invalid." Dan lowered his creaking bulk into the chair.

"I wish I'd known you were coming. I feel like a real intruder, using your office." Robin's discomfort was acute.

"No need for that." Dan's attempt to smile was partly successful. "Muriel and I are on our way to Marc Klein's island. He's turned it over to us for the next month or so. But we decided to visit our grandchildren on the way, and I couldn't pass up this opportunity."

"The whole staff will want to see you."

"Doctors won't allow it, and I've got to obey their orders."

Robin reached for the telephone.

"No need to warn them off," Dan said. "I'm sure Ellen has taken care of all that by now." He studied the younger man. "Congratulations on your marriage, and good luck this season. I've felt I've let you down. And the Cougars."

"A coronary was hardly your fault."

"I'm not so sure," Dan said. "I let my ambitions run away with me, you know. I discovered that sitting behind that desk was much tougher than running a team on the field. Maybe I'll get some zip after I pick up a little weight, but right now I feel I'm well out of the rat race. Which isn't to say I don't care what happens to the Cougars. This team is important to me."

Robin didn't know how much to limit the conversation, but could not let himself forget he was dealing with a man who had suffered a coronary attack.

Dan saw him hesitate. "I know about all your trades," he said, sounding sympathetic, "and I have a pretty fair idea how much you've had to pay your new player personnel. Not from Ellen, though. She's the most honorable person in football."

"I don't expect you to approve of what I've done," Robin said cautiously.

"This is your team, not mine. I can commend a couple of your deals. Byron Jeffers is a great addition to any team, and Adam Renewzski will pay off for you, even though he has a money-grubbing attitude I detest. I should have gotten rid of Tony Zimmerman years ago, I suppose, but I was weak. He'd played for me too long, and I felt loyal to him, even though he's a real troublemaker. I wrote to Mal last month that I think you've done a first-rate job of housecleaning."

"Thanks, Dan." The support of Mal Ferguson was of primary importance.

"I guess I shouldn't question the wisdom of unloading Ted Marcus. I believe I could have kept his radicalism under wraps, but I can't blame you for feeling otherwise. Collins is no Marcus, but he'll plug the hole. As nearly as I can tell, you've made just one mistake, Robin. Fred Finch."

Robin wanted to defend himself with vigor, but confined his reply to a simple, "We needed a first-string quarterback."

"Hjalmar Sorensen did a great job at Peoria last year. Which isn't to say he'd have come through in his first season with the big boys." Grannett rested both hands on the top of his walking stick. "I can't deny your need for a top-grade quarterback. But not Finch! I could have had him before he went to Baltimore, but I ducked. He's a rotten apple who can ruin your entire barrel."

"I'm aware of the risks," Robin said, "but I also believe he can become the biggest drawing card in the game, once he develops the right attitude."

"Oh, he has all the skills. Every team in the N.F.L. is conscious of that much. But how do you haul him into line?"

"Carrot and stick," Robin said.

"You've been feeding him carrots?"

"Lots of them. A one-year contract that doubles his salary, along with a promise of a bonus and a long-range contract

[135]

if he delivers. A big sales pitch on what a superstar he'll be if he behaves."

"What about the stick?" Dan waggled his cane.

"I've shown it to him, but I haven't used it on his backside, other than to let him know I'm in charge of this office and Mal runs the team. I've told him not to flaunt the sexpot who has been living with him, but otherwise I haven't gotten tough."

Dan was silent for a time. "Do you want some advice from an old man who may have seen his last active days in football?"

"I'll be grateful for any help you can give me," Robin said.

"Crack down on Finch as soon as possible, even if you have to invent a reason. Make sure he understands you're the boss, and that you won't tolerate any of his nonsense. Don't leave his disciplining to Mal. Finch sulks when a coach spanks him, so Mal should be the one who builds his ego, while you turn him over your knee. I wouldn't be able to tolerate somebody who has all that talent and no self-discipline, but more power to you if you can bring it off, Robin. Everybody in the league has dreamed of winning a championship with Finch, but you're the one who bought him—and must make him produce."

The door opened, and Ellen Hibbs looked in. "Your fifteen minutes are up, Uncle Danny."

The old man was disappointed. "So soon?"

"You promised to be good," she said.

Robin had no intention of following his advice, but knew how much Grannett had been enjoying their talk. "This is good for him. And for me."

Ellen's glance was withering. "Mr. Klein's car and chauffeur are waiting in front of the building."

Dan hauled himself to his feet. "I'm not complaining. I'm grateful to be alive." He held out his hand to Robin. "I'll be following you on the air and in the newspapers. They're going to humor me by allowing me that much. Good luck."

Robin wondered how he could refrain from adding, "You'll need all the luck you can get."

*   *   *

The town of Lincoln, Illinois, dozed in the heat of a midday June sun, and only the adolescents ventured out-of-doors to ride their bicycles or play games of baseball and tennis. The swimming pool at the country club was crowded, as were the private pools, where matrons sat together under oversized umbrellas and chatted while their children swam, splashed and shouted. Soon the more substantial male citizens would leave their air-conditioned offices in their air-conditioned cars and would drive to their air-conditioned homes for lunch; no restaurants worthy of the name were open at noon, so those who could afford the luxury of driving home did not hesitate to avail themselves of the privilege.

On the outskirts of Lincoln stood the cornfields that stretched out to the horizon across the flat, rich earth of the prairie, the tasseled stalks stirring faintly in the searing breeze. Due west of the town, however, a group of modern, gray buildings of stone cut off the view of the prairie. This was the campus of Central Illinois College, which had closed its doors to the student body for the summer, and it appeared as deserted as the oak- and elm-lined streets of the town.

But activities on the practice field at the stadium, an edifice of twelve thousand seats, more than made up for the quiet elsewhere. There, behind closed gates, twenty-seven Cougar rookies and nine free agents, experienced players without affiliation, were in their fifth day of workouts under the watchful eyes of the coaching staff. Clad only in shorts, undershirts, thick socks and cleated football shoes, one group was jogging endlessly around the running track while another did calisthenics. In a far corner was the only evidence that these athletes were football players: a tall young man wearing a bright red shirt that identified him as a quarterback was lobbing a ball to each of two companions in turn, and they raced down the field, running uneven patterns as they reached into the air for his passes.

The heat was so intense that it struck Robin like a physical blow as he left his car, identified himself to the uniformed campus policeman on watch at the gate and wandered into the stadium. This was the time of year everyone in the business awaited as eagerly as the fans, but Robin paid no attention to the sweating young men, and shielding his eyes from the sun with his hands, he finally saw Mal Ferguson, in sweat pants, a sport shirt and a long, peaked baseball cap, across the field. Just walking the short distance caused him to perspire, and he removed his jacket, hauled down his necktie and unbuttoned his collar.

Ferguson grinned as he moved toward him. "Welcome to Sizzle City," he said.

"Anybody down with sunstroke or heat prostration?" Robin asked as they shook hands.

"Not yet. Nobody has dropped except the two who went home yesterday."

"I got your notification last night." Robin looked at the joggers, knowing that no more than a dozen of the first-year men and free agents would make the squad. Most of the fortunates would be rewarded with contracts that would guarantee them incomes of less than ten thousand dollars for the year, and it was difficult to imagine why they bothered. "Is it always this hot?"

"Next month," Mal said, "will be worse."

"No wonder I got these facilities for a bargain."

"It's just as bad at Joliet University."

"Even so," Robin said, "maybe I should have rented quarters in the woods of northern Wisconsin."

Ferguson shook his head. "Weather like this is good for football. It separates the men from the boys mighty fast."

Ferguson was a different man on the field, Robin thought, and was encouraged by his tough attitude. "How does Sorenson look?" Again he shaded his eyes and squinted at the quarterback.

"Not too bad. He just started throwing yesterday."

Robin watched the man who, if his plans jelled, would become the second-string quarterback. "Quick release."

"Yes, he has a good wrist. Something that can't be taught."

"Plenty of power, too."

[138]

"Too much at this stage. The crazy kid is trying to show off for us." Ferguson raised a bull horn to his mouth. "Sorenson! Hold it down to twenty-five yards. Absolute maximum until next week. You trying to ruin your pitching arm?" Lowering the bull horn, he fumed in silence for a moment. "Goddam children, all of them. He knows he has a job, but he can't resist trying to make an impression, now that you're here."

As Robin well knew, no coach appreciated the presence of the general manager at rookie camp. "I can take the hint, Mal. I just came down for a quick look, and I'm driving back to Chicago this afternoon."

"Don't leave on my account," Mal said, and grinned. "Any improvement in ticket sales?"

"None. They stink. Blanchard keeps telling me he can hypo them, but I won't put him in charge until he shows me some concrete results. The pace will pick up after the veterans report. How are the press quarters?"

"Pretty fair. They've got air conditioning as good as mine."

"Fine. That should induce them to write some rosy reports. Beginning this afternoon, when Fred Finch arrives."

"He isn't coming today," Mal said quietly.

"We've already told the press he's due before supper tonight, and some photographers are driving down this afternoon. So is a television camera team. Fred knows all that. Publicity notified him yesterday."

"All the same, he won't be here," Mal said.

Robin stared at him.

"He called me from Baltimore this morning to say he needed a couple of extra days."

"What was his excuse?"

"He didn't make any."

In his anger Robin forgot the heat. He and Ferguson had worked out a new and intricate system requiring veteran back-field men and offensive ends to report for training in accordance with a staggered schedule that would enable the first-string players who were new to each other to become acquainted

[139]

before they began working with their linemen. The whole plan hinged on the varsity quarterback, who had been summoned several days earlier than the rest so he would be in top physical condition when they arrived.

Dan Grannett had been right, Robin told himself; the only way Finch could be handled by the front office would be to crack down on him. "Where's a telephone, Mal?"

"In the office they've given me, behind the locker rooms." Ferguson asked no questions as he pointed to a solid structure of gray stone under the stands.

Still oblivious to the weather, Robin hurried off, and was so preoccupied he failed to notice a drop in temperature of forty degrees in the air-conditioned office. He found Finch's Baltimore number in the little address book he always carried, and tapped a foot impatiently as he dialed it.

The instrument at the other end of the wire was lifted after the second ring, and a cheerful man's voice answered.

"Fred, this is Robin Stephens."

"Hiya, boss!" The quarterback seemed genuinely pleased to hear from him. "How's tricks?"

"Lousy, thanks to you. I just now got to training camp and heard you aren't coming today."

There was a brief pause. "I can't make it today, Robin. I'm going to be tied up here until Saturday, maybe Sunday. You know how it is." Fred Finch lost none of his poise.

"No, I'm afraid I don't," Robin said. "Our whole plan to get the Cougars moving this season depends on having you here. By tonight. When you were ordered to report."

"I'd have been on time if some personal problems hadn't come up." The quarterback sounded aggrieved. "You know I wouldn't let you down deliberately."

Robin made no reply when there was a pause at the other end of the line.

"Between us," Finch said, "I'm having some trouble with Martie. She's going up to New York while I'm at camp, but she doesn't want to leave until the weekend, and—"

well knew, he and his staff were resented when they interfered in the realm of the coaching staff, and he took care not to step beyond the invisible boundary of responsibility. "Do any of these boys look particularly good?" he asked the group.

The assistants left the reply to the head coach. "That Simmons," he said, "is as fast as Hayes of Dallas, he can cut without twisting his ankles, and for a boy who had only a year of intercollegiate competition at Grambling, he has fairly sticky hands. He still shows a tendency to look away from the ball when it's in the air, but if we can cure him of the habit he'll be an All-Pro candidate in two or three years."

"Any nuggets in the line?"

The assistant coach in charge of the defensive team took up the burden. "I have a couple of monsters who don't look too God-awful," he said cautiously. "Particularly a free agent who was turned loose by Atlanta. But it's too early to tell."

"Has anybody checked the Falcons to hear what they say about him?"

"I called Atlanta yesterday," Mal said, "and they rate him okay. They're loaded with offensive guards, so they cut him free at the end of last season. We may be picking up a bargain, but I don't want to count on it until we see him in scrimmage for a couple of weeks."

"How soon do you start body-contact work?" Robin wanted to know.

"Light scrimmages begin on Monday."

Robin nodded and glanced at his watch. By now Fred Finch would be on his way to the airport, if he was giving in to the ultimatum.

Mal caught his eye, but said nothing, and signaled to the waiter for another pot of coffee.

Robin knew what he was thinking: no experienced general manager would have allowed himself to be caught in a bind that made his future, as well as the team's, dependent on the ability of a single player to produce results. Unfortunately or otherwise, he had elected to use a short-cut, and he would have to curb and encourage the temperamental Fred Finch if he expected to continue his career in football.

While the coaches continued to talk, the players, who had scattered to their rooms, rested for an hour before resuming practice. Ferguson indicated his appreciation of Robin's delicacy by inviting him to attend the session, and he wandered out onto the field after making several telephone calls to the office in Chicago.

Many players were lined up in front of tackling dummies, and several units were hopping over obstacle courses, activities which kept them busy for the better part of an hour. One end of the practice football field was in shadows now, and when Robin saw the young quarterback, Sorensen, jogging toward the goal posts, accompanied by a heavy-set center and several tall ends, he strolled toward them. He paused at the sidelines, where Ferguson joined him.

"I thought you'd like to see Hjalmar and Simmons in action for yourself," the coach said.

"Snap the ball on the third 'hup,' Joe," Sorensen said to the center, and called a set of imaginary signals.

Simmons raced down the field, his leg muscles rippling as his cleats dug into the black earth, and the football came at him like a bullet from a distance of twenty yards, but was a trifle too high for him to catch.

"Try the straight fly pattern again," Mal directed through his bull horn. "And wait a split-second longer before you release, Hjalmar."

The pass was repeated, and this time the young quarterback and the even younger end connected.

Robin forced a smile. "Well," he said, "maybe it won't be the end of the world if Fred Finch doesn't show up."

He continued to watch the rookies and free agents until the end of the session, but he lacked the coaches' knowledge of the fine points of the game, and consequently was in no position to judge the individual merits of the players. A general manager could use his own judgment when he bought and sold, traded for players or obtained them in the college draft, but there his direct responsibility ended and he was forced to rely on the coaching staff.

The Cougars' coaches were Dan Grannett men, cut in old Mr. Football's mold and trained by him, and their attitude toward the game was apparent in everything they said and did. They were low-pressure operators, men who rarely shouted, seldom lost theim tempers and never cursed at the players. Dedicated to football, they regarded their profession as a game, and were happy to be earning their living doing what they liked. Observing them on the field, and again at the dinner table, where they demolished steaks as enormous as those consumed by their oversized charges, Robin couldn't help wondering whether he would have been wiser to make a deal for a quarterback less flamboyant than Fred Finch. In spite of all the uproar over the wholesale change in player personnel this season, the Cougars would be no better than their field staff, and the coaches, reflecting Dan's love for football, were not men who would tolerate selfishness and erraticism from any man, even a quarterback who, if he lived up to his potential, might lead the team to an American Conference championship in two or three years.

The players were served a fruit gelatin for dessert, but the coaches were privileged to eat ice cream, if they wished, and several ordered it. Robin, who was trying to be careful of his weight, settled for a cup of coffee into which he dropped a saccharin tablet, and had just taken his first sip when an assistant trainer came to the table. "Fred Finch has just arrived," he announced. "We're taking him up to his room."

Robin had won a battle, but knew it was just the first of many, and felt no gratification. "I think I'll drive back to Chicago right now, without seeing Freddie," he told Mal. "I don't want him to think I'm gloating."

The idea of holding a get-acquainted party for the veterans and their families prior to the opening of the regular training camp originated over drinks in the cocktail lounge in the building adjacent to the Cougar offices. Some said it was Minerva Stephens who first broached the scheme, saying that the holdovers and the newcomers from other teams would appreciate the opportunity to meet as individuals, rather than as football players. Others said Ellen Hibbs provided the original spark, but the half-dozen members of the office staff who were present agreed that both girls were enthusiastic.

Robin improved on the plan, and renting a resort near Lake Geneva, Wisconsin, for the purpose, sent invitations to all of the veterans who had signed for the season. The affair was scheduled to last for twenty-four hours, and facilities were available for swimming, golf, tennis and softball. Only football, by unspoken agreement, was prohibited. Mal Ferguson surprised Robin by giving the party his hearty endorsement, and even agreed to leave rookie camp with his two principal assistants and their wives in order to attend. Marcus Aurelius Klein, probably responding to Ellen's private influence, agreed to make a token appearance on the second night.

The party opened with a dinner in a series of private rooms on the second floor of the resort. The smaller children were taken in hand by trained members of the hotel staff, and a special room was set aside for the teen-agers, which made it possible for the adults to shed at least some of their responsibilities. Drinks and canapés were served in a gold-and-white anteroom, where the arriving players, their wives and the dates of the bachelors were greeted by Acting General Manager and Mrs. Stephens, and Head Coach and Mrs. Ferguson.

Minerva had chosen to wear a floor-length dress for the occasion, but when she moved it proved to be anything but demure, falling away to a point high on her thighs. Robin had raised an eyebrow when he had seen it, but she had silenced him with a sharp, "No lectures! Remember, I know a lot of the fellows and their wives already, so they know how I dress!"

One of the first to arrive was the gigantic Byron Jeffers, accompanied by his tiny wife, a model for *Ebony*, and the defensive end enveloped Robin in his renowned bear hug, lifting him several feet off the ground. "Baby," he announced with an enthusiasm that was generic before the aches of training camp dampened a player's spirits, "this is going to be our year!"

Others were more subdued. The Polish-born Adam Renewzski, supposedly the most accurate soccer-style kicker in football, clicked his heels as he greeted his hosts and created a ripple of excitement as he kissed the hands of his hostesses. Several of the guests endowed with highly developed senses of timing later claimed he lingered far longer over Minerva's hand than over that of the motherly Mrs. Ferguson.

Most of the guests were already assembled when Hal Helmsley made his entrance, resplendent in linen trousers, turtleneck and jacket in matching shades of bright red. And conversation died away as everyone strained to watch the drama of his meeting with his former wife and her new husband. All three of the principals acquitted themselves handsomely. Hal kissed Minerva on the cheek with the warmth one bestows on an old friend, and she responded in kind; then he grinned and chatted as he shook hands with Robin, who was equally cordial. Those who had hoped to see a display of fireworks were disappointed.

It took Fred Finch, who had not yet proved himself, to upstage the superstar. Released from training camp at noon of that day so he could attend, he was the last to arrive, coming in with a scantily clad Martie on his arm just as the party was about to move from the cocktail lounge to the dining room.

"Hiya, warden!" he said jovially to the head coach. "Thanks for springing me. Greetings, fellow sufferers to be," he shouted to the assembled players. "Eat, drink and be merry, because you're sure headed for liniment alley!"

The players greeted his mild humor with a roar of laughter, proving to both Robin and Ferguson that he had the capacity for leadership, if he cared to exercise it.

Fred was polite when he shook hands with Robin, but his manner was reserved, indicating he had not forgotten the threat that had brought him to training camp on time. He did not thaw until he was presented to Minerva, and then his attentiveness, his quick smile indicated an appreciation of her charms.

Martie more than made up for his coolness toward Robin,

however. The redhead threw herself into the arms of the acting general manager, embarrassing him by planting a long kiss full on his mouth and pressing closer to him than the amenities required. At least a dozen people noted that Robin had to wipe her lipstick from his mouth with a handkerchief as the party adjourned to the dining room, and these same observers also saw that Mrs. Stephens seemed unmoved by the incident. She continued to smile, and, as she walked beside her husband to their table, she chatted with him animatedly.

Had any lip readers been present, however, they would have known better. "That chick is too much," Minerva said. "Who is she?"

"Finch's girl." Robin tried to hide his discomfort.

"Obviously."

"She's a football groupie who has been around the league for about three years," he added.

Minerva continued to smile. "It figures," she said, and seemed to lose all interest in the subject.

It had been agreed there would be no speeches, but at the end of the meal Coach Ferguson asked the players to introduce themselves, and began with his superstar.

"Helmsley," Hal said. "Fullback. I've spent ten days in camp, and let me tell you, we're going to have us a backfield this season!"

"Atta way to go, baby!" a flankerback shouted.

Most players were content to echo Byron Jeffers' simple statement. The All-Pro defensive end contented himself with, "Jeffers. Lineman."

But Fred Finch felt compelled to take advantage of the opportunity to make a speech, and everyone noted that while most of the players confined themselves to beer, he was holding a highball in one hand. "You see before you," he said, standing easily at his place, "a refugee from a slave farm. I say this even though our genial slave driver, ole Massa Ferguson, is sitting over there. I've spent almost a month in camp, so I'm in rare trim, I can tell you. With luck, I may be able to heave a ball five to ten yards. Seriously, I've been working with the backfield and the ends, and we've got ourselves a great gang. If the guys up front will give us the blocking, and if defense will hold the enemy to reasonable scores, there's no telling how far we can go this year!"

Everyone applauded, and Robin exchanged a quick glance with Mal Ferguson. If this was a demonstration of the field leadership the quarterback could provide, the trade for him would be well worth all the agony it had caused.

Then Finch spoiled the good effect he had created. "But this, fellow slaves, is no night to think of football. Tonight we're free men—free to drink ourselves silly, free to make love, free to kick up one hell of a storm."

There were a few faint whistles of approval, mingled with a scattering of applause, but most of the players looked embarrassed. Ferguson announced there would be dancing in a room on the ground floor, and the dinner ended. Most of the women went off to the various ladies' rooms to freshen their make-up, while the men gathered in small groups as they drifted down the stairs.

Minerva ordinarily would have been one of the first to leave, but she stayed close beside Robin, even though he seemed anxious to say something in private to Mal. But she was waiting for someone, and not until she saw Fred Finch's red-haired friend making her way to the ladies' room at the rear of the bar did she depart. Then, taking her time, she followed, and sat next to the other girl in front of a long mirror. For a few moments they busied themselves with mascara, eyeliner, foundation and lipstick, and neither spoke.

Finally Minerva broke the silence. "You're Finch's girl."

"Uh-huh."

"I guess you don't remember me."

Martie squinted at the blonde, made a brief attempt to jog her memory, and then shrugged her bare shoulders. "I've met a lot of people tonight," she said without apology.

"I," Minerva told her, "am Mrs. Robin Stephens."

"Oh, sure. Now I remember you. Although I guess I never

did get to say hello to you when we came in tonight." She smiled as she remembered her arrival.

Minerva continued to speak softly. "I just hope you won't forget you're Finch's girl."

Martie stared at her, then bridled. "Exactly what is that supposed to mean?"

"Interpret it as you please." Minerva returned the stare, taking a cigarette from a case in her ⌐houlder bag and lighting it without looking at it.

"It so happens," Martie said with heavy dignity, "that I'm a friend of Robin's." She spoke his name slowly, with relish. "We were friends before you married him."

"So I gathered earlier tonight." Minerva pushed her chair away from the vanity and stood.

Martie immediately rose, too.

Minerva quickly realized her mistake: the other girl was the better part of a head taller. "I know most of my husband's good friends," she said, and only her increased rate of breathing indicated that she was upset.

Martie continued to regard her coolly. "So now you've met another."

"Don't get any flaky ideas, that's all. We'll all be chums if you'll keep in mind, from now on, that I'm the wife of the general manager."

Martie's laugh was mocking. "How could I ever forget that Robin is the lord high bossman of this outfit? Of course," she added condescendingly, "I suppose if I was your age, I'd be nervous around younger, pretty girls, too."

Minerva had to restrain herself from clawing off the other's dress, but she did not lose her temper, and managed to look Martie up and down, her manner indicating pity as well as contempt. "Baby, it's like the guys say. This is going to be a long, long season."

4

The intra-squad scrimmage on the last day of training camp was a resounding success that thrilled a crowd of seven thousand persons who paid one dollar each for the privilege of attending. Of far greater importance was the reaction of the sports reporters who watched the regulars sweep to a 34–0 victory over the substitutes. Fred Finch passed for two touchdowns, one of them a heave of more than fifty yards to Miner Simmons, Hal Helmsley scored another on a four-yard plunge inside left tackle, and Adam Renewzski kicked two field goals. The surprise of the day, however, was a rookie, the Cougars' seventeenth draft choice, Oliver Olson, an unheralded halfback from Penn State, who gained eighty-nine yards from scrimmage in twelve attempts, blocked superbly, and not only caught five passes, but scored the final touchdown on a 27-yard twisting run after catching a short pass in the flat.

"Don't look now," the Chicago *Tribune* said in its report of the scrimmage, "but as of this afternoon the Cougar first-stringers, playing a semi-game against their own bench-warmers, served notice on the AFL that they might be contenders this year. Hal Helmsley, as expected, was superb, and Freddie Finch, as hoped, kept him company. But it was the third member of the backfield, halfback Oliver Olson, a rookie and a nobody, who had Mal Ferguson and his coaching staff leaping with joy. If today's scrimmage was any criterion, Olson is a shoo-in for Rookie of the Year honors."

The *Sun-Times* was only a shade more restrained: "Many miles of turf will be chewed between now and Super Bowl time in January, but—as of today—Head Coach Mal Ferguson's varsity looked like champions. Hal Helmsley is paid to be great, and he was. An inexperienced second-string secondary made Fearless Fred Finch look like the Cougars' answer to every Hall of Fame quarterback, and the highly touted Adam Renewzski put on one of his patented exhibitions of flawless place-kicking. But he averaged only 37 yards on his punts, which is so-so by NFL standards, and the hero of the day, a rookie named Oliver Olson, who squirmed and dodged through platoons of eager-beaver Cougar subs who will be trimmed from the roster ere long, may not fare as well against professional opponents who understand the primitive science of open-field tackling."

Even Phil Donegan was willing to give the team its due, more or less, on his regular nightly sportscast. "The Cougars," he said, "made like real football players this afternoon. But don't start pestering acting General Manager Robin Stephens for post-season championship game seats just yet. A few match-ups in coming weeks against some big leaguers will tell whether Stephens is a resident genius or, as many observers suspect, whether Dan Grannett will be forced to cut short his recuperation to salvage what he can of a Stephens-made mess."

After breaking camp, the players, with the exception of a few older, married men, gave themselves a beer-drinking party of monumental proportions. The following Monday they reported for work at the practice field Ellen Hibbs had rented for the duration of the exhibition game season from the University of Chicago.

Robin was on hand for the beginning of the season at 10:00 A.M., and consequently did not reach his own office until noon.

There he discovered that his mail was heavy and that an unusually large number of telephone calls had come in during the morning. But he had no chance to answer any of them before Chuck Blanchard hurried into his office.

"Boss," the happy public relations director said, "I'll bet I've fifty newspapers and television queries about that Olson kid since Saturday's scrimmage!"

"Well, soft-pedal any information you send out on him," Robin said.

"How come?"

"He was running through butter the other day, and Mal doesn't want to give him any build-up whatever until we see how he makes out against the Cardinals, the Bears and Dallas in the first three exhibition season games."

"Olson happens to have captured the imagination of the press!" Blanchard was indignant.

"Mal is running his team," Robin said quietly, "and he has my unqualified support. So we'll do this his way."

"I don't think you understand, boss." Blanchard was respectful, but held his ground. "The switchboard has been jammed with requests for season tickets, and a bag and a half of mail has come in today. Olson is the big draw, even bigger than Finch!"

"Mal is bringing the kid along slowly," Robin said, exercising patience. "If we scream we have an unheralded star, other teams will start pointing their defense toward him, and his flame could be snuffed out before he has a chance to develop."

Blanchard stiffened. "This is the first day we've had requests for seats in any decent number."

"I've said all along that sales will take care of themselves when the team starts to jell."

The publicity man paused for a long count before he replied. "Maybe I'm just jittery about sales because no one person is in charge."

It was true that the vacancy had not yet been filled, but Robin had been delaying making an appointment until he found the right man for the job. He saw no need, however, to offer Blanchard an explanation. "For the present," he said, "we're going to have plenty of vacant seats on our hands, no matter who runs the box office. If we concentrate on the team, sales will take care of themselves."

"Not quite," Blanchard declared. "At least six hundred requests have piled up over the weekend, and they've got to be arranged in some sort of priority."

His argument was valid, Robin thought. "You're still nagging me for the appointment?"

"Somebody has to run that show."

"Okay." Robin reached a decision. "If you can handle ticket sales in addition to your regular duties, you're in temporary charge of the box office. Only until I get the right person to move in permanently, though."

"Fair enough, boss." Blanchard tried to sound matter-of-fact, but it was obvious he was pleased.

Robin was so busy it was not until that evening that he wondered, fleetingly, why a man would be so pleased to add to his responsibilities and work load when he was receiving no additional compensation.

The hopes of die-hard Cougar partisans were deflated that Saturday night, when the team played its first exhibition game of the season against the Cardinals in St. Louis. The score was a lopsided 42–6, and only Adam Renewzski distinguished himself by kicking two long field goals. Fred Finch, who played only in the first half, completed only five of thirteen passes for a miserable sixty-three yards, and Hal Helmsley, who carried the ball nine times, was held to twenty-one yards from scrimmage. Oliver Olson looked like any other rookie, carrying the ball three times for a net loss of eight yards, and lost possession of the ball to the Cardinals on a fumble. Hjalmar Sorensen, the second-string quarterback, proved ineffectual, too, completing only two short passes in eight attempts. The defensive team made an equally poor showing, and although Byron Jeffers held up his end of the line, his efforts were more than nullified by Big Horse Collins, who stumbled all over the field and allowed himself to be taken out of almost every play.

"The Cougars," a sepulchral Phil Donegan told his WWW audience, "are living up to our expectations. I don't think you'll lose money if you bet on them to wind up the season in the American Conference cellar."

The following Friday night the team played the Cowboys in Dallas, and seemed to become completely unhinged, losing by a score of 58–3. The Cougars' only score came on a desperation field goal of fifty-three yards made by Adam Renewzski, whose teammates played like rank amateurs. Fred Finch could neither organize an offensive drive nor find his receivers, and Hjalmar Sorensen, who replaced him for the second half, was equally inept. Hal Helmsley played dispiritedly, and young Olson, who saw action only in the third quarter, did nothing of note. The defense fell apart, too, and even Byron Jeffers looked like a rookie on a minor-league team.

"We hope," wrote a sports columnist in the *Daily News* the next day, "that Dan Grannett's family and friends aren't allowing him to read the newspapers or watch the boob tube. Even as strong a man as Danny would suffer a relapse."

The third of the pre-season games was important to both teams, even though coaches and players alike insisted to the press that it was just another exhibition match. The Cougars were playing the Bears, in Chicago, and the rivalry of the city's two teams was so intense that all seats had been sold months earlier. Robin had just completed negotiations for the building of the new lakefront stadium, which would not be ready until the next year, so the game was played at ancient Soldier's Field before a capacity crowd of 102,467 people.

Bear fans enjoyed their Sunday afternoon outing as they watched their team coast to an easy 17–0 victory, although the regulars were withdrawn midway through the second period and did not return. The best that could be said for the Cougars was that their defense showed some signs of jelling. But their offense was handcuffed, both of their quarterbacks played poorly and even Hal Helmsley was so discouraged that the Bears' second- and third-stringers held him to minor gains.

By the second half Cougar fans were chanting, "We want Marcus! We want Ted!" Whenever the team made a first down, an event that occurred only four times during the long afternoon, the crowd cheered ironically, and loud boos greeted Fred Finch every time he trotted off the field.

Coach Ferguson ordered the dressing room doors locked to all outsiders after the game, and the players showered and dressed hurriedly, then departed by little-used side doors. A few of the veterans conversed in low tones, but most were as silent as the first-year men, and the atmosphere was funereal.

Robin put Minerva in a taxi and sent her home, then joined Ferguson, carefully avoiding the players' locker room on his way in. "Mal," he said, "Blanchard is still holding the press at bay out there, but they're going to break down the doors any minute."

The head coach's smile was weary. "I'm stalling until all the players are gone," he said.

"Good idea."

"Stick around for the press conference, will you, Robin? I may need you to help pick up the pieces."

"Whatever you say, Mal." Robin opened the bottom desk drawer, found a bottle of bourbon and helped himself to a stiff drink. "Want one?"

"I'll wait until I get home—and then I may get plastered. For the first time in about twenty years." Mal looked into the locker room, saw it was empty and called out to the waiting Blanchard at the far end of the corridor, "Let the wolves in, Chuck."

When the reporters filed into the office they saw a smiling Ferguson seated behind the desk, looking as though he didn't have a care in the world. Standing inconspicuously in a corner, scribbling in a small notebook and apparently oblivious to the scene around him, was acting General Manager Stephens, who did not look up.

"Sorry to keep you waiting, gentlemen," Mal said, and sounded cheerful.

"What were you doing, sweeping out the dead bodies?" one of the newsmen demanded.

No one laughed.

"I suppose you want a general statement, gentlemen," Mal said. "Here you go. While no coach and no team enjoy losing, the exhibition season is a time to work out kinks. The Cougars are a new team, and most of our players are just learning to play together. The members of my staff and I think they're showing signs of coordination, and we have no reason to be dissatisfied with their performances. I believe you'll soon begin to see very definite signs of improvement."

Robin, who continued to make meaningless scribbles in his notebook, was filled with admiration for Ferguson, who was handling one of the most difficult assignments in the business with the aplomb of a real professional.

"Why did your guys lose today?" someone wanted to know.

"Because the Bears scored seventeen points, and we didn't score any. That's obvious. Let me hasten to add that the Bears have been playing together as a unit for a long time. Most of our players weren't even acquainted with each other until a few weeks ago."

"Mal," a columnist for *Chicago Today* asked, "is it true you read the Riot Act to the boys just now?"

"I did no such thing." Ferguson's annoyance was genuine. "Both our offensive and defensive teams are adjusting to a new style of play, and they can't do it overnight, or even in a month or two."

"How soon do you expect to start winning?" a *Sun-Times* man wanted to know.

"It won't be as long as some of you sad characters seem to think." Mal recovered his poise, and with it his good humor.

Phil Donegan took a step forward. "Where will the Cougars wind up this season, Mal? As champions, or in the cellar?"

"I'm a football coach, Phil, not a fortune teller."

Donegan transferred his attention to Robin. "Maybe the G.M. can tell us something."

"Certainly." Robin smiled, but braced himself.

"Are you satisfied with all of your trades, Mr. Stephens?"

"Completely. I have full confidence in our players, just as I have in Coach Ferguson."

"Then you aren't planning to mastermind any more great trades before the regular season begins?"

"As of this moment, we're planning to start the present season with players who are currently on the roster. I'm not ruling out a possible trade if somebody came along and wanted to make us a present of a couple of All-Pros, but we have no active deals in the works, and we also have none in mind, Mr. Donegan."

"What place in the standings do *you* predict for the Cougars this season?" Donegan demanded.

"I don't." Robin curbed his temper.

"But you still think Finch and Collins are worth the loss of Ted Marcus?"

"I believe the trades we've made speak for themselves," Robin said.

"They sure as hell do." Donegan made no attempt to hide his contempt as he stalked out.

There was a long moment of embarrassed silence before Ferguson said, "If there's nothing else, gentlemen, my wife is waiting for me in our car."

The reporters departed. Chuck Blanchard would have remained, but a single glance from Robin sent him on his way, too.

Robin closed the door. "I wonder when the team really will start to jell."

"I wish to God I knew." Mal sighed.

"Can you pinpoint the problem?"

"No, and that's the hell of it. Our defense really was better today, although I hate to think what might have happened if the Bears had kept their regulars in the lineup longer. Our offense puzzles me, Rob. I worked with them myself all week, and technically they've shown enormous improvement. They looked great in scrimmages on Wednesday and Thursday, but this afternoon they just fell apart out there. Nothing worked right, and they kept dragging their tails."

Robin helped himself to another drink and started to pace the length of the office. "I've seen it happen before, and not just in football. No matter what the sport, a team doesn't roll until it gains confidence in itself."

"I don't think this problem is a question of confidence," Mal said. "Helmsley knows what he can do. Finch has enough confidence for ten men. Everybody in the offensive line is a veteran, and so are the flanker and wide receiver. Only Olson and Simmons are still a little damp behind the ears, but they're developing fast. No, it isn't confidence that's lacking."

"Then I'm damned if I understand what's wrong," Robin said.

"This may be a premature judgment," Ferguson said, speaking slowly. "But if I had to put a finger on the problem, I'd say they're lacking the spark that would fuse them."

The problem was not a new one, and frequently arose when players from a number of organizations were brought together for the first time. "Somehow," Robin said, "they've got to begin to recognize the fact that they're a *team*."

The head coach stared at his oversized hands. "They're pros, so they take pride in their work, but so far they're out to win their individual jobs. They haven't yet gained the sense of pulling together."

"How do they get that feeling?" Robin knew the question was foolish before he asked it, but it annoyed him, as a businessman, to be forced to deal with the intangible that could only be identified as team spirit. Certainly he couldn't admit to Ferguson that he had always denied the need for that ephemeral, emotional quality in professional players.

"If I knew the answer," Mal said, "I'd be the resident genius of the year. There's nothing I can do to spark them that I haven't already tried. My staff can't do it, and neither can you."

Robin felt an unfamiliar wave of discouragement well up in him. "I suppose if Dan Grannett were here and made some of his inspirational speeches—"

"That might light the fire," Mal admitted. "Or it could fall flat. Don't start blaming yourself, Rob. I've been in this game a lot longer than you, certainly in my end of it. And if there's one thing I know for certain it's that the players will have to develop their own sense of unity. Either they're a bunch of individuals earning paychecks, or—and I don't care how corny this sounds—they're members of a team who believe in their own destiny."

Robin remembered a remark attributed to the late Vince Lombardi, that nobody in football was more helpless than the general manager of a team that failed to jell.

"Why am I waiting until I get home before I have that first drink?" Mal asked, and reached for the bottle. "Who knows? If we don't turn these guys around, I may well become an alcoholic."

The Cougars played their best football of the year in the first half of their exhibition game with the Washington Redskins, holding their foes scoreless while running up twenty-seven points. But in the second half both offense and defense fell apart, and they permitted the Skins to score four touchdowns in twelve minutes, so they lost, 28-27. "If they'll just remember the first half," Mal Ferguson said, "we'll be all right."

But the players couldn't put the catastrophic second half out of their minds, and the following week they made their most miserable showing of the exhibition season, losing to the San Diego Chargers of their own Conference by a score of 43-3,

Adam Renewzski's fourth-quarter field goal saving them from another humiliating shutout. Then they traveled to Green Bay, Wisconsin for their last pre-season game, and fifty thousand rabid Packer partisans jeered them without rancor as they bowed, 33–7, in a match that was no contest.

The post-game silence in the Cougar dressing room and on the team bus was deafening. Hal Helmsley and Big Horse Collins played gin rummy to pass the time, but most of the others stared out of the windows. A battered Fred Finch, who had been thrown for losses nine times, leaned back in his seat with his eyes closed, but no one knew whether he was sleeping or was merely seeking privacy.

The regular season was scheduled to begin in two weeks, so Mal Ferguson gave the team a forty-eight hour furlough. The coaches held their regular Monday post-mortem, however, and Robin sat in on the meeting as an observer. "The most I can say for the boys," Mal told his staff, "is that they haven't panicked. Yet. I'd shake up the varsity if it would do us any good, but the subs are falling on their cans even harder than the regulars, so I'm afraid we'll have to sweat it out."

At lunch that day in the Wrigley Building restaurant, Robin presented a smiling, confident façade for the benefit of the television and radio executives who made the place their head-quarters. He concealed the fact that he had no appetite by ordering a small salad, and that night he tried to release his frustrations by becoming involved in a meaningless fight with Minerva, who showed her good sense by refusing to reply to him and going off to bed.

The following midmorning his secretary came into his office and closed the door behind her. "I've just heard via the grapevine," she said, "that Dan Grannett is not only in town, but in the building. He and Ellen Hibbs are upstairs right now, seeing Mr. Klein."

Robin managed a weak grin. "Batten down the hatches," he said.

It did not occur to him that Dan might want a word with

him, so he was surprised, an hour later, when Patricia buzzed him on the intercom.

"Mr. Grannett would like to see you, if you aren't too busy."

"Too busy? Hardly!" He hoped he sounded cordial, and was glad he had a moment to compose himself.

Dan Grannett, heavily tanned and at least ten pounds heavier than he had been when last in Chicago, did not smile as he shook hands. "Robin," he said as he took a seat on the leather couch, "I don't believe in acting behind any man's back. Or holding back in telling him to his face what I've said about him to somebody else. I've just come from Marc Klein's office."

Robin tried to assume an expression of polite, faint surprise.

"As a matter of fact, I called Ellen right after the Green Bay game and asked her to set up an appointment with Marc for me."

Ellen, Robin thought, owed him the courtesy of telling him what she was doing, but he supposed he couldn't blame her. Dan was still her permanent boss as well as her mentor.

"I don't mind telling you I've been pretty upset by the worst exhibition season in Cougar history," Dan said.

"You aren't the only one."

Mr. Football ignored the younger man's remark. "I've begged the doctors to let me come back to work immediately. That's how serious I think this situation is. But they won't listen to me, so I'm condemned to spend the season on the sidelines. I couldn't have picked a worse time to be recuperating from a heart attack."

Robin could think of no bland reply, so he remained silent.

"What eats me, as I told Marc Klein just now, is that the Cougars are still my team. My name is still closely identified with the organization."

"I don't think you need to worry too much about being branded with the rest of us." Robin tried not to allow any bitterness to creep into his voice. "Phil Donegan and your other friends in the sports fraternity have made it very clear to the public that you're in no way responsible for the poor showing we've made so far."

Grannett shook his massive head. "That's very kind of them, but it doesn't make me feel any better. The Cougars have been my life for a long time."

Robin warned himself not to become embroiled in a fight with the man who, even in temporary retirement, exerted enormous influence.

"I've been making my own analysis of the team," Dan continued, "based on the videotapes I've seen of your exhibition games."

Ellen, Robin knew, had broken the rules by supplying Grannett with the tapes, but it would be difficult to chastise her for her display of loyalty.

"The defense became unhinged when you traded away Ted Marcus. Collins is a fair enough player, and I'm sure Mal can help him achieve his maximum potential, but he's no Marcus. Byron Jeffers is a first-rate addition, but he's playing an individual star's game."

"The boys are just becoming accustomed to working together, you know." Robin expressed his protest mildly.

"The real trouble with the defense," Dan continued, "is that the offense offers them no incentive. Helmsley is the best fullback the game has seen since Jim Brown and Jimmy Taylor, but he's become lackadaisical. Young Olson can become a fine halfback, but he needs guidance. On the field, from fellow players. Renewzski is all right, of course, and although Simmons is a sloppy blocker, he has good moves and can grow into a fair enough end. I have no major criticism of your offensive line, either."

Robin braced himself for what he knew was coming.

"The key to your whole problem is Fred Finch. I wouldn't have taken him if the Colts had handed him to me free. I sure wouldn't have traded for him, and I wouldn't have gone out of my mind by giving up Ted Marcus for him!"

Robin realized he could no longer allow himself to be browbeaten. "I haven't lost faith in Freddie, and I still think he'll vindicate my judgment when he finds himself."

[163]

"He's nothing but a journeyman quarterback who has had years to find himself. Look at his record in the league."

"His potential—"

"There's no place in professional football," Grannett said, interrupting incisively, "for any player who consistently fails to live up to his supposed potential. That's Finch, and what he's done for you during the exhibition season proves I'm right."

Robin could not agree that Finch's showing to date was proof he couldn't make the grade. "Suppose we had gone with young Sorensen, as you had planned to do. He's had several airings, and you've got to admit he's still green."

"But we had Tony Zimmerman to back him up and teach him. That was your other big mistake, as I told Marc. You shouldn't have gotten rid of Tony."

"I don't believe there's any place in football of today for an active racist." Robin felt his temper begin to rise. "I want no part of any bigot, white or black."

"Zimmerman was tamped down nicely," Grannett said. "And the way he felt off the field was his own business."

"All the same, Danny, he carried his prejudices onto the field, and the Blacks on the team resented him."

"In my opinion you were looking for trouble where none existed." Mr. Football hauled himself to his feet. "I didn't come here to quarrel with you, and my doctors would give me hell—as would Muriel—if they knew I had gone this far. I just wanted you to know what I said to Marc Klein this morning. I wanted the record made clear."

"It's your privilege," Robin said, taking care not to raise his voice, "to ask the owner to fire me. I just hope you don't expect me to thank you for your candor."

Grannett's level eyes seemed to bore into the younger man. "You're wrong. I didn't—and wouldn't—think of suggesting that Marc get rid of you now. The beginning of the regular season is no time to find another temporary general manager. Not only would the front office fall apart, but nobody competent would want to be saddled with any share of the blame for this year's failure."

"I'll just remind you," Robin said, "that exhibition games don't count in the standings. The regular season hasn't even started yet, so I can't accept your charge that the Cougars have failed. Or that I've failed. Wait until the end of the year before you start pinning nasty labels on me!" Ushering his visitor to the door, Robin felt little of the confidence that his attitude or words indicated.

The Cougars resumed practice on the Wednesday after Labor Day and began to point toward the opening game of the regular season against the New England Patriots at Foxboro, Massachusetts, where the newest stadium in the National Football League was located. Under the best of circumstances the Cougars were not a strong drawing card, and their lack of success in exhibition games reduced their box-office power still more. So Robin congratulated himself, after talking to the Patriots' office in Boston, when he learned that aside from the pre-sold season tickets, approximately fifty percent of the seats available for individual games would be occupied.

For the rest of the week Robin stayed away from practice, hoping the team had started to jell yet afraid the players were still mired in the swamps of their own making. By late Saturday afternoon he could no longer tolerate the suspense, and drove out to the campus of the University of Chicago on the South Side for a seemingly casual visit. By the time he arrived, however, the field was deserted. This was the last day the university's facilities were being used, so assistant trainers were busily packing away equipment, and Robin did not halt as he made his way through the labyrinth of small locker rooms ordinarily used for intramural sports.

As he walked down the aisle at one side of cubicles, however, he suddenly realized that one of the players had remained behind. A dejected figure in undershirt and trousers was hunched on a bench facing an open locker, his chin cupped in his hands as he stared into space.

"Hi, Freddie," Robin called.

Fred Finch raised his head with an effort. "Coach said we stunk up the field, so he let everybody out early. You've missed him."

Robin moved closer and leaned against a bank of lockers. "What are you doing here, then?"

"Thinking," the quarterback replied bleakly.

It was obvious he was depressed and needed help. "Anything I can do to help?"

Fred started to shake his head, then changed his mind. "Yeah. Listen to me for a minute, and don't interrupt. You've been damn decent to me, Mr. Stephens, and I wish to hell I could live up to your faith in me. But I'm smelling up the place, and I'm wondering whether to quit."

Robin sucked in his breath, but sounded casual. "And do what?"

"I can get some kind of a job. Back in college I had a job summers as skipper of a charter boat in Florida. You know, for deep-sea fishing, and I think I could latch on there for awhile."

"You spend more in a week on your girl," Robin said, trying to sound jovial, "than you could earn in a month as a charter-boat captain."

"What girl?" Fred's mouth twisted and managed to look bloodless.

Quickly piecing together the situation, Robin knew what had happened. Not only had Fearless Freddie made a miserable showing during the exhibition season, but had fought with the redhead.

"If you want to know how Martie is getting along," the quarterback continued, "don't come to me. Go see the great place kicker."

"She's—become chummy with Renewzski?"

"Do you need a blueprint, for God's sake?" Fred sounded

angry, but the anguish in his eyes was real. "She's shacking up with the son-of-a-bitch!"

Robin knew the blow to his key player's fragile ego had been catastrophically damaging, and was more than someone of his temperament could tolerate. The Cougars' slender hopes were riding on this young man with a yo-yo temperament, and in his present mood there was no telling what he might do. "Where are you headed right now?"

Fred shrugged. "I drove out here with one of the guys, so I'll either take a taxi back to the Loop or head for one of the bars near the campus. I can tie one on in this neighborhood just as easily as I can downtown."

Robin went through the motions of stifling a pseudo-yawn. "Finish dressing," he said, "and I'll give you a lift."

Fred took his time getting ready and cleaning out his locker, so another quarter of an hour passed before they walked together to Robin's car. Both were silent as Robin threaded through traffic on the Outer Drive, and Fred's attitude was that of a man who no longer cared what became of him. Robin knew it would be useless to explain that the redhead was indifferent to his accomplishments as a player, and that her departure from his bed and board had no direct connection with his abysmal training-season record.

A vague plan began to form in Robin's mind, and he drove straight to his own apartment building, leaving the car with the doorman. Fred started to protest, but was overruled. "We're here, so you may as well come up for a quick drink. My liquor is as good as any bar's."

Minerva, who was clad in a skimpy halter top and very short shorts, was surprised to see the unexpected guest, but greeted him cordially and sought no explanation from her husband until they had a moment alone in the kitchen. "He's not only been playing lousy football," Robin explained, "but the redheaded chick left him for Adam Renewzski, and he's ready to turn in his shoulder pads."

She realized at once how badly her husband would be crippled if his number-one quarterback, for whom he had traded away a superstar, gave up football. "Leave him to me, sweetie," she said, squeezing her husband's hand. "I may not know much, but I sure understand the vanity of an offensive backfield man."

It was a near-miracle to see Fred's morose hostilities gradually drain away. He scarcely touched the gin and tonic he had requested, turning instead to the beer that Minerva tactfully placed on the coffee table before him. She waited the better part of an hour before insisting that the guest remain for dinner, and when Fred consented after a token struggle, Robin began to feel a trifle easier in his own mind. Minerva, he told himself, was a marvel. Ordinarily she would not dream of cooking a meal on a Saturday evening, but she made it appear that they always ate at home.

They adjourned to the kitchen, where she outlined the menu: steaks, baked potatoes, salad and raisin pie.

Robin excused himself, went into their bedroom and looked up Adam Renewzski's telephone number, which he dialed. "I want you to meet me at the office in ten minutes," he told the surprised place-kicker, whose protests he ignored, and then wandered back into the living room. "Freddie," he said, "do me a favor and give Min a hand at the stove, will you? I've got to dash out on an emergency, but I'll be back soon."

Minerva asked no questions of her husband as she shepherded their guest into the kitchen.

Only one elevator was running in the office building, and Robin used his key for the first time as he let himself into the Cougars' suite and snapped on the lights. He waited for more than twenty minutes, pacing his office, before a belligerent Adam Renewzski finally showed up.

"What could be so important that it interrupts plans for a big Saturday night?" the player demanded.

Robin had decided to take a blunt approach. "I hear you have a new roommate."

Renewzski smirked slightly, then stiffened. "That," he said, "happens to be my private business."

"I'm making it mine," Robin replied, "because it affects the team. I'm sure you know that Martie was living with Fred Finch before she moved in with you."

"If Finch was not man enough to hang on to her, that is his problem."

"Nobody could be that much of a man, or would want to be. I know something about the young lady, and she's a castrating little bitch."

"I enjoy her company," Renewzski said, retreating into the formal shell of the European.

"Freddie," Robin said, "is pretty uptight. Not because of you, but because she took up with another player on the same team. Renewzski, I'm going to lay it on the line. Fred Finch has enough troubles, and one more may break him. The Cougars need him, playing the brand of football he's capable of playing. A brand that will earn you one hell of a lot more money in two or three years, when the Cougars start winning championships. So I want you to get rid of the girl. Throw her out. She won't starve."

"There is a player on the Dolphins who pesters her to join him," Renewzski said, his eyes dark. "But you ask too much."

"You know you can get all the tail you want," Robin said. "But it does too much damage when it's at Freddie's expense. You're a big boy, but he's still an emotional child. I'm reluctant to get tough, Renewzski, and I'm not the sort who goes around threatening people. But I'll be forced to report this matter to the Commissioner unless you break off with her, and I'll be compelled to tell him that a serious scandal is threatening the future of professional football."

"You would do it," the place-kicker muttered. "I truly believe you would."

"Don't put me to the test."

Renewzski bowed from the waist. "Mr. Stephens, you are a bastard and a shit."

"That's the best definition of a general manager I've heard since I was given my job." Robin began to snap off lights and guided him to the door. "Offer Martie her plane fare to Miami," he said. "First class. I'll reimburse you with a general voucher. And if it will make it easier to kiss her off with a gift, the Cougars will contribute two hundred dollars toward anything you want to buy for her."

In spite of his indignation Renewzski laughed. "If front-office scheming won championships," he said, "the Cougars would go all the way to the Super Bowl this very year."

Robin returned home in a taxi, and found a thoroughly relaxed Fred Finch, several empty beer cans on the coffee table in front of him, as he sat comfortably beside Minerva on the living room divan. He was telling her the story of his life, and she appeared to be so interested, so sympathetic that not even the return of her husband halted the quarterback's flow of words.

Fred talked all through dinner and far beyond it, recounting in detail every football triumph he had ever enjoyed in high school, in college, and on a far more limited basis, as a professional. Robin's mind wandered, and he sometimes forced himself to stroll around the apartment so he wouldn't fall asleep. But Minerva seemed totally absorbed by the recital, and further demonstrated her supposed fascination by asking appropriate, intelligent questions at intervals.

Fred was still jovially expansive when he departed after midnight, his desire to quit football forgotten.

"Honey," Robin said as he and Minerva headed toward their bedroom and began to undress, "you were terrific. You did more to change his mood in a few hours than I could accomplish if I worked on him for a solid month."

Minerva shrugged, then unzipped her dress. "Freddie is lonely, that's all. And like so many players, he confuses his public image with his personal identity."

"Well, you slugged like hell."

"It wasn't that difficult, sweetie. He has the same vulnerability that made me stay with Hal as long as I did. I feel sorry for poor little Freddie."

Robin sat down to remove his shoes. "Whatever your feelings, you prevented a crisis, and I'll never forget it. Anyway, we're getting a break. The problem will end very quickly." He told her about his meeting with Adam Renewzski.

Minerva's eyes appeared to grow larger. "Maybe the immediate crisis is ended," she said, "but there will be others. Lots of them, now that Freddie has found a soft shoulder he thinks he can cry on."

Robin looked at her. "We can do without the complications of Fred Finch falling in love with you!"

"That will never happen," she assured him. "He's like Hal —so infatuated with himself that he can never fall in love with anyone else. But he *does* need a woman who will listen to him, pat his hand and help him keep his shaky balance." She donned an abbreviated, semitransparent nightgown.

Robin hesitated. "Will you mind—if he's elected you to be his new mama?"

She smiled at him. "Only if it bothers you, Rob."

He couldn't remember when he had felt closer to her, and grinned at her. "We've launched a joint campaign to preserve the equilibrium of Fearless Freddie Finch, such as it is, to win the Super Bowl game for the Cougars—and to prevent my head from being severed from the rest of me on the chopping block."

That night their love-making was more impassioned, more mutually gratifying than it had been in a long time.

Robin and Minerva were invited to fly with Marcus Aurelius Klein and a large party of his friends on a private jet to Massachusetts for the opening game, and neither were surprised to find that Ellen Hibbs was an unobtrusive fellow passenger. Neither she nor Klein mentioned Dan Grannett's recent visit, and Klein expressed complete confidence that the Cougars had turned the corner, insisting on placing one-thousand-dollar bets on the team with each of a number of friends accompanying him.

Minerva sat with the Klein party in the boxes reserved for the Cougars' owner on ground level at the fifty-yard line. But Robin preferred the vantage point of the press box at the top of the stadium from which an assistant coach and a scout acted as spotters for the team.

The Cougars, wearing their new traveling uniforms of white, with blue trim, were warming up on the field, and from a distance, at least, they looked energetic and alert. But Robin was distracted by the empty patches in the new stadium. His practiced eye scanned the amphitheater, and it pained him to realize there were at least ten thousand unoccupied seats. Thanks to the Cougars' exhibition-season record, the fans were showing a distinct lack of interest in the newly reconstituted team.

The Patriots won the toss and elected to receive, but could not advance the ball, and were forced to punt. The Cougars took over on their own 29-yard line, and on the second play from scrimmage, Hal Helmsley fumbled. There was a wild scramble for the ball, which was scooped up by a Patriot defensive back, who promptly went into the end zone. A successful place kick made the score 7–0.

The Patriots kicked off, and Oliver Olson ran the ball back eighteen yeards to his own twenty-five. The Cougars were stopped on two ground plays, and on third down Fred Finch put the ball in the air. It was intercepted by the same Patriot back who had scored a few moments earlier, and he repeated his feat. Again the point-after-touchdown was successful, and the score was 14–0.

Thereafter both defensive teams played almost perfect football for the rest of the day, and there was no further scoring. Hal Helmsley accumulated only forty-two yards from scrimmage, Oliver Olson was stopped cold, and Fearless Freddie's passing record was abominable. He had only seven completions out of twenty-two attempts, for a gain of seventy-eight yards. The best that could be said for the Cougars was that the defensive team had jelled, but even that accomplishment was blighted by the knowledge that the Patriots had one of the weakest offensives in the American Conference.

Robin reached the locker room just in time to see Marcus Aurelius Klein making a token appearance. The owner was unaccompanied, his friends staying behind so they wouldn't embarrass him, and his smile was forced as he greeted the players. Robin took him aside for a moment.

"Marc," he said, "I'll appreciate it if you'll take Minerva back to Chicago—without me. I've decided to fly back with the team."

The owner made no comment, but there was a faint gleam of sardonic approval in his eyes.

A few members of the defensive team chatted quietly as the players settled themselves on their chartered airplane an hour later, but members of the offensive squad were glum and withdrawn. Fred Finch reached up occasionally to touch a bandage across the bridge of his nose, but otherwise sat motionless as he stared out of his window prior to takeoff. Hal Helmsley appeared to be asleep, Adam Renewzski looked bored, and Miner Simmons, who had not caught a single pass all afternoon, glowered at the seat in front of him.

Robin took a place beside a tired Mal Ferguson in the first-class section, where the coaches sat, and waited until they were airborne before he spoke. "Mal," he said, "would you mind if I address a very few well-chosen words to our heroes?"

The head coach shrugged. "Help yourself. I have a few remarks of my own to make, but I'll gladly give you first crack at them."

Robin immediately rose and went to the rear, behind the compartment where the hostesses were preparing drinks and dinner. At his request one of them gave him a microphone, and he moved with it into the tourist section, where the lethargic players were sitting.

"Give me your attention for just a moment," he said. "I don't know how many of you are planning to retire this year," he said, "but from the looks of it, nobody on the Cougars wants to stay in football. I know you won't be able to hold your jobs on this team, and nobody else will want you, either. It doesn't make me very happy that you're driving me out of the game, but I'm not vindictive, and I won't try to sell life insurance to any of you. My real reason, of course, is that I don't believe any of you are good risks."

Turning away quickly, he handed the microphone to Mal Ferguson, who had come up behind him.

The head coach was equally abrupt. "You'll need a day off tomorrow to recuperate from your hard labors of this afternoon," he said. "So we'll go back to work on Tuesday. If any of you are curious, we'll open our home season next Sunday against the Houston Oilers. The game we'll be playing is football. Anyway, that's what it is called."

Byron Jeffers hauled himself to his feet, his bulk filling the aisle. "Hold on a minute, Coach," he called, and limped forward. "What time is practice on Tuesday?"

"The same as always. 10:00 A.M."

"Thanks." Jeffers took the microphone, and fiddled for a moment with the on-off switch. "Did anybody miss that?" he boomed. "Ten on Tuesday morning, like always. Only this week there's something different. I'm calling a private team meeting for 9:00 A.M. sharp. In the locker room. Players only. No coaches, no trainers, no front-office people. Just us." He paused, his black eyes challenging as he looked up and down the aisle at his comrades. "I'll have a roster, and I'm going to take attendance. Any of you guys who don't show up—and on time—will be answerable to me, personally. And I guarantee you that anybody I've got to meet under the stands won't be in condition to play in next Sunday's game." Thrusting the microphone into the head coach's hand, he moved slowly back to his seat, a big, angry man who was defying the thirty-nine others on the active roster and the eight members of the taxi squad to disobey his command.

Robin and Mal exchanged a quick glance as they returned to

their seats. Neither spoke, but there was no need for conversation. The initiative Jeffers had taken in calling a team meeting was the first positive sign they had seen, and if some of the other players shared his feeling of lost professional pride, there was an outside chance that the team might improve.

The telephone in the Stephens apartment rang shortly before Robin left for the office. He was sipping coffee in the kitchen and reading the scathing accounts of the previous day's game in the morning newspapers, so Minerva answered the call in the bedroom. A moment later she joined him.

"Freddie Finch is on the wire," she said. "He wants to return our dinner of the other evening, and he's invited us to go out with him tonight."

Robin shook his head. "I can't make it," he said. "I've got to sit in on the coach's meeting after they go through the film clips of yesterday's catastrophe."

"Of course. I forgot." Minerva started out of the kitchen. "I'll tell Freddie."

Robin called her back. "I hate to turn him down when he's reaching out for sympathy and friendship."

"So do I." She ran a hand through her tousled blond hair. "After that terrible game he played yesterday, he must be feeling lower than dirt."

"He wants the soothing balm from you, honey, not from me," Robin said.

She stared at him for a moment as she tugged the belt of her short, lightweight dressing gown tighter. "Are you suggesting that I go to dinner with him and hold his hand?"

"Only if you feel like playing the Good Samaritan. I'm not sure anything will help Freddie play a first-rate game of football these days, but it can't do any harm to give him another ego-building treatment."

Minerva lighted a cigarette and inhaled deeply. "You're quite sure you don't mind, sweetie?"

Robin's gaze was steady as he looked at her over the rim of

his coffee cup. "I don't know any reason I should. You've never given me cause to mind."

"That's the nicest compliment you've ever paid me." She leaned down to kiss him, then went off to the bedroom.

Robin returned to the blistering story of the Patriots game in the *Tribune,* and was engrossed in it when Minerva rejoined him. "This is just brutal," he said, "but I can't blame the reporters or the public or anybody else for being down on us. You're married to the man who is personally responsible for putting together the very worst team in all of professional football."

Minerva poured him another cup of coffee. "There's nothing wrong that a few victories won't cure."

"Unfortunately," he replied bitterly, "there are no junior colleges on this season's Cougar schedule. What time are you meeting Freddie?"

"He'll come here for me around six."

Robin nodded. "Good. Then you should be through feeding him Mrs. Stephens' homemade sunshine and self-confidence pills by the time I get home. Which should be around eleven."

"Oh, I'll be home long before then, I'm sure," Minerva said.

He smiled at her. "Honey, I'm grateful to you for service beyond the call of marital duty. I don't think anybody can build a fire under the slob, but we're stuck with him, and at least you might be able to prevent him from throwing himself out of a skyscraper window. Not that I'd mind too much if he did—but we'll need him until I can pick up another quarterback on waivers, or buy one from some other outfit's minor-league team. Freddie may not be worth much, but the rules of the game require us to put eleven men in uniform on the field. You'll notice I carefully didn't say eleven players."

Minerva didn't want to give the impression that she expected a festive evening, so she deliberately dressed in a sweater, mini-skirt, wide leather belt and matching boots, the sort of attire she would wear if she were going shopping alone. But Fred Finch was so morose when he came to the apartment for her that he didn't appear to notice how she had dressed. He took her for dinner to Don Roth's Blackhawk, where the portions of first-rate beef were large enough to satisfy even the appetites of professional athletes. Gradually, under her subtle ministrations, his spirits improved, and after dinner they took a taxi to the Rush Street nightclub district, where they wandered into a place that neither knew.

There, sitting in a narrow booth, where Minerva sipped brandy and Fred drank beer, he thawed still more. Experience had taught her how to help a player dispel the memories of a game that haunted him, and he relived the nightmare play by play.

"You're too hard on yourself," Minerva said when he was done. "The kind of game you played yesterday won't win you any trophies, but it wasn't all your fault. Your line didn't stop the Patriot rush, so your throws were hurried, and when you did get rid of the ball, your receivers were covered. You were handicapped by a rookie halfback who doesn't really understand a blocking assignment, and I knew on your first series of plays that Hal wasn't really trying."

Fred couldn't argue the point with Helmsley's former wife. "You make it sound as though I played a good game," he said, his expression wistful.

"You did. Under awful handicaps." He sounded so much like a little boy that she unconsciously stroked his hand.

Her touch jarred Fred, who sat bolt upright for a moment, then inched closer to her on the wooden bench where they were sitting side by side.

Minerva recognized her error the instant she blundered, and knew that she alone was to blame. She was exceptionally attractive, her companion was leaning on her for emotional support, and she should have anticipated his reaction, knowing he would misinterpret the gesture.

"When Martie left me," he said, "I felt sure I was on the skids. And yesterday's mess made it even worse. But you really don't think I'm hopeless, huh?"

"In my book," Minerva lied, "you're terrific." She had allowed herself to be trapped in a situation from which it would be difficult to escape without further injuring his already bruised ego, thereby more than negating whatever good she might be accomplishing.

Fred signaled to the waiter for refills, and casually draped an arm across her shoulders. For the moment, at least, he was forgetting she was the wife of the Cougars' general manager, and knew only that she was an exceptionally pretty girl who admired him.

Minerva felt compelled to maintain a conversation. "I may not know football, but I do understand players, and I could tell you where you've goofed."

"Go ahead." He began to slide his hand under her arm.

"You've been too concerned with setting individual marks. You've forgotten your team will work that much harder for you if you show them you're the boss."

"You think that would do it?"

"I'm positive!" She tried to ignore the hand creeping toward her breast. "A dynamo like you has leadership written all over you. But I've seen you with the guys, and you're too diffident. Let them know who's in charge."

"I'm in charge," Fred said, grinning, and his hand closed over her breast.

This evening, of all nights, Minerva told herself, she should have been sensible enough to wear a bra. It would be easy enough to free herself in a public place, even if they were the only customers who had as yet shown up, but she couldn't reject him without destroying the very qualities in him that she was trying to create.

With his free hand Fred tilted her chin upward and kissed her, his tongue immediately probing.

Minerva's only conscious thought was that she had not realized, until this moment, how much she loved Robin.

He prolonged the kiss until she managed to extricate herself. "We're not invisible," she said, annoyed with her inability to control her short breath. "And somebody here might recognize us."

Fred agreed, and reluctantly released her.

Minerva downed her brandy in a single swallow.

"Have another at my place," he said, and signaled for the check.

The situation was rapidly moving out of control. "I can't go there," she said.

"It's just around the corner. And besides, it wouldn't be right at your house." Fred made his only, oblique reference to her marriage.

Minerva applied fresh lipstick and tried to think of a way out that would not damage his already injured vanity.

"It's been a long time," he said, taking her arm as they reached the street, "since a great chick like you really thought I was okay. You want to know something? You restore a fellow's faith in himself."

Nothing else he might have said could have disrupted her defenses so completely, and Minerva made no protest as he led her to his third-floor walk-up apartment. Abandoning all thought of escape, she decided to make the best of what had developed into an unavoidable situation. So, when the front door closed behind them, she made no protest as Fed kissed and pawed her, his hands roaming feverishly.

He released her, suddenly and unexpectedly, and pointed toward the open door of a bedroom. "I'll find you that brandy while you get ready," he said.

Minerva caught only a glimpse of an untidy living room before she walked into an equally cluttered bedroom. If she were clever, she thought, she could extricate herself from the unsavory mess, but her mind was a blank. All she knew was that she had allowed herself to be maneuvered into a spot: the future of the Cougars well might depend on her willingness to submit to Fred Finch and to pretend she enjoyed his love-making.

Her head ached and her hands trembled slightly as she pulled off her sweater and skirt, removed her boots and then divested herself of her pantyhose and panties. Naked now as she sat on the edge of the bed, she shivered slightly, even though the room was warm.

When Fred appeared, bringing her a water tumbler half-filled with brandy, she saw that he, too, had undressed. Her only thought was that she had never known a man with so little body hair.

Accepting the brandy, she was careful to swallow no more than a small sip. She would be smashed if she emptied the glass, and she wanted to be in control of herself, not only now but later, when she would see Robin.

Fred snapped on a bright overhead light. "Groping in the dark is no damn fun," he said, and threw himself at her as though he were tackling an opposing player on the football field.

His impetuous ardor was somewhat surprising, but Minerva submitted with as much grace as she could muster, simulating mounting passion as she allowed his hands to travel freely. Fred, it soon became evident, lacked the patience for prolonged preliminaries, and soon indicated he wanted to enter her.

But there was a problem, made familiar by her years of marriage to Hal. Fred, in spite of his desire, was not ready and needed help. Her eyes closed, Minerva slid a hand up his thigh and began to manipulate his penis, alternately teasing and withdrawing. It was strange, she thought, how many atheletes were so anxious to create an aura of invincible virility that they actually impaired their manhood.

"Now," Fred muttered. "I can't wait any longer."

She allowed him to mount her, guided him and then went through the old, familiar routine of pretending he was sweeping her to a climax. As a lover he was inept, clumsy and juvenile, and she enjoyed no physical sensation whatever; in fact, her only feeling was one of shame.

They separated as quickly as they had come together, and Minerva allowed herself the luxury of another sip of brandy before she began to dress.

"How was it?" Fred demanded.

She forced herself to return his gaze, and tried to speak with an air of sincerity. "I've never known anything like it," she said.

He chuckled, then whistled under his breath as he pulled on his clothes. "I guess," he said, "you'll be free for dinner again next Monday night."

"That all depends." She slipped into her sweater and skirt before hauling on her boots, and weighed each word with great care. "Dinner is fine, but it stops there."

Fred looked hurt. "How come?"

"No sensible person deliberately plays Russian roulette with atomic bullets," Minerva said. "We don't want a scandal. Think of what the talk would do to your career. Quarterbacks are national heroes, and are supposed to lead clean lives."

"Who'd know?"

Moving to a small mirror above a chest of drawers, she began to repair her make-up. "We might get away with it a few times, but eventually the whole truth would come out. Because I wouldn't be able to keep it to myself, if for no other reason. There isn't a girl on earth who could be that close to you— regularly—without blowing her mind and letting the whole world in on the secret."

Her reply, she saw, watching his reflection in the mirror, satisfied his almost boundless ego.

"Well," he said, "I can see your point. But any time you want more than dinner, just let me know."

"I'll remember," Minerva said.

Fred walked her back to the Stephens apartment, and she said good night to him at the entrance to the building. The presence of the doorman made it possible for her to escape with no more than a handshake.

Uncertain whether to laugh or cry when she was surrounded by belongings she knew, she took a hot bath, scrubbing herself vigorously, but still felt unclean. Under no circumstances could she allow herself to take another drink, so she propped herself up in bed and tried to read. Robin was late, and at 11:30 P.M. she finally turned off the lights.

A few minutes later she heard him open the front door and move softly into the apartment, but she kept her eyes closed and pretended she had fallen asleep. Perhaps it would be easier to face him in the morning, when she could confine herself to the remark that she had done everything in her power to aid the Cougars by restoring Fred Finch's bruised vanity.

Byron Jeffers and Big Horse Collins, each armed with a roster, stationed themselves at the two locker-room entrances and checked off names as the players straggled in. Both were grim, strangely silent, and their attitude communicated itself to the others, so there was only desultory conversation as the men gathered in front of their lockers.

At precisely 9:00 A.M. Jeffers called, "Into the trainers' room. We'll meet there."

They obeyed him without question, and as he marched to the far end of the room, Adam Renewzski straggled in.

"You're late," Collins growled.

The place-kicker intended to reply humorously, but the expression in the bigger man's eyes discouraged him.

"Nine o'clock," Jeffers said, "means nine o'clock. From now on we're doing things together around here, and anybody who doesn't like it can get the hell off the team. Including you, Renewzski. Do you dig me?"

"Every syllable," Adam Renewzski said.

"Defense didn't come out of Sunday's game smelling too bad," Jeffers said. "Although we weren't balls of fire, either, so let's not bust our spines slapping each other on the back. Compared to offense, though, we were great. What do you say for yourselves, offense?"

To the surprise of most of his teammates, Fred Finch jumped down from the trainer's table on which he had just made himself comfortable, and threaded his way toward the heavyset lineman. "Nobody smelled up the ball park worse than I did on Sunday," he said. "I'm offering no excuses. I smelled, and that's that. What's more, I take full responsibility for the entire offensive team."

"Wait a minute," Hal Helmsley shouted. "That's not fair."

Fred wheeled and pointed a finger at the fullback. "I'm calling the signals," he said, then turned back to Jeffers. "What's your complaint, buddy?"

The big man, who outweighed him by seventy pounds, was too astonished by his temerity to reply.

"We know we've got to haul ourselves off our butts and start slugging together," Fred said. "We know we've made ourselves look like horses' asses ever since training camp. We also know we have nobody but ourselves to blame. But we don't need any inspirational speeches or any bully-boy shit from defense. We're professional football players, every goddam last one of us, so let's cut the crap short and get out on the field for a workout."

Members of the offensive team began to cheer.

Byron Jeffers grinned down at the quarterback. "You miserable little punk," he said, "I think you might turn out to be an okay guy."

Fred shook his hand, then called out above the growing noise. "Into your uniforms, you guys. Maybe offense can teach defense a few new tricks. What do you say?"

Miner Simmons' roar echoed through the adjoining locker room. "Atta way to go, Freddie baby!"

When the coaches arrived for the session that was supposed to begin at 10:00, they were astonished to find their charges already on the field, the offensive and defensive regulars locked in a vicious scrimmage. Mal Ferguson was reluctant to interfere, not wanting to dampen his charges' new-found enthusiasm, but finally was forced to intervene for fear some of the players might suffer injuries that would put them out of action for the coming Sunday's game.

The difference in the attitudes of both squads was apparent all through the morning. Finch barked his signals with self-confident precision, talked furiously in the huddles and kept the offense on the move. His spirit was contagious, and Hjalmar Sorensen showed the same fiery vigor when he took over at quarterback. The line moved forward as one man at the snap of the ball, Hal Helmsley recovered the spring in his stride that made him so dangerous, and young Olson ripped off several long gains in broken field running. The defense became deadly, too, with Jeffers and Collins conferring hastily between plays, making assignments and demanding that no man give less than his best. They raged at any colleague who missed a tackle, failed to take out his man or hit sloppily, and the coaches wisely refrained from interfering, confining themselves to the prevention of unnecessary mayhem.

At noon, when the scrimmage ended, the players voluntarily ran seven laps around the field, a chore all professionals ordinarily loathed, and then jogged to the locker room. There Fred Finch approach Ferguson. "Coach," he said, "the guys will be happier if you don't go over the film clips of the Patriot game with us. We know we stunk, that we did everything wrong. So maybe we could save time by holding our first skull session for this Sunday instead. That'll give us a good head start for the Oiler game. Okay?"

Ferguson agreed, and retired to his private sanctum to call the front office. "Don't look now," he told Robin, "and don't hold your breath. But it could be there's a light at the end of a long tunnel."

* * *

The newspaper commentators were unanimous in their agreement that the Cougars who took the field against the Houston Oilers that Sunday looked like a different team. The offense, brilliantly directed by Fred Finch for the first three quarters, rolled up forty-two points, with Fearless Freddie completing twenty-three out of twenty-nine passes and pitching for two touchdowns. Hjalmar Sorensen, who replaced him for the final quarter, made an impressive showing, too, completing six out of seven and passing for yet another touchdown. Hal Helmsley had one of the more spectacular days of his career, gaining 197 yards on the ground, going into the Oiler end zone twice and catching several passes. Young Olson also contributed his share, making seventy-eight yards from scrimmage, and bringing the audience that only half-filled the stadium to its feet with a 93-yard scoring kickoff return.

The defense found itself, too, holding the Oilers to a single field goal from the 42-yard line and allowing no penetration into Cougar territory beyond their 38-yard line. Jeffers and Collins were everywhere, and a new hero appeared in the person of Eddie Brown, a defensive back who weighed only 180 pounds. He intercepted three Oiler passes, proved adept at crashing through the opposing line on safety blitzes, and was responsible for sixteen tackles.

"Either the Oilers are a far worse team this year than anyone has realized," the *Sun-Times* said, "or the Cougars are a far better team than even their most enthusiastic supporters have dared to hope."

Only Phil Donegan sounded a sour note. "The Cougars enjoyed their lucky Sunday," he told his vast WWW audience. "Through some fluke they all ran in the right direction and blocked at the same time. The Oilers, who are first rate, were so demoralized by the sight of their opponents imagining they were a football team that the gladiators from Houston forgot to play the game. But we predict that all will return to normal this coming Sunday, when the poor Cougars travel to Bloomington, Minnesota, for a mismatch with the highly touted Vikings, one of the best aggregations in the National Conference. We shudder to think of what will happen when the Cougar running backs and tricky passers meet that Viking stone wall. Or what the Viking meat-grinder offense will do to the Cougars who tackle people for a living. Local fans should rejoice because they won't be able to be on hand for the brutal letdown."

On the Monday night following the Oiler game, Minerva Stephens went with Fred Finch to Maxim's, a Chicago replica of the renowned Paris restaurant, for a leisurely dinner. Fred was recognized, and for the first time since he had joined the Cougars, his meal in a public place was interrupted by requests for his autograph. Then, in accordance with Minerva's request, Fred took her straight home after they left the restaurant, and they parted in the lobby.

Robin was in high spirits when he came home soon thereafter. "The films of yesterday's game make the boys look great," he said, "and we're already starting to build up a sale for the game with the Colts two weeks from now. Whatever it is you're doing to pump confidence into Freddie—keep it up, honey!"

Minerva managed a smile, but could not speak.

An early autumn rain that swept down from Canada drenched Minneapolis and St. Paul on Saturday night and Sunday morning. The stadium, located between the two metropolitan centers, was sodden, even though tarpaulins had been laid on the field to protect it. By noon the rains eased off and the sun made intermittent attempts to appear, but most commentators agreed with the analysis of Phil Donegan, who told his WWW-TV audience that both teams would be forced to forget their aerial attacks and stay on the ground.

It was quiet in the Cougars' quarters when Robin stopped in for a few moments before the team took the field. Players were lined up outside the trainers' room, waiting to have their ankles, legs and knees taped under the supervision of Dr. Scudder, and there was little horseplay. A few members of the kickoff and punt-return specialty squad were listening to rock music on a radio in front of one of the lockers, but everyone else seemed preoccupied. Hjalmar Sorensen sat in front of his locker, studying his play book, and Adam Renewzski was reading a thick biography of a Polish patriot. Several members of the defensive varsity appeared to be napping, and Hal Helmsley rounded up the offensive regulars, who went into a private huddle in a corner. None of the coaches accompanied them, and Fred Finch seemed to be doing most of the talking.

Owner Marcus Aurelius Klein, who was also paying a token visit to the locker room, asked Mal Ferguson the question that was on everyone's mind. "How does it look, Coach?"

Mal shrugged. "I never make predictions before a game," he said.

Klein slipped his arm through Robin's, and they left together. "Ferguson is damn touchy today," Klein said, and frowned.

"I can't blame him," Robin replied. "What we do out there today may set the pattern for the rest of the season. Either last week's victory was a fluke, or the team really may have found itself. We'll soon find out." He paused as they came into the open, and studied the crowd that was moving into the stands.

His intensity made the owner smile. "Counting on a sellout today, Robin?"

"Not a chance. The Vikings' treasurer says they're about seven thousand seats light, and it would be worse if the Vikings didn't have so many full-season ticket holders. But we'll do fine at home next week—provided we make a decent showing today."

Minerva was waiting for him, and accompanied him to the press box, having elected to sit under cover in case the rain started again. Robin bought her a program, and when the players of both teams appeared for their warm-ups, she checked off names against the numbers she saw on the field below.

"Right about now," she said, "I always get a funny feeling in my tummy, and it doesn't go away until after the opening kickoff. Does that happen to you?"

Robin shook his head. "The only thing that upsets my

stomach," he said, "is the sight of empty seats." He and a very few others who regarded football as a strictly business venture, he thought, probably were the only people in the stadium who felt no sense of anticipatory excitement prior to the beginning of a game.

The Cougars won the toss, and elected to receive. They ran back the opening kickoff from the goal line to their own eighteen-yard line, and on the first play from scrimmage Fred Finch surprised virtually everyone in the stadium, including his own coaches, by ignoring the sloppy footing and taking to the air. Olson faked a buck into the line, Helmsley circled out of the backfield and caught a perfectly thrown pass on his thirty-seven, then picked up an additional nine yards on his own. On the next play Finch moved the ball into Viking territory by flipping a short pass to Miner Simmons in the flat, and the end drove to the thirty-yard line before he was downed. With the fans still settling in their seats, Finch threw again to Helmsley, picking him up on the Viking four-yard line, and the big full-back went in for a touchdown, standing up. Renewzski made the conversion, and the stunned crowd realized that the Cougars were leading, 7–0.

Lightning struck again shortly before the end of the first quarter when Finch, passing to his ends and mixing his plays expertly, drove to the Viking ten; Helmsley, who was also demonstrating that his expertise of the previous week had not been accidental, drove for the touchdown, and again Renewzski converted.

The score was 14–0, and the Vikings were helpless until the final moments of the first half, when a field goal gave them three points.

Robin went down to the locker room at half time, and was surprised to discover that the pre-game atmosphere still prevailed. The players were quiet, listening without comment to the critiques of the coaching staff, and seemed almost subdued as as they trotted back onto the field.

In the third quarter Finch brought a hostile crowd to its feet, cheering him, when he connected with a 69-yard pass to Olson in the end zone, making the score 21–3 after Renewzski again converted. The Cougar defense continued to perform miracles against what was generally considered the strongest running offensive in the National Conference, and the Vikings could only get on the scoreboard via two more field goals. The inter-Conference game ended with the Cougars on the heavy end of a lopsided 21–9 score.

The players were pleased with themselves, but their joy was muted. The offensive and defensive squads voted game balls to Fred Finch and Big Horse Collins, but both insisted the honor belonged to the whole team, and the trophies, duly inscribed, were placed on display in the locker room. Robin, who had watched the proceedings with the coaches, offered to buy a trophy case out of his own pocket, and the players promptly accepted.

"We'll need it," Byron Jeffers said, expressing what appeared to be a common sentiment, "after we play the Colts."

The Monday newspapers were lavish in their praise of the newly awakened Cougars, and a columnist in *Chicago Today* said the team was no flash-in-the-pan, and might be a contender for season's honors in the central division of the American Conference. The sportscasters were generous, too, and only Phil Donegan remained reserved.

"Two victories won by a team that has been put together with spit and a prayer," he said on his Monday-night telecast, "are no indication that the Cougars will escape permanently from the cellar berth for which they seem slated. So don't order your Super Bowl seats just yet."

On Tuesday evening Robin Stephens, Mal Ferguson and their wives dined together at a restaurant, and both men expressed guarded optimism regarding the team's future. Robin and Minerva returned home just in time to tune in Donegan's program on WWW-TV.

"An off-the-field crisis," Donegan said at the end of his program, "threatens to jeopardize the remarkable two-game winning streak amassed by the Cougars. Rumors of a romance between one of the key players in the team's so-called drive and a certain lady have been verified. At least, they are being seen together in public. What creates the potential danger to harmony in Cougarland is the fact the lady was formerly married to another key player in the Cougar line-up, and currently is the wife of a team executive. The storm signals are flying, and the odds favoring the Colts should rise for this Sunday's game."

"The son-of-a-bitch," Robin said, and snapped off the set.

Minerva was white-faced, and sat unmoving.

Robin immediately went to the telephone, and called the television station's studio. Identifying himself, he demanded to speak to the sportscaster, and after a brief wait he heard the familiar, deep voice at the other end of the line. "Donegan," he said, "you can cut me up all you please, and you can call the Cougars every name in the book if that will make you happy. But leave my wife out of your vendetta! For your information, I work on Monday nights, and Fred Finch has been keeping my wife company by taking her to dinner. With my full knowledge and approval. There's no romance between them, I assure you. My wife wouldn't allow Finch—or anyone else—to even hold her hand!"

Minerva averted her face.

"No," Robin said, "I'm not asking for a public retraction. I see no reason to give a lie additional exposure. But from now on, leave my wife out of your attacks on the Cougars!" He slammed the telephone into its cradle, then went to Minerva and stroked her shoulder. "I'm sorry, honey."

She fought back her tears. "I don't mean to be upset, but I wasn't prepared for anything like that."

"There's no reason you should have been prepared. Where was it you and Freddie ate last night? You told me, but I forgot."

"The Cape Cod room. At the Drake."

His eyes were narrowed. "See anybody there you know?"

"I told you. Frannie Healey and her husband. I went to school with her, and they came over to the table for a minute or two."

Robin shook his head. "I mean, anybody in sports. One of Phil Donegan's assistants, maybe."

Minerva shook her head.

"Think hard. Anyone connected with the team?"

For a long moment she was silent. "I just remembered. Chuck Blanchard was sitting at the bar as we left."

Robin's mind was working rapidly. "He saw you?"

"Oh, sure. We waved to him, and he waved back." She was still badly shaken. "Rob, I'd better stop going out to dinner with Freddie on Monday nights."

He couldn't blame her for being fearful, but he wanted her to understand the entire situation. "I have no intention of forcing you to see him every week. But you've been a tremendous help to him. I can't swear that your brand of medicine is what's changed him, but look at his record these past few weeks. Myself, I'm convinced Freddie doesn't function on all cylinders unless some sympathetic gal listens to his woes and mothers him."

Minerva was tempted to blurt out the truth, but Freddie had been controlling himself admirably, and she felt there was little chance their relationship would become intimate again. Provided she didn't panic or cause Freddie to become disturbed, there was every valid reason to hope she could maintain the present equilibrium. "I don't mind the Monday-night dinners—too much," she said.

"I think I can promise you there won't be any more of this loose gossip," he said.

"Then I'll keep meeting him—as long as it helps you, Rob. Finch means even less to me than Hal. But I want you to get credit for a good season."

"The Cougars," Robin said, "are going to start improving in

many ways." He knew she couldn't understand that front-office support could be as important as the team's achievements on the field, so he didn't bother to explain. It was difficult enough not to indulge in conjecture himself, and all he knew at the moment was that the morning would be the busiest he had spent since joining the Cougar organization.

5

"Pat," Robin told his secretary, "I want you to make a check in depth with the central ticket sales office on our situation for this Sunday's game. Find out how many seats were allotted, how many have been sold to date and how many are still sitting in the racks."

Patricia Thompson scribbled in her stenographer's notebook, then looked up. "Mr. Blanchard may have all those figures already," she said.

"Maybe so, but under no circumstances do I want you to go to Blanchard—or his office—for them. I'm not asking you to work surreptitiously, behind Chuck Blanchard's back, but I'll appreciate your discretion. I'd prefer he doesn't know about our inquiries for the present."

She had learned, in the months she had worked for him, that it was useless to question him when he elected to be oblique. So she confined herself to technical essentials. "How soon will you want a report?"

Robin glanced at his watch. "Before lunch, certainly." He saw her dismayed expression and laughed. "Getting this data for me is going to be much easier than you realize. Our entire ticket program is computerized now, you know, so one of the girls in central sales who is familiar with the operation of the machine can give you everything we need by pushing a few buttons."

Patricia was relieved. "Why didn't you say so in the first place?" she demanded, and stalked out before he could reply.

Robin's smile died on his lips, and he stared out of his windows at the Chicago skyline, unable to concentrate on the routine tasks that awaited him. He curbed the desire to pace, but could not prevent himself from drumming on his desk. Finally, after a wait of about thirty minutes that seemed much longer, the secretary returned with several long strips of paper, on which various figures were typed.

"They ran the projection through the machine three times, in three different ways," she said, "and the results were identical each time."

Robin scanned the figures. "Ask Miss Hibbs to drop whatever she may be doing and come in immediately. And tell Mr. Blanchard to stand by. I'll want to see him before he goes out to lunch."

A few moments later Ellen Hibbs appeared, raising an eyebrow. "Don't tell me the Colts have stolen a copy of our offensive-play book," she said with a laugh.

Robin remained grim. "I want your help," he said. "I'll appreciate information as accurate as you can give me."

His unrelenting air surprised her, but she nodded as she dropped into a chair and smoothed her skirt.

"Did Chuck Blanchard ever approach Dan Grannett and request the job of ticket sales manager? Search your memory carefully."

"I don't have to," Ellen said. "Chuck must have gone to him at least three times in the year before Uncle Danny was taken ill."

"Why didn't Dan give him the assignment?"

She hesitated.

"This isn't just curiosity," Robin said.

"All right. I hate being a hatchet woman, but I'll level with you. Uncle Danny never trusted him. And I'll anticipate your next question. Chuck is a good public-relations man, so he wasn't fired."

Robin gazed up at the ceiling. "To the best of your knowledge, has Blanchard ever ever expressed a desire to become general manager some day?"

"I can't give you a direct answer to that one," Ellen said. "He's always been careful talking to me. Partly because of Uncle Danny and partly because he knows about Marc and me."

"If you had your back to the wall and had to give me a flat yes or no," Robin persisted, "which would it be?"

"I'd have to say yes. I believe he's dropped casual hints to Marc from time to time. But don't quote me on hearsay evidence."

"All this is for background purposes only." Robin threw her the computer ribbons. "These are the sales projections for the Baltimore game."

Ellen studied the figures and looked shocked.

Robin pressed an intercom key. "Ask Mr. Blanchard to come in, please."

"I'll fold up my tent and steal away," Ellen said, rising to her feet.

He waved her back to her chair. "I'll want you as a third party, as a witness. Feel free to join in the conversation whenever you like, but there's no need for you to shoot off if you want to keep quiet."

Blanchard tapped at the door, then bustled into the room. "We've had requests for press-box space this Sunday from a half-dozen more out-of-town newspapers," he said. "Our boys are beginning to create a stir."

"Sit down," Robin told him, and picked up the computer ribbon. "Twenty-three hundred seats for Sunday's game—all of them between the forty-yard markers on both sides of the field —are missing."

Blanchard's face showed polite surprise. "That's hard to believe."

[195]

"All of the allocations to the various sales offices and to the brokers were countersigned by you," Robin said. "And no one other than you had the authority to determine the allocations."

Blanchard's round face reddened. "What is it you're trying to prove against me?" he demanded.

"So far," Robin replied, his voice deceptively calm, "I merely want to know what's become of twenty-three hundred of the best seats in the stadium."

"I couldn't possibly tell you offhand. I'll have to look into it."

"The figures were determined by a triple run through the computer."

"I'll find out what I can," Blanchard said.

Robin glanced at Ellen, then turned back to the other man. "I don't believe that will be necessary. The seats were removed from the racks, and illegally turned over to scalpers—who are selling them for thirty dollars per pair beyond the authorized price. The scalper keeps five to ten dollars of the loot, and hands over the rest to his mentor. It's a situation that always crops up when an athletic team shows promise or a hit show comes to town."

"You can't prove a thing against me," Blanchard said.

Ellen felt compelled to speak. "You aren't on trial, Chuck," she said, "but anyone familiar with the business knows precisely what you've done."

"So admit it," Robin added, "and let's bring an extremely unpleasant discussion to an end."

Blanchard clamped an unlighted cigar between his teeth. "Sue me!" he said.

"I prefer to accept your resignation, effective immediately," Robin told him.

"You can't do this to me, Stephens!" Blanchard was defiant. "You can't force me to quit!"

"I'm hoping you won't make it necessary for me to bring this situation into the open. If I do, I'll also have to mention the unsavory fact that you've been feeding personal gossip about me to Phil Donegan—because you've wanted a crack at my job."

Blanchard's façade cracked open. "Who told you—"

"Never mind. I know."

The publicity man recovered his bravado. "But you can't prove that against me, either. Donegan never reveals his sources of information."

"I don't care to quibble with you." Robin looked at his watch. "I'll give you one minute to decide. Resign—with severance pay—and we'll issue a dignified announcement. Or I'll throw you out on your butt. Then I'll send a full report to every team owner and general manager in the National Football League."

Blanchard turned to the girl. "You hear that, Ellen? He's threatening to blacklist me."

"One minute," Robin said. "Time in."

There was a long silence, and no one moved, but Blanchard suddenly heaved himself to his feet. "Screw you, Stephens," he said. "Have my severance voucher sent to my office. I don't trust you, so I won't go without it." He left quickly, slamming the door behind him.

"Ellen," Robin said quietly, "I'd like you to take charge of ticket sales. I hate to bring in someone from the outside, now that the season is well under way. And I don't know how much any of Blanchard's assistants can be trusted."

"It's a nasty job," Ellen said with a sigh. "But I'll do it. I can see you don't have much choice."

"Thanks. I know I can rely on you. And I'm afraid you'll have to start by recalling as many of the missing twenty-three hundred seats as you can dig up. The demand for the Baltimore game is still growing."

"I'll do what I can, which means I'd better not loiter." Ellen rose, started toward the door and then turned. "Donegan's vicious remarks on the air last night must have been sparked by Chuck."

"They were."

"Forgive my curiosity, but how did you know?"

"I didn't," Robin said. "The whole puzzle fitted together so perfectly that I bluffed Blanchard just now. I figured he was too weak to stand up to me, especially with you sitting in, so I gambled—and won."

"Marc is right." Ellen smiled wryly. "He says there's more to you than meets the eye."

Mal Ferguson closed the practice sessions for the Baltimore game to all visitors, including the press. The sports reporters and commentators reacted as anticipated with a critical barrage. "The Cougars are taking themselves seriously after winning a grand total of two games," the *Daily News* said. "Perhaps they think they're champions." Phil Donegan was even more scathing. "Robin Stephens, Mal Ferguson and their minions are leading an Alice-in-Wonderland existence these days," he told his huge television following. "But the Colts should restore them to the world of reality with a resounding thump on Sunday afternoon. As most of you out there know, I seldom make specific predictions on a game, but I'm going all out this time. I'm picking the Colts by twenty-one points."

The front office was too busy to pay any attention to the press, television and radio barrage. The demand by prominent citizens for seats became so insistent that Robin instructed his secretary to tell all callers he was out. Some of the pressure was eased by Ellen Hibbs, who worked furiously and managed to recover twelve hundred of the seats that Chuck Blanchard had distributed to scalpers. The rest, she reported, had already been sold, and consequently there was no way to regain possession of them.

The team remained relaxed all week, and a self-appointed "morale squad" pinned all adverse newspaper clippings to a bulletin board in the locker room. A substitute lineman had made a tape recording of Phil Donegan's prediction, and played it immediately before the players went out onto the field each day.

On Friday morning Fred Finch twisted his ankle during a workout, but Dr. Scudder immediately prescribed whirlpool baths, and by Saturday morning the swelling began to recede. "With any luck," the team physician said, "Finch should be able to play the better part of tomorrow's game."

Every seat in the stadium was sold by midmorning on Saturday, but the pressure remained intense, and Robin ordered the office closed for the weekend at noon so the staff could obtain relief. He met Minerva for lunch, and hoping he would not be pestered, he took her to a German restaurant on the North side that was neither fashionable nor well known.

"Invite some friends to share the box with you tomorrow," he said. "I'm sure anyone you know will jump at the chance."

"I was hoping I could watch the game with you from the press box," she said.

He shook his head. "Mal has invited me to join the team on the bench."

Minerva raised a delicate eyebrow. "How come?"

"He feels that a greater rapport with the front office will help achieve a greater solidarity. In plain language, my presence will encourage the players to try harder because I'll be a reminder of the new contracts they'll sign after the season for next year."

"It's a smart gimmick," she replied. "Of course, Dan Grannett showed up often on the field—and made the boys nervous."

"I don't intend to make a habit of sitting on the bench," Robin said. "And before I forget it, you may not want to go out to the stadium as early as I'm planning to go."

"That's okay." She was splurging on lentil soup, one of her favorites, even though it was fattening. "I'll take a taxi."

"Good. I have an unpleasant little assignment I've given myself, and now that I've made up my mind about it, I'm anxious to get it out of the way." Even though guests at other tables were not within earshot, Robin lowered his voice. "My thoughts have been jelling ever since I fired Chuck Blanchard. I'm certain

he'll be vindictive—which means I'm willing to bet he'll feed
more poison to Phil Donegan. And as much as I dislike Donegan,
I'm afraid I've got to have a word with him. I'll tackle him in
the broadcast booth before he goes on the air."

Minerva's spoon was poised in midair. "What are you going
to talk to him about?"

"You and me, principally."

She lost her appetite.

"I don't care how hard he attacks me professionally. But my
private life is my own, and what my wife does—including her
choice of a dinner companion on a night when I'm working—
is her business. It isn't Donegan's or his listeners'."

"I wish," Minerva said, "you'd leave well enough alone."

"I want to get him off our backs, that's all."

"Suppose he gets even nastier."

"How can he?" Robin demanded. "He's virtually accused you
of infidelity already."

"I—I'd hate to have him snooping around." Minerva stared
down at the red-and-white checked tablecloth.

"That's where we've got him. Let him snoop, Min. We have
nothing to hide."

She lighted a cigarette in the hope that he wouldn't see how
upset she was becoming. If she ever intended to tell him about
her slip with Freddie, now was the time to do it, but she lacked
the courage. Robin might forgive her, or it could mean the end
of their marriage. She knew he was possessive, that he would
find it difficult to forget the incident, and she was unwilling to
jeopardize their entire future together, even though her guilt
would be relieved.

Robin started to reassure her, but something in her expression
silenced him, and as he looked at her an ugly suspicion formed
in his mind. He had no proof, and didn't want to make an
accusation without it; on the other hand, he had no desire to
bring the matter into the open, even with a measure of cause.
Their marriage was working out reasonably successfully, and
he would be wise to leave well enough alone. However, it

would be wrong to take unecessary chances, even though he could not believe she found someone as shallow as Fred Finch attractive. All the same, his presence at the Monday night coaches' meetings was not mandatory, so he could leave a little early this coming week, and would join Minerva and Finch. He felt sure he would know, when he saw them together, whether the unpleasant thought that popped into his head was justified.

"Leave Donegan to me and don't worry about him," he said lightly, ostensibly dismissing the subject.

There was a strong hint of autumn in the stiff breeze that blew in off Lake Michigan on Sunday morning, but an early October sun appeared around 10:00 A.M., and the day promised to be ideal for football. Robin and Minerva slept late, and then, while she prepared a large breakfast, the only meal they would eat before evening, he took his cup of coffee to the telephone in their bedroom and called Mal Ferguson at the hotel where the team always stayed for twenty-four hours prior to a home game.

"How is your quarterback's ankle?" he asked without preamble.

"Doc Scudder is still hoping he'll be all right," Mal replied. "There's some tenderness, apparently, but they'll tape the hell out of the ankle—and hope for the best."

"You're not planning to mention the injury to the press?"

"Hell, no!" The head coach was emphatic. "If the Colts know Finch is under par, they'll put on a far heavier pass rush!"

"That's what I figured," a relieved Robin said. "I'll see you out at the stadium."

After breakfast he took his time shaving and dressing, and a little before noon he departed, arranging to meet Minerva in the coaches' conference room under the stands at the end of the game. Traffic was still fairly light, and the taxi deposited him at the main gate after a ride of only fifteen minutes; soon it would take three times that long to reach the ball park.

Technicians were setting up their equipment in the WWW-

TV booth when Robin climbed to the press box at the top of the stadium, and Phil Donegan had not yet arrived. So Robin wandered into the public-relations quarters at the end of the corridor, where a buffet lunch was being served to members of the working press. Helping himself to a cardboard container of coffee, he noted that Howard Bailey, the former assistant who had been promoted to head the department when Blanchard had been discharged, was handling himself with the poise of a veteran. He greeted each of the reporters by name, then chatted for a few minutes before passing along a thick sheaf of publicity handouts that included up-to-date statistics on each player's record for the season to date.

Phil Donegan was one of the last to arrive, and after handing his trenchcoat to one of the innumerable assistants who were always in attendance on a major television personality, he helped himself to a ham and cheese sandwich and a glass of beer.

Robin didn't want to give him time to become engrossed in another conversation during the brief period that remained before he went on the air, and therefore joined him immediately. "Phil," he said, "I'd like a word with you."

The sportscaster followed him to a far corner of the room, a sardonic smile on his lips.

"You're entitled to think what you please about my team," Robin said. "I hope we'll make you eat your words, naturally, but that's beside the point. It's your privilege to think I've put together a collection of stumblebums, and to hate my guts for it."

Donegan took a large bite of his sandwich, then chewed and swallowed it before he replied. "There's nothing I'd enjoy more than seeing the Cougars develop into championship material," he said. "My disagreement with you is on the methods."

"That's fair enough, too. There's just one thing I ask of you. As you undoubtedly know, I had to let Chuck Blanchard go this week. Not because I learned he was passing along personal vitriol to you, hard though that may be to believe. He was discharged because of business irregularities I prefer not to discuss. Be that as it may, he's certain to come to you with more malicious gossip—if he hasn't already. I'll be grateful to you if you'll lay off my private life. And my wife's. She has no connection with the team except through me, socially. The fact that she may be acquainted with this player or that is irrelevant, and so is the fact that she was once married to Hal."

"I don't believe in spreading malice for its own sake," Donegan said. "But I do think there's been a lowering of certain standards ever since Danny Grannett was forced to step aside, and that change is reflected in the kind of team you put on the field. Some individuals become symbols of the decline, or so it seems to me. And that's why I don't regard anything I've said on the air as personal."

Robin found it difficult to control his temper. "I'm not going to argue with you, Phil, and I have no intention of threatening you. Hang me if the Cougars fall apart. Pour on the pressure until Marc Klein is forced to boot me out. But stop making hints about my wife on the air, or you'll force me to deal with you as one guy to another, not as the acting general manager of the Cougars who is required to handle an eminent sportscaster with kid gloves!"

An expression of reluctant admiration crept into Donegan's eyes. "You may make the worst trades in football, Stephens, but I've got to hand it to you. There aren't many people in this town with the guts to wave a fist under my nose!" Suddenly he grinned. "You may have heard that I've picked the Colts this afternoon—by three touchdowns."

"I believe someone did call it to my attention," Robin said.

"Well, if I'm wrong—if your sterling gang of egomaniacs and misfits win today's game, and prove they're a football team, not an aggregation of freaks—I'll apologize to you on the air. I'll do more than that. Say the word, and I'll kiss your ass in public!"

Scanning the stands from the vantage point of the fifty-yard hash marker, Robin had the satisfaction of seeing that the last seats in the huge stadium were filling, and he knew that within a short time the largest crowd in Cougar history would occupy every place. For the first time since he had joined the organization he enjoyed the indulgence of a favorite exercise in mental gymnastics, that of estimating the home team's share of the receipts. He allowed nothing to interfere, and was scarcely aware of the appearance of both teams or of the cheers that greeted them.

The Colts were alert, aggressive and sharp, and their self-confidence showed as they warmed up. Linemen slammed into each other, the thud of shoulder pads reverberating through the amphitheater, but the behemoths continued to smile, losing neither their physical balance nor their poise. The Cougars seemed drab by comparison, running through their brief pre-game drill with quiet, almost absent-minded precision. Fred Finch and Hjalmar Sorensen loosened their throwing arms on the sidelines, both reflecting a cool indifference to the crowd, their opponents or the possible significance of the game.

The appearance of Finch made Robin uneasy, and he glanced inadvertently in the direction of Minerva's box. His wife was conspicuous in a bright red suit, trimmed at the collar and cuffs with silver fox, and he not only saw her instantly, but realized she had been watching him, not Fred Finch. He waved, and Minerva responded by blowing him a kiss.

Mal Ferguson, wearing a windbreaker with old pants, cleated shoes and a baseball cap with a long peak, approached his acting general manager. "All's well so far," he said. "The Colts have no idea that Finch is suffering from a gimpy ankle. I've forbidden him to limp before the second half."

A noted musical comedy star, who was appearing in the Chicago company of the previous year's biggest New York success, sang "The Star-Spangled Banner," and the players trotted onto the field. The Colts had won the toss and had elected to receive; a 27-yard return of the opening kickoff brought them to their own thirty-three, and without delay they went to work. True to the traditions established over many years by the great Johnny Unitas, the Baltimore offensive team quickly set up its passing game, and in eight plays crossed the Cougar goal, a conversion making the score 7–0.

The Cougars took the ball on their own goal and returned it for a niggardly eight yards, putting Fred Finch in a spot on his initial play from scrimmage. He sent Helmsley into the line on a fake, intending to unleash a long pass, but the Colt defenders anticipated the play, and after chasing Finch all over the field, finally dropped him for a two-yard loss. Adding insult to injury, his former teammates showed mock solicitude as they hauled him to his feet again.

The Cougar quarterback merely smiled at his tormentors, but repeated the same play immediately, and made it good for eighteen yards. Then, mixing Helmsley's sure-fire power plays with his own passing, he took the Cougars the length of the field in twelve plays, sending his fullback crashing over the goal line from the one-yard line. Renewzski's kick tied the score at 7–7.

The Cougar bench erupted. "Atta way to go, offense!" "Right on!"

Robin, sitting in the second of two rows of benches, felt an unaccustomed stir of excitement. Only eight minutes of the first quarter had passed, but his team was holding its own. The players, knowing what they could do, shouted encouragement to each other, but it occurred to Robin, for the first time, that the Cougars had a chance to win the game.

Neither team scored again until the inexperience of the home team gave the Colts a break early in the second quarter. A Baltimore punt sailed over the head of Olson into the end zone, and instead of allowing it to rest there, which would have meant an automatic touchback that would have placed it on the Cougar twenty, the rookie wanted action. He chased the ball, scooped it up and started forward, but was smothered behind his goal by a swarm of Colts. The score was 9–7.

The visitors struck again within the next five minutes, a long run and another pass giving them their second touchdown and conversion, and the score was 16–7. It appeared that the emerging Cougars had more than met their match, and were destined to sink back into helpless anonymity.

Robin did not accompany the coaching staff and sobered players into the dressing room at half time, knowing that Ferguson would want to address his charges in private. Minerva was making her way down the ramp, her husband saw, so he moved over to the base of the stadium and passed through the police lines so he could join her.

"What's the matter with those guys?" she demanded. "They act like they've got lead in their tails."

Her partisanship amused Robin. "Maybe they have," he said. "Do you want to go up to the press box for a snack?"

"They make me so sick I couldn't eat!"

He laughed, took her arm and led her to a refreshment booth under the stands. After buying a beer and a hot dog for himself and a container of black coffee for Minerva, he watched with satisfaction as a large crowd was fed quickly, in an orderly manner. Nothing was more important than patron comfort, and the Cougars would receive a gratifyingly large percentage of the receipts taken in by the refreshments concessionaire.

"Look at the way that mob is being handled!" he said. "Our cut for the day may run as high as ten thousand."

Minerva inhaled deeply on her cigarette, then sipped her coffee. "Sometimes," she said, "I think I'm married to a human cash register."

"Could be." He was enjoying his cold beer.

"I keep wondering if the game itself is ever going to mean anything to you."

Robin studied the huge throngs moving up and down the ramps. "I'll be happy with anything the players do, just so long as we continue to sell every last seat in the house!"

It was Minerva's turn to be amused, and she shook her head as they moved back toward the ramp. "Give 'em hell!" she said as they parted.

The Cougars were trotting back onto the field by the time Robin returned to the bench. Many of them looked like angry, chastised little boys, so it was apparent that Mal Ferguson had not spared their feelings. Even Byron Jeffers and some of the other veterans were scowling.

Oliver Olson seemed determined to win the dubious honor of being labeled the goat of the game. He took the ball on his own goal line as the Colts kicked off to open the second half, but was hit so hard he fumbled on his own ten, and the visitors gained possession of the ball. Olson had been knocked unconscious, and was carried from the field suffering from a slight concussion and a shoulder separation that would keep him out of action for a number of weeks. At least he was spared the misery of seeing the Colts race into the end zone again on the first play from scrimmage, making the score 23–7.

Again the visitors kicked off, and Olson was replaced on the offensive team by Greg Baines, a veteran halfback with six years of professional experience who had been picked up as a free agent. All through the third quarter the Cougar offense sputtered; on some series Helmsley gained ground consistently, but Finch could not locate his receivers. Then the quarterback and his ends began to click, but Helmsley was stopped cold at the line of scrimmage. The Cougar defense, which had played first-rate ball all day, continued to hold Baltimore, and it appeared that the day's scoring was ended.

On their first offensive series in the final quarter, however, the Cougar offense suddenly came to life. Finch engineered five successful completions in a row, Helmsley ripped off a number of long gains on the ground, and Baines, the new halfback, proved his worth by blocking effectively, then moving into the flat for several of Finch's short passes. Two minutes after the unexpected drive began the score was 23–14 when Baines caught a Finch pass in the end zone.

The Cougar defense went onto the field grimly, determined to regain possession of the ball as soon as possible, and Robin, unable to sit still any longer, began to pace up and down behind the bench. Somewhat to his own astonishment he was joining the players on the sidelines who were shouting encouragement to their comrades on the field. He laughed at his own exuberance, then looked up into the stands to see if Minerva was aware of his new-found enthusiasm.

Not only was she too busy watching the teams on the field to be aware of what her husband was doing, but Robin almost missed one of the key plays of the game. The Colts made the mistake of trying to run a ground play over Byron Jeffers, but the end shook off two blockers, then made such a jarring tackle that the ball popped out of the arms of the Baltimore fullback. Big Horse Collins snatched the elusive ball out of the air, and remembering his own, distant days as a high-school running back, he plowed fourteen yards up the field before being hauled down.

Robin's wild shouts mingled with those of the men on the bench and the Cougar fans in the stands as the offensive team trotted onto the field. Finch remained behind for a few moments, conferring with Mal Ferguson on strategy, and then ran out to the huddle. On the first play of the series the entire offensive team faked a halfback-trap play up the middle. Then Finch rolled out to his left, and executing one of the most difficult maneuvers a quarterback could perform, simultaneously threw the ball far downfield to his right. Hal Helmsley had drifted into the Colt secondary after faking a block, then had turned on steam, and was running at full tilt as he caught the ball over his shoulder. The pass was good for thirty-nine yards, and Helmsley ran twenty-six more into the visitors' end zone. The score was 23–21.

Less than four minutes of the final quarter remained, and Baltimore made a supreme effort to protect its slender, two-point lead. Colt running backs bucked repeatedly into the line while the Cougar defenders fought and clawed for the ball. There was pandemonium in the stadium, and Robin, standing on one of the benches, heard himself shouting with the other Cougars, "Defense! Defense! Steal that ball!"

The Colts were forced to punt with only 1:03 left to be played, and the Cougars took the ball on their own twenty-three, where the receiver was downed immediately. Only fifty-five seconds remained. Virtually everyone in the stadium expected Finch to pass, but Helmsley carried on an off-tackle slant, and in a brilliant, twisting run reached midfield. Only forty seconds left to be played, and Finch called for time before hurrying to the sidelines for a talk with his coach.

Robin's throat ached and there was a rip in the sleeve of his vaguely recalled having been pounded on the back by a 290-pound substitute defensive tackle during Helmsley's run, but neither then nor later could he recall feeling the beating.

On two successive passes Finch took the ball to the Colt 27-yard line, and there used his last time-out call. Fourteen seconds were left, and everyone in the stadium was standing as Adam Renewzski trotted onto the field to try a place-kick from a sharp angle. Sorensen, whom he preferred to the first-string quarterback as a ball-holder, accompanied him.

When time was called the Cougars stalled as long as they dared, and when only four seconds remained, Renewzski put the ball into the air. Seventy-one thousand people were silent for a moment, and then went mad when the referee signaled that the effort had succeeded. The score was 24–23 in favor of the Cougars, and spectators poured onto the field. Three seconds of playing time remained, however, and after a long delay the police and the corps of highly trained ushers succeeded in clearing the field.

Renewzski boomed the ball deep into the Colt end zone, and the officials brought it out to the twenty-yard line. On the first play from scrimmage the gun sounded, and the Cougars, to the astonishment of a dazed and delirious crowd, had won by a single point.

Robin, his necktie askew, the rip in his coat considerably longer, raced across the field with the players, then sprinted with them into the tunnel that led to the locker room. Behind him he could hear the steady roar of the mob, and he knew the goal posts would be torn down, a gesture that would cost the Cougars several hundred dollars, but he did not care. The team had come from behind to win in a photo finish, and his own elation was as great as that of the men who had played in the game.

The bedlam in the locker room seemed unending. Offensive and defensive teams squirted beer and soft drinks at each other, then soused the coaching staff. Robin was not spared, and neither was a rumpled Marc Klein, who had needed the help of a flying squad of police to work his way through the crowd. Grown men wept, hugged each other and danced together across the slippery floor of the locker room, and the din became unbearable when a dozen players began to beat on the metal doors of their lockers with cleated shoes. The Cougars had moved into a tie with the Kansas City Chiefs for first place in their division, and as the *Tribune* noted the next morning, "The joy of the victorious gladiators was not only unconfined, it spilled out under the stands in a flow that looked suspiciously like a mixture of beer, soda pop and buckets of shower-water, which is precisely what it was."

The wives and girls of Cougar officials and players gathered in the coaches' conference room to await their disheveled heroes, and every man was soundly kissed as he entered. Robin, who had tried to tidy his appearance, was one of the last, and a score of attractive women surrounded him. He escaped in time to see Minerva enthusiastically kissing her first husband, before several others bore down on Hal. His face covered with lipstick smears, Robin approached his wife, whose mascara-smudged cheeks indicated she had been weeping with joy. They embraced, and there was no need for an exchange of words. It was as obvious to Minerva as it was to her husband himself that he had made an emotional commitment to the Cougar cause.

Marc Klein invited the players, coaches, executives and their ladies to his near North Side town house for an impromptu celebration. Robin and Minerva stopped off briefly at their own apartment for a change of clothes, and by the time they reached Klein's house they found the party in full swing. Bartenders were busily dispensing drinks, the kitchen staff was working frantically in an attempt to cope with an emergency created by more than one hundred unexpected guests, and the contents of entire freezers were being emptied to provide a meal.

A beaming host stood at the entrance to the baronial, sunken living room, Ellen Hibbs beside him, and greeted new arrivals effusively. He embraced Minerva, while Ellen surprised Robin by kissing him, and then Klein pumped the hand of his acting general manager. "You're the one who put this gang together," he said. "No matter what this team does the rest of the season, you deserve one hell of a lot of credit."

"I think we'll win some more games," Robin said cautiously.

Klein roared with laughter. "You *think* we will? I'm giving seven points when we play the Jets next week in New York!"

This was no time, Robin thought, to tell him his optimism might be unwarranted, and that the following Sunday's game against one of the most efficient and explosive teams in football would be critical. This was an evening when everyone could let down the bars for a few hours, enjoy the victory and let the future take care of itself.

Maids circulated with canapés, Klein's liquor cellar appeared to be limitless, and the mood of the guests began to soar. Someone found the stereo and a pile of records, and soon many of the younger people were dancing, the players happily ignoring their supposed physical exhaustion.

Robin took advantage of the gathering to tidy up some loose business ends that would have required his attention at the office the following morning. Moving as far as he could from any of the booming, strategically placed stereo speakers, he accepted the breakdown of the day's box-office receipts from Ellen, then brought Mal Ferguson and Howard Bailey together to settle details of the press conference they would call the following afternoon. Finally he had a chance to exchange a few words in private with the head coach.

"How is young Olson?"

"He'll miss at least three games, maybe four," Mal said. "Doc Scudder will give us a more detailed report when he gets here from the hospital."

Robin absently watched couples dancing on the far side of the room, aware that Minerva was creating something of a stir as she danced with Hal Helmsley. "Do you want me to shop around for another halfback, Mal? Now that we seem to have gained some substance, you might want a replacement."

Ferguson considered the suggestion for a moment, then shook his head. "Baines played a great game today."

"Yes, he did. The best performance I've ever seen him make in the years he's been kicking around the league."

"Well, I don't want to ruin whatever self-confidence he's built up by bringing in an outsider. I don't suppose it would do any harm to find out who might be available, just in case Greg Baines falls apart on us, but I'm inclined—for the moment—to string along with him."

"Fair enough." Robin grinned. "After what we did today, so many teams are going to take us seriously as contenders that they'll be reluctant to sell or trade us anybody worth playing."

Mal lowered his voice. "I don't want to dampen any spirits," he said. "But strictly between us, I don't regard us as serious contenders. Not yet. The odds against our reaching the play-offs are pretty high."

"I'm afraid I feel the same way," Robin replied. "I was carried away this afternoon when we came from behind to win, I must admit. We looked like champions, and we played like champions. That should help ticket sales for the next few home games, and I can't ask for more. But one of these weeks we're going to start taking our lumps again."

"As individuals," Mal said, "these men are as competent as any in the game. But they haven't played together long enough to have created a strong team unity, and I expect them to fall apart again when the going gets really rough."

Robin nodded, but was only half-listening. Fred Finch had

cut in on Minerva, and was dancing with her. It wasn't easy to watch them while pretending to take no notice of them, but Robin continued to chat with the head coach, even forcing himself to smile. Gradually his tension eased and he was able to relax again: Minerva's attitude toward her partner was pleasant but impersonal, and Finch, who obviously thought of himself as a superb dancer, was too busy trying to impress the cluster of younger players and their wives forming his audience to concentrate on Min. Apparently she was his mother confessor, as he called her, but that was all, and Robin felt a trifle ashamed of himself for having entertained doubts about his wife.

A gargantuan buffet dinner was served about two hours after the party began, and those of Marc Klein's business friends who had never before seen football players demolish food were astonished. Steaming casseroles and platters of cold meats disappeared almost as fast as the servants brought them to the dining table. Entire loaves of bread vanished, but the athletes avoided the potatoes and several dishes with rich sauces. Some continued to drink beer, while others switched to milk, which was served in large pitchers.

Robin, who ate in a quiet corner with Minerva, was pleased when he noted that very few of the players had been drinking hard liquor. It was tacitly understood that training rules had been suspended for the night, but the men were professionals, nine more games remained to be played on their regular schedule, and they knew they had to stay in good physical condition if they hoped to survive on the field for the rest of the season.

"Why do you keep looking at your watch?" Minerva asked. "We're not going anywhere else."

"Phil Donegan's Sunday night show goes on the air earlier than his weekday program. And it's about time for him." Leaving his plate, he took her hand. "Come along."

They found that Mal, Marc Klein and Ellen Hibbs had preceded them into the book-lined study, where a wall panel opened at the touch of a button to reveal a color television console. Phil

Donegan had just gone on the air, and was giving the scores of the afternoon's football games.

Marc poured brandy for the newcomers, and the conversation in the room died away as Donegan said, "The biggest upset of the day took place here in Chicago, where Mal Ferguson's remarkable Cougars came from behind, and in the last minute of play beat the highly touted Baltimore Colts by a score of twenty-four to twenty-three. I'll have more to say about those amazing Cougars in a few minutes."

Robin broke the silence in the study. "Well," he said, "Hallelujah. I didn't think the day would ever come when Donegan would change his tune."

"The team changed it for him," Klein said.

Minerva was on the verge of remarking that there was more behind Donegan's change of heart than the others knew.

But Robin silenced her with an almost imperceptible shake of his head. He had divined what she had intended to say, but he could take no credit for the sportscaster's change of attitude. The team alone had been responsible, and it was a coincidence that he had made it his business to talk to Donegan before the game.

After a sixty-second break for a commercial, Donegan came back on the air, and the camera moved in for a close-up. "Ladies and gentlemen," he said. "I doubt if any follower of the Chicago Cougars has felt worse than I have over the loss of Dan Grannett to the team this season. As a player, a coach and ultimately as a general manager, Mr. Football was an inspiration to everyone who has ever known him. I watched with dismay that became sheer horror as Grannett's replacement, acting general manager Robin Stephens, methodically broke up the team of the future Danny was trying to build. No one deplored more than I the change in the spirit the Cougars have long represented. I believe I've been Robin Stephens' most consistent and most severe critic."

Minerva quietly squeezed her husband's hand.

"But tonight," Donegan continued, "I'm eating humble pie. Stephens and I had a chat before today's game, and when he first sought me out, I thought he planned to take a swing at me. He didn't. He asked me, in effect, not to judge the Cougars prematurely or too harshly.

"Well, he was right, and I offer him an apology this evening, as I promised him I would if the Cougars won today. And what a victory it was! Oh, the troops may need seasoning for another year or two before they begin winning gold and silver footballs for owner Marcus Klein, but Robin Stephens and Coach Mal Ferguson have formed the nucleus of a scrappy organization that never quits. I salute everyone connected with the Cougars, and I send this message to Stephens. You've made me a true believer."

Another commercial appeared before Donegan showed his audience film clips of highlights of the day's action.

Minerva impulsively kissed her husband, and Mal solemnly shook his hand. "Donegan," he said, "isn't as big a bastard as I thought."

Marc Klein slapped his acting general manager on the back. "You rascal! You didn't tell me you'd bearded the lion today!"

Robin could afford to shrug modestly. If the team hadn't won, Donegan would still be ripping him apart on his telecasts.

Ellen wandered across the room and poured more brandy into her snifter.

Catching a glimpse of her face, Robin saw that her lips were compressed and her eyes were bleak. He should have known how she'd feel, of course, but he had been unprepared for her reaction, and was startled to discover she was upset by the public praise Donegan had heaped on him. Only Dan Grannett, in her opinion, deserved honors for Cougar accomplishments, and she resented the credit given anyone else. It would be wise to remember her feelings, and to brace himself for possible complications.

*　　*　　*

[215]

On Monday evening Robin cut short his attendance at the meeting of the coaches to join Minerva and Fred Finch at the Blackhawk, where they were finishing dinner. He rationalized his appearance on the grounds that he wanted to end any lingering gossip about his wife and the Cougar quarterback. But his real reason, he knew, was to assure himself beyond any last doubts that his own suspicions had been unjustified.

Feeling rather foolish, he had to admit that he could find nothing untoward in Min's relationship with Finch. She obviously had come to know him well, she laughed with forced heartiness at his jokes, and she lost no opportunity to build his ego, but her husband could detect no intimacy in the friendship.

"Did you know," Minerva asked him, "that the Associated Press poll named Freddie the quarterback of the week?"

"That's great," Robin said warmly. "But let me be the last to say I told you so, Fred."

Finch struck a thoughtful pose. "The Colts are behind us," he said. "As I was telling Min at dinner, now we've got to start getting ready for the Jets. I dreamed up some new plays today, and I just hope Coach will let me try them out in scrimmage."

Robin had no intention of saying anything that could be interpreted as approval; Mal was master in his own domain, and wouldn't appreciate a general manager's interference. "Why don't you talk to him tomorrow? He wants to win this Sunday's game, too, you know."

"So he does," Finch replied with an air of discovery.

Later, after returning home, Robin made an oblique apology to Minerva for his doubts. "Finch's vanity is so insufferable that I wish I hadn't involved you in operation nursemaid."

Minerva understood what he was really saying. "If I didn't feel sorry for him, he'd bore me." That, she thought, was the truth.

"If he can keep playing as he's done these past three weeks," Robin said, "nobody will have the right to feel sorry for him. He'll become one of the richest and most famous young men in the country."

"I'll still pity him," Minerva said, "because his outlook is so limited. He's so busy admiring Fred Finch, analyzing Fred Finch and girding Fred Finch for future battles that he doesn't realize there's anyone else in the world. So he doesn't even know what he's missing!" Nothing, she reflected, could induce her to repeat her own moment of weakness.

Late Friday afternoon the Cougars flew to New York in their chartered plane, and as Minerva had elected not to attend Sunday's game with the Jets at Shea Stadium, Robin flew with the team. But he went his own way as soon as they landed at La Guardia Airport, and believing that someone in his position should maintain a distance between himself and the players, he did not accompany the team on their chartered buses into Manhattan. Instead he took a taxi to the same hotel, and went straight to the suite that had been reserved for him.

As he had anticipated, a large stack of telephone messages awaited him, most of them requests for seats at Shea on Sunday. He sorted through the pile, putting aside the more important, including several friends of Marc Klein, whose names he recognized. Then, after speaking to the treasurer of the Jets and arranging that the tickets be held, he methodically returned the calls of those whom he was helping. Nothing that had happened all week made him more conscious of the new status the Cougars had achieved. Had the Colts beaten them, he knew, there would have been virtually no requests for tickets awaiting him.

He had to hurry to the Press Box, an East Side restaurant favored by the sporting fraternity, so he wouldn't be late for a dinner engagement with several old friends from the Giants' front office. Fortified by liberal libations of bourbon and a large steak, he spent a thoroughly enjoyable evening. A number of sports reporters he had known for years came to the table to congratulate him on the Cougars' showing, and several of football's more enthusiastic, wealthy followers, for whom he had reserved seats in the past, insisted on sending drinks to his table.

It was great, Robin thought, to be hailed as a success when

he returned home, and he savored every moment of his triumph. No one knew better than he, however, that if the Cougars lost on Sunday, those who hailed him the most vociferously tonight would be the first to give him the cold shoulder. But that knowledge in no way diminished his sense of pleasure, and he allowed himself to drink more than he knew he could safely handle.

His liquor consumption didn't matter, he told himself as he strolled back to the hotel shortly after midnight. There was no need for him to accompany the team to Shea for their light workout in the morning, and he could sleep an hour or two later than usual. He had nothing on the agenda until noon, when he would attend the lunch being given by the Cougar publicity department for the Chicago sportswriters and commentators.

One of the assistant coaches was sitting in a far corner of the lobby, trying to appear invisible behind an opened newspaper as he kept watch for any players who might be breaking Ferguson's curfew. He grinned, raising a hand, and Robin returned the wave.

The presence of the assistant coach decided Robin against stopping at the bar for a nightcap, which he neither needed nor really wanted. Perhaps he should have insisted that Minerva accompany him to New York, even though she hated out-of-town football weekends. This was one of those rare nights when he felt like celebrating a personal triumph, no matter how fleeting it might be, and he disliked the idea of returning alone to the large suite.

As he let himself into the sitting room Robin heard someone in the adjoining bedroom, and before he could recover from his initial shock, a familiar redheaded girl wearing a tight-fitting, very short dress of green velvet came to greet him. Fred Finch's former mistress was the last person he had expected to see.

"Surprise!" Martie called, and as she moved toward him he saw she was holding a half-filled highball glass in one hand.

"How did you get in here?" Robin demanded.

"You're too much, darling. I've been around, and I've yet to see the hotel staff that won't let me into any room." She brushed back a long lock of copper hair and laughed. "If you must know, I told them I was your wife."

"That's just dandy," he replied, wincing. "I wonder if you realize that every last member of the Cougar organization knows my wife. And I'm sure a great many of them know you, too."

"But I'm here to see you, not the rest of the Cougars." She sat on a white divan, allowing her skirt to ride high on her thighs. "You don't look very glad to see me."

"I'm overwhelmed." Robin was afraid the incident would find its way into print if he ejected her or asked the hotel management to throw her out.

"That's a cute little ice machine over there in the corner, and I found a quart of bourbon in your luggage, just where I knew it would be. I hope you don't mind my helping myself while I waited for you."

"Be my guest," he said.

"I forgot my manners. Let me get you a drink, too." She jumped to her feet, took a glass from a cupboard, and after filling it with ice, went off to the bedroom to add whisky to it.

Obviously this was no ordinary visit, and Robin decided to play along until he discovered Martie's reasons for coming to see him.

"Thanks," he said as she handed him his drink, and he raised his glass in a token toast.

She returned the gesture, then sat on the divan again and patted the place beside her.

Robin knew he had consumed too much bourbon to maintain total self-control in the presence of such a provocatively appealing woman, so he deliberately took a chair opposite her.

"You haven't even asked me what I'm doing in New York," Martie said, pouting, "so I guess I'll have to tell you anyway. I moved here right after I left Chicago. I have a friend. On the Jets."

He was not surprised. "Small world, isn't it?"

She ignored his irony, or perhaps she failed to understand it. "I don't like New York. In other towns everybody turns to look at me on the street, but here I'm just one of a million pretty girls. I like it better in Baltimore and Chicago, and Florida is much more fun." She took a cigarette from her handbag and waited for him to light it.

Robin was too far to reach across the coffee table, and was forced to stand; as he bent toward her with the lighted match, the scent of her perfume almost overpowered him.

Martie knew he had become more sharply aware of her, and smiled. "Good stuff, isn't it? A friend of mine brought me a huge bottle of it from Paris."

"Sure," Robin said flatly, "it's sensational."

The girl studied the glowing end of the cigarette. "You asked me right off why I came here. I want you to help me."

"How?" He raised his invisible guard still higher.

"I made a mistake when I left Freddie Finch, and I want to go back to him."

"Finch is doing okay without you! So leave him alone!" Robin didn't realize how harshly he spoke.

Martie remained calm, her green eyes guileless. "I knew you'd be a roadblock. You wanted to bust up Freddie and me from the day you signed him to a Cougar contract."

"Look, Martie," Robin said, leaning forward in his chair. "For the past few weeks Fred Finch has been playing top-grade football. He can become a big star if he keeps his balance, which means he doesn't need a chick like you messing up his life."

"What's wrong with me?" She ran a hand down across her breast, side and thigh.

"You lived with him for months. So I don't have to tell you he needs a girl who tells him he's the greatest."

"Day and night," she agreed.

"You went along with him for awhile, but then you got tired of praising him, and you walked out. Who says you won't do it again?"

Her mascara-rimmed eyes were unblinking. "Who says I'm going to stay with him forever this time?"

"If you'll just leave him alone until the end of the season—"

"By then every gal in the country who follows football will be trying to get her hooks into him! Maybe you don't know what a big attraction all that publicity he's getting can be! Or the money he'll make during the off-season!"

At least she was frank, he thought, but that was no consolation as he groped for a way to handle her.

"Maybe you can hide Freddie somewhere between now and kickoff time on Sunday," Martie said, reading his mind, "but you can't keep him out of circulation permanently. Sooner or later he'll come to the surface, and when he does, I'll be there. If you think he won't want me back, just watch him when I snap my fingers!"

"I'm not disputing your power over him," Robin said. "I'm just making a request for Finch's good."

"Uh-huh. And because of all the money the Cougars will rake in if he stays on the beam."

Robin saw no reason to deny the obvious. "Of course."

"I'm no freak," Martie said. "I have some common sense. Enough to know I've got to look after myself while I still have my face and figure. If I don't take care of me now, nobody else will do it for me when I start to fade."

He began to suspect she had a specific deal in mind, and did not interrupt.

"I'm thirsty," she said abruptly, staring at her empty glass.

Robin went to the bedroom for the bottle, poured her a refill and added ice.

"I hate to drink by myself," she said.

He poured more bourbon into his own glass, even though he was already feeling his drinks.

"This time around," Martie said, "I'm going to hang onto Freddie until I get my cut, which will be at least a year. You'll have to give him a raise for next season if he keeps burning up the Conference, and I'll want my fair share."

"In other words," Robin said, "you're planning to stay with him through the rest of this season, the winter and spring, and then all of next season."

Martie forced him to light her another cigarette, then playfully blew the smoke at him. "That's what I have in mind, kind of, but I'm not promising."

"Why not?"

"Because you know I can keep him happy, and that knowledge ought to be worth something to you."

She was suggesting blackmail of sorts, and Robin saw no reason to deal politely with her. "Exactly what's on your mind?"

"A diamond watch and matching diamond band I saw at Tiffany's this week," she said promptly. "Together they cost eight thousand, and they're gorgeous."

He tried not to let her see his agitation. "Suppose the Cougars bought them for you, very quietly and off the record. What would prevent you from leaving Finch again the very next day?"

"I knew that's how you'd figure it. Pay off after I produce, and I have my own way of making sure you will."

"You'll be responsible for Fred's batting average. If he falls down on the job, there will be no payoff."

"He'll produce, never fear." Martie was supremely self-confident.

No one, Minerva included, could keep the redhead and Finch apart if she was determined to snag him again, so Robin knew he had no real choice and would be compelled to gamble. "Okay," he said, "you've made yourself a deal."

"You won't be sorry." Martie stretched and stood. "Now we'll sign the contract before you can change your mind." She unzipped her dress and, in virtually the same motion, stepped out of it.

The startled Robin saw she was wearing only pantyhose and shoes, and decided a good-natured approach would cause the least fuss and resentment. "Do me a favor, and get to hell out of here." It was an effort not to look at her large, firm breasts.

"Not until we've sealed our bargain." She removed several pins from her red hair, which tumbled down across her bare shoulders. "Then I've got something on you if you try to back out of the deal."

"You think of everything."

"Including a scream so loud, if you don't play along my way, that it'll bring every house detective in the hotel to your door in the next two minutes." Showing no concern, Martie casually peeled off her pantystockings.

Robin took a large swallow of the stiff drink for which he had no need.

She came toward him, smiling and completely naked, her hips undulating. "But nobody is going to play rough." Catching hold of his head, she pushed it between her legs, simultaneously thrusting her pelvis forward. "Because I dare you to tell me you don't like the games that you and I play." She maintained a firm pressure on the back of his head.

Unable to stop himself, Robin buried his face in the warm mound and slid his hands around her body to grasp her firm buttocks.

Again she undulated, murmuring, "This is fun."

Alcohol and mounting desire were making it difficult for Robin to think clearly. He knew he was being unfaithful to Minerva, and despised himself for it, even though he tried to excuse himself on the grounds that he had been trapped and had no alternative. A few minutes earlier he could have found some way to avoid Martie's advances, but it was too late now to do anything but give in to the erotic impulses that inundated him.

His tongue darted out and in, caressing and teasing, and the girl responded by grasping his head with both hands. It was difficult to breathe, but he no longer cared, and his ministrations became more intense.

Martie began to jerk convulsively, her moans keeping time to the thrusts of her body as she lost all control. Then, suddenly, she went limp, and releasing Robin, moved back to the divan, where she gulped the better portion of her drink.

"You're good at doing that," she said. "I had a hunch you would be. Now it's my turn, and you know I'm good, so get your clothes off."

He was so aroused he obeyed, his hands trembling as he undressed.

Martie sat facing him, and beckoned.

Powerless to halt himself, he went to her, and allowed her to do what she pleased with him.

She was the first to recover her equilibrium, and went off to the bedroom for more liquor.

"I don't think I can drink any more," Robin said.

"You need a little nightcap, because we're going to bed together and sleep until morning. So we'll be ready for more fun and games."

He was too weary and drunk to protest, but he knew, as she led him off to the bedroom, that she was spending the entire night with him so he could not change his mind about their deal.

It was axiomatic in all professional sports that New York demanded winners, that the crowds in the largest city in the United States were generous to the teams that won championships for them, but were vicious when their representatives on the field failed to produce for them. The fans who filled every seat in Shea Stadium were convinced the Jets would win another Super Bowl, and roars of approval greeted each of their players as the home team was introduced. Always unabashedly partisan, most of the spectators did not even bother to applaud politely when the Cougars came onto the field.

Robin sat alone in the booth high above the crowd that was reserved for the visiting general manager, and tried to concentrate on the players as they lined up for the opening kickoff. But it wasn't easy. More than twenty-four hours had passed since Martie had finally walked out of his hotel suite, leaving him tired and disgusted with himself after their prolonged orgy, but he found it difficult to put her out of his mind. She had used sex to beat him in a game of wits, and he was committed beyond recall to the bargain they had made.

Yesterday afternoon, he knew, Martie had "accidentally" come face to face with Fred Finch in the hotel lobby as he had returned to the hotel after practice, timing her move to perfection. They had chatted for some minutes, and last night had dined together before an assistant coach, who had made it his business to eat in the same restaurant, had carted Fred back to his bachelor quarters. But the die was undoubtedly cast, and Robin felt certain she would travel to Chicago with him on the same airplane tomorrow. She had reminded him, in a telephone call this morning, that she expected him to stay over another night so he could meet her at Tiffany's in the morning to take care of a purchase there. If Finch fell apart, he thought gloomily, he would have no one but himself to blame.

It quickly became evident after the Cougars received the ball on the opening kickoff, however, that Finch was in command of himself and his team. The Jet defenders keyed on Hal Helmsley, so Finch gave the ball repeatedly to Greg Baines, whose long runs on off-tackle slashes made it possible for Finch to throw the ball thirty yards to Miner Simmons for the day's first touchdown.

No commentator had expected a high-scoring game, as both defensive teams were regarded as first-rate, but neither could contain the driving offense of their opponents, and at the end of the first half the score was tied, 21–21.

Robin paid a quick visit to the locker room, then returned to his booth for a solitary cup of coffee, and was sipping it when Phil Donegan opened the door.

"I want a brief chat with you," the sportscaster said, "but I'm going back on the air in a little over two minutes. What flight are you taking back to Chicago tonight?"

"I'm not," Robin said. "I've got to stay over for some business

[225]

here in the morning. I hope to be home by early afternoon."

"Call me at home as soon as you get in." Donegan scribbled a number on a card. "I'll be there all day."

The gesture was so unusual that Robin knew it was unnecessary for him to mention the obvious importance of whatever was on his mind.

The second half of the game caused him to forget Donegan for the time being. The Jets changed their defense, holding their linebackers until the Cougars committed themselves on each play. Finch read the situation, and immediately altered his own tactics by alternating passes just beyond the linebackers' territories with delayed-draw plays in which he sent Helmsley barreling up the middle. The Cougars scored two more touchdowns before their hosts could recover, making the score 35–21.

But the Jets proved their mettle by coming back with another touchdown of their own, then made two field goals, and with the score now 35–34, Robin was reminded of the previous week's single-point victory over the Colts.

In the final quarter, however, Fred Finch gave himself a margin of safety by driving for yet another touchdown on three long-pass plays. The score was 42–34, and remained unchanged for the rest of the game as the Cougar defense managed to contain several desperate Jet drives.

Robin's shirt was soaked with perspiration, and he felt weak as he made his way down to the dressing room. "Today," he told a happy Marc Klein when they met in Coach Ferguson's office, "is the day *I've* become a true believer. It wouldn't surprise me too much if we go all the way. This year. Anyway, I sure know one thing. By Tuesday morning there won't be a seat left for the Kansas City game!"

On Monday, the football statistics that Robin read at noon on board the airplane to Chicago helped to neutralize the bitter taste in his mouth caused by the transaction at Tiffany's and the subsequent hiring of a joint safety-deposit box with Martie.

All that remained now was to charge off the expenditure of $8,000 to the general manager's special fund when he reached his office.

Hal Helmsley, Robin read, was the leading ground gainer in the American Conference to date for the season, and Fred Finch stood head and shoulders above all other quarterbacks in yardage gained, passes completed and aerial touchdowns. Even *The New York Times* conceded that they were the dark-horse team of the year.

Calling Minerva as soon as he reached his office, Robin told her, "I'll come home early tonight so I can see you before you go off to dinner with Fred Finch." Then, before returning any of the calls that had accumulated during his absence, he dialed Phil Donegan's private number.

"What time are you leaving the office this afternoon?" the sportscaster asked.

"No later than five."

"Make it a half-hour earlier, and stop off here for a quick drink—and some food for thought."

Robin left an unfinished pile of work on his desk in order to leave the office at 4:30 P.M., and the knowledge that he had not replied to scores of ticket requests for the coming Sunday's game with the Chiefs made him feel guilty. Attention to detail was responsible for an executive's success, and he seldom shirked his routine obligations.

Phil Donegan came to the door of the apartment himself, and led his visitor to a small room crowded with plaques, framed testimonials and other awards he had won in his long career as a broadcaster.

Robin refused the offer of a drink. "I'm in a real whirl today. I want to get home for a little while to see my wife before I go on to the coaches' weekly dinner meeting."

Donegan proved to be understanding. "Okay, we'll skip the amenities. Robin, I called you because all hell is about to break loose, and whatever momentum the Cougars have gained in the past month can be lost overnight. In fact, they may go right down the drain when the sword falls."

Show business people were inclined to dramatize even trivial matters, so Robin reserved judgment.

"Never mind my source of information, but a certain matter has been reported to the Commissioner's office, and the principals are going to be called in tomorrow morning. Morton will give you a last-minute ring and tell you to be there, too."

"It isn't a gambling charge, I hope."

Donegan shook his head. "You undoubtedly know that Hal Helmsley and Gerald Collins are sharing an apartment. As I understand it, the Horse moved into Hal's old place."

"That's what I've heard." The players' living arrangements in Chicago were their own business, and he failed to see why the office of the Commissioner should be concerned.

"Hal and Collins," the sportscaster said, "aren't just sharing the place. They've shacked up together in more ways than one."

Minerva had told Robin in some detail about her first husband's homosexual tendencies, so the revelation wasn't too surprising, although he hadn't realized that Collins was that way, too. But the situation required an immediate, spirited defense. "How can anybody be positive enough about a thing like that to make a definite accusation, Phil?"

Donegan shrugged. "You'll have to take my word for it. A detailed set of charges citing chapter and verse has been submitted to Commissioner Morton."

"I think," Robin said, "I detect the busybody hand of Chuck Blanchard in all this."

"You've mentioned his name. I haven't."

"I wish you'd do the Cougars one more favor, Phil. The next time you see Blanchard, tell him if he doesn't lay off, I'll see to it he never gets another job in football."

"I'll pass along the word," Donegan promised.

"As to this fag business, it seems to me that what Hal and Big Horse do in their private lives is their own damn business. They've both been playing great football. Hal is ahead of his record of last year, and is certain to do even better—unless he breaks a leg. And I think you'll admit that Horse is filling the middle linebacker spot so well that nobody has missed the supposedly indispensable Ted Marcus."

"I have no quarrel with them as football players or as individuals," Donegan said. "And I certainly have no intention of breaking this story on my own initiative. I'm no Boy Scout, but Commissioner M. J. Morton is, and don't forget it. If he cracks down on two of your star players because he insists that the purity of football's image be maintained for the sake of America's young, or whatever, it becomes news. When that happens, I've got to tell the public the facts, and so does every other reporter. I'm sorry, Robin, but that's the way it has to be."

"I'm aware of your obligations as a newsman, and I wouldn't ask you or anyone else to muzzle himself. But what I don't understand is why there should be a big fuss now. Homosexuality is nothing new in football, or in any other professional sport. Men who take pride in their bodies often fall into homosexual patterns that may be temporary or permanent, depending on the individual." Robin warmed to his theme. "So why pick on Hal and Collins, even if some sort of conclusive evidence has been found that will make a charge against them stick?"

"Well," Donegan said, "as the story has been told to me, they've been flagrantly indiscreet. You'll recall the case of an N.F.L. team several years ago that caused a lot of rumors when some of the players stayed behind in the locker room for an orgy after a number of games. They shielded their activities from the outside world, so nothing could be done about them."

Robin heaved himself to his feet. "I appreciate the warning," he said. "Maybe I'll have myself fitted for a helmet and shoulder pads before I hear from the Commissioner tomorrow morning."

A brief taxi ride brought him to his own apartment building, and his mind was whirling as he stepped off the elevator. Minerva greeted him warmly, but she had something on her mind, too.

"I'm not meeting Freddie for dinner," she said. "He called me a few minutes ago to say he had to cancel the date, but he didn't tell me why."

Martie, Robin thought, had returned to Chicago. "I think I can explain, honey, after we try to tamp down a crisis that's even more urgent." He told her about his meeting with Donegan.

"I'm not surprised," she said. "Hal simply doesn't give a damn."

Robin telephoned Mal Ferguson, broke the news to him and promised to do what he could when he saw the Commissioner. Then he dialed the Helmsley-Collins apartment, and Hal answered.

Mincing no words, Robin told him what to expect in the morning.

As Minerva had predicted, Hal laughed. "Maybe it'll be a meeting that will make history," he said. "Or maybe we can push the Commissioner back into the woodwork. Either way it will be great fun."

Minerva had a stiff drink of bourbon waiting for her husband when he finished his call, and had mixed a martini for herself.

"I don't know how to handle a situation like this," Robin confessed, sipping his drink.

"You'll have to play it by ear, that's all."

"I guess." He stared at an engraving on the far wall, then sighed. "Four victories in a row were too good to be true. Now lightning has really hit the outhouse."

"What else?"

He told her about the return of Martie, omitting only his own sexual encounter with her.

Minerva was silent for a moment. "I'm glad Freddie doesn't need me as a hand-holder any more. I can't stand that redhead, she's so greedy, but she'll treat him like a king as long as she knows that more and more money will be rolling in. I hate to think of how fast she'll dump him if his play is just so-so for a few Sundays and the Cougars start to lose again."

"She'll cut him loose in a hurry and make him a free agent before he even knows what's happened to him. Which could destroy him before another rescue operation can be organized."

"You really understand the bitch," Minerva said, sipping her drink.

Robin was silent for a long moment, then said, "I should." Giving himself no chance to lose his courage and back down, he told her, in general, about the intimate nature of his encounter with Martie.

Minerva's face grew pale, and she made no comment, but again sipped her drink.

"I make no excuses," Robin said. "It's true I had too much to drink, but that didn't give me the license to act as I did. I could also claim that Martie seduced me, but I'm a big boy, and I accept full responsibility for my conduct."

Minerva's fingers trembled slightly as she lighted a cigarette. "Did you—have a good time with her?"

"When you've been driving a car for hours," Robin said, "you suddenly realize you're hungry, so you stop in at a little roadside barbecue stand and stuff on a couple of hamburgers and some French fries. By the time you get back in the car, you aren't hungry any more because you realize the hamburgers were badly cooked and the potatoes were greasy."

She nodded, appearing to grasp his meaning.

"I'm a half-generation too old for infidelity," Robin said. "I know that a lot of young people who are married think nothing of playing around, and some of them actually claim the variety improves their marriages. But I'm not built that way. The new system doesn't work for me, and I'm willing to pay for my mistake. I'll accept any decision you make."

It was Minerva's turn to be silent for some moments. "I can understand," she said at last, "how a person can be trapped in a situation and not be able to escape. It can happen to anyone."

Robin was stunned by her generosity. Then, peering at her, he saw bright spots of color burning in her cheeks, and caught his breath. "You, too?"

She inclined her head. "The first night I had dinner with

Freddie. I made sure it didn't happen again." Suddenly the words became a torrent. "You just don't know how much I've wanted to tell you, Rob, or how often I've tried. I've felt cheap and degraded—"

"So have I," he interrupted.

Minerva stubbed out her cigarette and lighted another. "There's one thing that's beyond me."

"I know. You and I played around together while you were still married to Hal, but it didn't bother either of us."

"I guess," she said, "there was something different about the way we felt toward each other."

Robin tried to smile, but his face felt stiff. "For a man and a woman who had a semi-shotgun marriage, we seem to have come a long way."

Minerva drained her martini.

"I'm not going to the coaches' meeting. I have something far more important to do. Go fix your lipstick so I can take you out to dinner." He stood, finishing his own drink, and felt as though an unbearable burden had been taken from him.

"Wait."

He looked at her.

"Before we go anywhere or say anything more, Mr. Stephens, Mrs. Stephens wants you to make violent love to her."

Hal Helmsley and Gerald Collins, deliberately dressed alike in turtleneck sweaters, plain slacks and low-cut cowboy boots, slouched in easy chairs on either side of Commissioner M. J. Morton's desk. Big Horse Collins started at the ceiling, while Hal, vastly amused but trying not to laugh, looked straight at the man who was the final authority in all matters pertaining to professional football.

Robin Stephens tried to appear composed, and was glad no one knew his insides were leaping. A scandal could hurt ticket sales, at the very least, and if two key players were forced to leave the team the Cougars would suffer irreparable injury.

Commissioner Morton was reading from a document written

by a member of his staff, and his voice was as dry as his manner was pedantic. At off-season meetings with the owners and general managers he was jovial, took an occasional highball and even slapped an occasional back, but in his dealings with players he was invariably severe. Perhaps he was even more withdrawn than usual because he found the subject of this meeting distasteful.

The facts, as he presented them, were clear. On two successive Monday evenings, apartment-mates Helmsley and Collins exchanged intimate gestures and caresses in a bar, where they were seen by others. Therefore their conduct had been offensive, and they had damaged the image cultivated by everyone associated with professional football.

When the Commissioner came to the end of the report, he put the document aside and removed his glasses. "Do any of you care to deny the facts, as presented, or make some other comments?"

Robin replied quickly, before either of the players could speak. "It seems to me that the so-called 'crimes' mentioned in this investigation have been exaggerated. The alleged fact—and for purposes of this discussion I'm willing to accept it as a fact —that one of these young men patted the other on his rear end doesn't mean he's a homosexual or indulged in a definitively homosexual gesture. It could have been friendly, humorous, ironic—whatever." The point, he thought, would be difficult to dispute.

Big Horse Collins promptly tunneled under him. "Bullshit," he said. "I like Hal's ass and he likes mine, so it does mean something if we stroke each other on the butt. What your spies didn't mention in their report, Mr. Commissioner, is that we did all kinds of things to each other that your gumshoes didn't notice. For instance, it drives Hal nuts if somebody diddles with him. So, on both the nights your reports talk about, I unzipped him. I not only got him hard, but I damn near drove him through a wall." The big man laughed at the memory.

Hal grinned, too. "My friend over there presents a one-sided

[233]

case. Sure I got horny. Who wouldn't. But I got even. You never saw anybody more sensitive to goosing than Horse!"

Robin fervently wished both players would learn the benefits of keeping quiet. They might have escaped without penalties had they remained silent, but they were admitting far more than the charges contained.

The Commissioner could not stem his indignation. "Both of you admit you've committed a series of unnatural acts."

"Not so fast," Robin said desperately. "Any remark accepted and recorded here requires verification. And both of these boys have acquired sufficient credentials in football to be heard with respect. I know them better than you, Commissioner. They're a pair of great kidders, and neither of us knows how much they're saying for effect, trying to irritate us."

"Thanks for the helping hand," Hal said, "but we don't need it. If you're looking for solid proof, Commissioner, a friend of ours took a picture of us going down on each other one night. Maybe you'd like a set of prints for your files."

Robin made a last attempt to cover up for the pair. "Hal's sense of humor," he said, "is sometimes exaggerated."

The two players were remorseless. "Your report made one big mistake, Commissioner. It called the bar where we had a little fun with each other a public place. Well, it isn't all that public. We don't believe in flaunting our relationship in front of straights who become offended and don't understand. Both of the incidents that gave your investigators such hot pants took place in gay bars. Where the things we did are mild by comparison with some of the other things that go on there."

Robin tried to make the best of a questionable position. "You heard that, Commissioner? They spent both evenings at a homosexual bar. They did nothing to offend the public at large!"

Morton had never dealt with a similar dilemma in his years as Commissioner. "I won't deny the possibility of mitigating circumstances," he said uncertainly.

Hal became annoyed. "You've got it all wrong. Just because

we like to go to bed together occasionally doesn't make us degenerates. We also ball girls from time to time, and we like that, too. I'm not saying Horse and I are in love with each other—"

"Hardly." Collins' voice was a deep growl. "It's far too soon to tell. If we're still hitting it off a year from now, that'll be plenty time enough to decide whether to make some joint investments and go into a permanent partnership."

Commissioner Morton was stunned. "Are you trying to tell me you wouldn't be upset if this office reveals that you're homosexuals?"

"Forgive the cliché," Hal Helmsley said, "but gay is good. We aren't ashamed of our friendship, and we sure as hell don't try to hide it."

"Maybe a lot of people aren't yet ready to accept our kind of freedom," Collins added, "but that's their tough luck. You won't hurt us by making disclosures about us. And if you shock a lot of people who are still prejudiced and narrow, it's tough-titty for them. And for you." Smiling complacently, he slouched in his chair again.

For a moment Robin thought the Commissioner would suffer a stroke of apoplexy, and couldn't blame him. The pair were not only frank in admitting their relationship, but seemed unable to realize they were behaving immorally. So their attitude made it almost impossible to curb or punish them.

"What does the Cougar organization think of all this?" Morton demanded, turning to the team's acting general manager.

"Hal is the best fullback in the game today," Robin said. "And Horse is doing so much more for us than we'd hoped that we wouldn't even listen to a deal offering us Ted Marcus in an even trade. What I think of their personal life is as irrelevant as whatever you may think of it, Commissioner. I don't happen to approve—for me. But what they choose to do on their own time is none of my business. I pay them to play football, which they're doing, and I have no desire to interfere in their off-the-field lives. Who cares if they're homosexuals? I defy you to name me an owner who wouldn't trade for either of them tomorrow."

Commissioner Morton had the grace to recognize defeat. "Hereafter," he told the two players, "stay away from homosexual bars and keep your hands to yourselves in public. I'm putting official warnings in your personnel files, and you'll pay a stiff penalty if you're called in here again on the same charges. Now—go back to work—and play football."

6

"WE'RE TRUE BELIEVERS," a sign on the bulletin board in the Cougar dressing room said, and every member of the squad signed his name to the article of faith. Proving they were men of their words, they blasted the Kansas City Chiefs into oblivion that Sunday. Finch passed for five touchdowns, Helmsley gained almost two hundred yards from scrimmage, scoring twice more, and Renewzski booted three field goals through the posts. The Cougar defenders made their best showing of the season, holding their opponents to a single touchdown and conversion, and one field goal. The final score was 58–10, and as the *Sun-Times* remarked the following morning, every American citizen who lived within a 300-mile radius of Chicago became an unqualified, bona fide true believer, too.

Late in the third quarter Finch was knocked unconscious by a blitzing safetyman, and Sorensen, his replacement, performed with admirable efficiency, driving to the three-yard line for one of Helmsley's touchdowns, and moving deep into Kansas City territory again, which enabled Renewzski to make good his last field goal. The star quarterback, as the press unanimously referred to Finch, suffered a mild concussion from which he recovered within a few hours. He was held overnight at the hospital as a precautionary measure, and was released the following morning.

That week he carried a light work load in preparation for an out-of-town game to be played with the Cincinnati Bengals. Martie scrupulously kept her promise to Robin, and not only lavished tender care on Finch at home, but called for him after practice each day to make certain he did not exert himself.

He played only the first half of the Cincinnati game, but that was enough, as he passed for two touchdowns and directed a drive for a third that enabled Helmsley and Baines to carry the ball for long gains, with the former plunging over the goal. The Bengals fought valiantly, but could do no better than rack up two touchdowns and a field goal, which made the final score 21–17. The Cougars had won six games in a row now, after losing their opener, so the attention of football fans everywhere was riveted on the team. And the Chicago cup of joy overflowed when a publicity department statistician made the happy discovery that Adam Renewzski had not yet missed a conversion attempt or a field goal. The ranks of Cougar true believers proliferated throughout the United States.

The Bengal game was notable in yet another way, marking the first time Dan Grannett had seen the team in action all season. It was announced just before the game that he was present, as he happened to be visiting a sister and brother-in-law in Covington, Kentucky, across the Ohio River from Cincinnati. He was introduced to the crowd and received a thunderous ovation, but refused to speak, and contented himself with doffing his hat.

Many of the Cougars looked at him curiously when the play carried them to a place on the field near his box. To them he was a legend, a larger-than-life person they had never met, and they were surprised to see that, in spite of his heavy tan, he looked frail huddled in his topcoat. Robin, who watched the game from his usual press-box perch, expected Dan to visit the locker room after the game, and was surprised when he failed to make an appearance there.

Marc Klein gave him no chance to ask Mal Ferguson if he

knew what had become of Grannett, however. Grasping Robin's arm and drawing him into a corridor, beyond the delirium of the players' victory celebration, the owner was curt. "Fly back to Chicago with me," he said. "I'm sending the rest of my party on another aircraft, so we'll be alone."

Three-quarters of an hour later Robin sat in a comfortable, overstuffed seat on the private jet. A stewardess served high-balls as soon as they were airborne, and Klein wasted no time.

"I made the mistake of taking Ellen to Danny's box and sitting there through the entire second half. What an earful I got!"

Robin wondered what had become of Ellen, but thought it diplomatic not to inquire.

"Danny is a great old guy," Marc said, glancing out at the breaking cloud cover. "But I'm afraid his illness has soured him. He did nothing but bitch about you and the team. And Ellen was no help," he added, a hint of exasperation in his voice. "I don't know whether she could have tamped him down, but she might have tried. Instead of encouraging him."

Robin spoke with care. "I know Dan was upset when we blew game after game during the exhibition season. But when we're winning week after week and have become the talk of the whole country, it makes no sense."

"Not to me and not to you, maybe," Marc said. "But it does to Dan Grannett. And to Ellen."

"What are his objections?"

"You've put together a team that has flash, but no substance. The object in building a football team is to establish a dynasty, but some of the players you've brought us are only good for a few more years before they'll have to retire. Byron Jeffers for one. Renewzski for another."

"Jeffers is good for at least five more years, barring serious injury, and Adam Renewzski will be around a lot longer than that!"

Marc raised a hand. "You don't have to blast at me, Rob. I'm with you. I'm just repeating what Dan Grannett and his echo were saying during the second half."

Robin could afford to be magnanimous. "I'm sorry Dan feels

that way. We've put together a solid team, and I know we can make improvements in it for next year."

The owner leaned forward, grasped his shoulder and shook him. "Dan is jealous, that's all. He's turned pea-green because you're doing better with his Cougars than he ever did."

"Those are the breaks."

"There's more than luck involved. No matter what we do during the rest of the season, you've created a fighting, aggressive team." They were flying high above the clouds now, and Marc stared out at the weak autumn sun. "I wouldn't be surprised if Ellen has told Danny about some of my thoughts for next year."

Robin had been careful never to think about the future, much less mention it.

"When Dan gets an okay from the doctors to come back to work," Marc said, "I've been considering bringing him upstairs as a vice president of the parent corporation. He can take it easy, spend no more than a few hours at his desk every day, and he'll be available for occasional visits to some of the plants around the country."

"I don't think he'd be too enthusiastic over that kind of a life," Robin said.

The owner's face hardened. "A speech by Dan Grannett at an employees' banquet would be great for morale. As for Danny, he's lucky he's alive, lucky I haven't sent him into complete retirement on a pension and still luckier that I'll be giving him the opportunity to talk about his favorite subject. Not that anything is definitely settled," he added.

Robin understood: if the Cougars continued to burn up the National Football League, he would be offered a contract as general manager in his own right, but if they slipped badly between now and the end of the season, Klein was reserving the right to look elsewhere for a new top executive.

Ellen Hibbs failed to appear at the office on Monday, and a staff of assistants handled the requests for tickets to Sunday's home game with the Buffalo Bills. Robin thought she might be ill, and tried a number of times to reach her at home, but she did not answer her telephone. She finally showed up at noon on Tuesday, and went straight to Robin's office without stopping off to leave her coat, gloves and shoulder bag in her own.

"I hate to leave you short-handed in the middle of the season," she said, "but I'm submitting my resignation, effective immediately—as soon as I go upstairs and break the news to Marc."

Perhaps no individual was indispensable, but Ellen, more than anyone else, was needed to insure that the front office would continue to function smoothly. "If you'll tell me what's wrong," Robin said, "perhaps we can work out our differences."

"I owe my allegiance to Uncle Danny's Cougars, not yours," she said, and marched off to the bank of elevators that would take her to the tower.

Marc Klein was cleaning up his morning's work prior to acting as host at a business lunch in his private dining room, but he had Ellen sent in immediately when she was announced.

"Where the hell have you been?" he demanded, his manner frigid.

"I wanted to go off by myself to think after Sunday's game," Ellen said. "And I've made up my mind. I've told Robin Stephens just now that I'm resigning."

"Because Dan Grannett is jealous, and it makes you feel too guilty to be working for his successor."

"We've gone 'round and 'round on this too often, Marc. There's nothing to be gained by repeating the way we feel."

"By now you know my stand." Klein stood, deeply offended. "I've made it clear to you that if you leave the Cougars, you and I are finished, too."

"You know I can't buy your love-me-love-my-dog philosophy, Marc." Ellen was one of those rare young women who looked even more attractive when she was angry.

"You're twisting basic facts. Either you give me your primary loyalty, or you go off and sulk with Dan. I have no conflict with him, but you apparently see this situation his way, which is your privilege."

"I'm also aware of the consequences," Ellen said.

Marc's expression was bleak. "I've never asked anyone to stay on with me, either in business or in my personal life. Anyone who wants to leave soon becomes useless to me. I've never varied from the principle in my dealings with anyone, and I don't intend to begin now!"

"I'm sorry, but you're entitled to your feelings, just as I am to mine." She extended her hand. "Let's not break up on a sour note. We've had too much fun together."

He ignored her gesture. "I'm already late for a meeting," he said.

Ellen turned and left. Hurrying downstairs to her own office, she began to pack her personal belongings.

There she was interrupted by Patricia Thompson. "Mr. Stephens asked me to keep watch, and to tell you he'd like to see you."

"I'm here," Ellen said curtly.

A few moments later Robin sauntered in, his eyes revealing the tension he was trying to hide. He watched Ellen filling a cardboard carton, then remarked casually, "The least you can do is let me buy you a farewell lunch."

She didn't want to appear boorish by rejecting a gracious gesture, and reluctantly agreed.

They went to the Wrigley Building restaurant, where they sat at a corner table, and conversation was stilted until the waiter brought them a second round of drinks.

"For your information," Robin said quietly, "I'm not accepting your resignation."

"You can't stop me from going!" Ellen retorted. "Oh, I know—you can make it impossible for me to get another job in football. I've seen the blacklist in operation. But who says I want to stay in football? And you can't make me change my mind by refusing to give me my terminal pay, either. I know all the tricks."

"I have no intention of using any tricks," Robin said. "Since we're both rational people, I hope I can persuade you to stay. I've been told Dan Grannett is unhappy because the team I've

[242]

put together is doing better than any of his Cougar teams ever did. Well, I think he's being foolish, and I feel sorry for him. But what he feels and what I feel alters no fundamental. The fact is that I'm not competing with Dan Grannett. My team is competing with the other ball clubs in the American and National Conferences. So I can't see why you'd be made to suffer conflicting loyalties if you stay."

He realized her relationship with Klein was a major factor, but thought it wiser not to fish in waters that were out of bounds. "So my position is simple," he continued. "If you walk out, I'm in a nasty spot. There's no one in the organization who can be moved up to run ticket sales, and the chaos would be worse if I brought in an outsider who would have to learn all the little peculiarities of our system before he could function efficiently. But ticket sales aside, you take care of more odds and ends than I can count. I don't mind telling you I was leery of a woman in an executive job in this business when I first came to the Cougars, but I'd have been lost without you. And I sure will be if you walk out now."

Ellen refused to return his gaze, and stared over the heads of the restaurant's other guests. "Uncle Danny urged me not to leave," she said. "I want to make that part very plain."

"Of course. He knew the office would fall apart without you. If we were a cellar team, it might not matter too much. But we've become a championship contender, so all the pressures are greater. A heavier demand for seats. More complicated relations with the press, including the hotel reservations and all the rest for increasing numbers of out-of-town reporters. The sudden increase in the number of scouts from other teams who visit us. The complications with manufacturers and advertising agencies who want to pay us for endorsements. The list is endless, and is growing larger."

"I've known I'd be playing a dirty trick on you," Ellen said. "But how can I help you when Uncle Danny is sitting down on that island off the Georgia coast, eating his heart out week after week?"

"You aren't doing anything for me," Robin said, his voice becoming sharp. "You're doing a job and being well paid for it. On the basis of a verbal understanding that I consider as binding as a written contract. If you want to quit at the end of the season, that's up to you. But I won't let you leave now!"

"I was hoping you'd let me go without making a fuss."

"I would if I could. I don't enjoy arm-twisting, and I can't force myself to beg. All I can do is ask you to be sensible."

Ellen slowly turned her glass. "You wouldn't try to hold me after the season is over?"

"I don't know that I'll have any authority after the season!"

"Uncle Danny believes you will. He's convinced you're going to be running the Cougars for a long time."

"I'm flattered. All I can do is promise you that—if it's my show—I won't try to keep you against your will or better judgment. I'd want a month's notice, which is fair. And in return I'd recommend you to any other team as the most competent executive I've ever known in the football business."

She was silent for a time, then turned to him. "All right," she said. "I'll stay. Provided you can square it with Marc Klein."

Rarely had Robin felt so uncomfortable. He was caught between Marcus Aurelius Klein and his mistress, a position he had long tried to avoid, but he had no choice, even though he was treading on delicate ground.

"Marc," he said to the industrialist who restlessly paced the penthouse office, "I don't need to tell you that no business runs itself, that no company is any better than its administration. No matter what the Cougars do on the field—and the boys continue to surprise me every week—we're in for major trouble if the office stops functioning efficiently. Ticket sales are already a major headache, and the problem becomes worse with every game we win."

"I'll let you borrow anybody you want from the corporate treasurer's and comptroller's offices," Klein said.

"They'd be no help. This is a job that requires a knowledge

of box-office management, combined with the technique of turning people away without making enemies of them. It can't be learned overnight."

"Then go out and hire the best in the business. Anybody you want, and pay him accordingly."

"I already have the best in the business," Robin said, and drew in his breath. "I've persuaded Ellen to stay if you'll give your approval."

Marc stared at him with hostile eyes. "Quite the persuader, aren't you?"

"We need her."

"It's a hell of a way to run an office when the whole place goes up in smoke if one person walks out!"

Robin refused to be browbeaten. "You forget that I inherited the Cougars' office set-up. The system wasn't mine, and I've tried to work within the limitations of what was handed to me."

"Are you telling me you'd reorganize the front office if you stayed on permanently as general manager?"

"Immediately! Too much was concentrated in Ellen's hands." Robin decided to speak bluntly. "But she was Dan Grannett's protégé—and your girl. So *my* hands were tied."

"She isn't my girl now," Klein said.

"I couldn't care less," Robin said. "I'm interested in her only because she's an extraordinarily competent assistant general manager. A title she should have had long ago."

"When an executive or a woman shows loyalty to someone other than me, I lose interest," Klein replied. "Maybe that's petty of me, but it's the way I am."

Robin leaned back in his padded chair, his manner deceptively casual. "I assume you'd like to see us win the American Conference title this year. Maybe go on to win the Super Bowl and become the world's champions."

"My God!" Klein stopped pacing and stared hard at him. "You ought to know there are few things in this world that I want more!"

"I'm not promising you a title—because I can't. But I give

you my word that if Mal Ferguson and I—each of us in his own way—can maintain the head of steam we've generated, we'll have a good shot at a championship. We've moved faster and farther so far this season than I dared let myself hope. But a professional football team is a complicated mechanism, and a breakdown in one of its component parts, even a minor breakdown in a minor part, can throw the entire machinery out of whack."

"I find it difficult to swallow the notion that we won't win a championship unless Ellen Hibbs stays on the job!"

"That isn't what I said," Robin replied. "I just want it clearly understood that if there's a foul-up in one of the areas where she's had responsibility, it could change the tempo. For instance, she's been doing a superb job handling the scouts from other teams. If they become disgruntled and pass the word that we're nine-day wonders on the verge of collapse, that attitude will find its way into print. Not in Chicago, maybe, but in other cities. The players will hear about it. They always do. And if this team of ours ever loses confidence in itself, forty true believers will be transformed into forty journeymen gooks!"

"No matter how you put it," Klein said, "the facts are the same. If I want a shot at a title this year, I've got to take up with Ellen where we left off."

"I have no voice in her personal relationship with you, Marc, and I want none. All I'm requesting is your approval to keep her in the job she's tried to quit. She won't stay without your okay."

"What goes on between a man and a woman," Klein said with a wry laugh, "is even more complicated than a football team. Take my word for it, if Ellen keeps her office key, she'll also hang on to her key to my house."

"Then I want no voice in the decision," Robin said. "My judgments were based only on what was good for business."

Marc dropped into a chair, and too weary to sit upright, rested his head against the back. "The world is filled with women," he said, "most of them ready to grab at a guy in my boots. Every race. Young and old. Beautiful, brilliant, sexy, whatever a man wants. But a championship football team is something else. No matter how much money you sink in a club, you never know whether it will win or lose, and nobody can draw you a blueprint of success." He roused himself. "Don't repeat any of our conversation to Ellen. Just tell her how glad I am that she's decided to stay."

Another crisis had been overcome, and Robin should have felt relieved, but his pity for Marc Klein was so great he had no room within him for any other emotion.

The Cougars extended their winning streak to six consecutive games, defeating the Buffalo Bills by a score of 20–7. Finch and Helmsley again shared offensive honors, and Ron Belotti, the 290-pound center, blocked so effectively and opened such enormous holes for his running backs that the press voted him the player of the game.

The Bengals came to Chicago for a return game, which was played on Saturday night because it was being televised for a national audience. No one had suspected, when the schedule-makers had drawn up their matches, that this would be the season's closest-scoring game between well-matched opponents.

A 52-yard pass, Finch to Helmsley, set up the Cougars' first score, and the Bengals retaliated in kind. The game became a seesaw battle between two defending lines, and neither side scored again until the last quarter, when Finch drilled another long pass to Helmsley, who punched across the goal line with it. Young Olson was healthy again, but could not break into the game, thanks to the first-rate job Greg Baines was doing. The final score was 14–7, and thousands of patrons in the sell-out crowd poured onto the field and tore down the new goalposts for souvenirs.

"The true believers are the miracle team of the year," the News declared the following day, and on Tuesday a team of reporters and photographers appeared to do a long feature piece for Sports Illustrated. On Wednesday Fred Finch had a fight with his girl, who threatened to leave him again, and Robin was forced to drop everything else on his desk to deal with Martie. He called the redhead into his office, and there read the Riot Act to her.

"Stick to your bargain," he said.

Martie looked at him, and then unpacked her luggage.

On Thursday the team from *Sports Illustrated* converged on Robin in his office for an interview. "Why in your opinion, are the Cougars upsetting all of the experts' prophecies this year?"

"Because they're playing the game as it should be played. They're blocking and tackling better than any team since Lombardi's Green Bay Packers of the sixties."

"Which players would you single out as exceptional, Mr. Stephens?"

"Helmsley and Finch are stars, and so are Jeffers and Collins. Baines has plugged a hole at halfback, and Belotti may be our biggest unsung hero at center. But you can't give credit to a handful on the team. There are forty Cougars on the squad, and all forty of them are pulling their weight. They're in harness together, all of them tugging in the same direction, and that's why we're winning games."

"Mr. Stephens, do you think the Cougars are going to win the championship?"

"Don't ask me that question. See Coach Ferguson."

"But you must have thoughts of your own on the subject."

Robin grinned at his visitors. "We play our football one game at a time, Sunday by Sunday. But you can put me on record as being a true believer."

He was telling the truth, he realized, not merely saying what was expected of him for publication. His "Cougar fever," as the newspapers described the enthusiasm sweeping Chicago, had become chronic, and it was unlikely that he would ever again think of football exclusively as a business enterprise. Certainly the players were proving to him, week after week, that emotional factors were as important in the achievement of victory as technical skills.

Forty men were winning games because they believed in

themselves and each other. Fred Finch was living up to his potential as a quarterback and leader because his ego had been bolstered, first by one girl, then by another. Big Horse Collins was enjoying the best season of his career because his teammates had confidence in him, and Byron Jeffers, long an All-Pro, had developed a new spirit of leadership as captain of the defensive team.

"These guys," Robin told Minerva, "are making a hash of my theory that football is nothing more or less than a major facet of the entertainment industry. I haven't seen this kind of rah-rah since I was in college, and even there you were considered pretty unsophisticated and raw if you cheered too loudly."

"Ever since I first met Hal," she replied, "all he cared about was improving his personal statistics. But I honestly don't believe he cares that much about his own records this season."

"He doesn't. Which is why he'll be five hundred yards ahead of himself as a ground-gainer, and is smashing records as a pass-catcher out of the backfield."

"Is there any chance we'll go all the way, Rob?"

"I'm discovering I'm superstitious. I don't let myself look that far ahead. But I'm beginning to think we've got a real chance—unless something comes along and knocks us cockeyed. We've survived every serious blow so far, and the question now is how much longer our luck will be good."

Cougar luck and skill combined to win the team its eighth victory in a row when they beat the Chiefs in a rematch played in a heavy, cold downpour. The ball was so slippery the game was marked by repeated fumbles on both sides; the Chiefs failed to capitalize on their opponents' errors, while the Cougars took full advantage of every break, and that difference was the margin for a 15–6 victory. Fred Finch, who could gain only 106 yards in the air with a water-logged ball, recovered four fumbles in deep mud, and his teammates rewarded him with a new nickname, Water Rat.

A steady, growing hysteria gripped Chicago, and it reached its peak when the Cougars trounced the Houston Oilers by a score of 38–14. All of the Cougar regulars distinguished themselves, and the final touchdown was engineered by the substitutes who played all of the fourth quarter. "Even if the Cougars become as inept as they were at the beginning of the season and lose all the rest of their games," Phil Donegan said on his telecast, "their nine-to-one record so far virtually assures them of a place in the play-offs."

As a promotion stunt Robin ordered one hundred thousand lapel buttons bearing the legend, *"I'm a TRUE BELIEVER,"* and the demand for them was so great that he called the manufacturer and asked for an additional three hundred thousand. The key players in the team's drive were in such demand for appearances on television and radio interview programs that Mal Ferguson was forced to crack down, and banned all such visits until the season ended. "You're football players," he reminded them in a brief locker-room speech. "If you want to be show business personalities, you'll have to do it on your town time in the off-season."

Robin had seen very little of Marc Klein since the owner had papered over his differences with Ellen Hibbs, and suspected that Klein might be annoyed with him because of the part he had played in the matter. But the Cougars' record spoke for itself, so he was only mildly concerned.

Finally, two days before the Cougars played host to the Los Angeles Rams in an interconference game, he was summoned to the penthouse, where a brusque Marc Klein awaited him.

"We've tried to get you the three additional boxes you wanted for Sunday," Robin said, "but I'm afraid we can't produce them for you. The house has been a clean sellout for the past ten days, and we wouldn't be able to come up with as much as one box, even if we went to the brokers and tried to buy them back at scalpers' prices."

"I'm disappointed," Marc said, "but that's still the best news I've had all day. Here." He threw a sheaf of papers in a blue binder across the desk. "You may want to glance at this."

"What is it?"

"A three-year contract, engaging you as general manager. At a salary of sixty thousand a year. With the right to hire and fire in the front office as you see fit, and giving you the power to make any player deals you wish. It's more or less the same basic set-up we had with Dan Grannett."

Robin tried to appear calm. "Why are you offering this to me now, Marc, rather than at the end of the season?"

"You'll be still more expensive if we keep winning, but the team has done so well that I can't get you any cheaper if we begin to lose. So I see no sense in waiting. Take the agreement to a lawyer, if you like, but don't let him sit on it. I want to get this thing wrapped up. We'll call a press conference next week to announce it."

"I trust you're planning to sign Mal Ferguson to a new contract, too."

"Certainly!"

"Then I'd very much like an announcement covering both of us made at the same time," Robin said. "Mal and I work together in a form of partnership, and a dual-contract signing would help symbolize our relationship."

A faint smile creased Marc's face. "For a guy who was proud of being a rugged individualist, you're sure a team man."

"I've been getting religion on Sunday afternoons. Does Dan Grannett know you're giving me the job, Marc?"

"Not yet. Which means I've said nothing to Ellen. She'd be on the long-distance telephone to him in two minutes flat."

Robin hesitated. "I'd hate to have him learn about it in the newspapers or on the air."

"I don't think he'd show you the same courtesy if your positions were reversed. Poor old Danny isn't overly fond of you these days."

"That's understandable." Again Robin pushed into a sphere that, strictly speaking, was none of his business. "May I ask your plans for Dan?"

"I intend to give him a choice. He can retire outright on a

[251]

generous pension. Or he can take the vice presidency of the parent company I mentioned to you. If he wants the job, Ellen can move in with him as his office manager. She'd love it, and it would end my personal obligation to her."

"If I can," Robin said, "I want to keep her on the Cougar payroll for the next year. She does a fine job, and she's worth more money." He saw the owner's dour expression, and added, "If it would help you, I'll be glad to spell things out when I make her the offer. She'll understand she's getting an executive position—with no private strings attached."

"Fair enough. She's a clinger, but she's far from stupid, and I'm sure she can take a hint."

"There's one thing more," Robin said. "I'd very much like Dan Grannett to know in advance of any publicity—or any possible leak—that I'm moving into his job."

Marc shrugged. "He'll be here for the game with the Rams, as I just found out today."

"Then I'd like to tell him myself," Robin said.

"Are you a glutton for unpleasant scenes?"

"No, and I'm not making a grandstand play, either. Dan has a great many friends in the business, more than anyone else in football. If I can get to him first, maybe I can draw some of the poison out of his fangs, and he won't go around the industry damning me."

"I'm glad to see success hasn't spoiled your ability to think of every angle," Marc said, his voice dry. "Dan and Muriel are coming to my house for dinner tomorrow night, and I was procrastinating in my own mind about telling him because I want a relaxed evening."

"In that case," Robin said, "maybe Ellen will set up a date for tomorrow afternoon, and I can see him before he goes to your place."

Marc's grin was ironic. "Good luck," was all he said.

Football enthusiasts from New York and Miami who always followed winners were chatting in the spacious lobby of the

Drake Hotel. Many of them were acquainted with Robin, as were sportsmen from southern California who had come to Chicago for the game with the Rams. So he was forced to halt repeatedly for a handshake and an exchange of pleasantries as he made his way to the bank of elevators inside the hotel's south entrance.

The Grannett suite afforded a view of Lake Michigan, with the curve of Oak Street beach directly below, but Dan was wasting no time looking at the scenery. Newspapers were everywhere in the sitting room, all of them opened to the sports pages. His greeting was perfunctory, but his grip was as firm as it had been before he had suffered his heart attack.

"You're looking like a guy who's been having a great time in the sun," Robin said.

"I've brought my golf score down to the upper seventies, but that's been my only accomplishment." Dan invited his visitor to sit by jabbing a thick forefinger in the direction of a chair.

"I'd like to say hello to Muriel while I'm here."

"She and Ellen have gone shopping." Dan made no effort to converse.

"As Ellen may have told you, we put on a huge search for a box, and we have one for you tomorrow afternoon, if you want to use it. If you prefer the press accommodations, you can share my box, of course. Or you may want to sit with the team."

"Why would I want to do that?" the old man demanded, raising his voice. "It's your team, Stephens, not mine!"

The outburst was so sudden that Robin was unprepared for it, but he had no intention of allowing himself to be drawn into an argument, and shrugged. "As you will," he said.

Dan looked grim and made no further comment. He offered his visitor no refreshments, and his attitude was plain. He did not regard this as a social occasion.

The best play to call, Robin decided, would be one utterly lacking in subterfuge, an undisguised plunge into the center of the line. "Dan," he said, "word has drifted back to me that you've been unhappy with me, and I'm sorry to hear it."

"I had a building program for the Cougars," the old man said, "and you destroyed it."

"I was lucky enough to speed it up," Robin said. "A record of nine wins and only one loss at this point in the schedule isn't bad."

"You've won games with flashy players who aren't my idea of sound football men."

"If you mean Finch, he may go over three thousand yards in passage completions, and he's passed for twenty-one touchdowns so far. He's also been a grand field general, as the record proves."

"He's living with a woman who isn't his wife, and I have reason to believe she's had similar affairs with other players. Your kicker, Renewzski, has no humility. Baines uses his knees and elbows too freely when the officials aren't looking. Collins uses language I never permitted on the field. The list is quite long, and I could go on and on. But why bother? You get the point, I'm sure."

"It would be beneath both of us if I tried to defend my players," Robin said.

"Character," Dan replied, "has always been as important to me as winning games. Football builds character!"

It was impossible for Robin to remain silent. "By the time a player leaves college and gets into pro ball, his character is formed. The name of the game is winning!"

"You have your approach, Stephens, and I have mine. We think and operate on different levels, which is why it won't be possible for us to work together." Dan paused for a moment. "I'm sorry I must speak so bluntly, but if you knew me better you'd realize that's my way. I'm saying all this to you now, well before the season ends, so you'll have enough time to—"

"Just a minute." Robin held up a hand. "Before you go too far with this, Dan, I've been offered a contract, in my own right, as general manager of the Cougars. And I'm accepting it."

The old man's eyes bulged as he glared at his successor. "You sneaky little son-of-a-bitch! You tunneled under me and stole my job while I was sick!"

With a great effort Robin managed to keep his voice down to a conversational level. "I was given your job on a temporary basis when you were taken ill. So I hardly connived for it. I did what I believed to be right, and I was fortunate enough to transform a losing team into a winning team. Call it luck, if you like. Or say I've done it with the wrong kind of players. The simple fact of the matter is that the Cougars have won nine games and lost only one. They've never before won more than seven in an entire season."

"You wouldn't know what I mean by standards!"

Robin didn't want him to become so excited he might suffer another heart attack. "Look here, Dan," he said, rising. "I've always thought you're a grand guy, and I still think so. I happen to know Marc Klein isn't going to throw you out in the cold. He'll tell you what he has in mind. All I can say is that I admire you, and I'd like to part as friends. Don't blame me, please, because football is a young man's game—in the front office as well as on the field. It isn't my fault that times have changed and have made a new approach necessary."

Dan turned his back to his visitor, walked to the windows and looked down at the always busy traffic on Lake Shore Drive.

Robin realized he had said enough, perhaps too much, so he left without speaking again.

The Cougars-Rams encounter was called the game of the week by most commentators, and lived up to its billing. Los Angeles scored a touchdown and conversion early in the first quarter to take a seven-point lead, and by half time that slender margin looked enormous. Three Finch passes were picked off by the Rams' defensive backs, and the Cougar quarterback was dumped behind the line four times, suffering his worst indignities of the season. The Ram line smothered Helmsley, holding him to a total yardage from scrimmage of thirty-seven yards, and the fans jeered as the players left the field.

Mal Ferguson made a series of adjustments during the half-time break, with the offensive squad receiving the bulk of the coaches' attention. Meanwhile Dan Grannett, who had chosen to sit in a box, was introduced to the crowd, and the spectators who occupied every seat in the stadium gave him a standing ovation that lasted for almost two minutes. Minerva Stephens, sitting beside her husband in his press-box booth, was indignant. "You'd think from the fuss they're making that he had something to do with the team's success," she said.

In the third quarter Finch revealed a simple but effective change in tactics: he turned his halfback loose in off-tackle slants, and Greg Baines proved equal to the opportunity, finally breaking away for a touchdown in a gallop of forty-six yards. Renewzski kept his record intact by kicking for the extra point, and the score was tied at 7–7. On the next series of plays the Rams carried the ball to midfield, where the Cougars held, and Olson returned the Los Angeles punt to his own thirty. There Finch began a new drive, and with the Ram defense off-balance, mixed passes and running plays in a march that carried the Cougars to the Ram eighteen. There the defense stiffened, and on fourth down Renewzski was called in to attempt a field goal.

Robin stood, scarcely breathing until the ball sailed squarely between the uprights, and not until then did he realize he was gripping Minerva's arm. The score was 10–7 in favor of the Cougars, and the three-point difference loomed larger with each passing minute. The Cougar defense was brilliant, and its offense, unable to move the ball again, stalled for time whenever the home team gained possession. The score remained unchanged when the final gun sounded.

Although the day was chilly, Robin discovered that his shirt was soaked with perspiration, and he felt a trifle weak. "I feel," he told Minerva with a sheepish laugh, "as though I was out there on the field, playing the whole sixty minutes."

Several members of the press noted, but did not comment in print on the fact that Dan Grannett left the stadium immediately after the game, and did not drop in to see either the coaches or the players.

During the next week Mal Ferguson fought against the team's almost inevitable psychological letdown by scheduling only light practice sessions. One of the regular offensive guards, Roosevelt Garcia, had been put on the injured list after the game, so a substitute was moved up to the first team and a member of the taxi squad was activated as a replacement.

The following Sunday the Cougars enjoyed their easiest victory of the season, romping over the Buffalo Bills in a rematch by a a score of 38–7. The regulars left at half time, enjoying a lead of 21–0, and the substitutes, playing the entire second half, distinguished themselves on both offense and defense. Sorensen's passing record for the day surpassed Finch's, and Olson's 139 yards gained from scrimmage led the running backs. "The Cougars, who now enjoy a won-lost record of 11–1, can do no wrong, it seems, no matter what players they send onto the field," the *Sun-Times* observed.

In the next two weeks the bandwagon of the big blue team continued to roll forward. The Cougars defeated the Denver Broncos by an emphatic 28–7, then proved they were masters of the Bengals in the two teams' second game of the year by winning handily, 35–14. A dazzling and unexpected 13–1 season's record assured Chicago of a place in the play-offs, and Coach Ferguson revealed that, rather than risk injury to any of his key players, they would sit on the bench when the Cougars flew to San Diego to meet the Chargers. However, as Hal Helmsley needed only twenty-six yards to achieve a regular season's total of 1,500 yards, it was assumed he would make an appearance that would enable him to accomplish that mark.

When Robin reached his office on Monday morning after the victory over the Bengals, Super Bowl excitement was in the air. He pushed aside sheafs of congratulatory telegrams, called in Ellen Hibbs and told her to get him a breakdown of the seating capacity at the Orange Bowl in Miami, where the first of the play-off games would be staged, and then started to read the scouts' reports of the preceding Saturday's college games. As he and Mal Ferguson well knew, it was not too early to begin making an intensive in-depth study of the players who would be submitted for professional consideration in the forthcoming college draft, which would be held in late January.

Patricia interrupted her employer, and looked agitated. "I'm sorry, but Commissioner Morton wants to see you."

Robin looked up from the papers that were piled several inches deep on his desk. "When?"

"Without delay, his secretary said."

"Did she tell you why?"

"No. I tried to find out, but she was either playing it coy or else she didn't know. All I could get out of her was that Mr. Morton wants you right away."

He stood, sighed and went to the closet for his topcoat. "It's bound to be another of those dandy little emergencies the Commissioner dreams up to justify the existence—and the expense—of his office."

Mal Ferguson, two of his assistants and Dr. Scudder were already sitting in the reception room at league headquarters when Robin walked in, but none of them had any idea why they had been summoned. Within minutes Cougar players began to arrive, many of them resenting the call because it spoiled their holiday. Soon the reception room was crammed, but they continued to pour in, and when Robin saw veterans and rookies, regulars and substitutes, he knew something major was in the wind.

A number of the younger players became boisterous, and when a group began to play touch ball with a large ceramic ashtray, Ferguson felt impelled to restore order. Then a secretary materialized at the inner door, and when she called, "Dr. Scudder, please," the players fell silent.

Robin exchanged a glance with the head coach, then shrugged. Neither knew the reason for the unusual call, and both were too experienced to speculate.

After a quarter of an hour the secretary reappeared. "Mr. Stephens, please."

Robin followed her down a long corridor, and she ushered him into an oak-paneled conference room. At the far end of the chamber five men were sitting at a long table, and in front of each of them was a microphone. Commissioner Morton had the place in the center, his two deputies flanked him, and a pair of strangers sat at either end. In front of the table was a smaller table, on which yet another microphone stood, and Robin noted that a secretary was seated at one side, a notebook in hand.

"Please sit down, Mr. Stephens," the Commissioner said, waving the newcomer to the smaller table. "It is my duty to tell you that everything being said here this morning is being recorded and transcribed. I don't believe you've met two members of this panel, Dr. William Hodges of the Rush Medical School faculty, and Dr. Emanuel Levy of the University of Illinois Medical School, both of whom have consented to act as consultants to the Office of the Commissioner. If you wish, you are entitled to be represented this morning by legal counsel."

"I won't know whether or not I want a lawyer until I learn whether I'm being accused of breaking a law."

"This is an official hearing, but you may regard it as preliminary in nature. No formal charges have been lodged—as yet —against the Cougars as a team, or against any individual connected with it. The extent of your own involvement, if any, will be determined this morning."

Robin seated himself at the smaller table and faced the solemn quintet. "For the moment," he said, "I'll waive legal representation."

"Very well." The Commissioner leaned forward. "Will you tell us, Mr. Stephens, whatever you may know about the use of drugs by the playing members of your team?"

Robin made no attempt to conceal his astonishment. "What drugs?"

"That, sir, is what we want to learn from you."

Before the irritated Robin could reply, one of the deputies intervened. "The Office of the Commissioner," he said, "has received evidence to the effect that Cougar player personnel have been offered drugs prior to each game in order to increase their aptitude for football."

"If I knew of any such drug, I'd suggest that the owners, general managers and coaches of other teams use them," Robin said. "The Cougars play a good enough brand of football to get along without drugs, thanks."

One of the physicians seemed to appreciate his humor, and smiled, but the others remained stone-faced.

"You claim to be unaware of this practice, Mr. Stephens?" Morton asked.

"I claim nothing," Robin said. "I make the flat statement, gentlemen, that to the best of my belief and knowledge, this allegation is hogwash. Speaking for myself, I've never heard of any drugs being offered to any member of the Cougar team, I've never seen any player either being offered or taking any drugs, and I've never known any of our players to be under the influence of drugs." The secretary, he saw, was scribbling furiously in her notebook, and he also suspected that the microphones were attached to a tape recorder.

"If drugs were offered to your players, Mr. Stephens, would you know that fact?"

"After a season that has already seen us through fourteen games," the annoyed Robin said, "I'm positive someone would have called the matter to my attention. If you don't know it, Commissioner, a football team is like a family. Sooner or later everybody learns the business of everyone else. Now sir, may I know who is supposed to be pushing this dope onto my team?"

"Please hold yourself available if we want to question you further this afternoon, Mr. Stephens," the Commissioner said.

"And we'll be grateful if you'll leave by the side door, where you'll find a bank of elevators. We're hoping that all contact can be avoided between those whom we've seen and those who haven't yet been questioned."

Robin stood and went to the door. "In my opinion, Commissioner," he said, "you and these gentlemen are wasting your time."

Still annoyed, he made his way to the elevators, where he found Dr. Scudder pacing up and down.

"I've been waiting for you," the agitated physician said.

Robin called his attention to two members of the Commissioner's staff, who were also waiting for an elevator and seemed to be taking a coffee break. "Let's go over to my office," Robin suggested. "We can be there in five minutes."

Scudder nodded and remained tight-lipped. A distinguished physician with a lucrative private practice, he was a football enthusiast who had served the team for a number of years because it gave him an inside approach to the game that most fans were denied. He was amiable, always even-tempered, and never before had Robin seen him so upset.

When they reached the inner sanctum of the general manager in the Cougar suite, Dr. Scudder exploded. "That stupid bastard is the absolute end," he said. "Do you know why he has a sputtering Roman candle up his rear?"

"I can't imagine," Robin said.

"Because we do precisely what every other team in professional football does. We make amphetamines available to players who want them before a game."

Robin had been vaguely aware of the practice, but it was obvious he needed to know more. "What amphetamines, Gene?"

"Dexadrine, mainly. The boys call them pep pills or greenies. The trainers hand them out."

"Can any player get them?"

"No, I've specifically forbidden several of the boys to use

them because amphetamines would be harmful to them. The trainers know who is allowed to have them and who isn't."

"Is there any record kept of the pills that are dispensed?"

"My God, now you sound like that idiot, Morton!"

"Sorry."

Scudder smiled apologetically. "I don't mean to chew you out, Rob. Naturally we keep complete records. The trainers turn over a list to me every week, and we keep the pills under lock and key at all times. Nobody fools around with amphetamines!"

Before Robin could continue his questioning, a wildly angry Mal Ferguson stalked into the office. "I figured you came back here! I just threatened to punch Morton's teeth out through the back of his head! The son-of-a-bitch is trying to claim our actions have been illegal, but he's full of shit!"

Robin waved him to a chair. "We're just hashing out this whole thing. Can they make a charge of illegality stick, Gene?"

"From a strictly medical standpoint, no. They can't," Scudder said. "I'm the medical authority, and in my judgment the pills could be given to the boys without harm."

"Every team in the league hands out greenies!" Ferguson said, still fuming.

Robin glanced at his watch. "Mal, your schedule is already knocked cockeyed for the day, so I suggest you get together with your staff to watch the film clips. Gene and I will handle this situation, and you can tell any of the players who come to you that they aren't to worry, either."

Eventually a somewhat mollified Mal Ferguson went off to his delayed day-long meeting with the members of his coaching staff.

By then Dr. Scudder's sense of humor had been restored. "So you and I will be the sacrificial lambs who voluntarily cast ourselves into the lion's den. Do you have some sort of strategy in mind?"

"Not yet," Robin said. "All I know is that nobody can threaten to kick the Commissioner in the teeth without causing still more trouble for himself. You and I can't afford the luxury of losing our tempers."

"I can't help wondering," the physician said, "what prompts a man to *want* to be general manager of a professional football team."

"Now that you mention it, I find it hard to think of a reason myself."

7

Robin was again entitled to the protection of legal counsel when he and Dr. Scudder made their second appearance before the Commissioner, but he deliberately refrained from calling in the Cougars' lawyers. He intended to rely on psychology rather than on the team's rights under the law, and consequently reasoned that his defense would be far more effective if he appeared alone before Morton and the board.

"Gentlemen," he said when he was called back to the hearing room, "you surprised me this morning when you made your charges against the Cougars. One reason you caught me off guard, so to speak, is because I can't believe that you think our situation is unique. Surely you know that if we're guilty, so is every team in the National Football League. I challenge you, gentlemen. Walk into the locker room of any team before any game on any Sunday chosen at random, and you'll find that pep pills are made available to players who want them."

One of the Commissioner's deputies nodded. "He's right, you know."

"If the practice is wrong—and I make no attempt to defend it," Robin said, "make a blanket regulation ordering all of us to stop. But don't single out one team for punishment. Don't make an example of the Cougars—or any other organization."

"What upsets me," Commissioner Morton said, "are the implications of drug use. It disturbs me that athletes who should be setting an example for American youth are leaning on drugs in order to improve their game."

"The philosophy of football, like that of every other professional sport," Robin said, "is schizophrenic. We're in the entertainment industry, providing amusement and relaxation to the public. For profit. At the same time, however, we're playing a game that requires certain mental and physical skills. And we compete in accordance with the Anglo-Saxon standards of good sportsmanship that have been developed over many centuries. So we're trapped, all of us, the players, the coaches, the physicians and trainers, the businessmen and other front-office experts. And you gentlemen who supervise and arbitrate and administer.

"Is football primarily a business or a sport? Until a few weeks ago I'd have stood here before you and told you it's exclusively a very big business. But I've seen the Cougars mesh, I've watched them win thirteen consecutive games, and I recognize the emotional qualities that have made this accomplishment possible.

"So we succeed when we treat football as a sport, but we can't forget, or allow ourselves us to forget, that it gives us our living. The players suffer the worst financial vulnerability, as they've got to earn as much as possible within a few years. Wanting the maximum in achievement, they try to increase their proficiency by using pep pills.

"This situation, let me emphasize, is not unique to football. Professional basketball players rely on amphetamines. So do tennis players, baseball players and many others. Let me also point out that these athletes break no laws, since they take the pills under medical supervision.

"I have just one more point to make, gentlemen. I've never heard of any professional athlete becoming addicted to amphetamines because he has used them before a game to increase his

[265]

proficiency. I suspect—and you physicians may want to verify this in detail with Dr. Scudder—that the benefits an athlete derives from the use of pep pills are psychological rather than physical, since the dosages they take are too small, generally speaking, to give them greater stamina."

There was a silence as Commissioner Morton looked at each of his colleagues in turn. "Thank you, Mr. Stephens," he said. "Will you wait outside?"

A secretary took Robin to an office, and Dr. Scudder joined him there after twenty minutes of questioning by the board. Neither could guess what the outcome of the hearing might be, and they agreed that the inability to appeal an adverse decision to a higher authority made the position of the Cougars particularly difficult. The word of the Commissioner was final.

After a wait of almost an hour, Robin was called back to the board room.

"Mr. Stephens," Commissioner Morton said, "my decision— with which my advisers unanimously agree—is to take no action against the Cougars at the present time."

Robin felt great relief.

"I intend to call a meeting of the physicians for all teams in the league after the season ends, and thereafter I'll formulate new regulations that will safeguard the health of the players. In the meantime, I suggest that amphetamines no longer be made available to the members of your team."

"If you make a similar suggestion to every other team in the league," Robin replied, "we'll gladly comply. But if we're the only team to whom you're making the suggestion, I must respectfully decline. We've come a long way in one year, and a championship is within our grasp. So I won't do anything that will be a psychological handicap to my team."

Even the stenographer who was taking the record of the proceedings in shorthand was stunned. No one present could recall an occasion when a "suggestion" made by the Commissioner had been defied by any representative of any professional football team.

But Morton demonstrated that, contrary to a popular rumor, he was human. "Your point is well taken, Mr. Stephens. I must say that the players aren't the only members of the Cougar organization who have acquired a fighting spirit."

The letdown that so many of the experts had been predicting for weeks became painfully evident in the first quarter of the San Diego game, when the Cougar second team took the field to give the regulars a breather. The Chargers scored a touchdown and a field goal, holding the Cougars to insignificant gains. Coach Ferguson sent his regulars onto the field to rectify the damage in the second quarter, but they were as inept as the substitutes had been. San Diego scored a second touchdown, the celebrated Cougar offense sputtered and died, and at half time the score was 17–0.

It appeared that the Cougars would end the regular season as ineptly as they had started it, but the pride of men who believed in themselves and their ability to accomplish miracles reasserted itself in the second half. Ferguson had intended to put his second team on the field again, but the regulars demanded the right to play, and he wisely gave in to them. The defense threw the Chargers seventeen yards closer to their own goal on the first series of plays, and then Finch, Helmsley and company took over, marching to a touchdown in nine plays. After the ball changed hands the defense again behaved maniacally, and downed San Diego behind their goal, making the score 17–9.

Hal Helmsley ripped off a 46-yard run on an up-the-middle trap play, then Finch threw thirty-two yards to Baines for the second touchdown, and the Cougars trailed by a single point. San Diego was unimpressed by the visitors' record, and held firm until only five minutes of playing time remained in the final quarter. Finch advanced the ball to the Charger thirty-two, but was stymied there, and Renewzski came in to kick a field goal. The Cougars squeaked to a 19–17 victory, ending the regular season with an almost unbelievable 14–1 record.

Training regulations were relaxed on the homeward flight, and

Ron Belotti coined a new slogan after consuming his sixth beer. "By God," he shouted, "we're invincible! Even when we goof, there's nobody that can beat us!"

Phil Donegan began calling the team "the invincibles" on his telecast the following night, and sportswriters throughout the United States and Canada immediately followed his example. The following Saturday the Cougars were playing host to the Denver Broncos in the first of the play-off games, and the demand for seats was so great that the switchboard was swamped all day, and Robin refused to take any telephone calls.

On Thursday he revealed a surprise. He had ordered a survey made by a national opinion-sampling organization, and the study showed that the unexpected surge of the Cougars during the long season had created unprecedented national interest in the sport, resulting in dramatically increased television audiences everywhere. "I'm convinced" he wrote to Marc Klein in a memo, "that we can up the TV ante by at least 15 percent for next season. I'm forwarding this opinion to the owners and general managers of all teams, and anticipate no difficulty in obtaining 100% support when the industry negotiates next year's contracts."

On Saturday afternoon the Broncos demonstrated that they had become true believers and accepted the new Cougar slogan. Showing little of the drive and finesse they had demonstrated through the season, the Broncos played sloppily, the Cougars capitalized on their mistakes and the home team won a handy 35–7 victory.

Coach Ferguson gave his players a twenty-four-hour holiday, and Robin confirmed the tentative arrangements he had made to use the facilities of the University of Maryland for the next week. On Sunday night the team flew to Baltimore, where the game that would determine the championship of the American Conference would be played the following Saturday.

Representatives of the mass communications media descended on Baltimore, and the coaches of both teams were forced to hold daily press conferences. Adam Renewzski was suffering from a slight head cold, and enjoyed the dubious pleasure of learning, in print and on the air, that he was so seriously ill he might miss the game. And a defensive tackle for the Colts, who was involved in a minor automobile accident, was subject to similar treatment. His health was perfect, but the newspaper, radio and television reporters insisted he had been incapacitated by whiplash injuries to his neck and shoulders.

An enterprising syndicated columnist interviewed Ted Marcus, the All-Pro linebacker, who was quoted as saying, "I'll make the Cougars sorry they traded me. I'm going gunning for Helmsley, Finch and Baines."

The Cougars' dressing room blossomed with copies of the interview. Clippings appeared at once on the Cougars' bulletin boards, and Ferguson, who was trying to contain the hostilities of his players prior to the game, issued an order preventing them from granting press interviews until they gained his specific approval. The climate became milder, the members of both teams having found it was dangerous to build up the feud in public.

In private, however, key members of the Cougar squad fumed. "I'm going to roll over Marcus so hard," Helmsley said, "that he'll quit football and take up golf. It's okay with me if he hates our management, but the players didn't trade him, so why take it out on guys who thought he was their friend?"

Fred Finch said nothing for publication, even before Coach Ferguson issued his ban on interviews, and was equally silent in private conversations with his teammates. But he had grown tired of being asked whether he planned to make Baltimore sorry he had been traded before being given a fair chance to play. He was grim in practice, concentrating so hard that the other members of the squad became tense.

Big Horse Collins also contributed to the growing pressure. "I know I'm not allowed to shoot off," he said, "but it burns me that not one Baltimore reporter has even given me a chance to say, 'No comment.' Maybe they've forgotten I used to play in this town, so I'll have to remind them."

On Friday morning Robin and his wife flew to Baltimore, Minerva resplendent in a new fur coat he had purchased for her after signing his new three-year contract. That afternoon she remained in their hotel suite, supervising preparations for a cocktail party they would give that evening for visiting team owners, general managers and coaches. Meanwhile Robin rented a car and drove to the campus of the university, where he had to prove his identity before he was admitted to the Cougars' closely guarded practice session.

There he found Mal Ferguson and his staff close to panic, and understood their concern after watching the team in action. Both offensive and defensive squads were jumping offsides repeatedly, missing tackles and clipping on blocking plays. "What's eating them, Mal?" he asked.

"Championship fever," Ferguson replied. "They've come too far too fast, and they can't take the heat. It looks like they'll blow tomorrow's game for sure."

Robin had anticipated the development, and was not surprised. "Don't let anybody leave after practice," he said. "I want five minutes with the whole team."

The players were unusually quiet as they came off the field, so Robin gave them ample opportunity to grow calmer in the showers before he assembled the squad at one end of the locker room.

"They're so uptight," Mal Ferguson said, "that I hope you'll take it easy. A pep talk might do them more harm than good."

Robin grinned at him, but said nothing until the players were clustered on the nearest benches. "You fellows are tired and don't want to hear any speeches," he said, "so I'll make this brief. According to front-office calculations, the winners of tomorrow's game will pick up about ten thousand dollars per man, while the losers will be paid about seven thousand. The Cougar management isn't indifferent to money, as most of you discovered during contract negotiations. But you guys have paid off for us, and we've made far more this year than expected. Marc Klein and I had a little chat yesterday, and he's authorized me to pay a bonus of three thousand—today—to every player, taxi-squad member and coach, with two thousand to every trainer.

"That means you'll make out as well as the Colts, even if you lose. We aren't philanthropists, you understand. We're just giving you a chance to concentrate on football instead of your wallets." He took a thick sheaf of certified checks from his attaché case, threw them onto a bench and walked out before the surprised players could respond.

Mal Ferguson's quick smile told him he had struck precisely the right note.

The public relations departments of the Colts and Cougars held a joint press party at which the liquor flowed freely and mountains of catered delicacies were served. But the affair broke up early because most of the reporters and commentators hoped to pick up some tidbits from the Stephens affair for the league brass. An enterprising Chicago *Tribune* reporter had heard that Dan and Muriel Grannett had been invited, and a sports columnist for the Baltimore *Sun* had been told that Mr. Football was electing to absent himself from his successor's party. So a large number of reporters were on hand when guests began to emerge from the Stephens' suite.

Even those owners and general managers who were willing to cooperate with the press, television and radio were of no help, admitting they had no idea who had been invited. The reporters were granted an unexpected opportunity to learn something when Minerva Stephens accompanied several guests into the hotel corridor, and she found herself surrounded by clamoring newsmen who wanted to know whether the Grannetts had been asked and whether they had put in an appearance.

Minerva proved she was capable of responding in a manner worthy of a general manager's wife. "This has been an informal, private party," she said, smiling calmly. "We're issuing no guest list."

Among the last to leave were the Cougars' owner, Marc

Klein and assistant general manager Ellen Hibbs, and Klein was affable but silent as they ran the gauntlet of questioners. But Ellen, whose loyalty to Dan Grannett was well known to many of the reporters, became white-faced as she and her escort pushed past the newsmen.

Eventually it became obvious that the Grannetts had not shown up, and this fact, combined with Ellen's attitude, may have been responsible for the conclusions drawn by the newsmen. On the day of the game the newspapers and airwaves were flooded with stories to the effect that Dan Grannett, now a vice president of Marcus Aurelius Klein's parent organization, had snubbed his successor. The report gained substance when he failed to make an appearance at the game itself.

During the usual ceremonies preceding the opening kickoff the photographers spotted the photogenic Minerva Stephens sitting in a box with her husband, and she reluctantly posed for several shots. Then the teams came on the field, and everyone in the stands, including the Vice President of the United States and several Senators, as well as prominent sports and show business personalities, was forgotten.

The Cougars took possession of the ball on their own twenty-yard line after the opening kickoff, and on the first play from scrimmage Fred Finch faded back to pass. But Ted Marcus blasted through the Cougar offensive line and dropped the quarterback for a five-yard loss, to the delight of a partisan crowd. Finch called the same play again, and this time Hal Helmsley put such a vicious block on Marcus that the Baltimore linebacker was very slow in hauling himself to his feet. Those were the opening moves in a grueling duel that lasted the entire afternoon.

Big Horse Collins made good his private boast, and every Baltimore fan was aware of his presence on the field: in the first half he made eight tackles, five assists and snuffed out a Colt threat just before the end of the half with a pass interception on his own 23-yard line. Byron Jeffers and the other members of the Cougar defensive team also played their best game of the season, and defensive back Eddie Brown broke up eight Colt pass plays.

The Baltimore defense was equally effective, and the Cougar offense could generate little steam. When Helmsley made short gains on the ground, Finch's passing was off the target. Then the line gave the Cougar quarterback more time, and he began to find his receivers on short passes, but the Colt front four, supported by a rapacious Ted Marcus, bottled up Helmsley. Neither side was able to score.

A band marched onto the field at half time, and a worried Marc Klein left his guests while he made his way to his general manager's box. "I don't like the looks of this, Rob," he said.

"Both teams have too strong an offensive potential to be corked all afternoon. Sooner or later somebody is going to break this game wide open."

"Will we do it or will they?"

Robin forced a smile. "Two of the best teams in football are out there, Marc. Only an idiot would predict the outcome of this game." The morning newspapers had reported that the odds were even.

"We have a fourteen-week momentum going for us," Klein said stubbornly.

"Or against us. Sooner or later we're going to lose a game. Even a true believer knows this winning streak will be snapped."

"But not today—and not in the Super Bowl!"

It was Robin's duty to remain objective and dispassionate. "One of the fascinations of football is that any team in the league is capable of beating any other on any given weekend. Match these teams again next week, and today's winner well could be next week's loser."

Marc's smile was wry. "I should have known better than to come to you for encouragement. Mr. Ice Water."

"That's not true," Minerva said, interrupting them. "He shouted himself silly all through the half."

"Unfortunately," Robin said, "that is beside the point. A season is successful only as long as a team wins. One loss spoils the year, no matter what may have gone before, and that's particularly true in the post-season championship games. I'm just trying to prevent any of us from getting our hopes up too high. In fact, no matter what the outcome today, I intend to sit down with Mal Ferguson this coming week to talk about some trades that will strengthen us at positions where we're shaky."

"I'm going to be a true believer to the end," Marc said as he departed.

"So am I," Robin told Minerva, "even though I'm not supposed to feel that way."

Midway through the third quarter the Colts mountained a sustained drive that carried them to the Cougars' 26-yard line, their deepest penetration of the day, and there they bogged down. But a field-goal try was successful, in spite of the fierce rush led by Byron Jeffers in an attempt to block the kick, and the score was 3–0.

It appeared as though the Cougars would be unable to move into Colt territory, and after nine minutes of the final quarter had passed, members of the press corps were beginning to write about the most stunning defeat of the season. Then, suddenly, the tide turned. Finch carried eighteen yards to his own forty-seven on a surprise quarterback sneak, and Helmsley burst through the defensive line on the next play to the Colt forty. A pass to a wide receiver was good for six yards, and a Finch flip to Baines in the flat picked up another ten.

With the ball on the Colt twenty-four, easily within Adam Renewzski's range, it appeared certain that the Cougars could tie the score. But Finch and his cohorts wanted victory, not a tie that might carry the game into overtime. With the relatively few Cougar fans in the stands screaming for a touchdown, Finch executed one of his favorite maneuvers, fading to his left, then passing to his right. Hal Helmsley seemed to burst through a knot of Colt defenders, and arrived on the ten-yard line at the same instant the softly thrown pass arrived there. He gathered it into his arms, lowered his head and thundered down the sidelines, crossing the goal line with the nearest Colt defender at least seven yards behind him. The Cougar bench emptied as Helmsley's teammates carried him in triumph to the water cooler, and Finch received similar treatment as he trotted off the field. Renewzski made good his conversion, and the score was 7–3 in the Cougars' favor.

Baltimore made a desperate attempt to score a touchdown, attempting a trick end-around and a complicated screen play as well as several long passes. But the Chicago defenders held firm, and the game ended with the score unchanged. The Cougars were the champions of the American Conference, bound for the Super Bowl.

The newsmen were admitted to the locker room after game balls had been awarded to the offensive and defensive units, and had been added to the crowded trophy case. The quiet was startling, and virtually every reporter commented at length on the seeming calm of the new champions. The tired players sipped beer or soft drinks as they dressed, and there was no horseplay.

"We're saving the champagne until we beat the winner of tomorrow's National Conference championship game in the Super Bowl," Byron Jeffers explained.

"Which would you rather play?" one of the reporters asked. "The Giants or the Vikings?"

"We don't give a damn," Horse Collins snapped. "We're glad to take on either of them."

A number of newsmen surrounded Finch and Helmsley, but both were uncommunicative, and both refused to be regarded as heroes. "We did what we were supposed to do," Helmsley said.

"It took eleven men to score that touchdown, not two," Finch added.

Ron Belotti thrust himself into the conversation. "We're a team!" he roared in his deep bass voice. "We're forty guys who win games together, and we can lick anybody else! We'll prove it two weeks from tomorrow in the Super Bowl!"

To the astonishment of the press and other visitors, the Cougars suddenly came alive, and the locker room erupted as players cheered, banged on lockers with cleated shoes and jumped onto benches, waving their arms and brandishing fists.

Robin, who stood at one end of the room with Marc Klein, watching the demonstration, felt his own heart beginning to pound. "I haven't let myself hope they could bring it off. But you know something, Marc? They will! The true-believer line is more than a publicity slogan. These boys are actually convinced they're invincible, the best in the business, and for the first time I agree with them. Maybe it's crazy, but these fellows who were total strangers to each other a half-year ago are going to win the Super Bowl game and make themselves the champions of the world!"

The Minnesota Vikings defeated the New York Giants in a hotly contested game that was forced into overtime play, and became the National Conference champions. Every football commentator began to analyze the comparative strengths and weaknesses of the two teams that would meet two weeks later in the Super Bowl game, which would be held in New Orleans. Mal Ferguson immediately followed tradition and issued a firm order prohibiting his players from granting interviews unless a member of the Cougars' public-relations staff was present. Under no circumstances did he want someone to blunder into making a provocative statement that would arouse the ire of the Vikings and give them an added incentive.

As it was, the members of both squads had ample reason to want victory. In addition to the obvious fact that the winners would be hailed as football's best, the total sellout of all seats for the game guaranteed that a crowd in excess of eighty-three thousand would be on hand. Robin ordered an immediate financial breakdown made, and then checked with the office of the Commissioner for verification. He learned that each member of the winning team would be awarded a purse of $15,500, while each of the losers would earn $8,000. The difference was large enough to insure that even those veterans who had become too jaded to feel the emotion known as team spirit would be anxious to win.

Before returning to Chicago from Baltimore, Coach Ferguson gave his charges a seventy-two-hour furlough, ordering them to report in midweek at the New Orleans motel Robin had engaged immediately after the team had won the American Conference championship. Training season rules would be in effect for the ten days prior to the climactic game, Ferguson announced, and the players would not be allowed to live with their wives and families. Accommodations would be available for the ladies at a motel only a short distance from the team's quarters, but the athletes would be required to eat all meals with the team and would be subjected to a nightly bed check.

Robin returned to Chicago, where Coach Ferguson joined him, and together they made a preliminary study of the computerized scouting reports on the college players who would be drafted soon after the Super Bowl. The two Conference championship teams presumably needed the least help, and therefore drew last for the new players, so Robin and Mal concentrated their attention on young men from the less publicized schools, knowing that those who had been press headliners would be taken by other teams before the Cougars had an opportunity to bid.

Relaxing together over a drink after two grueling days, Mal Ferguson finally lost some of the reserve that had characterized his relations with Robin from the beginning. "I'm of two minds," he said. "I'm tempted to give the offense some new plays, but I don't want to take too many chances. They've done marvels for guys who've never worked together until this season, and I wonder if I ought to stick with the plays we've used all year."

"If you're asking my advice, I wish you wouldn't," Robin said. "I haven't consulted you on the details of the new stadium, and I don't want to butt in where I'm no more than a fairly well-informed amateur."

"Hell, you wouldn't be butting in." Mal's grin was tired. "So much of this business of mine is guesswork. A great coach can look like a bum when his team doesn't jell, and a mediocre coach can become a wonder boy when his players pull in the same direction."

"If you think you're mediocre, you're wrong. So wrong, in fact, that I'm offering you a new contract," Robin said. "It'll have blanks in it, and you fill them in. Three years, five years, whatever you want. Name your own salary. And if there are any special terms you want, put them in, too. I make just one reservation. I won't give up any of my own authority on trades and college drafts."

"After the results we had this year, I wouldn't either, if I were in your shoes," Mal said.

Robin laughed. "Maybe I'm the one who's had dumb luck, but we might be able to do it again, and it's worth the try."

"Sure is. And I'm grateful for your confidence in me." Mal leaned forward, pushing his glass to one side of the table. "I'll tell you something, Rob. I hated your guts when you first took over as general manager."

"What else is new?"

"Well, I did, and I couldn't have been more mistaken. You and I have formed a team that's as solid as the team we've put on the field."

Robin nodded. "We sure have, and it's the cooperation of the front office and the coaching staff that really makes or breaks a team."

"I feel sorry as hell for poor old Danny, but I wish he'd stop giving us bad publicity by staying away from these championship games."

"I can't criticize him," Robin said. "I just hope I'll have the good sense to know when to retire. Assuming I'm still in football by then."

"You'll be around for a long time," Mal told him.

"I have my new contract for the next few years, sure. But nobody will go around saluting me as the General Manager of the Year if we lose at New Orleans."

"Win, lose or tie there, you'll be around. You have the feel for the game, and the guts."

"To tell you the truth," Robin said, "I'm tired. When I look back at all the crises we've had this season—"

"There are crises every season. Problems that only the general manager and the head coach know about. Get yourself a good rest when you go on your vacation, because the merry-go-round for next season will be whirling at top speed by the time you get back."

"I know you're right, so I'll buy that advice." Robin paid for their drinks and they walked together to the elevators, where they would part, with Robin returning to his office and Mal going home for twenty-four hours before joining the team.

"When will we see you in New Orleans?" the head coach asked.

"I'm flying down Saturday night or Sunday morning. Incidentally, I'll be staying at the place where we're putting up families. I'll have Minerva with me, and the players would resent it if we took a room in their place—when they're not allowed to live with their families."

"You really do think of all the angles," Mal said as they shook hands.

"When I'm able to look ahead, I try to. How do you think we're going to make out in the big game, Mal?"

"Officially or unofficially?"

"Off the record and between us."

Mal's broad shoulders rose and fell. "I've always said that anybody who bets on a football game is crazy. There's no sport that's less predictable. And this is one game I honestly can't figure. On the basis of experience, the Vikings have the edge. If our boys keep believing they're invincible, that gives us an advantage. What scares me is what will happen if they find out they're human, just like everybody else. The guy who plays over his head consistently, season after season, becomes a great star and finds himself in the Hall of Fame ten years later. The ordinary football player has a great year when he's self-confident, and then slips back to normal."

"Are you suggesting we're playing over our heads?"

"Maybe, but not necessarily. We have two all-time players in Helmsley and Jeffers. Renewzski is marvelously consistent, like a robot, but he has no heart. Whether boys like Finch and Collins and Eddie Brown are real stars, I don't know. I'll give you my opinion after we see how they do for the next couple of seasons. Belotti has come on fast this year, and should be first-class for the rest of his career. If you look at Greg Baines' record, he's done more this season than he accomplished anywhere else in any two seasons. So I don't know how we'll make out in the Super Bowl. All I can tell you is I'm not missing church the next couple of Sundays!"

Fred Finch was one of the last players to arrive in New Orleans, and when he finally reached the motel, less than an hour before the curfew, he appeared listless, had lost weight, and there were dark circles under his eyes. Within minutes he was summoned to Coach Ferguson's suite.

"What happened to you?"

"I've been celebrating the victory over Baltimore," Finch said, "and maybe I was too enthusiastic."

"You and your girl?"

"Yeah, Martie was with me. I dropped her off at the place down the road just now."

Ferguson minced no words. "So you've spent the past seventy-two hours drinking too much, staying out too late at night and screwing."

"Something like that." The quarterback was sheepish.

The boy was one of those narcissistic, perennial adolescents who wouldn't settle down until an emotionally mature wife provided him with an anchor, Mal thought. He would discuss the problem with Robin, who would see to it that Finch married the right girl during the off-season. The Cougars were fortunate they had a general manager who could cope effectively with such problems.

"Freddie," Ferguson said, "you're excused from practice tomorrow morning. Go to a Turkish bath and sweat all that alcohol out of your system. I'll give you three days to regain the weight you've lost, and if you miss my deadline I'm fining you five hundred dollars a day until you catch up."

Finch accepted the orders, but not until the following afternoon did he learn the nature of his punishment for breaking training rules. Hjalmar Sorensen guided the regulars through a long offensive drill, and the next morning was again placed in charge. Newspapers from coast to coast responded with appropriate headlines: FINCH, COUGAR STAR, IS BENCHED.

In his limited appearances throughout the season Sorensen had proved he was a big-league quarterback, but he was not in a class with his predecessor, and the public echoed the comments of the experts. Some gamblers had been offering even money on the game, but the odds changed very quickly, and in Las Vegas, Miami and other cities where gambling was a regular part of the citizens' lives, the odds shifted, and the Vikings became 5–3 favorites.

At the end of his second day's treatment, Finch went to Ferguson. "Please don't bench me, Coach," he said. "I know I behaved like a freak-out after we beat the Colts, but you've got to give me another chance. I can run the team better than Hjalmar can, and the Vikings will whip us if I'm on the sidelines."

Not until Saturday did Ferguson relent. That afternoon the regulars celebrated the return of their star quarterback by tearing large holes in the ranks of the defense during a hard, prolonged scrimmage. That night, after Robin arrived in New Orleans, Mal discussed the problem with him.

"I've known all along that the redhead is a disturbing influence on Finch," Robin said, "but I was hoping she'd keep his feet on the ground for another season." In spite of his deal with Martie, he owed her no loyalty, and with any luck in the months ahead, he might find Finch a sensible, ego-feeding wife. Perhaps Minerva would assist in the search, but one thing was certain: no matter how much Finch needed direct help, Minerva would not be on hand to give it to him.

On the Tuesday before the big game, a reporter who paid a visit to Dan Grannett on the island off the coast of Georgia brought back a story that made national headlines. "It's true that I'm going to work for Marc Klein in a new capacity after the first of the year," Mr. Football told him, "but my opinions are still my own. I think the Vikings are a better team, and will win on Sunday."

On Wednesday Miner Simmons was knocked unconscious in practice, and it was feared, at first, that he would be forced to miss the game. But he was released from the hospital the next morning, and an hour later he rejoined the rest of the team for practice.

On Friday Ellen Hibbs came to Robin in his motel suite. "No matter whether we win or lose on Sunday," she told him, "I'm resigning from the Cougar organization, effective Monday morning. I'm leaving football, and I'm giving up what's become a very uncomfortable relationship with Marc. Whether I'm right or wrong doesn't matter. I can't go through life making myself miserable by acting against Uncle Danny's best interests."

On Saturday evening, a scant seventeen hours before game time, a telephone call from the White House threw the stadium authorities, the local police and the general managers of both teams into a sudden panic. The President of the United States had decided to fly to New Orleans for the game. Security plans were drawn up hastily under the supervision of the resident Secret Service agent, and the general managers shuffled the seating arrangements they had made for celebrities in many walks of life in order to find appropriate accommodations for the Presidential party of twenty-four persons, not counting a Secret Service detail of sixteen men.

Early Sunday morning a light rain fell, to the consternation of fans everywhere, but a tarpaulin protected the playing field, a warm sun came out around 9:00 A.M., and aided by a brisk wind, produced a perfect, dry field. An hour later the players ate hearty breakfasts, then retired to their rooms to rest for two hours before climbing onto their respective team buses for the ride to the stadium. The physicians for both squads reported their were no major casualties and no one was ill.

The teams arrived at the stadium at noon, and the trainers began the laborious process of taping arms and legs, wrists and ankles, sore shoulders and backs. Thirty minutes before game time Phil Donegan informed a television audience estimated at eighty-five million persons that the sun was shining in a cloudless sky, the temperature was 63 degrees, the field was dry and the wind had died away to become a faint breeze that would be a negligible influence on kickers.

The Vikings, the first team on the field, were greeted by a standing ovation, in which the President of the United States joined. Since New Orleans was a National Conference city, most of the local fans were Viking partisans. The President impartially joined in the applause when the Cougars trotted onto the field in their green uniforms with white trim, and the Chicago rooters tried to make up in volume what they lacked in numbers.

Robin Stephens was interviewed by one of the roving television reporters as he and his wife made their way to their box, and for public consumption, at least, his enthusiasm was unqualified. "We've come a long way this season," he said. "I fully expect the Cougars to take that last step this afternoon—and go all the way. The Vikings are good, no question about that, but all true believers know the Cougars are invincible."

Minnesota won the toss, and elected to receive. Renewzski boomed a kick into the end zone, where the ball was downed, and play began on the Viking twenty. The National Conference champions made one first down, reaching their own thirty-six, before they were forced to punt. Oliver Olson suffered a case of jitters and fumbled the ball on his punt return. There was a wild scramble, and a Cougar interior lineman recovered on his four-yard line. Fred Finch was in a hole, and unable to pass so close to his own goal line, and sent Helmsley barreling into the line on two successive plays, then tried Baines on an off-tackle slant. On fourth down the ball rested on the Cougar five. A tremendous punt by Renewzski took a Chicago bounce as it landed, and came to rest on the Viking thirty, ending the threat.

Neither team was able to score in the first quarter, but five minutes after the second quarter began, the usually dependable Eddie Brown missed his assignment on a pass play, and a Viking receiver caught a 52-yard bomb, then ran another twenty-one yards to the Cougar eleven. Before the defenders could rally, Minnesota punched across the goal for a touchdown and added a conversion. The Cougar defense was still stalled, and the score was 7–0 as Chicago took the ball for its final series of downs. With less than one minute to play in the half, a blitzing Minnesota linebacker shook off his blockers, and catching Finch ten yards behind the line of scrimmage, knocked him to the ground with such force that the quarterback lay still. He was carried off the field on a stretcher, Sorensen replaced him, and the half ended with the Cougars still in the doldrums.

As soon as the intermission began, Robin hurried off to the locker room, where the players of the offensive and defensive squads were listening to critical analyses given by the coaches. Mal Ferguson was standing in an inner room, talking with Dr. Scudder, and as Robin joined them he saw the physician was dismantling a hypodermic syringe and needle.

"The Doc says Finch can play," Mal declared.

"Hopefully," Eugene Scudder said, "the worst that happened to Finch was that he had the breath knocked out of him. The trainers are putting a half-inch of tape on his ribs, and I've given him a little something to clear his head. He says he wants to play, and I don't intend to stop him."

Robin couldn't help thinking ahead to the next season. "He has no broken bones?"

"Not to my knowledge. We'll take him to the hospital for X-rays, of course. *After* the second half."

Robin looked into the trainer's room, where Finch was sitting on a table, submitting to the ministrations of trainers who were applying yards of broad adhesive tape to his torso. "Give 'em hell this half, boy!" he called. Moments later, as he returned to his seat, Robin took care to compose his features. Too many people would jump to conclusions if they saw he was worried.

Olson redeemed himself as the second half began, and repeatedly reversing his field, took the ball from his own one-yard line to the Viking forty-eight. On the first play from scrimmage Hal Helmsley burst through a gaping hole in the Minnesota line opened for him by his center and guards, and after carrying the ball for nine yards, inexplicably dropped it. Minnesota recovered, and the Cougar drive came to an abrupt end.

Robin glanced at Minerva, then looked at Marc Klein in the adjoining box, and read his own fear in their eyes. Their belief in the invincibility of the Cougars was shaken, as was his.

Neither side was able to advance until the latter portion of the third quarter, when the Vikings carried to the Cougar forty-six, and a perfectly placed field goal sailed through the uprights to give them a 10–0 lead.

If Fred Finch was suffering from the blow he had received earlier, he allowed no one to know it. Cursing his teammates in the huddle, he took possession on his own twenty, and prodding the others as hard as he whipped himself, he drove the offensive unit forward. His short passes connected, and Helmsley, furious with himself for dropping the ball, ripped off gains of five to sixteen yards every time he carried.

Finally, with the ball resting on the Viking eleven on second down, Finch wasted no time in the huddle. "Two-green-seven," he said, meaning the fullback would carry over left tackle. "Put it in, Hal. We're tired of playing catch-up ball."

Helmsley obliged by running over half the Viking team into the end zone. Renewzski's kick was good, and the score was a far more respectable 10–7.

The last quarter was one of the most memorable in Super Bowl history. After several fruitless exchanges of punts the Cougars took possession on their own goal line, and Finch directed a drive that carried to midfield. Again he mixed his plays craftily, alternating punishing runs by Helmsley with short passes, and it appeared as though the Cougars were on their way to another score. But the Viking defense stiffened, and on fourth down Adam Renewzski trotted onto the field to try a 55-yard field goal.

Everyone in the stands stood in silence to watch the attempt, and Cougar partisans became delirious when the ball sailed squarely between the goal posts. The score was now 10–10, and a wildly excited Phil Donegan, forgetting that television commentators were expected to be impartial, told eighty-five million members of his audience, "How do you like *that*, true believers! The Cougars don't know when they're beaten! They really are invincible!"

But the Vikings also refused to admit defeat, and after eight minutes of play in the final quarter they staged a rally of their own, marching eighty-one yards to a touchdown in twelve plays. The score was 17–10, and with only two and one-half minutes of playing time remaining, the Cougars launched their final offensive, hoping to tie the score and force the game into an overtime period.

Finch, standing on his twelve, threw a perfect strike to Miner Simmons, who caught the ball on the Cougar forty-nine, and was immediately downed. Virtually no one in the stands realized that Finch, who had been crushed by two Viking defenders at almost the instant he released the ball, had not risen from the ground.

Dr. Scudder went onto the field himself, and a brief examination convinced him the quarterback was not capable of finishing the game. Belotti and Helmsley half-supported Finch as he went to the sidelines to the accompaniment of sustained cheers from the crowd, and it was apparent that he was protesting the decision to take him out. Sorenson replaced him, but the pressure on the substitute was too great, and he could not spark a new march.

Instead he was thrown for a loss on third down while trying to pass, and had to eat the ball on his own thirty-nine. Not even Adam Renewzski could kick a field goal of sixty-five yards, so Sorensen attempted another pass on fourth down, and when it was batted away from the receiver, the hopes of the Cougars died. Minnesota played out the clock for the last ninety seconds in spite of frantic efforts by the Cougar defense to regain possession of the ball, and when the final gun sounded the score was still 17–10. The Vikings were the National Football League champions, the best team in the world.

Minerva was weeping, smudging her face with mascara, but not caring, and Robin put an arm around her shoulders. There were tears in his eyes, too, he discovered, and he felt as though his world had come to an end. Unable to shut all thought from his mind, he remembered what he had told Marc: a team that won its post-season championship games could boast a successful year, but a team that lost was a failure.

The fact that the Cougars had clawed their way to the top from nowhere was irrelevant now, and their 14–1 regular season record had no meaning. All through the months to come, newspaper reporters and television-radio commentators would refer to the Cougars as the champions of the American Conference, but the phrase was hollow. The Cougars were second-best, vanquished by the world's champions, the Vikings.

His arm still encircling his wife, Robin started toward the locker room, where he would make the expected, obligatory remarks to the downhearted players. But, in spite of his own depression and weariness, his mind was working at its usual pace. The completion of the Cougars' new stadium before next season would mean there would be twenty thousand additional seats to sell every week, so the team had to be good.

Scouting reports on a guard who had been playing for an obscure little college in western Pennsylvania rated him as tremendous, ready to play regularly on a professional team, and Robin was determined to snag him. In the draft, if possible, in a trade if someone else got him first. The addition of a star outside linebacker would make the defense virtually airtight, Mal had said, and with several good defensive backs coming up from the minor leagues, Eddie Brown was expendable trade

[287]

bait. One way or another, patching and dealing, scraping and wheeling, he would put together a still better team during the winter months ahead.

Then, perhaps, another miracle could be created. All of them —he and his staff, Mal and his coaches, and above all, the players —might be able to create a new aura of invincibility, in which all of them could believe.

"Don't let it get you down, honey," he said. "We'll win the big one next year."

A light appeared in Minerva's misty eyes, and she leaned against him as they walked. "Sure, we will," she said.